HIDDEN ON THE FENS

A totally addictive crime thriller filled with stunning twists

JOY ELLIS

Detective Nikki Galena Book 11

JOFFE BOOKS

First published 2020
Joffe Books, London
www.joffebooks.com

Please join our mailing list to receive free Kindle crime thriller, detective, and mystery books and new releases. Join now and don't miss out on the next bargain book. We are one of the UK's leading independent publishers of crime fiction.
www.joffebooks.com/contact/

ISBN: 978-1-78931-343-7

This book is dedicated to our
amazing friend, Julie Crunkhorn.
Your courage and strength inspire us all.

CHAPTER ONE

He stood with his eyes shut. A solitary figure incongruous in this landscape of endless fields, big sky and fast-moving river, its reeds waving in the endless breeze. This place was etched deep in his memory. He'd seen it every time he closed his eyes, all the time he'd been away.

Now he wanted to absorb the other aspects of the place, use his other senses to take in the sounds and smells of his native fens and devour them. He breathed deeply, inhaling the aroma of damp grass, the hint of wild camomile, the scent of sweet clover, the slight tangy whiff of diesel oil coming from a boat or possibly a tractor and, seeping through it all, the salty ozone drifting up from the Wash.

He sighed deeply, almost painfully, and then listened. The first sound was the call of a skylark somewhere above, the song continuing for maybe two minutes — a cascade of notes, an endless refrain, no phrase ever repeated. The song of freedom.

He felt a tear forming, but he refused to open his eyes and allow it to escape. He listened again and this time heard the hushed breeze from the river, the tiny trickles of water as it lapped against the muddy bank. He heard a murmur of engine noise, almost too far away to identify but undoubtedly farm machinery of some kind, and seagulls, their mournful cry suddenly replaced by the echoing peeping noise of a lone avocet.

How he'd missed this. He opened his eyes and stared and stared at the vista laid out before him, along with every sensory gift it had to offer.

There had been days and nights when he doubted that he'd ever see this place again.

The temptation to end it all had sometimes been almost overpowering. He would never have believed that he had the strength in him, but he had found it and come through. He had survived.

Now he was back. He wiped his eyes, the earlier emotion fading and a new one slowly taking its place like a seedling forging its way up to the light. He had not been to blame for his lost years, but someone had and that someone needed to be taught a lesson. Karma. It was only right. What goes around, comes around. Or as his father used to say, "Sow the wind, reap the whirlwind." For the first time in years, he smiled. How apt this was, and he would prove it.

* * *

Sergeant Niall Farrow eyed the man on the other side of the police station reception desk, wondering why he seemed vaguely familiar. He was around forty, tall, with thick dark hair and a close-cut beard, and was wearing jeans, a blue Oxford shirt and a half-jacket.

'I don't want to waste police time, Sergeant Farrow, but I think someone is targeting my parents.'

Niall took note of the cultured tones and decided that this man was no timewaster. His voice and his expression all conveyed serious concern.

'Let's take this into an interview room, sir, and you can tell me why you think this.' Niall led the man to an empty room and ushered him inside.

They sat down and he asked the man his name.

'Richard Howard, Sergeant, and my parents are Duncan and Aurelia Howard.'

The names rang bells, but annoyingly he couldn't place them. 'And where do they live?'

'Sedgebrook House, Jacob's Fen.'

Niall looked up, surprised. 'I live in Jacob's Fen, but I don't recall a Sedgebrook House.'

Richard Howard smiled. 'Not surprising. Unless you're a real old Yellowbelly, you wouldn't even know it was there. As you know, Jacob's Fen is a tiny village, but the fen itself covers a very big area. Their house is located down a lane about a quarter of a mile past the old Hobbs Mill.'

Niall frowned. They could see the deserted hulk that was Hobbs Mill across the fields from their bedroom window, but it seemed to be on a road to nowhere and so far he and his wife Tamsin had never got around to walking that way. Their evening dog walks always took them in the opposite direction, on a prettier route along the edge of a waterway, or into the little village for a pint before making their way home. 'So, can you tell me why you are concerned about them, sir?'

'They didn't want to tell me what was happening,' Howard said. 'I think my dad put it down to Mum getting a bit forgetful with age, although that's far from the truth — she's still as sharp as a tack. So I don't know how long this has been going on, but possibly a few weeks. Initially, things kept disappearing, or moving.' He frowned. 'Like the planted tubs of flowers, which are usually in a line under the lounge window, all moved to one end of the house and arranged into a kind of cross design. Then the axe that's always left in the log store disappeared. Mum found a bundle of flowers and herbs tied to the front door knocker. Washing has gone missing off the line. Silly things, weird things, but to my mind, they were worrying.' He gave Niall an anxious smile. 'I wasn't going to come to you. I thought it must be bored kids or something, and that I was overreacting, but when they got up this morning, my father found this on the doorstep.' He reached into the bag he had been carrying and took out

3

something carefully packaged in bubble wrap. He laid it on the table, peeled back the wrap, and revealed a knife.

Niall exhaled and leaned forward. It was a cruel-looking weapon and unlike anything he'd ever seen before. It wasn't the kind of thing a thug would carry, and it certainly wasn't military. The long wavy blade and intricate carved black handle inset with enamel and semi-precious stones had something ancient about them. It looked expensive, antique.

'My mother was terribly distressed when she saw it but refused to say why. It was as though she recognised it.' Richard shook his head. 'All she would say was that it was a witch's knife.' He ran his hand through his hair. 'I don't understand this at all.'

Niall stared at it. 'Have you touched it, sir, especially the handle?'

'No. As soon as they found it my parents rang me and when I saw it, I wondered about fingerprints so I picked it up with the bubble wrap.'

'Good thinking. If it's alright with you, sir, I'll keep it for the time being and run it through our lab.' Niall went to the door and asked a PC to fetch him an evidence bag. When he was once again seated, he said, 'I'll get a car out there later today.' He stopped. 'Second thoughts, I'll go myself, on my way home. Will you be there?'

'No, Sergeant, I have to get back to work. I've lost enough time today. I look after the Sedgebrook Estate Farm out at Jacob's Fen. My parents have no interest in it, so I manage it for them, and I need to make use of every hour of daylight at the moment. We are clearing an old copse and changing the layout of the fields. But don't worry, my mother might be distressed but despite what my father says, believe me, they are both fully in command of their faculties! They both still lecture on occasions. I suspect they'll open up to you better without me there.' He paused, then gave Niall a rather apologetic grin. 'Be prepared, Sergeant Farrow, they are a tad eccentric, and their subjects are esoteric, to say the least.'

'Okay. If I could have a contact number for them, and for you, sir, I'll phone them and stop by to have a chat. I'll ring and update you tomorrow.' Niall would have liked to reassure Richard that it was probably just young tricksters, but he was pretty sure it wasn't. Jacob's Fen had a population of under two hundred, and they were scattered over miles of farming land. He had never seen a gang of kids hanging around anywhere. There was no public transport and no school, and the few children that did live there were taken to and from school by bus. There was a tiny pub and little else. Plus, how would kids get out there? On bikes? But it would be a long old ride and where the hell would they have got this creepy knife? No, it didn't fit.

Richard stood up. 'I really appreciate it, thank you.'

Niall went back to the office and rang Tamsin. It took her a while to answer.

'Sorry, babe. Hope this isn't a difficult time.'

Tamsin laughed. 'Oh, not at all, I'm just up to my knees in the middle of a stream checking water quality, that's all.'

'Oh. In waders, I hope.'

'No, my bikini. Of course I'm in waders!'

Niall laughed. 'Look, I won't keep you. First, I'm going to be a bit late tonight. I'm calling in on an old couple on my way home. And second, what does esoteric mean?'

'Esoteric? That's a big word for a copper.' Tamsin laughed again.

'I don't want to look a prat by asking someone here, not that I think any of my PCs will know anyway.'

'You've heard of Google, I suppose? It means obscure stuff usually, something you need specialist knowledge to understand. Why, babe?' Tamsin asked.

'Oh dear. Well, this old couple I mentioned, I'm told they lecture on esoteric subjects. I'm going to be way out of my depth, aren't I?' Niall sighed.

'Then rely on your boyish charm, my darling. It worked on me, didn't it? So I'm sure you can win over a couple of wrinklies. Now, I have to go before I drown. See you at supper. Love you.'

Niall ended the call, smiling. Before they married, Tamsin, having studied environmental science, had worked on a Woodlands Trust project. After a short time spent making their Fenland cottage into a proper home, she joined a local company that was working with farmers to achieve agricultural biodiversity. She was now doing three days a week and loving it. A bonus was that she could take their dog Skipper to work with her.

'Have you got a minute, Niall?'

He looked up to see his father-in-law, DS Joseph Easter, smiling at him from the doorway.

'Yes, sir, of course. Come in.' It had taken him a long while to feel comfortable calling his hero "Dad," but now he liked saying it — although never at work, of course.

Joseph entered and closed the door behind him but still kept his voice low. 'Nikki and I wondered if you and Tam could come to dinner tomorrow evening?'

Joseph and DI Nikki Galena had not made it known that they were in a relationship. If it were to get out, they would be forced to stop working together and one of them would have to move to a different area. They had forged a very good, tight-knit team and they didn't want to let that go, so the couple concealed their close association to preserve the status quo. Niall grinned. 'We'd love to. Is it a special occasion?'

'Nikki's mother wants to talk to us about something, so she's called a family pow-wow. And as you know, we don't turn Eve down lightly. We said we'll hold it at Cloud Cottage Farm, and I'll be cooking, so you might like to pass that on to my little veggie daughter.'

'She'll like that. You're a great cook.' Niall's eyes fell on the knife sitting on his desk, waiting to go to forensics. 'While you're here, you've travelled a lot. Have you ever seen anything like this?' He handed Joseph the sealed evidence bag.

Joseph let out a long, low whistle, 'That's a type of *athame*! Where the hell did you find that?'

'It was left on someone's doorstep. And what's an ath . . . athame?' Niall asked.

'It's a ritualistic knife used in Wicca, or witchcraft.' Joseph was regarding the design carefully.

'Right.' Niall nodded. 'Well, apparently it scared the life out of the woman whose step it was left on. According to her son, she said, "It's a witch's knife," and clammed up.'

'Really! Not many people would know what they were.' Joseph pulled a face. 'So, what are you doing about it?'

'Going to visit her and her husband as soon as my shift finishes. It's only a mile past our cottage in Jacob's Fen. I can't say I'm particularly comfortable with what is happening to them. Tam spends a lot of time alone at home. I'd hate to think we have some screwball roaming the lanes.'

'Want some company?' Joseph's eyes were bright with interest.

'Would I ever! Her son beefed them up to be a couple of eccentric academics and as I'm but a humble plod, unlike you, Detective Sergeant Easter, I'd really appreciate it.'

'Right, I'll follow you over there. Give me a bell when you are ready to leave. Oh, and shall I tell Eve we are on for tomorrow?'

'Absolutely. See you later.' Niall was hugely relieved. He was perfectly comfortable with police matters but anything academic made him uneasy. Plus, Joseph had known what the knife was, and that would help enormously.

He picked up the knife and went to find someone to take it over to forensics for him. *Witches? On Jacob's Fen? Oh, please!*

* * *

DI Nikki Galena cursed softly, pushed the pile of reports away from her and stretched. Two months ago they had faced one of the darkest investigations of her career and still the paperwork went on. She wanted the whole thing over, including the court case. It had drained the whole team and everyone else involved, and although they were slowly recovering, she needed to be able to draw a line under that traumatic case and move on.

At a knock on her door, she straightened up and tried to look business-like. Then she saw it was DC Cat Cullen, and she relaxed.

Cat flopped into the chair opposite Nikki and scowled. 'Boss, that case you've got me on is a right pain in the arse. He's going to walk, I just know it. The CPS are going to say there's not enough evidence and the bastard is going to get away with it.'

Cat and Dave were working on an investigation involving a sexual predator targeting older women who'd recently lost their husbands. He'd already got off scot-free once before, due to lack of admissible evidence and it had come down to his word against the victim's.

'I so wanted this one to go well, not only because the dirty sod should pay for what he's done but because it's Dave's final case before he retires.'

Nikki understood what she meant. Personally, she'd have the predator castrated, but apparently that wasn't permissible in these "enlightened" times, and she too would have liked to see Dave Harris bow out on a high. Dave had been part of her amazing team for years. He had retired once before but came back full time as a civilian interviewing officer. Now he was leaving for real, and Nikki was going to miss him. His age had given him expertise and knowledge that was going to be impossible to replace. 'There's time yet, Cat. You just need to find a couple of other women the bastard's come on to and pray they step up and help take him down.'

'I know, I know, but I'm terrified he'll find a way to wriggle out of it, like the snake that he is.'

'As soon as I've tied up this lot,' Nikki indicated to the reports, 'Joseph and I will pitch in too. I want this pervert off the streets as much as you. The thought of someone preying on women my mother's age turns my stomach.'

'Thanks, boss, I appreciate it. I just want to prevent him getting to yet another grieving widow, although if I do actually get my hands on him, I might be looking for another job.' Cat gave her boss a ferocious look. 'It could involve sharp knives and no anaesthetic.'

'Sounds pretty fair to me but as I'd hate to lose you, rein the temper in and be the consummate professional that you are.'

'If I must.' Cat gave her a tired smile. 'But no promises.'

Cat seemed far from her normal exuberant self, and Nikki had a feeling that it wasn't the case alone that was bugging her. 'You okay, Cat?'

For a moment Cat didn't answer, then she gave a long sigh. 'Same old problem . . . do we, don't we?'

Nikki smiled at her. 'You both know what I think. But it's entirely down to the two of you.' For some while now, Cat had been going out with another member of their team, DC Ben Radley. They were already living together, and to Nikki's mind they were perfectly suited. But they had yet to set a firm date for the wedding because they were both scared that their demanding jobs could become an issue.

'I've seen so many failed marriages, all because of the kind of work we do,' said Cat, 'and I don't want that to happen to Ben and me.' She looked thoroughly miserable.

'Why should it?' Nikki asked. 'Half those failed marriages you are talking about came about because the copper husband was playing away on night shifts, and Ben Radley is *not* going to do that. He loves you to bits. I mean, you are totally committed to each other and already living under the same roof, so where's the problem?'

Cat shrugged. 'Put like that . . .'

'Exactly. So, shall I get my diary out? I'll need some new clothes but I absolutely draw the line at a hat, okay?'

Cat laughed. 'You are excused the hat. I know I'm being paranoid, but it's so important to me, well, to both of us. As you know, Ben's been married before and he wants to get it right this time.'

'It wasn't his fault last time either, Cat. That was simply a tragedy that had a bad outcome. No one's fault.' Nikki really didn't want to think about that time. It dredged up sad memories of her own. Both she and Ben had suffered the loss of their daughters.

'Sorry, ma'am, I wasn't thinking.' Cat looked anxious. 'I didn't mean to upset you.'

'You didn't, so don't worry. Bad things happen to good people. We need to accept that we can't alter what has already happened and move on.' It sounded good, only, moving on and away from her precious Hannah was never going to happen. Nikki pushed away the sadness and gave Cat a big grin. 'My advice to you is, one, go find some mud that will stick to your pervert, and two, get together with Ben and your diary, set a bloody date and put us all out of our misery!'

Cat stood up, looking a lot brighter.

CHAPTER TWO

Sedgebrook House was a far cry from what Niall had expected. He couldn't fathom out why he had never seen it before — it was so big. Then, as they drew nearer, he began to understand. From his side of the fen he would see only a tall stand of trees that completely obscured the lovely old period property from view. He guessed the building was listed, but he knew very little about architecture. Extensive gardens, from which a vista of trees, shrubs and flowerbeds stretched away for what Niall thought must be a couple of acres at least, and then it was farmland as far as the eye could see.

He pulled into the drive and waited until he saw Joseph's Ford Kuga 4x4 behind him.

'Impressive,' said Joseph, emerging from his vehicle, 'if a little overgrown.'

'Tamsin would love it, wouldn't she? I can hear her now: "Perfect habitat for birds, butterflies, insects and so many of our native living creatures. Just wonderful!"' He rolled his eyes in mock exasperation, and affection. Tamsin adored the natural world and had awakened a whole new appreciation of the fenlands in him.

As they approached the door, he noticed the decorative flowerpots lining the front of the house. He guessed that these were the ones that had been moved. He raised an eyebrow. Whoever had shifted that lot must have been strong.

He rang the bell and they heard loud barking, then footsteps, and a deep voice yelling at the dogs to get in their beds and stay there.

As the door opened, it was clear that the creatures had absolutely no intention of doing anything of the sort.

Joseph smiled broadly at them, saying through the deafening barks, 'Hey, dachshunds! I love these little guys! Great characters.'

Niall wasn't quite so sure. He liked his dogs a bit bigger and calmer, like his Skipper, a German Shepherd cross Labrador.

Eventually the owner managed to herd them into the kitchen and close the door. 'Sorry about that, gentlemen. Wonderful housedogs and terribly loyal, but a tad on the stubborn side and wary of strangers. Anyway, come in, come in.'

Niall wondered how someone had managed to move those pots without disturbing the dogs. He'd save that question for later.

They were ushered into a sitting room and told to sit down while Duncan Howard went to find his wife.

'Inside doesn't quite match the exterior, does it?' said Joseph in a low voice after he had gone.

It was true. Niall had expected elegant, yet Sedgebrook House was anything but. He looked around and took in the pot plants on every windowsill, along with some beautiful rock and crystal specimens. Two walls were covered entirely in paintings, as well as all manner of books, academic magazines and papers scattered on shelves and tables and strewn around in piles on the floor. The furniture had obviously once been expensive, now it was what you might call "well-loved," with slightly sagging armchairs and sofas covered with unmatched cushions, all bearing a fine covering of dog hair. 'It's lived in, I'll give it that.'

'I do love that.' Joseph was looking at a big ornate Victorian cast-iron fireplace, bordered with decorative Victorian tiles. 'I can see a roaring fire blazing in there on a cold winter's evening.'

Niall could almost hear logs spitting and crackling.

Joseph went to examine the pictures. 'All landscapes,' he said softly, 'very good ones too.'

Out of his depth again, Niall was even more grateful that his father-in-law had decided to tag along.

Finally, Duncan returned, closely followed by a willowy woman wearing an old short-sleeved Ralph Lauren polo top, a canvas half-jacket with bulging pockets, and a pair of faded chinos with mud stains around the hems.

Peeling off her grubby gardening gloves, she smiled at them apologetically. 'Sorry about the state I'm in, gentlemen. Goose and I were trying to prevent the Russian vine strangling the gazebo to death. I swear the damned stuff really does grow a mile a minute.'

'Goose is the gardener,' added Duncan, seemingly accustomed to pointing out the vagaries in his wife's stories.

'Well, I'm sure they didn't think he was my solicitor, dear, or a passing vagrant.'

This was followed by a rather lengthy stream of amicable bickering between the couple. It looked like the interview could well last some time.

Niall hastily interjected, 'Mr and Mrs Howard, as you know, your son came to see us today. I wonder if you would be kind enough to tell us about these recent incidents?'

After much discussion, the Howards listed six separate occasions when things had been disturbed — failing to mention the knife. Niall temporarily let that go and asked them if they had any idea who might be behind these petty and annoying incidents.

They both agreed that they had no idea.

'Mind you, you've upset a good few people in the past, Aurelia,' said Duncan thoughtfully. 'You don't suffer fools gladly, and you don't have much patience with shallow types.' He shrugged. 'Maybe you've upset one of your students?'

'Oh, for heaven's sake, Duncan! As if one of them is going to drive all the way out here to rearrange my garden planters! They have minds of their own. If I upset them, and I do occasionally, they tell me. So far none of them has threatened to steal my clothes from the washing line.' Aurelia Howard flopped down into an overstuffed armchair and glowered at her husband.

'Just a thought,' he said mildly.

Niall could see Duncan in an academic gown, but not Aurelia. 'What are your subjects, if I might ask?'

Duncan answered first. 'Geology and mineralogy. I'm semi-retired now, but I still lecture occasionally. I specialise in the Jurassic period and the geology of the North Yorkshire Coast.'

Joseph indicated some of the beautiful specimens. 'So I see, sir. You have some amazing rocks and crystals.'

'You really like them?' asked Duncan, brightening up.

'I do, sir. When I was a kid, I used to go beachcombing and hunting for fossils. One of my favourite pastimes was searching for quartz and amethyst in the slag heaps behind the old tin mines in Cornwall. I've still got some of the treasures I found as a boy.'

'Goodness me! How refreshing! You must come around one day and let me show you my private collection.' Duncan had come alive. 'I have one or two very rare pieces that I think would fascinate you, Detective Sergeant. Especially a particularly beautiful specimen of Dioptase — that's a copper cyclosilicate with an intense emerald green colour, it's quite—'

'Oh Lord, now you've got him started. We'll get nowhere with my laundry thief.' Aurelia raised her eyebrows in mock horror. 'Oh, and I lecture in psychology, specialising in the effects of folklore and superstition on modern society.' She turned to Joseph, 'But I doubt you'll be too interested in *that*, young man.'

'On the contrary, Mrs Howard. I've travelled extensively in the past and have seen first-hand the influence of superstitious beliefs on both behaviour and health. It's a fascinating subject.' Joseph bestowed an earnest expression on the woman, and Niall saw her soften visibly.

'However,' Joseph added, 'right now we have a job to do. Mrs Howard, why would someone leave an athame on your doorstep?'

Aurelia Howard stared at him. 'I . . . I don't know.'

'There has to be a connection with your particular field of expertise, wouldn't you say?' prompted Joseph.

'How do you know about the athame?' Her voice was now low, all its bombastic authority gone.

'An old investigation involving a Wiccan woman, Mrs Howard. I learned a lot about that particular religion, and the traditions of witchcraft. It dispelled a lot of the misconceptions I held about it and I discovered a peaceful, balanced way of life that is based on nature and integrity.'

'Are you sure you're a policeman?' Duncan asked.

Joseph smiled. 'I'm a human being, sir, and a very inquisitive one. A pretty good reason for choosing to be a detective, I think.'

'And a very good one at that,' added Niall, failing to keep the pride out of his voice.

'A very unusual one, to be sure.' Duncan shook his head.

'The thing is, Mrs Howard, as far as I recall, one of their tenets is "Harm None," and that is the whole of the law. The witch's knife is part of a box of ritual tools. It is not used for actual physical cutting, is it? It is used for cutting energy. So it shouldn't have alarmed you. Why were you so upset by it then?'

'Because I don't believe that it was sent with pure intentions,' she said softly. 'As in every part of society, Wicca has its good and bad elements. You yourselves have the odd corrupt officer, do you not?'

'I'd be a fool to deny that,' said Joseph.

'Exactly. Some would use witchcraft to control and frighten, instead of offering peace and tranquillity.'

15

'Do you know who sent the knife?' asked Niall.

She shook her head slowly. 'No, I'm afraid I don't. I just know that someone does not wish me well.'

Niall began to worry about the old couple. They lived so far out on Jacob's Fen and were pretty well isolated. His own cottage was just a few minutes' drive away, but he'd never known they were there. 'Does your son live at home?' he asked.

'Oh no. Richard lives a couple of villages away,' said Duncan. 'And our other two sons are abroad. Neither of them has Richard's love for the land.'

'Which is why we made him farm manager,' added Aurelia. 'This will all be his one day.' There was a wistfulness in her voice.

'What about the dogs? Wouldn't they bark if someone was snooping around?' Niall asked.

'To be honest, they bark such a lot that we tend to think it's just a fox or cat that's set them off. Maybe we'll take more notice in the future,' said Duncan.

For a few moments no one spoke. 'Sadly, I can't allocate a watch on your home,' said Niall. 'It's too far out to do a drive by. However, I live close by, so I'll be particularly vigilant regarding strange vehicles in the area and should things escalate, we'll think again.' He took a card from his wallet and scribbled a number on the back. 'That's my mobile and my home landline. If anything worries you, ring me.'

He and Joseph stood up.

'We'll make enquiries in the area,' said Joseph. 'See if anyone has noticed any strangers around here recently, but as Sergeant Farrow said, do ring if you are at all concerned.'

They left to a cacophony of barking and a loud voice yelling, 'Rheinhardt! Manfred! Helmut! Get in your beds and for heaven's sake, put a sock in it!'

* * *

On their way out, Niall asked Joseph to come and see him and Tamsin before he went home.

Joseph didn't need asking twice. By now, his daughter Tamsin had been around for years, but he still felt he had a lot of catching up to do. He'd seen little of her in her childhood. As a Special Forces soldier, he was rarely at home and even when he was, she had hated him for his job. She had considered him a murderer and it had broken Joseph's heart.

'Try and stop me. See you there.'

Tamsin opened the cottage door and seeing her father, ran forward and gave him a hug. Joseph closed his eyes briefly. Miracles did happen.

He patted a bouncing Skipper, followed her inside and looked around. 'Every time I come here, there's something new!' He indicated the cooker. 'That's a Rangemaster, isn't it?'

Tamsin beamed at him. 'My dream. We've been saving up for it. It's a refurb, but it looks like new, doesn't it? I love it.' She ran a hand over it lovingly. 'And so does Skip. I keep finding him curled up in front of it. Now Niall can finish the tiling and the kitchen will be complete at last.'

'This place is a credit to both of you. You've worked so hard.'

Tamsin smiled. 'With some sterling help from my father, as I recall.'

'Made a change from chasing bad guys, and I got more tea than I do at work.' Niall stepped in, made a fuss of the dog and then hugged his wife.

Tam laughed. 'I see you've got your priorities right. Dog first, then the wife.'

Niall kissed her. 'He's pushier. We've been in a really interesting house, just five minutes up the road.'

He and Joseph told her about Sedgebrook House, the dachshunds and the Howards.

'Howard? That's Richard Howard's parents, isn't it?' Tamsin said casually.

Niall looked surprised. 'You know him?'

'From work. He's trying to get the biodiversity right on his farm. You know, wildlife corridors, field margins, dyke maintenance and copses. I'm going out to see him tomorrow as it happens, so maybe I'll get a look at your old house.' Tamsin poured boiling water into mugs. 'I've only spoken to him on the phone so far but he's a breath of fresh air. He's already stopped using herbicides and is farming totally organically, which is fantastic for the plants and insects.'

'Right, well, that's a coincidence.'

Niall looked slightly uncomfortable. Joseph imagined that he wouldn't want Tamsin wandering around the Sedgebrook Farm Estate if some crazed warlock was lurking about, casting evil spells on Aurelia Howard.

'Are you going alone?' asked Niall, a little too casually.

'Niall Farrow! You're jealous! Think I might run off with Richard Howard, do you?'

Joseph laughed. 'Sorry to disappoint you, Tam, but I think he's concerned for your safety.'

'Rats! And there was me thinking . . .' She gave a mock frown. 'Anyway, I haven't seen him yet. He might be as ugly as sin and have terrible habits.'

'Actually, he's a good-looking man, although I hate to admit it,' grumbled Niall, 'But Dad's right. Just be on your guard, and if you see anything out of the ordinary while you're there, you phone me, okay?'

Tamsin handed them their tea. 'I will, and I promise not to look at handsome Richard.'

'I didn't actually say *handsome* . . .'

Joseph watched this exchange with a smile. He'd been stunned, and not a little concerned, when Tamsin had told him that she was marrying a policeman. She had always equated the police with the armed forces, but now she had come full circle. Tamsin Farrow was a very supportive police wife and under her ministrations young, gung-ho PC Farrow had become a responsible and competent sergeant and husband.

Joseph drained his mug. 'Better get back to Cloud Fen. You know how Nikki gets when her dinner's late. She does love her food.'

'Just hates cooking it,' added Tamsin. 'Lucky you're such a handy chef.'

'Hey, that reminds me. Tomorrow night, our place, family dinner, seven thirty, and bring Skipper.' Joseph stood up. 'I've got a new veggie recipe that I'm making especially for you.'

'Great! Love to Nikki and see you both tomorrow.'

Joseph drove back across the fen towards the main road. Like Niall, he also felt apprehensive. This area was pretty remote, and two people he loved were a long way from help if they needed it.

His previous good humour faded, to be replaced by anxiety. Objectively, some joker stealing washing and moving plant pots was very small fry, but he had a feeling that Aurelia Howard had not been wrong when she said that someone did not wish her well. And considering that Niall and Tamsin were the Howards' nearest neighbours it made them vulnerable too.

By the time he reached Cloud Cottage Farm, he had decided to ask Nikki if he could take some time to help Niall clear this mystery up as soon as possible. It was certainly not a CID matter by any stretch of the imagination, but possibly a day or two spent making some enquiries of a few people that he knew could speed things up, and then Niall could bring it to a close, hopefully with an arrest or at least a serious warning.

He locked his car, hoping that he was overreacting. Coppers, he reasoned, always suspected the worst of people, but sometimes they were proved wrong. So why couldn't he shake the thought that this was just the tip of an iceberg? And his daughter and son-in-law were right on collision course.

He pushed open the front door and hurried in. 'Nikki? I'm home . . . and I need to ask a favour.'

CHAPTER THREE

Tamsin was up even earlier than Niall, and by the time he was awake, she was showered, dressed, and singing softly to herself as she placed a mug of tea on his bedside table.

Niall grinned at her sleepily. 'Perfect start to the day, a beautiful woman serenading me *and* bearing gifts.'

She returned the smile. 'And there it ends, sunshine. Ten minutes and I'm off.'

'Why?' He rubbed his eyes and blinked at her.

With his tousled hair and bewildered expression, he reminded her of a small boy. 'You know what these farmers are like. Up with the lark and grabbing every moment of daylight at this time of year.' She sat down on the bed next to him. 'Like most farmers, Richard Howard has a mammoth amount of stuff to contend with. So, early start.' She leaned forward and kissed him. 'And that means I finish early. Skip can stay here this morning and grab a few zeds, and I'll come home and let him out at lunchtime. Win-win all round.'

He pulled her towards him and they kissed.

'You take care, Tam.' His seriousness of the evening before had returned. 'Keep vigilant. We are pretty sure some-one is watching Aurelia Howard and we can only assume the motive is malicious.'

She nodded. 'I will, darling, I promise. If I see the slightest thing that bothers me, I'll ring you immediately.'

It was a short journey to work, just a mile up the road, but into new territory. She slowed as she drove past Sedgebrook House and wondered how on earth she had never seen this impressive building and its incredible rambling gardens before.

The barns and farm estate office were about five hundred yards further on. She was impressed by the cleanliness and neatness of the place. Richard Howard obviously kept a tight rein and was pretty proud of his business.

As she stepped out of her car, he strode towards her, hand outstretched.

Niall had been right, he was a good-looking man.

'I'm Richard. Good to meet you in person, and grateful for your turning out so early.'

Tamsin smiled. 'Hardly an effort, us practically being neighbours. I had no idea you were here.'

Richard laughed. 'You are not alone. There is absolutely no reason to drive down here unless you are coming to Sedgebrook. The road ends on our land and all the paths, pads and access lanes are purely for the farmworkers and machinery. When we were kids, we used to say that Sedgebrook was built at the end of the world and if you went any further, you would fall off the edge.'

Tamsin stared over the acres of arable farmland. She saw only a row of pylons stretching towards the horizon and a couple of small copses of tight-knit trees, and understood exactly how a child might see this place. 'It's a lot of land.'

'Not as much as it was,' replied Richard. 'Some was sold off in my grandfather's day. Even so, we are still around one hundred and sixty hectares.'

Tamsin did a quick calculation. 'Wow! That's four hundred acres?'

He nodded. 'Quite enough for me, thank you. I want to get this right, I mean not just as a profitable farm, but ecologically.'

'So, tell me, how can I help?' said Tamsin.

'It's about the copses. Especially the one you can see out there. It's called Hob's End, Lord knows why.' He pointed across a long field to where a large overgrown cluster of trees and bushes formed a dark green cushion on the horizon. 'I understand about regular cleaning of the ditches, the field margin management, and I'm learning about increasing wild pollinators without losing productive land, but I know nothing about trees and copses — what helps and what doesn't, what to keep and what to cull, or what I should be doing with them.' He looked towards his Land Rover. 'Shall we take a look at it? It hasn't been touched for as long as I can remember. Right now, I've got a small team of men and women who are prepared to tackle clearing it, with your help and advice. Two of them should be out there now.'

'I'll be interested to see it.' Tamsin followed him to his vehicle. 'I'm sure you know that the government provides a Farm Woodland Payment scheme for keeping a percentage of your fields in a natural or reforested state. It's hugely important, helps your crops and reduces field pests and soil erosion.'

'It will help, no question about that.'

Tamsin got in. 'Of course, it could be one of those areas that cannot be farmed for some reason, so it's simply been left. We have found that some areas are either too boggy or full of rocks to cultivate, so over the years the trees have taken over.'

'You could be right. Hob's End Copse was overgrown even when I was a bairn.'

A few minutes later they were parking up on the edge of the field where the copse was situated.

'We're taking away all the old broken-down fencing and scrubby stuff that surrounds the area and cutting a swathe of grass margin that will be left to naturalise. What I really want to know is, should we clear the whole area and replant, or cut back and manage what is already here?' he asked.

Tamsin walked across to the edge of the trees and stared at it. It appeared almost impenetrable. 'I'm going to have to get in there before I can assess it, Mr Howard.'

'Please call me Richard. "Mr Howard" makes me feel like my father.'

'Okay, Richard it is, and I'm Tamsin. You've also met my husband, Sergeant Niall Farrow, at Greenborough Police Station so this is all a bit of a coincidence.'

'A good one, I'm sure.' He lowered his voice, even though there was no one in the immediate vicinity. 'I'm not sure if he told you, but I went to see him because someone has been hanging around my parents' home and being a nuisance, a rather worrying kind of nuisance.'

'He didn't go into detail, but as we live on the doorstep, he told me to keep my eyes open for anything out of the ordinary while I was here.' She gave him a small smile. 'I'm really sorry for your parents, Richard. It's a horrid thing to happen.'

They walked around the perimeter of the copse, and soon Tamsin saw an off-road vehicle and a flat-back Toyota truck parked up close to the tree line.

As they approached, a man called out to Richard, 'Over here, sir, we've found something a bit odd.'

The man was in his twenties, his long dirty blond hair tied back in a bandana. He wore worker trousers, steel toe cap safety boots and a Greenpeace T-shirt.

'On our way, Leigh.' Richard pointed to her. 'And this is Tamsin, originally from the Woodland Trust, now working with us ignorant farmers.' He turned back to her. 'Leigh Peacock. He's a volunteer from the village, and a Save the Planet enthusiast.'

'Good for you, Leigh, I'm with you there.' Tamsin smiled warmly at the young man. 'So, what have you found that's odd?'

'A pathway, recently used.'

'In this tangled mess?' exclaimed Richard disbelievingly. 'Are you sure it's not badger tracks?'

'Positive, unless Bill Badger is wearing size-ten heavy-soled boots. Come and see.' Leigh loped off towards a small area that had recently been cleared of nettles and elder. 'We took down the broken fenceposts and started winding up the rusty wire that was hanging from them and Claire noticed a spot where the undergrowth had been flattened.'

They walked over to where a woman was standing staring into the copse. She looked up, shook her hair and frowned. 'Who on earth would want to try to access this jungle?' Seeing Tamsin, she stopped and grinned. 'Sorry, I'm Claire Rhodes, one of the victims, er, volunteers, that Leigh has kidnapped to help him re-educate farmers — and work our socks off into the bargain.'

She was a tall, friendly-looking woman with startling green eyes and wavy auburn hair.

From the hint of an accent, Tamsin guessed she had Irish blood in her somewhere.

'What do you make of this?' Claire said.

Tamsin wasn't sure. 'Better check it out. The only reason I'd try and get in, other than the one I'm here for, would be if my dog had run off and I was afraid he'd get snarled up in brambles.'

'Fair point,' said Claire. 'Or maybe if I was a poacher.' She turned to Richard. 'Do you get much trouble from poachers here?'

Richard shook his head. 'Not really. Had a few guys out here one night looking for rabbit or pheasant, and we've had the odd bit of hare-coursing over the years, but nothing too dramatic.'

'You'd never find your way into this at night,' said Tamsin, stepping over the fence line. 'Let's see if this leads right in.' She pulled a few large branches aside and followed the track. Leigh had been right, there were boot prints. Now she was really puzzled. It didn't make sense. It led nowhere, so why go in?

Carefully following the boot tracks, she soon realised that the path was widening out, and, yes, it had been used recently. There were fresh cuts in the branches, and in several places brambles and plants had been hacked away and left in heaps. 'No one else has been here with the same intention as me, have they?' she asked Richard. 'Like Woodland Trust people or someone from another agency like mine?'

'Absolutely not,' grunted Richard, fighting his way through the bushes to catch her up. 'This is weird.'

'You haven't had any naturalists ask if they can track badgers or muntjacs across your land?'

Again the answer was negative. 'No one has my permission to be here. The only people recently were a metal detecting club. I allowed them access onto some of the other fields after we'd done the first plough. And that's it.'

Tamsin pushed forward. The recently cut path was accessible, with care, but the ancient trees and all the tangled brambles and elder bushes were getting denser. After a while, she guessed they must be getting close to the centre of the copse, but she still had no idea why someone had taken the time and energy to cut a way through.

'Hold it.' She stopped and stepped off the path and into some thick overgrowth, 'There are some rocks or stones here, so maybe it was originally ground that wasn't farmable.'

Leigh followed her through. 'They're not just stones. That's a wall.'

She looked closer. 'It's even more than that, Leigh, it's a building of some kind — well, the remains of one.'

'Let's go further down the track,' called out Claire. 'It might show us more.'

A few seconds later they came to a halt.

'Good God!' Richard exclaimed. 'A derelict cottage!'

Tamsin found it hard to believe, but there it was, almost completely covered by trees, foliage, and eroded soil, with the upstairs all but gone, and with just a chimney stack rising up amongst the trees, entirely enveloped by dark green ivy. She let out a long low whistle. 'I've never seen anything like this in my life.'

'And the path leads directly to the door, so someone knew about this place, didn't they?' said Claire, darkly.

No one spoke, then Richard whispered, 'I've lived or worked here all my life. I must have been past the copse almost every day and I never knew this existed.'

'We should talk to your father and mother,' suggested Tamsin. 'Surely they knew about it?'

'It's very old,' said Claire, 'I'm guessing from around the turn of the century, but what puzzles me is who has been coming here now?'

'And possibly still is,' added Leigh.

Tamsin thought of the fresh cuts in the branches. Someone had been here, possibly as recently as the day before. She narrowed her eyes and took in the moss-covered stonework, the rotting woodwork and the grimy opaque glass, or what was left of it. She wanted to see inside.

She moved towards the door, the others following her. Richard called out, 'Wait! I have a duty of care while you are on my land, and this place looks like a death trap to me.'

'Oh, come on!' Claire burst out. 'We are all big boys and girls. You can't not let us go inside! We are dying to know what's going on. Please?'

'I agree, Richard,' Tamsin said. 'We'll be careful and I take full responsibility for myself.'

'Ditto,' chimed in Leigh. 'I *have* to see inside that hovel!'

'Okay, but let me go in first.'

Richard moved forward quickly, with Tamsin close behind.

'Oil on the door hinges?' Richard said almost to himself. He pushed the weathered and warped door open and stepped inside.

Over his shoulder, Tamsin saw that they were in the kitchen. So this must have been the back of the cottage. She gazed around. If you disregarded the debris, it was still recognisable as an old rural cottage kitchen.

There was a rusty coal-fired range set in a recessed fireplace with a high stone mantle shelf, and on the stove were a dusty old kettle and a dented saucepan with a lid. In the centre of the room stood a heavy wooden table with the remains of some hardback chairs around it. There had been a butler sink, but it was cracked and broken and lay tilted to one side on the floor. A mould-covered ridged, wooden draining board still hung drunkenly from the wall from one remaining fitting, and several dented and battered oil lamps were scattered about the room. Big hooks were fixed to the ceiling in the region of the fireplace, no doubt for suspending cooking pans or drying herbs.

Conspicuous as a beacon in the night was an area on the table that had been wiped and cleaned and was now home to a Tupperware box of digestive biscuits and a large bottle of spring water.

Tamsin looked at the others. They were all silently staring at those two commonplace objects as if they had freshly arrived from an alien planet.

'You've had visitors,' said Leigh shortly.

'So it appears,' murmured Richard.

He looked worried, and Tamsin was certain that it was connected to his reason for going to the police station. Was the person who had made a camp here the one who had threatened Richard's mother? Tamsin decided not to say anything in front of Leigh and Claire. She would ask him later.

'It could just be a vagrant. Maybe some old Yellowbelly who knew about this cottage from donkey's years ago,' suggested Leigh, sounding unconvinced.

'Right, so he spends hours, maybe days, clearing a path and getting inside, just to drink water and nibble digestives?' Claire laughed. 'I don't think so.'

Tamsin looked towards the only other door in the kitchen. 'Well, we can't get upstairs, but maybe we should look around the rest of the ground floor?'

Richard opened the door.

It was clear that this had been the sitting room, the best room in the house. A big open fireplace remained, and rags that had once been curtains still hung at the broken windows. A staircase led up from a corner of the room and disappeared into nowhere. The roof of the floor above was totally gone, and branches and greenery had taken its place. Tamsin could see daylight. Like the rest of the place, it had fallen into ruin.

Except that one area had been completely cleared and occupying it was a bright blue, pop-up, one-man tent.

'Last time I saw one of those was at Glastonbury,' declared Leigh.

For the first time, Tamsin felt a twinge of fear. Niall had said to ring him if she saw anything remotely out of the ordinary, and this qualified in spades. And this tent probably belonged to the person who was targeting Sedgebrook House. She looked across to Richard and knew he was thinking the same thing.

'Maybe we should leave everything untouched,' said Tamsin. 'The police might need to gather evidence from it.' She used her iPhone to take some photos of the room and the tent, just in case its owner returned and removed it before anyone else could see it.

'Good idea,' said Leigh. 'We may never see something like this again. The whole cottage looks as if it's been constructed of living trees and growing plants. It's awesome.'

'Nature will always take back what we stole from it,' said Claire almost reverently. 'As you say, awesome.'

'Can I ask you guys to keep any pictures you take to yourselves for a while, please?' Richard sounded anxious. 'We are not sure what we are dealing with here, so it might be better to keep this quiet until we know more.'

Tamsin agreed, though of course she would be showing Niall.

'Sure thing,' said Leigh.

Claire nodded. 'Of course. So what do you want us to do here? Continue, or hold off the clearing?'

Richard looked at Tamsin. 'What do you reckon?'

She thought for a moment and then said, 'I'd say back off for a day or so. I'll do my check, as we are here now, then you decide when we've thoroughly inspected the copse.'

'That's what I think too,' said Richard. 'So, if you guys just finish up with that fencing and wire, you can shoot off and I'll ring you tomorrow.' He looked at them apologetically. 'Sorry about this, I hope it's not too much of a pain.'

Leigh grinned. 'No sweat. Got plenty to do. We're organising a demo against excess plastic in supermarkets. We'll see you in a day or so.'

They made their way back to the field, where Leigh and Claire set about finishing the job of tying off the wire and stacking the broken fence posts. Tamsin asked Richard if he wanted to join her in checking out the copse.

'I need to get back to work fairly soon,' he said, 'but I'm certainly not leaving you out here alone. And I want a word with you anyway.'

Tamsin nodded, and they walked a short distance from the others.

After a few moments, he said, 'This could well be connected to the threats to my parents, couldn't it?'

'If it's okay with you, I'll ring Niall and tell him about the cottage and your squatter,' Tamsin said.

'Absolutely. Please do.' Richard shook his head. 'You have no idea how surprised I am that we found that cottage. I'm pretty sure even my parents don't know about it. Certainly, no one's ever mentioned it. And how on earth did the owner of that tent know it was there?'

'I've been wondering that myself. That path was cut directly to the cottage, it wasn't just someone hoping to sneak into the copse and pitch their tent away from prying eyes. That was deliberate.'

'Make that call, Tamsin. This is giving me the creeps.'

CHAPTER FOUR

Cat Cullen and Dave Harris sat in their car outside a house in a small village a couple of miles from Greenborough. The village was called Old Fleeting and up until a year ago, had been a tiny hamlet with no amenities other than a bus that ran about four times a day. Now it was a maze of new housing that had attracted incomers from all over, especially the South, because of its affordability. Cat and Ben had looked at one of the classy little estates themselves, which were outside the town but close enough to not worry about the commute to work. A brand new three-bedroom detached house with garden and garage would have cost in the region of £225,000, and the properties were being snapped up as soon as they went on the market. Once again, they couldn't make up their minds. The houses had a lot going for them. They were well built with fitted kitchens and an en-suite attached to the master bedroom, but neither of them really wanted to live in the heart of a new development, no matter how "desirable" the houses were.

The place they were watching right now was a smart little detached bungalow. The garden was neat, almost artificial looking, with orderly rows of bedding plants, all perfect matching colours and uniform heights, surrounding a perfectly rectangular lawn with an ornamental bird bath in the centre.

'Blimey! He must use nail scissors to get the edges of that lawn to look like that! And it's so green I'm wondering if I'm looking at AstroTurf,' Dave said.

'I'm surprised he has time for gardening, what with all his other activities — dirty bastard,' growled Cat.

Dave laughed. 'What happened to innocent until proven guilty?'

'He's as innocent as Jack the Ripper, and you know it, Dave Harris.'

'Just saying . . .'

'You're in a good mood this morning, mate,' she said.

'That's true.' He turned and looked at her, 'Don't tell the others just yet, because I'm still in two minds about it, but I might be moving.'

Cat's eyes widened. 'But you've lived in that house for eons!'

'Exactly, and I'm thinking it's time to move on.' He smiled at her. 'My Margaret and I were really happy there. It was a proper family home back then, but when she got ill, the place got neglected. I never had time for everything and, well, I guess it's just not the same now she's gone.'

'Where would you go?'

'That's the good bit. I've been offered a cottage in the Cressy Old Hall estate.'

'What? That toffee-nosed git, Clive Cressy-Lawson, is giving you a cottage?' she spluttered.

'He's not that bad! After I've retired I'm going to help him out with security. He's finally decided to open the Old Hall to the public and he's offered me the job, with a cottage thrown in.' Dave beamed at her. 'I just love that place, even though it's had more than its fair share of notoriety.'

'I'll bloody well say it has!' Cat recalled their last murder enquiry. 'Hey, if you like it there, it's not a million miles from town. We'll still be able to keep in touch, won't we?'

'As if I'd ever lose contact with you, Catkin.' He patted her arm affectionately. 'And it's only about fifteen minutes from the nick, so . . . ?'

'Coffee and a Danish once a week?'

'Deal!' He looked back at the bungalow. 'By the way, shouldn't we be working?'

'I suppose so.' She set her jaw. 'Actually, yes, I want us to nail this son of a bitch before you walk off into the sunset.'

'Then we better get a move on. I'm off in two weeks.'

'I'm pleased you don't look sad, Dave. It's going to be a big wrench losing you and I'd hate it if you were really cut up about it.' She was going to be devastated at losing her old partner but she wasn't going to lay that on him.

'I've done my bit for Queen and Country, kid. I'm ready for some me time. There are some things I'd like to do, and the Old Hall will keep me busy part of the time. Clive said I can rent the cottage permanently, even if I decide to back out of the job after a while. So, with the proceeds of the house sale and my police pension, I reckon I'll survive, don't you?'

'You sure will, my friend, and good luck to you,' she said. 'Now, as a little leaving present, let's see if we can nail Mr Vernon Deacon, shall we? If he sticks to his usual schedule, he won't be home for over an hour, and I want to see what the neighbours think about him. Ready?'

Dave opened his door. 'And willing.'

* * *

Nikki had given Joseph two days to help Niall with his inquiry, and then she wanted him on the Deacon case with Cat. He was now motoring towards Jacob's Fen to see this mysterious overgrown cottage in Hob's End Copse. It was a miracle how close he and Tamsin had become recently. For years, she had been lost to him, and winning her back had been far from easy. His girl had very strong ideals and he was aware that if he failed to live up to them, he might lose her for ever.

He found her on the perimeter of the copse, talking to a tall, attractive man who just had to be Richard Howard.

She looked surprised to see him. 'Hi, Dad. Didn't realise this warranted a detective sergeant.'

'It doesn't,' he said, 'so don't get the wrong impression. I'm simply doing your husband a favour as all the foot soldiers are busy.'

'As you are here now, DS Easter, would you think it rude if I got back to work? I just didn't want Tamsin out here alone. My other two volunteers have already left, and this whole thing is making me very anxious.' Richard Howard did indeed look concerned.

'No problem. Tam can show me this cottage, and then we'll get away ourselves.'

Howard's vehicle moved off in the direction of the estate yard.

Joseph turned to his daughter, 'Right. Let's take a look at the Gingerbread House.'

'Back to witches, huh, Dad? Believe me, you're not far out, it's pretty spooky.' She led him to a small gap in the undergrowth and they pushed through into a roughly cleared pathway.

As they proceeded, it became clear to Joseph why Tamsin had felt so uneasy. You had to know exactly where you were going and what you would find when you got there, to make the effort to clear such a direct route through the wood. This was either ancient local knowledge, or an educated guess about something you'd been told about.

They walked on in silence, pushing back branches and trying to avoid getting snagged by vicious thorny brambles.

'Nearly there,' called back Tamsin, forging ahead.

And indeed, it was like something out of a fairy tale. It seemed to have been there forever, the stone, brick, wood, bark, branches, tangles of twisted ivy roots and foliage, all an organic part of the whole. It was the oddest fusion of man-made building and encroaching nature that he'd ever seen.

'We thought it could be turn of the century,' Tamsin said.

'Maybe older,' said Joseph. 'It's almost totally covered and engulfed by the wood, isn't it?' They both spoke in hushed tones.

'It's a bit clearer round the back. That's where we got in. Come on.'

She picked her way across the rubble and fallen stonework. 'This is the kitchen door.'

The interior smelt of damp and decay. It wasn't an unpleasant smell, more like age and leaf mould.

Tamsin indicated the table with its biscuit box and bottled water. 'Lunch?'

'More like safety rations, in case he gets caught without food or drink.' He walked around, inspecting everything. The stove was cold, but it would have been impossible to light a fire in any case. For a start, the chimney would have been blocked, and then the smoke would draw attention. Still, it was late summer and warm.

'The tent is through there.' Tamsin pointed to a door. 'In the sitting room.'

Joseph took out two pairs of nitrile protective gloves and passed one to Tamsin. 'Touch nothing unless I say so, okay?'

'You're making me feel like a scene-of-crime officer,' murmured Tamsin.

'Depending on what I find, you could well be a temporary one. Let's take a look.' He pushed the door open and went in.

The bright blue nylon tent was so incongruous it was hard to take in anything else. He recognised the make — good, but not expensive. It was zipped up tight and gave nothing away, like the closed expression of someone hiding a dirty secret.

Cautiously, he undid the flap and looked inside, aware as he did so of Tamsin hovering close to his shoulder.

All he could see was a sleeping bag and a couple of emergency foil survival blankets, and for a moment he felt disappointed, although he wasn't sure quite what he had been expecting.

'Oh,' said Tamsin, glaring at the sleeping bag. 'Is that all? I was hoping for something exciting.'

'Careful what you wish for, love,' warned Joseph.

She didn't answer. He lifted up the end of the padded sleeping bag. There was nothing concealed either in or beneath it.

Joseph backed out and gazed around the room. 'I wonder what drew him or her here?' he mused.

'Well, it certainly wasn't its modern conveniences and old-world charm,' said Tamsin dryly. 'He had to have known it was here, so maybe he'd been here in the past but a long time ago, before it got so overgrown.'

'From the stuff left in that kitchen, I'd say it's been uninhabited since before the Second World War,'

'And Richard Howard said he'd never even heard his parents talk about it, so it's probably been hidden for over seventy years.' She wrinkled her nose. 'It certainly smells that way.'

They returned to the kitchen. Like the tent, the water bottle and the Tupperware biscuit box looked so out of place amongst all the grime and dilapidation that they were startling.

'I suppose all we can do now is wait to see who comes back here and challenge him,' said Tamsin.

'We? I don't think so! Well, certainly not you,' Joseph said. 'Heaven knows what this person is up to, but ten to one, it's nothing good.'

'But we have to find out what's going on, Dad! I'm desperate to know.'

Joseph threw up his hands. 'Okay, okay. For starters, let's take a really close look at this cottage. Think like a detective, Tam. Something brought our intruder here, and as you say, it wasn't just somewhere warm and dry to spend a night, he came here purposely, so why?'

'Have you got a torch? It's pretty gloomy in here if we're looking for clues.'

She was right. The remaining windows were filthy and very little light penetrated through the trees or in the open back door. He took a pocket Maglite from his jacket and passed it to her.

Tamsin shone the torch beam into cupboards and corners. 'I'm wondering if he came back for something. If so, and if he didn't collect it already, it could still be here.'

'Good point.' Joseph smiled at her. This was a scenario he could never have dreamed of, not in a thousand years. Joseph Easter and Daughter, Crime Busters . . . He watched, almost bursting with happiness, as she carefully and perfectly seriously, searched for clues.

After a while, just as he was starting to think they would find nothing, she said, 'Dad? Why pitch the tent in the sitting room? It's got a great hole at the top of the staircase that is open to the elements. The kitchen is drier and there is plenty of room for that tent in here.'

'What are you thinking?'

'That maybe what he came for is in that room, so he's sleeping there to be closer to it.'

She had a very valid point. 'That's good deductive thinking, kid.' He led the way back into the sitting room. 'Let's take a closer look in here.'

'Dare we climb the stairs and look into the remains of the upstairs rooms?' she asked.

'I'll check. We don't want an accident stuck out here. Give me the torch for a moment.' Joseph took the Maglite from her and inspected the treads on the staircase. 'Hmm, some are pretty well rotten where the rain has come in. I'm pretty certain that no one else has attempted to get up these for decades. There are no footprints. They're a death trap, Tam.'

'Then he's not been up there?'

'No way.'

'So we look down here.' She held her hand out for the torch and began her version of a fingertip search of the derelict room.

Her solemnity made him want to laugh. Instead, he asked, 'Would I be right in thinking that there's no chance of a cellar in this part of the fen?'

'Not on this soft silt,' she said, 'and if this house was built a long time ago, they didn't even have foundations. Jacob's Fen is all reclaimed land, with no high spots that I know of.'

'Okay. Check around the fireplace, Tam. It used to be a favourite place for hiding things.'

'As in, up the chimney?' she asked. 'If so, it's over to you, Detective Sergeant. I've got to see Richard Howard later with my suggestions for the copse, and I don't want to turn up looking like the Little Chimney Sweep!'

Joseph took the torch from her and shone the beam slowly around the stone surround. He stopped. Someone had certainly placed their hands on the mantle-shelf, but that would be perfectly normal if they were using the cottage as a squat.

He bent down and shone the light up into the chimney flue. As he had expected, it was completely blocked. Nowhere to hide anything.

They searched for another ten minutes but found nothing.

'Disappointed,' muttered Tamsin. 'I was so sure about that.'

'I'm afraid a lot of detective work ends like this, but it has to be done, because . . .' He stopped. Something had caught his eye. 'Hold on.'

Close to the tent, one of the old quarry tiles was sticking up slightly. Joseph pushed the tent aside and saw that a square of four tiles had been disturbed. He handed the torch to Tamsin and dropped to his knees, ignoring the dirt and that he was wearing smart trousers. 'Shine it down here, Tam.'

It took little effort to raise the tiles. Beneath, he found a shallow space. Indeed, there were no foundations, simply rows of joists with ancient rotting floorboards across them and under that, hard ground. The tiles must have been added later.

'What is it, Dad?' Tamsin asked urgently.

'Someone has cut away a small area of old floorboard and fashioned a shallow recess underneath.' He leant forward and felt around beneath the floor. 'There's something here! Tam, I reckon you were right after all.'

He could feel a shape he vaguely recognised, something made of leather, with buckles. 'I think it's a school satchel.'

He pulled it out and stared at it. 'It's old, but not that old.'

'I had one like that,' said Tamsin, 'didn't I?'

'You did. You put stickers all over it and got told off by your teacher.' For a moment they were back in the bad old days, and he held his breath, afraid of her retort.

But Tamsin seemed totally engrossed in their find. 'Open it up.'

Reprieved, Joseph quickly changed his soiled protective gloves and undid the buckles. 'Photographs,' he murmured. 'Lots of them.'

'Let's go outside and see what they are,' Tamsin urged.

'I need to be careful. I'm not sure what we've found here, but if it turns out to be evidence, I have to watch out for cross-contamination.'

They went out into the fresh air and took some deep breaths. How the intruder actually slept there was a miracle, though Joseph reminded himself that he had slept in far worse places during his time as a soldier.

'I think we should take this back to my car,' he said. 'I've got a clean paper evidence sheet, so we can lay it out and look at the contents properly.'

With a swift glance back at the suddenly sinister old cottage, they made their way through the undergrowth to their vehicles.

Joseph unlocked the boot, took a large folded sheet of paper from a sealed plastic envelope and laid it on the floor of the boot. Then he carefully withdrew the large bundle of photographs from the old satchel.

Tamsin leaned closer. 'Looks like they're all of the same person. And there's press cuttings with her picture on too.' She looked up. 'Dad? What does this mean?'

Joseph's throat had gone dry. He knew who the girl was.

He swallowed. 'We have to report this immediately, seal the area and get forensics out here.'

Tamsin looked at him anxiously. 'You've gone pale, Dad! Who is she?'

He took a long deep breath. 'Her name is Jennifer Cowley. She went missing years ago. There was a manhunt for her abductor but her body was never found.'

'Why don't I remember that?'

'You were probably abroad with your mother, Tam. I doubt if it made the news in Switzerland or the States, or wherever you were at the time.'

They stared at the pictures in silence for a moment, until Joseph gathered himself and rang it in.

'Nikki's on her way,' he told Tamsin, 'and a whole team of SOCOs.' He was still shell-shocked. Whatever he'd expected to find, it wasn't this. 'You'd better ring Richard Howard, Tam, and tell him his land is about to get invaded by a whole convoy of emergency vehicles.'

Tamsin did as she was asked. 'He's on his way. What are you thinking, Dad?'

'You wouldn't want to know.'

'How old was she?'

'Nineteen, and very beautiful,' he said.

Tamsin nodded. 'I could see that from the photographs. Was she a Jacob's Fen local?'

'No, she was from Greenborough. She came from the Carborough Estate. Her parents still live there, as far as I know.'

Memories of the Carborough Estate swarmed into Joseph's mind. When he first arrived in Greenborough, he and Nikki had worked on a terrible murder case that had taken place there. The estate was much improved now, but back then it had been rough, very rough, and harboured a whole host of criminals. There were good people there too, and the Cowleys were just such a family. The case was long before his time, but it was still talked about at the station. When bodies are never recovered, even though everything points to murder, it leaves a black cloud hanging over the whole neighbourhood. These photographs were the first evidence of any kind to show up for years. It was an important discovery, which might lead to some real admissible evidence.

Father and daughter leaned against his car in silence, looking out over the tranquil rural landscape, both thinking about loss.

CHAPTER FIVE

'I'll save you the effort of knocking on more doors. You'll not get anyone to speak a bad word about Vernon in this road.'

Dave looked at his list of residents and decided that Mrs Doris Butters wasn't someone you argued with. She was solid, foursquare, with heavy shoulders, a squat build, a tight, iron-grey perm and a stony face. And she had no intention of letting him go until he fully appreciated that her opinions were the only ones worth listening to.

'Salt of the earth, that man, and if anyone says otherwise, they're a liar.'

'Well, that's very helpful, Mrs Butters. No one is casting aspersions on his character but if a complaint is made, we have to follow it up. You do understand?' He gave her his warmest smile and almost imperceptibly she seemed to defrost.

'No doubt you've got a job to do, but yer wasting yer time.' She folded her broad arms across her ample bosom. 'If it were that Dorothy Scuddles at number four who complained, she's a right chuckle-wit, so I'd takes no notice o' that one.'

'No one here has complained, Mrs Butters. This is not a local matter. Thank you for your help and good day to you.' Dave backed away fast.

He was back in their car and waiting for Cat to finish with her enquiry when a very different sort of woman approached him. She was tall, well-dressed and carefully made-up. He'd seen her earlier, talking to one of the other residents.

She glanced around before she stopped, and then in a low voice and very deliberately, she said, 'You don't dirty your own doorstep, Officer. If you want to know the real Vernon Deacon, talk to Carmel Brown. She lives next door to the Claridge Arms. She's just moved in. Little cottage with hanging baskets out front. She'll tell you a very different story.'

With that, she hurried away.

That sounded a bit more promising. Dave took out his notebook and scribbled down the name and location. He watched as the woman went into a bungalow at the far end of the cul-de-sac and also made a note of that, in case he needed to follow it up.

As soon as Cat returned, he passed on the woman's piece of advice.

'So what are we waiting for? Hop in, Davey-boy.'

'Your mystery woman has a point, hasn't she? You don't shit on your own doorstep, so he's gone to a lot of trouble to be Mr Charming to his gullible neighbours.' Cat eased the car out into the Old Fleeting village road. 'From what I've read about him, he's been at this nasty game for quite a long while, so he's had plenty of time to gather himself up a whole gaggle of respectable citizens, all prepared to swear that he's the victim of someone with a grudge against him.'

'That's what happened when we tried to nail him before, wasn't it?' asked Dave. 'A few very upright local notaries swore on oath that they would trust him with their lives.'

'*Their* lives. I wouldn't trust him with their granny's life, though. That's his target market — older women.' Cat spoke through gritted teeth.

'I'm looking forward to speaking to this Carmel Brown, aren't you?'

Cat slowed down as they approached the Claridge Arms. 'There it is, Honeysuckle Cottage. Let's hope she's at home.'

They parked in the pub car park and walked back to the cottage. As they went through the gate, they saw that the windows were open, and somewhere inside a radio was playing.

'Could be in luck, Catkin,' said Dave, and rang the doorbell.

'Yes?' Carmel Brown looked about sixty-five, maybe older, but she had beautiful chestnut brown hair with only the slightest hint of grey beginning to creep in. She had one of those startlingly attractive angular faces that makes you think of maturing film stars.

They held up their warrant cards and asked if they could have a few minutes of her time.

Looking puzzled, she invited them in.

'The place is a shambles, I'm afraid. I only moved in last week and I'm on my own, so it's something of a marathon finding homes for everything.' She looked rather sad. 'I downsized.'

Dave felt for her, suddenly realising that he would have to do a major cull of his own treasured possessions if he chose to move to Cressy Old Hall. The cottage was half the size of his present home.

Carmel Brown pointed to two armchairs. 'Please sit down. So, how can I help you, officers? Sorry, where are my manners? Can I make you some tea?'

Though he could have killed for a brew, Dave said no, and Cat explained the reason for their visit.

Dave noted how Carmel Brown blanched at the mention of Deacon's name. For a moment he thought she was going to ask them to leave, but then she closed her eyes and sighed. 'I really should have gone to the police at the time, but . . .' Her voice petered out.

'We understand,' Cat said. 'There are a hundred good reasons for not doing so. Crimes like these are horrible and very complicated, and most women don't wish to come forward.' She leant towards Carmel. 'How do you know Deacon?'

'Not from here. As I said, I've only just moved to the area, and I feel like packing up and moving out again now I know that he lives close by.' She fell silent.

'Where did you know him from?' prompted Dave.

'A village just this side of Saltern-le-Fen, called Kirk Deeping. I lived there with my husband Harry for over twenty years. Then Harry died. He had belonged to an Army Veterans' Club, and Deacon turned up supposedly to offer his condolences and any support and advice I needed about pensions and so on.' She grunted in disgust. 'And that's not all he offered me.'

Dave sensed Cat tense up. This was exactly what they had hoped to hear.

'Look, it was almost a year ago and until my friend Marian told me that he was living in the same new estate as her, I'd tried to put it behind me. I'm not sure that I want it all brought to the fore again, especially as I'm a newcomer here. Apart from Marian, I don't know a soul and I'm going to have to build new friendships if I am to stay.' She stared down at her feet, 'And being in my late sixties, that's not going to be easy.'

Dave shook his head. 'He's dangerous, Mrs Brown. He sexually assaulted another woman, but sadly, no one believes her.'

'Except us,' added Cat grimly. 'We know she's telling the truth, but it's his word against hers, and unfortunately, she's not the best of witnesses.'

Carmel Brown's expression darkened. 'He said if I told anyone, I'd just be laughed down. He had influential friends and an impeccable reputation, and who was I? Just a lonely woman who had lost her husband and was looking for solace. He said he would swear that I seduced him, and then he laughed and said no one in their right mind would ever take my word over his.'

Dave sighed. 'No wonder you didn't go to the police. But, Mrs Brown, we have to stop this predator. Would you help us now?'

She groaned. 'I really don't know. I'm not sure I'm strong enough.' She gave a little sob. 'I was so ashamed of what happened, and on top of losing my lovely Harry, it was just too awful for words.'

'What he's doing is wicked, Mrs Brown. He's destroying lives,' said Cat. 'He's preying on women when they're at their most vulnerable, assaulting them, getting away with it, then moving on to a new area and new victims. I'm desperately sorry for our other lady. She did find the courage to come forward, only to be labelled a neurotic. It's criminal and degrading.' Cat looked the woman directly in the eyes, 'One day he's going to pick on someone who can't put it behind her, and she won't be able to live with it. I want him locked up before that happens. Mrs Brown, I think you just might have the strength to help me do it.'

Dave noticed a tiny glint of steel appear in Carmel Brown's eyes. 'I'll think about it, officers, but no promises.'

They left and made their way back to the car. Cat smiled grimly. 'She's going to come on side, Dave, I know it.'

* * *

'As this is so far off the beaten track, Superintendent Cam Walker has decided to keep it lowkey, just until we know what to expect from your creepy cottage.' Nikki looked from Joseph to Tamsin, then down at the photos still spread out on the evidence sheet. 'Forensics are collecting these ASAP. I want to see the timeline, because at first glance it would seem that the photographer had been following Jennifer and took sneaky shots of her for quite a while.'

'And if he was stalking her, it's a good chance he abducted her,' Tamsin added. 'But is whoever took those photos the same person as pitched that tent, or did our squatter have a different agenda for coming here and knew nothing about that satchel?'

'My goodness, Tam, you really are your father's daughter, aren't you?' Nikki said.

'He told me to think like a detective and now I can't stop,' she complained. 'It's all consuming.'

'Well, I'm afraid you'll have to find a way to unconsume it, Tam. It's an official investigation now, and you are going to have to hand over to the professionals,' said Nikki.

'Damn!'

'Sorry, kid — protocol. But if it hadn't been for you, we might never have discovered these, so there's something to take with you. Niall will be dead proud.' Joseph gave her a hopeful grin. 'And don't forget I'm still cooking dinner tonight — the veggie special?'

Tamsin nodded, somewhat appeased. 'We'll be there, never fear. Now I guess I'd better go and talk to Richard.' She nodded in his direction. 'He seems devastated by all this.'

Nikki nodded. 'I'll be over to chat to him too, as soon as I've had a word with Joseph.' She watched Tamsin walk off, turned back to Joseph and lowered her voice. 'I'm asking for the cottage to be taken apart, brick by brick. If a body has remained undiscovered all these years, it's very well hidden, and oh boy, what better place to hide something than here?'

Joseph heaved in a big breath. 'I think she's here too. I've thought so ever since I found that satchel of photographs. I had the oddest feeling the moment I touched that leather, like . . .' He paused, searching for words, and looked at Niki almost apologetically. 'You'll laugh at me, but I had a sort of weird feeling, like a charge of energy, an electric shock.'

'You're right, I am going to laugh at you. Don't you go all spooky on me or I'll run screaming across the fields.' She was only half joking. Nikki had always been dismissive of anything even remotely supernatural. 'Back to the real world. What's your take on the state of that cottage structurally?'

Unruffled by her chiding, Joseph replied, 'The upstairs is totally unsafe. Most of it has collapsed and very little of the roof remains, but downstairs is still pretty sound. I think it's been protected by all that overgrowth.'

'I want to see it for myself, but Cam has asked if we can all keep clear until the SOCOs are ready to do a preliminary check, and he's sending a fire chief to assess safety.'

Joseph frowned. 'Shame. That all takes time. It's quite awesome, Nikki. The way the wood has encroached and almost covered it is like something from a fairy tale, albeit a rather dark one.'

'I've had enough of dark after our last case, thank you very much, Joseph Easter.' Nikki saw the fleeting look of discomfort and wished she hadn't mentioned it. That investigation had dragged them both into a very bad place, and it still haunted her.

'Me too,' he added quietly. 'But even so, this long-deserted cottage, hidden in the heart of Hob's End Copse, along with a witch's knife left on Sedgebrook House's doorstep, is bloody sinister. Oh, and the name Hob is an old nickname for the devil, as in hobgoblin. Hob's End has been used in several works of fiction to convey a place that has a sense of wrongness or evil about it.'

She shook her head. 'You really are a mine of information, aren't you? Even if it is pretty useless to the investigation.'

Joseph shrugged. 'If that poor lass is found here, you can bet your bottom dollar that it'll be plastered all over the papers. The press just love a horror story.'

'And you think they'd really know about this devil thing?' asked Nikki, mildly disbelieving.

'They'll know, believe me. They aren't all philistines.'

'And I am?'

Joseph grinned and pointed across the field. 'I think I've just been saved from having to answer that. Forensics are here.'

'Aren't you the lucky one.' Nikki straightened up. All this banter was just a way of postponing thinking about what they might be about to find. She shivered. This was big, no, this was massive. Jennifer Cowley's disappearance had been a complex case that had run for months, resulting in one man being convicted, even with the absence of a body. She recalled his name, even though it was long before her time as a DI. Patrick Shale. He had consistently fought the verdict, swearing that he was innocent. Even hardened and cynical police officers had been split into two camps over him. They all knew that he had been besotted with the girl, but very few believed he had killed her. His being found guilty had been a shock to everyone and had been a judgement that some found a travesty. Finding Jennifer Cowley might provide definitive answers to a whole shedload of questions. And that was apart from finally allowing the Cowley family to have some form of closure.

Nikki shook herself. She was getting carried away. This could just be the hiding place of a bag of pictures, end of story. 'Okay, let's get this show on the road.'

CHAPTER SIX

At six that evening, everyone was called off the search of the cottage. A summer storm was brewing and the skies were heavy and grey, with intermittent flashes of lightning flaring through them. In the wood, it was as dark as twilight and even though they had portable lighting it was deemed too dangerous to continue. They would resume the search at dawn.

'Nothing so far?' asked Joseph, as they walked back towards their vehicles.

'They've barely scratched the surface.' Nikki's answer was accompanied by an ominous rumble of thunder. She looked up. 'And we can do without a bloody downpour. They are throwing protective tarpaulins right across the roof, but even so.'

'One thing is for sure,' Joseph said. 'Our squatter won't be spending tonight in his cosy little one-man tent in the sitting room.'

'Tonight or any other night,' said Nikki grimly. 'One glance at the blue lights and he'll be out of here.'

'Uniform are covering all roads into Jacob's Fen, stopping and talking to everyone entering or leaving.' Not that he believed the squatter would come within a mile of the place.

Even the interest Tamsin and Howard and his volunteers had shown in the place would have been enough to make him very cautious indeed. 'It would've been good if we could have held off this search and just watched the estate until the squatter came back to his camp, but after finding those photos, well . . .'

'I know what you're saying, Joseph, but I had no option. The powers that be wanted us all over this like a rash, and they wanted that site contained immediately. If it's that lovely girl's last resting place, they want to know about it as quickly as possible, whether the squatter knew about her or not.'

A perimeter cordon had been placed around the copse, with uniformed officers stationed at intervals to prevent any unauthorised entry. To Joseph, looking back at the halogen lights and silently flashing blue lights, the scene had a surreal, dreamlike appearance. He felt almost guilty that he was off to cook dinner while other officers were working into the night.

'See you at home, Joseph,' whispered Nikki. 'I'll be right behind you, just as soon as I've reported back to Cam, okay?'

He smiled. 'Sure. I'll make a start on the feast.'

And she was off, the most important thing in his life.

* * *

Aurelia Howard paused on the stairs and looked through a long casement window, out across the fen. The huge dark grey clouds were almost apocalyptic, like a scene from a Turner painting. Lightning, both sheet and fork, added to the drama. The storms that came in at this time of the year, after a blazing hot day, were often spectacular, and they seemed to get caught in their little pocket of land at the edge of the Wash and rumble on for hours.

This evening's storm failed to inspire her. She found it threatening. She couldn't see the copse from this side of the house but she knew that if she went into their bedroom, she would see lights of a different kind. Bright cobalt blue and glaring orange, not signs of an apostolic coming but of a serious incident in this world.

Her heart sank. She was rarely afraid, but at this moment, Aurelia Howard was sick with apprehension. She still saw that athame lying on the doorstep. It was a warning, no question. She just didn't know what of. She did know, however, that she, and maybe the people close to her, were heading for perilous waters.

Who was out there? And why had they singled her out?

With a shudder, Aurelia turned and hurried back down the stairs to the warmth and light of the kitchen. But even there, surrounded by her precious dachshunds, she still felt cold inside.

* * *

Everyone arrived at once. Nikki had offered to open up the little-used dining room, but there was something so comfortable about eating in the old country kitchen that, instead, they gathered around the big pine table.

Her mother, Eve Anderson, had come with her old friend Wendy Avery, and both were chatting amicably with Tamsin and Niall. Nikki smiled to herself. She had spent many years looking after her daughter Hannah on her own. Hannah was gone, but now she had another wonderful family around her. Niall and Tam were like her own kids, her mother she adored, although she was an enigma, and Wendy had become a sort of favourite "auntie." Along with Joseph, she had all she needed, and could ask for nothing more, apart from having Hannah back.

Nikki never ceased to be amazed at how Joseph could manage to create a whole table of tempting food in what seemed like minutes. She herself needed several days' notice and an action plan simply to boil an egg. After the extraordinary day that they had had, it was good to unwind and be with the people they loved, but even so, Nikki's mind kept returning to Jennifer Cowley and the possibility of finally finding the girl. With an effort, she pushed those thoughts away and concentrated on her friends and family.

'So, why have you called this extraordinary general meeting, Mother?' she asked.

Eve lifted her glass in a toast. 'It was a good excuse to get invited to eat some of your Joseph's amazing food. Here's to the chef!'

They all raised a glass to Joseph, complimenting him on another triumph. Then Nikki said, 'Right, Mother, and the real reason?'

Eve glanced at Wendy. 'Well, you all know that Wendy and I accepted a short-term post working for Robert Richmond of Acacia House?'

There was a murmur of assent.

'You are restoring a Victorian botanical artist's old studio, aren't you?' asked Tamsin.

'That's right. He was also called Robert, and his work is amazing.' She turned to Tamsin. 'The thing is, he went missing and was never heard of again. A strange clause in his will stated that if he were to die his studio must remain exactly as it was. Now so much time has elapsed, the family have permission to restore it, and that's what Wendy and I are trying to do.'

'It's a bizarre job,' said Wendy. 'It's a big attic studio, and for all the world it's like he stepped out for a few moments and left everything where it was, right down to a half-finished glass of wine and a paint-splattered artist's smock.'

'Shades of the *Marie Celeste*. How long has he been gone?' asked Niall.

'Since before the First World War,' replied Eve. 'But what this is all about is this . . .'

Again, Nikki saw her mother turn fleetingly to Wendy. There was excitement in that look. She was up to something. Whenever Nikki saw that glint in her eyes, she knew she should be worried.

'His disappearance has bothered the family, particularly Robert, for decades, but in going through all of his art materials and notes and sketches, we think we've found some clues as to where he might have gone.'

'Wow! This is exciting,' exclaimed Tamsin.

'We think so,' said Wendy. 'And even better, Robert Richmond wants us to see if we can do a little sleuthing and follow up our possible clues.'

'All expenses paid,' added Eve. 'Our first port of call is the Lake District.'

'I knew it! You two cannot just chill out and do the leisurely retirement thing, can you? You have to be getting into mysteries, and that usually means trouble or danger. You are incorrigible!'

Eve smiled sweetly at her 'Can't deny that, but,' the smile widened, 'this time it is just an historical paper trail, a treasure hunt. And it could give the family answers to an unsolved puzzle that has been haunting them for generations.'

'I'm pretty sure it's risk free, Nikki.' Wendy gave her a wry smile. 'This time.'

'I'll believe that when I see it. You two have previous, remember?'

Everyone laughed. Eve and Wendy had formerly been in the military, as well as in the MOD, so their working lives had been intense, to say the least. Now, despite being "of mature years," as Eve liked to call it, neither seemed ready to settle down.

'So, when are you taking off?' asked Joseph, handing his daughter a third helping of his new veggie creation.

'End of next week, all being well.' Wendy said. 'We need to collate what we've discovered and do some computer searches, prepare as much as we can from here, make appointments and so on to keep the expenditure down.'

'Robert has insisted we stay in some swanky hotel that costs a fortune, though frankly we would have preferred to rough it a bit and pitch up wherever the clues take us.' Eve shrugged. 'And we might well finish up doing that, mightn't we, Wendy?'

'Most likely. It's not a holiday, after all.'

'I'd grab the luxury and enjoy your downtime,' said Nikki. She gave Joseph a sidelong glance and raised an eyebrow. 'Well, I would if someone offered *me* a swanky hotel break. Hmm, Joseph?'

'Hint, Dad, hint,' Tamsin said.

'Anytime you like! But you never want to let go of the reins at the nick! It won't fall to pieces if we take a few days away, you know.'

She did know, but the problem was getting the time together without causing tongues to wag. It just wasn't worth the risk. 'One day,' she said, rather sadly. 'But right now, it looks like we are going to have our hands full, yet again.'

And the conversation inevitably turned to the creepy cottage in Hob's End Copse.

'You do know Hob means devil?' said Eve.

'Bloody hell!' Nikki shook her head in disbelief. 'How come everyone knows these things but me!'

'Probably because you are grounded in the material. We like a little bit of magic sometimes,' Eve said.

'That makes me sound like a very boring person,' Nikki grumbled.

'Nikki Galena? Boring?' Joseph laughed. 'I don't think anyone could *ever* call you that!'

Before the laughter had subsided, Nikki's phone rang.

'Bugger!' She stood up. 'If that's bloody work . . .'

She took the call outside the room and was surprised to hear the voice of her good friend Professor Rory Wilkinson, the Home Office pathologist.

She knew at once that something was wrong. Rory was a fount of irrepressible humour, and rarely spoke seriously, but tonight he sounded anxious and quite on edge.

'Nikki, I hope I haven't interrupted anything too important?'

'Just dinner with Mum and the rest of the gang.' She paused. 'What's wrong, Rory?'

'It's those photographs of Jennifer Cowley that were found under the cottage floor.'

Nikki felt her stomach contract. 'Yes?'

'They vary in age, as you probably saw, indicating that the person who was stalking her had been watching her over a period of time. They also cut out pictures from the papers following her disappearance.' There was a silence. 'You probably wouldn't have looked at every photograph individually before you got them to forensics, but I looked at each one carefully, trying to work out the time sequence, and I hate to tell you this, but although most of those photos are of Jennifer, there are three pictures there of someone else. The second girl is so much like Jennifer that I almost believed it to be her, until I saw the difference in the hairstyle and clothing, plus they were taken with a digital camera and so were much sharper than the older ones, not that those had faded, having been kept in the dark. Worst of all, the second girl's photos are very recent. I guess you can see where I'm going with this?'

'Oh no. He's stalking another girl.' Nikki felt as if she had been sucker punched.

'Bit of a showstopper, isn't it?' said Rory. 'I'm sorry I interrupted your dinner, but I thought you should know straight away.'

'Absolutely. Of course.' Her head was spinning. 'Er, Rory? Could you get some copies of the second girl's photos for us, enlarged ones? We need to find and identify her fast, make sure she's okay.'

'I'll do it tonight and send them over first thing. All the originals are being processed for fingerprints, DNA, or any trace evidence. I should have some answers for you around midday tomorrow.'

Unaccustomed to this new, sombre Rory, Nikki was relieved when he continued, 'Give my love and kisses to your lovely dinner guests, especially that gorgeous Joseph. Tell him I still love him, even though my invite to dinner obviously got lost in the post.'

Nikki laughed. 'Sorry, Rory, next time for sure. This was sprung on us by my mother. She's off on another adventure, solving an historical mystery this time.'

'Heaven preserve us. What a woman! But regarding dinner, I'll hold you to that, Nikki Galena. That man is such a divine cook.'

'Lucky old me.'

'In more ways than one! Ahem. Now, I have to finish up here and get home or my lovely David will think I don't love him anymore.'

Nikki felt for David, Rory's partner, because where his profession was concerned, Rory was even more driven than her, if that were possible. 'Give him my love, and thanks for passing on the grim news. I'd better go fill in Joseph and Niall, and then ring the super. Night, Rory.'

'Nightie night, cherub. Sweet dreams.'

Sweet dreams? Sleepless night, more like. Among all the other unanswered questions surrounding those photographs was the worry that they might have a dangerous individual stalking an unknown young woman.

All eyes were upon her as she entered the room. 'Sorry, guys, police business. I need to talk to you, Joseph, and you, Niall, please?'

'Is it about the cottage in the copse?' asked Tamsin excitedly. 'Can't we hear it too?'

Nikki smiled at her. Tam's childlike enthusiasm was endearing. 'Not at the moment, Tam, I'm sorry.'

She turned and left the room. Joseph and Niall stood up, followed her into the lounge and closed the door after them. As she recounted what Rory had told her, their expressions grew steadily more concerned.

'But someone was convicted and incarcerated for that crime, weren't they?' asked Niall, 'Surely he'd still be inside? I certainly haven't had any notification of a recent release.'

'His name was Patrick Shale, and we need to check exactly where he is now,' said Nikki. 'If he's out, then maybe he's taken up where he left off, with a new victim in his sights.'

'Want me to do that now, Nikki?' Joseph said. 'I can phone Ben. He's the duty detective tonight.'

Nikki nodded. 'Yes, do it. We need to jump on this as fast as we can.'

'As soon as you get those photos, I'll get my troops onto finding this new girl,' Niall said emphatically. 'I'm assuming she's local? Maybe there will be something in the background of the photos that will give away where they were taken.'

Nikki had already considered that. 'I'm about to ring Cam Walker and ruin his evening. I think he'll say we have to presume that she's from round here and must move heaven and earth to discover who she is. Her pictures have been found along with those of a missing, ostensibly dead girl, so we have to talk to her as a matter of urgency and, if necessary, get her to a place of safety.'

'Will he give her image to the media, do you think?' queried Niall.

'I think he'll want to keep this quiet, rather than ignite a wildfire, just until we know if there's a reason for her pictures being found in that bag. But,' she shrugged, 'if we can't identify her, then he'll certainly plaster her face across every newspaper and TV screen in the country.'

Niall and Nikki sat in silence while Joseph phoned DC Ben Radley. Outside, the storm still rumbled around the night sky, and they heard the rain lashing the windows. Nikki kept picturing the cottage at Hob's End Copse. She had only managed to get a quick look at it before the weather warning came in, but now she imagined it buffeted by wind, battered by flailing tree branches and lit up by eerie flashes of lightning. It held secrets, dark ones, and she wondered what new horrors tomorrow would bring to light.

Joseph hung up, then flopped down onto the sofa. 'Ben's onto it now. He'll ring us the minute he knows anything. This has rather put a dampener on Eve's evening, hasn't it?'

Nikki sighed. 'They'll all be eaten up with curiosity. But for now, this has to stay between us, until we know more.'

'I'll be getting the third degree from Tamsin,' muttered Niall. 'She's never really seen the kind of thing we deal with before or realised just how all-consuming a case can become.

And now, after finding that cottage and those photos, well, she's hooked.'

Nikki saw the different expressions flit across Joseph's face. She felt for him. When she was younger, Tamsin had constantly belittled what they did, insisting that their priorities were misguided and going on about police brutality. Her criticism and disparaging remarks had caused Joseph a great deal of suffering, until, slowly, and after being caught up in a frightening situation herself, she had relented. She had now come full circle, a police wife with a completely different understanding of what their job entailed.

She looked at Joseph. 'I'll call Cam.'

As soon as Nikki finished talking to her superintendent, the phone rang again. It was Ben.

She listened to what he had to say, put the receiver down and turned to Joseph and Niall. She managed to keep her tone even. 'Patrick Shale was released three weeks ago from HMP Whitemoor Prison in Cambridgeshire. Ben can't get any more info until the world wakes up tomorrow, but there's every chance he's come back to our patch. He's lived here all his life.'

'And so it begins again,' whispered Joseph.

'God help us,' added Niall softly. 'We've barely got over the last cycle of violence.'

Nikki did her best to rally them. 'This time, guys, we're well ahead of the game, and we can nip it in the bud. We have photos of the possible victim, so we'll soon be able to find her.' She stood up, mentally crossing her fingers for a luck she professed not to believe in.

As she did so, there was an almighty clap of thunder. The lights flickered and went out, then came back on again. The thunder was above the house now, the sound deafening, making them all start. They all looked at each other and for a brief fraction of a second, Nikki saw fear in their eyes.

CHAPTER SEVEN

As dawn broke over Jacob's Fen, it was hard to imagine the violence of the previous night's summer storm. The vegetation still dripped, but an early sun promised to dry up all remaining traces in a matter of hours.

At Hob's End, the weary and bedraggled night-shift officers were relieved and the new shift prepared to pick up the threads of the day before. Forensics arrived just a few moments after Nikki and Joseph, and Nikki was surprised to see Professor Rory Wilkinson's bright green Citroen Dolly make its way to the temporary parking area.

'Didn't expect to see you here today. We have no gory body for you — so far,' Nikki said.

'I just had to see the place for myself,' he said. 'My SOCOs made it sound like a scene from Hansel and Gretel, and I so love fairy tales — the more gruesome the better. It'll be a break from delving around in dead people's abdominal cavities.'

'Beautifully put, Rory,' Nikki said, raising an eyebrow. 'I'm sure you'll find that it's certainly a one-off.'

'What's the plan of action for today?' asked the pathologist.

'Well, yesterday your team had just finished photographing the whole ground floor before anything is moved or handled.' Nikki took out her notebook. 'They've taken video footage too, which should give something of the atmosphere of the cottage. Then the investigation team had just moved in to start the search for evidence when we had the weather warning. I'm told the tarps they threw over the whole upper floor held out most of the bad weather. These have now been removed to let in some natural light, so now it's back to the hunt for physical evidence.'

'And when they've extracted all they can, we will be taking the cottage apart, brick by brick,' stated Joseph.

'Starting with the floorboards, no doubt.' Rory sounded thoughtful. 'After I'd seen those photos of Jennifer Cowley, I looked the old case over last night. I wonder if this witch's cottage really is her last resting place?'

'If it is, then she'll finally be released from the bloody witch's spell.' Nikki hoped they would find her, not for the accolades that would surely come their way for finding the missing girl after so many years, but simply to get her innocent body away from such a sinister place and lay it to rest.

They made their way along the newly widened and cleared pathway to where a movable barrier had been set up. A uniformed officer with a clipboard took their details and logged them in, pointing to a crate of fresh crime-scene suits. They pulled them on, and Rory stepped through the barrier and took his first look at the ruined cottage.

'Oh my! They weren't exaggerating, were they? This is awesome.' Eyes wide, he pushed his glasses further up onto the bridge of his nose. 'Do you know, I've seen thousands of crime scenes and some have freaked me out . . .' He threw them a warning glance, 'Although I'd *never* admit that in public, you understand. But this has to be one of the eeriest settings I've ever seen. It's the perfect location for an old Hammer Horror film. Picture it on a misty evening as night falls, with tendrils of fog creeping insidiously through the trees and shimmering in shafts of intermittent moonlight . . .'

'No thanks,' said Nikki. 'It's creepy enough as it is.' It was her first look inside too.

Silence fell as they stepped over the doorstep, each of them aware that they might be walking over a dead girl's grave. They moved around, careful not to touch or disturb anything, and sticking to the tread boards that had been laid out to keep contamination to a minimum.

'It's like one of those rural folk museums,' murmured Rory. 'Everything authentic and of an age.' He stared at an ancient strainer and some well-used metal measuring jugs. 'It's got to be around 1900. There are some old Kilner jars with God-knows-what still preserved in them. Those arrived in British kitchens at the end of the nineteenth century. Made in Yorkshire, you know.'

Nikki grinned. Rory knew the oddest things.

They looked through the door into the sitting room and saw the blue tent and the displaced quarry tile, where Joseph and Tamsin had discovered the satchel of photos. What else had the stalker put there for safe keeping?

'I've got a GPR scanner coming in,' Nikki said. 'Cam Walker okayed it as he's used that particular tech company before. It will save us hours of manual labour.'

'Ground-penetrating radar scanning. Cool.' Joseph looked impressed. 'Sensible move. Was it you who thought of that?'

'I have my moments, Easter.'

'For someone who even struggles with a digital display microwave, I'm frankly amazed.'

Nikki was not about to tell them that it had been Cam's idea, though she had a sneaking suspicion that they knew anyway.

'Professor Wilkinson? DI Galena? Can we come in and get on, please?' A SOCO and several cohorts were waiting in the outer doorway.

'Sure, we were just getting a feel for the place before it gets demolished,' said Nikki. 'Any trace evidence you come across of who has been using this place as a camping site, let me know immediately, okay?'

Back at the barrier, they disposed of their protective gear and dumped it in the bin provided. If they were called back in, they would need new coveralls, rather than traipse detritus from the wood and the rendezvous point back inside with them.

Rory ran a hand through his hair. 'I'd like to stay, but we are pretty busy back at the Greenborough Necropolis. Nothing as exciting as this, but people still die, and a lot of them need my services before they, or their nearest and dearest, can rest in peace. Plus, my dear Spike is away on yet another course, so I am without my best technician for a fortnight.'

'Don't worry, we'll contact you if we find any surprises or need your incomparable expertise down here in the woods.' Nikki strolled back to his car with him, leaving Joseph talking to the investigation team leader.

'Rory, this other girl. You said they were recent pictures. Do you think they could have been taken within the last three weeks?'

Rory glanced at his watch. 'They will already be in your office. You can look for yourself and while it's impossible to be sure, I'd say yes. There are trees in full leaf in the background and several other indicators that it's this season.' He looked at her quizzically, 'Why do you ask? Have you got someone in mind for the covert photographer?'

'Maybe. The man who was convicted of taking Jennifer was released from prison three weeks ago.'

Rory pulled a face. 'Not looking good then?'

'Very worrying. I've got Ben and Cat getting the info on him as we speak.' They stopped at his car. 'In fact, I'd better head back too. Thanks for sending the pictures. I'll get uniform onto tracing her as soon as I've seen them myself.' She turned back to find Joseph and called out, 'I'll keep in touch.'

'Absolutely. This is a fascinating one.'

She hurried along to where Joseph was still talking to one of the team. 'I'm going back to the factory. You stay here and update me every step of the way. I'll be back before lunch, but I need to get the girl in those photos identified and make sure the others are firing on all cylinders regarding Patrick Shale's whereabouts.'

He nodded. 'I've got this covered, don't worry. Oh, and Richard Howard is coming out in half an hour. He's given permission for us to raze the cottage to the ground if necessary and widen the track into the copse to allow access for vehicles or excavators.'

'Excellent. You deal with him. The techie with the scanner isn't due until this afternoon, so I'll be back for that. Take care, Joseph, I'll see you later.'

Nikki drove back through the sun-drenched fields of Jacob's Fen, wondering where all this was going. Unfortunately, there was no hurrying forensics. Due to the dirt and decay in the cottage, finding any new evidence about the squatter was going to be a painstaking process. The good thing was that it was quite a small area. They were concentrating on the tent and the items left on the kitchen table. With luck, their floor scan would be underway by mid-afternoon. And then they'd know.

Rory had summed it up well. She had mocked him, but there was no doubt — this was eerie. The place and its contents had a strange, chilly atmosphere clinging to it. It made her uneasy. Nikki liked things down to earth and wasn't accustomed to being affected by atmospheres.

With a grunt, she turned on the radio. Meatloaf was belting out "Bat out of Hell" at the top of his voice. Oh great. She changed channels and was greeted by Abba's "Dancing Queen". She turned up the volume and started to sing along, until she thought about the words.

She drove the rest of the way back in silence.

* * *

Cat cursed softly under her breath. Suddenly all her enquiries into the pervert, Vernon Deacon, had been put on hold. She understood why, but even so, she felt that she needed to keep up the pressure or once again he'd slip through the net. She glanced across to Ben's workstation and saw him stretch and yawn.

'Go home! You've done a whole night here and it's almost ten o'clock. You're out on your feet.'

'You underestimate my staying power, Cat Cullen.' He grinned at her lasciviously.

'Keep it clean, children.' Dave threw a balled-up piece of paper at Ben. 'I'm not sure I want to know about your staying power. It might be too much for me at my age.'

'I tell you, my friend, it's legendary.' Ben winked at Cat, who chose to ignore it.

'Honestly, Ben, get away and have some sleep. You're back on shift tonight again, don't forget.' When he got something between his teeth, Ben was like a terrier and refused to let go. 'I'll finish up what you're doing.'

'I'm waiting on one last call and then I'll go, I promise.'

But instead of Ben's, it was Cat's phone that rang. 'DC Cullen, can I help you?'

There was a short pause, and then she heard a soft voice say, 'Actually it's me who has decided to help you, DC Cullen. This is Carmel Brown. I've been thinking about that poor woman no one believes, and it's weighing on my conscience. I will make a formal complaint about Deacon, and to hell with the consequences. Someone has to stop that man.'

Cat mentally punched the air. 'That's the best thing I've heard all week, Mrs Brown. You are a diamond.'

'I'm not sure about that. I rather think I'm a coward for not coming forward earlier. Shall I come in to make my statement today, DC Cullen?'

'Please, and I'll deal with it personally. When would suit you?' She scribbled down the woman's name.

'Now might be good, before I lose my courage.'

'I'll be here. Just ask for me at the front desk. And thank you, Mrs Brown. What you are doing could finally stop that piece of rubbish for good.'

'That's the general idea,' said Carmel Brown dryly. 'I'll see you in around thirty minutes.' She rang off.

Cat let out a whoop of delight. 'Davey-boy! Our woman has come through for us! Carmel Brown is going to make a formal complaint about Deacon!'

Dave stuck a thumb in the air. 'Brilliant! Well done her! With her testimony, we might well nail him this time.'

'We might, old pal! You won't be able to actually slap the cuffs on that bastard yourself, not being a proper copper and all that, but I'll do it for you. I promise to make them just a bit too tight for his wrists.'

'It's a deal. And I'd have no objection if you made them even tighter.' Dave laughed.

'My pleasure,' Cat said. She turned back to her screen, 'I just need to tie up a few things, and then she should be here. Will you come with me, Dave? We'll do this together, okay?'

'Try and stop me.'

They smiled at each other. Nothing would give her more pleasure than having his last case end in success. Meanwhile, Ben was talking on the phone and scribbling copious notes on a pad. He finally put down the receiver and said, 'Found Patrick Shale! And he is from round here.' He leaned back and exhaled. 'He was advised to move out of the area — people have long memories — but he is still swearing his innocence. He says he was wrongly accused, so why should he run away from the place he loves?' He pulled a face. 'I'm not sure if he's courageous, evil or just plain stupid.'

'Personally, I'd go with stupid.' Nikki walked in the door. 'As you say, there will be some very bitter people around still wanting to know where he hid Jennifer's body.'

Ben stood up. 'Hello, boss. How's it going out at Hob's End?'

'Slow, so I've left Joseph to it. Ben Radley, why are you still here? You've done your bit, now bugger off. I can't be doing with sleep-deprived detectives on my team — well, not unless it's absolutely necessary.' She smiled at him. 'And well done for finding Shale. Let me have the details and I'll get it followed up.' She threw Cat an enquiring glance. 'And why do you and Dave look so smug, may I ask?'

Cat beamed at her. 'We finally have one of Vernon Deacon's victims who has the balls to tell it how it is. She's on her way in.'

Nikki nodded. 'Nice one, you two. Make sure there are no holes in this case for the CPS to find, and that your woman is totally reliable. We can't have him weaselling out yet again because she's been found to be unsound.'

'She's a sound woman all right, boss. She impressed us both,' said Dave. 'Even though he threatened her, she's decided that it's time he paid the price.'

'Then give her all the support you can. She's going to have times when she'll wish she'd never opened up to you, believe me. Keep her on-side and positive, okay?'

'You got it, boss. Can we be released from this background stuff on your stalker for the time being?'

She was relieved when Nikki nodded. 'Yes, stick with the Deacon investigation for now. It might change when we know what we are dealing with out at Hob's End, but you are making great progress, so keep up the momentum. You never know, a strong voice condemning him could encourage others to come forward.'

'Wouldn't that be something? We'll give this one all we've got, ma'am,' Cat said. 'You can rely on us.'

Nikki chuckled. 'I always do. But would you please tell that Ben Radley fella to sling his hook before I have him forcibly removed from the office.'

'You heard the lady. Do one!' Cat pointed to the door.

Ben handed Nikki a sheet of paper with all the details he'd collated. He looked at Dave helplessly. 'Don't you just hate it when they gang up on you?'

'I never argue with them, mate. Makes life a whole lot easier.'

'Sensible man,' Nikki said.

In the doorway she passed a civilian who called out, 'DC Cullen? There is a woman called Mrs Brown in the foyer for you.'

Cat beckoned to Dave, her eyes alight. 'This is it, Davey-boy. Let's go.'

* * *

Nikki looked at the address — Calthorpe Lane, in some-where called Langtoft. Less a village, Langtoft was more a scattering of houses a few miles outside Greenborough. She stared at it, trying to imagine where Calthorpe Lane was. It wasn't well known, so if he kept a low profile, Shale might just have avoided the heckling, the graffiti scrawled on his walls.

She sat down at her desk, and her attention was drawn to a large brown envelope marked in felt pen with her name in a beautiful cursive script. Rory liked to keep up appearances.

The copies of the photographs found in the satchel.

'Oh shit!' she whispered. For all the world, she could be looking at Jennifer Cowley.

The girl, whoever she was, looked to be in her late teens. She had very long, shiny, straight blonde hair, laughing eyes and a heart-shaped face. Slim, and wearing ripped jeans and a low-cut T-shirt, she was a modern-day Jennifer, no question.

Nikki knew that stalkers often had a "type," always choosing girls or women that had similar hair colour or fea-tures, but this was extraordinary. 'Who are you?' she said softly to the image, 'and where, because I really need to get you to safety.'

She looked closer at the three pictures. Rory was right, the season was the same, but was there anything to give her an idea of where the photos were taken? She laid the three copies in a row in front of her. One seemed to be taken as the girl walked down a garden path, but there was no house number or name on view. Another showed her walking along a tree-lined road. She frowned. Now, that one was vaguely familiar, but those streets tended to all look the same to her. The last showed more promise. It had an old building in the background. Again, it rang bells, but nothing specific.

Nikki grunted with frustration, then had a thought. Of course — Yvonne Collins! If anyone would recognise where this was, it was her. Yvonne had been a beat bobby here since time immemorial and though she was well past retirement age, somehow she had managed to hang on. Thank heavens! It was going to be tough enough losing Dave, let alone Vonnie as well. So far, she had been given two stays of execution. Nikki was pretty sure that the powers that be were afraid that Greenborough Police Station would collapse without her encyclopaedic knowledge of the town and its residents.

She picked up the phone and asked the back office if PC Yvonne Collins was on duty. The answer was yes, and luckily, she was in the station.

Nikki gathered up the photos and hurried out. Niall wanted them to give to his officers, so she'd kill two birds with one stone.

Downstairs, Yvonne looked closely at the pictures. 'I could be wrong, but I think we should take a look at the roads that back onto the recreation ground. They have lines of trees very much like this.' She pointed to one of the pictures. 'And good-sized front gardens too, like the one the girl is standing in.'

'Like Christchurch Road? Or Plymouth Avenue?' asked Nikki, vaguely recalling the lines of trees.

'Yes, but my money is on Pilgrim Terrace.' Yvonne nodded to herself. 'At the bottom of the terrace is the back of the cricket pavilion, and I'm certain that's what that wooden building is.'

'You're right! You really are a marvel, Vonnie.'

'Please tell my sergeant, ma'am. It won't do anything for my pension, if I ever get one, but sometimes he needs to be reminded of just what he'll be missing when I do go.'

Nikki laughed. 'Don't worry, he knows. But I'll tell him anyway.'

Yvonne continued to stare at the photos and was soon joined by a young rookie constable. She moved aside to give him a clearer view. 'Anyone you know, Kyle?'

The young man shook his head. 'Don't think so.'

'What about one of the Gately girls? Penny Gately's daughters all have that long white-blonde hair, don't they?'

'They do, and where they got those model good looks from, I have no idea. Penny's no oil painting and her old man looks like a WWE fighter, only uglier.'

Yvonne looked at Nikki apologetically. 'You haven't met my new crewmate, have you, ma'am? This is PC Kyle Adams, and he's under my wing for a few months, heaven help me.'

Kyle seemed to notice Nikki for the first time, and then the penny dropped.

Trying not to laugh at the kid's confusion and embarrassment, Nikki said, 'It's okay, PC Adams. Don't take too much notice of what the messroom says about me. Only some of it is true.'

He laughed nervously. Policemen were definitely getting younger these days, Nikki thought. With that baby face and flaming red hair, he looked no more than fifteen or sixteen. 'You're lucky to have Yvonne as your mentor, Constable. You won't find a better copper anywhere, so listen to her and you won't go far wrong.'

'That's exactly what Sergeant Farrow says, ma'am.'

'Then believe it.' She turned back to Yvonne. 'Can you get copies of these photos run off, please? Sergeant Farrow wants to circulate them, and I need some myself.'

'I'll get it done immediately.' Yvonne was still gazing at one picture in particular. 'If it's alright with you, we'll take a walk around to Penny Gately's home. It's just off Pilgrim Terrace. I think I know who this is.'

'Please do. Right away. I'll get someone else to sort the photocopies. Yvonne, this girl could be in grave danger. We have no idea what we are dealing with yet and I want her not only identified but brought in, and I want it done yesterday.'

'On our way, ma'am. I'll just let Niall, sorry, Sergeant Farrow, know our movements.' Yvonne turned to her young apprentice. 'Come on, mate. Look sharp.'

Nikki wondered what the force would do without old-style officers like Yvonne Collins. Young and enthusiastic was good, but without their older colleagues' experience and local knowledge, they would be lost.

CHAPTER EIGHT

Joseph was hungry. It felt like a long time since breakfast, and with the only things on offer being tea, coffee and packets of crisps, he was finding the tedious task of watching and waiting something of a bore. Joseph liked action. Although he knew that a large part of police work was made up of hours of simple observing and surveillance, he didn't have to enjoy it.

While he waited, he rang Tamsin.

'Dad? Have you rung to tell me what's going on?' she said.

'Sorry, sweetheart, just touching base. I'm out at Hob's End Copse, and I've been talking to Richard Howard. Would you give him a ring and give him your opinion on what to do with the copse? Only we could be demolishing the cottage and he's anxious to still do the right thing with what is left of the wood there.'

Tamsin sighed. 'The fact is, there is very little viable native stuff left there, Dad. I reckon it would be best thinned right down to just the few sustainable species, and then replanted. It would grow in a matter of a few years and then be easily maintained.'

'So if we ran a wider track in, we'd do no damage, eco-logically?' asked Joseph.

'I could come down and give you a professional opinion if you like?'

'Nice try, kid, but not just yet. Only authorised police officers are allowed in at present.'

'Oh, Dad! This is torture! I was there, wasn't I? *I* bloody well found the cottage! *We* found those photos, didn't we? Please don't cut me out!'

'Tamsin, I utterly understand and I promise that immediately we have some answers to a few questions that have arisen, I'll tell you all I can. Really I will. And I agree, we do owe you that much.'

'I'm not going to win, am I?'

''Fraid not, Tam. But you'll ring Richard?'

'Of course I will. I was going to anyway.' He heard the rustling of papers. 'I've just finished working out which trees to save and which to ditch. Introduced species are inclined to take over and kill the natives, and that's not good.'

'Same thing happened with human beings in the colonies.' A vision of Native Americans came to his mind.

'Exactly the same. But here we can do something about it without causing a war.'

They were wandering onto dangerous ground. With talk of wars came thoughts about soldiers and killing. He changed the subject. 'I'd better go do some work, sweetheart.' He paused. 'By the way, did he say anything to you about the threats to his parents?'

'Not really,' she said. 'He just said that if anything else happened, he would move back home for a little while.'

'Really? That could be useful. His village is almost five miles away, not a long distance but in an emergency, it is too far.'

After he'd rung off, he phoned Nikki and asked her to bring some sandwiches when she returned. She said she'd already thought of that and hoped to be with him in under an hour. She gave him a brief update, including the frustrating news that Yvonne Collins had a shrewd idea of who the girl in the pictures was, but there was no one at the family's address. Yvonne was going to continue to try until someone came back. In the meantime, she was snookered.

Joseph sighed. More waiting. He used to have eternal patience and could easily take his mind to another place as the hands of time moved slowly forward, but these days he seemed to be almost as impatient as Nikki, and that was saying something. Maybe it happened as you got older and began to realise that time was precious.

'Sarge! Got a mo?'

He dragged himself back to the present. 'Jim, what's up?'

PC Jim Waterman beckoned to him. 'Sorry, Sarge, but we've got a bloke here asking for the DI. Some techie? Got some equipment that she requested.'

'He's early, but that's fine. He can come this far, but nowhere near the cordon yet. Forensics are still working the site.' Joseph accompanied the uniformed officer to where the vehicles were parked. He was interested to see the scanner and how it worked. He had used something similar when he was in Special Forces but was sure that the new ones would be much improved.

Joseph went over and shook the man's hand. 'Thank you for coming out here. I'm Detective Sergeant Joseph Easter. Our boss will be here fairly soon. Meanwhile, can I get you a coffee?'

The technician, Len Beanland, accepted readily. 'Thanks. It's a bit of a trek down here from Newark, where we are based.' He looked around, puzzled. 'So what's going on, Sergeant? This is a pretty unusual place to need GPR. I was called in from another job and I haven't been given any details yet.'

Joseph took him across to the refreshments van. 'It's an odd one all right. Hopefully, you can save us a hell of a lot of spadework.' As he made the drinks, he explained about the cottage.

'Blimey! So I'm looking for a body?' Beanland's eyes were wide.

'Yep. That's exactly what you are looking for, and there's a pretty good chance you'll find one.'

'No shit! Well, that's a first. I'm usually called out to check for underground utilities like pipework or cables, or void spaces in construction.' He accepted a beaker of coffee and grinned. 'A mate of mine is always going on about once being sent to an archaeological dig of an old cemetery, but I think this probably beats that one hands down.'

Joseph was fractionally concerned that this guy was being flippant. After all, they were talking about a dead girl. Then he decided that finding himself in the middle of a crime scene had probably thrown him somewhat. 'It might help if we get your gear off the van and set it up before my DI arrives, then as soon as forensics allow us in, you can crack on.'

'Not much to set up, Sergeant. I've got top-of-the-range equipment which can be assembled on site in less than two minutes. The whole system comes in a flight case. As long as I can get a signal out here, reports can be delivered directly, connecting to a cell phone as a hotspot.'

Things had moved on. Joseph remembered hunting for UXBs with a big trolley-like piece of equipment that resembled a giant lawnmower.

'I've also got a handheld scanner, a bit like a resus pad, for difficult areas, should we need it. From what you say it could be useful?'

Beanland was acting more professionally now and Joseph relaxed. 'Excellent. I think we are safe to get it down to the cottage now. I've seen a couple of the forensic team pulling out, so we shouldn't have long to wait.'

As Beanland unpacked his van, Joseph went over to one of the SOCOs. 'What's the score, Thomas?'

'Got all we can, Sarge. It's the pits in there for trying to sort the evidence. We could be there all week and still be sifting through it.' He pulled off his mask. 'But we know you're keen to get in there, so we've prioritised as best we can. We might have to go back in if you find the hidden treasure that you're searching for.' He shrugged. 'I don't think there's anything more under that floor, but who knows?'

'That guy over there with a baseball cap and a hi-tech ground-penetrating radar system, that's who.'

'Ah, well, that will answer your questions, won't it?' He turned away, then hesitated. 'Take care in there, Sarge. One of the fire officers has been checking the structure and he's not too happy about it. Reckons all the comings and goings could be weakening it.'

'Thanks, Thomas. I'll go and get a situation report from him before we all go in.' Joseph didn't like the sound of that. The old building had probably survived thanks only to the surrounding trees and foliage, but now, shaken by the constant tread of heavy boots, it might not remain upright for long. Asking Len Beanland to hold on for him, Joseph hurried down the path and asked the nearest PC where the fire officer was.

'Over there, sir.' The PC pointed to a tall, muscular man talking with a scene-of-crime officer.

'Joseph Easter. It's Bill Thorne, isn't it?'

The big man smiled in recognition. 'Sure. We've crossed paths a few times. Remember that lunatic fire-starter on the patch a while back?'

'I certainly do. The SOCOs tell me you're concerned about the safety of the building.'

Thorne shrugged. 'The brick and stonework is unstable. I'm worried that if people go at that floor heavy handed like, well, they could find half the cottage caving in on them.'

'You know what we're looking for, Bill, don't you?'

'I do, and I'm sure you'll do it by the book, but forewarned and all that.'

Joseph nodded. 'I appreciate it. I'm planning on clearing everyone out, and just the DI, myself and the technician with the radar equipment will go in and scan the floor area.'

'Good idea, Joseph. I'll be out here if you need any advice. Before I got into this game, I was a structural surveyor, so I know my stuff. Just shout if anything bothers you.'

'Then maybe I'll extend the invitation to you as well, Bill. Your expertise could be invaluable, especially if the situation in there is unpredictable.'

'Pleasure. Give me a shout when you're ready, I'll be somewhere about.'

Joseph thanked the man and watched a SOCO making his way back out of the copse carrying all his equipment. Following him out, he saw Nikki's car coming across the field. Great. They could finally get to work. Could they be about to find the long lost Jennifer Cowley?

He introduced Nikki to Len Beanland, then took her aside to give her a brief report on what had been happening since she left.

'I agree about keeping the number of officers in there to a minimum, Joseph. It's a tiny cottage, and we don't need half the station lurching around in there. Just us and the fire officer is perfect.' She looked at him. 'Ready to go? Or grab that sandwich first?'

He wanted to say go, but forensics were still clearing out. 'Quick sandwich, then we'll have the scene to ourselves.'

She'd been to their local delicatessen and bought him his favourite roast beef and horseradish sandwich. He devoured it hungrily.

'I ate mine in the car on the way here,' said Nikki, leaning against the side of her vehicle. 'I can't believe we might be minutes away from finding that poor kid, can you?'

'I've been thinking of nothing else,' he said between mouthfuls. 'Poor Richard Howard is totally beside himself now he knows what we are looking for. I really feel for that guy. Depending on what we find, he says he wants the place razed to the ground.'

'Best thing,' murmured Nikki. 'No matter what we find, it's a death trap.'

One of the retreating SOCOs called out that they were done.

'Ready?' Nikki asked.

'Ready. I'll get our techie. Bill Thorne is already down at the cottage waiting for us. Let's do it.'

* * *

The Carmel Brown sitting opposite Dave and Cat today was a very different woman to the one they had met the day before. She was impeccably dressed, straight-backed and determined.

'I've spent most of the night searching my soul over this, officers, and I've decided that if I'm at all a decent human being, I have no choice. I'm haunted by that other poor woman suffering because she wasn't considered a reliable witness. If she went through what I did but isn't allowed to have her say, then it's no wonder she's a wreck. That man cannot be allowed to walk free and I'm going to be the one to stop him.'

Cat's hopes rose. 'I can't tell you how pleased we are to hear that, Mrs Brown.'

'We are also hoping that by you speaking out, others might be encouraged to come forward,' added Dave. 'It can happen like that. Sometimes it takes just one voice.'

'I'm hoping that myself — just in case I suffer a serious bout of self-doubt at any point.' She grimaced. 'I'm aware that it won't be plain sailing, but I am determined to see it through.' She paused for a moment then added, 'And I might just have some actual proof of his actions, but I need to think carefully before I swear to that.'

'Well, we are right beside you, Mrs Brown,' Dave assured her.

Cat leaned forward. 'Okay. Can I now ask you if you are willing to give a voluntary statement? This will be in the form of a victim's personal statement.'

'Absolutely.' Carman Brown's eyes narrowed. 'Every last detail.'

Cat took out a statement form from the folder she had brought with her. 'This will be a record of your evidence,

Carmel — of what you saw, heard and felt — and we'll get you to sign it to confirm that the contents are true. Are you alright with that?'

Carmel took a diary and some reading glasses from her handbag, 'Where would you like me to start?'

* * *

Nikki and Joseph had begun the search with high hopes, but now Len Beanland was on the last section of the floor and all the digital display screen showed was void space under the quarry tiles and in between the floorboards and the hard ground below.

'Sorry to tell you, guys, but there's nothing down there.' Len looked as disappointed as they felt. 'I'm sure you don't want to be told how to suck eggs, but what if your body had been stashed in the attic? When the roof slowly collapsed over time, it could have been dislodged and is now on that upper floor.'

Nikki didn't think this was a viable option but saw a hint of interest on Joseph's face. She nodded to him.

'Improbable, but it's a thought, isn't it?' Joseph turned to Nikki. 'I'm happy to give it a try. I know the stairs are all but gone but I reckon I can get up there, just far enough in to eyeball the state of play.'

Nikki's stomach tightened, but she knew that her feelings for Joseph must not get in the way of policing. Luckily, Bill Thorne saved her from having to decide.

'I'm sure you're more than capable, Joseph, but I saw that PC Lisa Jones is on duty outside. She's a volunteer instructor at the wall climbing centre at the Greenborough and before she moved down here to the flatlands, she was with a mountain rescue team in the Lakes. If anyone can get up there safely and not cause the remaining floor to collapse, it's her.'

Nikki breathed a sigh of relief. 'Joseph, go get her. Whatever, she'll be lighter than you, and if that staircase is as bad as it looks, you stand no chance.'

'Thanks for the vote of confidence, folks, but I have to agree.' He hurried out to the cordon and asked for someone to find Lisa and tell her to suit up and meet them in the cottage.

Five minutes later, PC Lisa Jones was carefully eyeing up her latest challenge. 'No sweat,' she said, all confidence, 'although I have to say that attempting something like this in a zoot suit will be a first.' She turned to Nikki. 'What am I looking for exactly, ma'am?'

Nikki looked at the lithe, wiry young woman and decided they had made a good choice. Lisa looked as though she weighed six stone wringing wet. 'Remains, Constable. Human remains. Bones, or anything else that really should not be in the bedroom of a deserted cottage. And, Lisa, ditch that protective suit, it's too dangerous. You can't be hampered by that thing, and frankly the level of contamination in this dump is off the scale anyway.'

'In any case, forensics have finished.' Joseph stared up into the gap at the top of the stairs and the blue sky above. 'Tell us what the condition of the top floor is, if you will, Lisa.'

Lisa nodded. 'Will do, Sarge.'

She pulled off the protective suit and checked that her shoes were tightly laced. 'If I'd known I'd be doing this I'd have brought my climbing shoes.'

Lisa approached the staircase. Then, after carefully checking the treads, she inched her way up, keeping to the edges of the steps. As they became more rotten, she tested the wall and the wood of the remaining landing banisters looking for hand and footholds. In no time at all, she had swung and worked her way up until she was perched on a solid piece of flooring, close to an outside wall.

'It's bad,' she called down. 'The landing is impassable, full of broken tiles and collapsed roof rafters, but I can see into the bedrooms, as most of the walls have crumbled. Half the wood has grown into here, ma'am! It's got a stranglehold on two old bedsteads and some broken furniture. There's even an old mirror still hanging on a partially demolished wall.' She paused and surveyed the area again. 'It's pretty creepy, but no body or bones that I can see.'

Nikki had expected little else. 'Then get back down, Lisa. You are giving me heart failure sitting up there like a fairy on a toadstool.'

'I'll just take a couple of pictures so you can see for yourselves.' Lisa pulled her phone from her pocket and took a sequence of shots. 'That will do.'

In seconds, she was back on terra firma. 'It's eerie up there. Looks like nature just ate up the house.'

'Getting its own back in a small way for the destruction of the Amazon rainforest,' muttered Joseph, echoing what his daughter would have said about it.

'Check out the images,' said Lisa, offering Nikki her phone.

Scrolling through them, Nikki saw exactly what the young constable meant. The chimney stack looked more like a tall column of tangled ivy than a manmade brick structure. The mirror hanging drunkenly on the wall was strangely poignant. Nikki mentally shook herself. *Get a grip, Galena.*

She handed the phone to Joseph and Bill in silence.

'I don't like the look of some of the remaining brickwork around that small bedroom fireplace,' Bill said anxiously. 'I'm wondering if securing that tarpaulin over the roof when the storm was on its way put strain on it. Look at those cracks! I think the less time we spend in here the better.'

'Forgive me for chiming in again, but what about me running the scanner over some of the outside area? Don't bodies regularly turn up under patios?' Beanland looked hopefully at Nikki.

'Apart from the fact that patios didn't exist that long ago, I reckon if the killer wanted to get rid of the body, he would have used a shallow grave in the heart of Hob's End Copse,' Nikki answered, with a smile at Beanland's enthusiasm.

'There is a backyard, complete with a cast-iron mangle,' chipped in Bill. 'Wouldn't hurt to run over it, would it? I mean, the equipment is right here.'

'Okay, give it a try. And, Lisa, thanks for your help, it was much appreciated. Now get out of here in case it comes down on top of us.' She paused. 'Could you email these photos to me?'

'No problem, ma'am.' Lisa collected up the discarded protective suit and hurried out, closely followed by Beanland and his scanner.

'Right, well . . .' Nikki stopped mid-sentence and frowned. She could hear something. A kind of shooshing sound. They looked at each other.

'What . . . ?' Joseph began, then stopped, listening hard.

A small cascade of twigs and bits of mortar and loose debris suddenly trickled into the grate of the big open fireplace.

'All that garbage from the trees is shifting.' Joseph moved towards Nikki, who was staring at the hearth.

'Maybe we should get—' Bill's words were cut short by a sudden rushing noise.

Nikki gasped.

A mass of plant debris and brick dust had showered her feet as it hit the grate and flew out over the floor, but what had caused her to gasp was the empty eye sockets of an upside-down skull.

'God Almighty!' Bill mouthed.

Joseph put his arms around Nikki and pulled her back. 'The bastard! He left her suspended in the shaft of the chimney stack.'

For what seemed like forever, they stood in silence staring at the macabre sight. Then Nikki found her voice. 'We have to get her out of there before the whole place comes down. She deserves better than this.'

She was back in police mode, even if her heart was still thundering in her chest.

Bill grabbed his phone. 'I'll get some of our guys out here with tools. If we just tug at her she'll disintegrate. We need to cut the brickwork away and release her slowly and gently, and hopefully intact.'

'Do it,' said Nikki. 'But first, I want Rory out here. This must be forensically photographed and dealt with properly — with him in charge, no one else.' She turned to Joseph. 'Better tell Beanland to forget his latest theory. We have our girl.'

It would not be official until Rory confirmed it, but Nikki knew. The body in the chimney was Jennifer Cowley.

Rory answered almost immediately, his voice sounding like Lurch, the spectral butler. 'You rang, Revered Detective Inspector?'

'I need your help, Rory, right now.'

'Well, that's concise and to the point, even for you. Sounds ominous.'

'It is.' She gave him the story, hoping that only she noticed the tremor in her voice.

'On my way. You hang on in there, dear heart.'

She ended the call and stared at the phone. She should ring Cam Walker, she *must* ring him, but right now, all she wanted to do was either cry, or kill someone. The fact that the killer had disposed of that lovely girl in such a despicable manner took her breath away. Stuffed head first down a chimney stack and left to rot.

Nikki didn't want to look at the skull. Neither did she want to see those oddly white teeth in the yellowing bones of the jaw. She did not want to see the lank strands of hair still attached to the cranium. But somehow she couldn't tear her eyes away. She'd seen death many times, and some of the bodies had been horrifically damaged, but the sudden shock of this had derailed her.

'Nikki?' Joseph's voice was soft. 'We need to get out of here. Bill has just said that it was probably all the activity over the last two days that started that movement in the chimney and the whole thing is ready to come down. It's too dangerous to stay. Let's go back to the cars and wait for Rory and his team to get here.'

'Some of those SOCOs won't even have got home yet,' she murmured. It didn't feel right leaving that poor soul suspended over the hearth, but she allowed herself to be led away. They couldn't risk someone being crushed beneath a falling ceiling or collapsing chimney.

As they walked back down the now well-trodden path, Joseph said, 'Strange, isn't it? After feeling so, well, so *elated* that we might finally find Jennifer and give her family some answers, the reality of seeing that body is utterly sobering.'

'We shouldn't be surprised at the things people are capable of, after everything we've witnessed over the years, but,' she shook her head sadly, 'it still sickens me to the core and makes me effing angry.'

Joseph smiled at her. 'Good. Proves that you're not hardened to it, because that's the day you hand in your notice.'

'Still a human being, after all the knocks?'

'Still a human being, Nikki Galena,' he said.

They walked the rest of the way in silence, each lost in thought. Nikki recalled those early days, before Joseph had come into her life, when, eaten up by grief, she had not felt like a human being at all. She had worked only to put drug dealers behind bars, and she hadn't been too fussy how she achieved it. Then Joseph Easter arrived at Greenborough, and everything changed. Even before she fell in love with him, he rekindled all the emotions that had made her a good copper. And a decent person.

'Look!' Joseph pointed to where a Lexus Hybrid was pulling in beside their own vehicle. 'Cam Walker.'

'I haven't even updated him yet,' exclaimed Nikki.

'Guess it was the ever-efficient bush telegraph.'

'Or he's suddenly developed second sight. But I think your guess will be closest.'

'Are you two okay?' asked Superintendent Cam Walker, even before he was out of his car. There was genuine concern in his voice.

'Shaken up, to be honest, but, yes, we're okay, Cam.' Nikki smiled wanly.

'Do we think it's her?' he asked quietly.

Nikki and Joseph both nodded. 'It has to be. After finding those photographs, I'd put money on it being our missing teenager. Our body has good teeth, Cam, and we have Jennifer's dental records on file. I expect that's the route Rory will take for identification.'

'Speaking of angels,' said Joseph, pointing across the fields. 'You can spot that lime green Citroen a mile away.'

'I need to see the scene.' Cam looked at Nikki. 'Are you up to going back in there?'

'We've been evacuated, Cam. Bill Thorne is worried about safety. He's organised a team to extract her, under Rory's instruction of course, but until they go in, he's asked us all to keep out.'

'Then I'll wait for them,' Cam stared past them, into the copse, 'It's an extraordinary scenario, isn't it? A hidden deserted cottage, camouflaged by a small wood, unknown to the world for generations, and then along we come and find a dead body. You couldn't make it up, could you?'

'Truth is stranger than fiction,' said Joseph.

'Why do we say that?' Nikki asked, never having thought about it before.

Joseph shrugged. 'One of Mark Twain's characters declared that it's because fiction is obliged to stick to possibilities. Truth isn't.'

'Very good point,' said Cam. 'Between us, I think we've seen some very strange things, don't you?'

They waited, keeping the tone of their conversation light, for which Nikki was grateful. After a while, she saw another emergency vehicle, this time from the fire service, tearing along the lane. 'Bill's team are here. Rory has Ella Jarvis the forensic photographer with him, so I reckon it's crunch time.'

Joseph took a deep breath. 'So begins the next chapter in this tale of the unexpected.'

CHAPTER NINE

Yvonne Collins and her new crewmate sat in their car outside where Penny Gately lived. It was an old-style terraced house, a little tired and in need of some maintenance on the roof and gutters, but it still appeared as though someone was trying to look after it. Bright curtains hung at the windows and some-one clearly made an effort to keep the brass house number and letterbox polished. Everything pointed to making do on a limited budget.

Yvonne knew that was exactly the case. 'You know the Gately family, don't you, Kyle?'

PC Kyle Adams was another local, born and bred in Greenborough. 'Not well, Vonnie. Penny's husband drinks at the same pub as my old man, and I've eyed up the eldest daughter once or twice.' He grinned at her, 'She's a smasher! Name's Adele. What a looker!'

'Could we concentrate on the matter at hand, lad, and not get caught up with your fantasy love life.' Yvonne grinned at him. 'I reckon those photographs are of the youngest girl. I think her name is Laurie. Am I right?'

'Laurie? Yes, I've heard of her, but I've never actually met her. I do know all three have long blonde hair and are very similar in looks, although Adele has the edge.'

'Your opinion, or a general consensus?'

'She's a beauty, Vonnie. Ask any of the lads, it's not just me. She could have the pick of anyone around here but she doesn't even have a boyfriend. Odd that.'

'Not odd, just sensible,' said Yvonne sagely. 'The girl clearly has a good head on her shoulders.'

'Mayhap.' Kyle had lapsed, as he often did, into the local dialect. Yvonne liked the sound of it. It made her feel at home.

'Cheer up, cherub, there could be an upside,' she said with a grin. 'We might well have to interview your gorgeous Adele.'

'Now there's a thing! Oh, and look who's coming up the road.' He nodded towards a hunched figure struggling towards them under the weight of several bulging shopping bags.

'Go give her a hand, Kyle.' Yvonne opened her car door and waved to the woman. 'Hi, Penny. Haven't seen you for a while. How are you?'

'Yvonne? Oh dear, nothing's happened, has it?'

Yvonne didn't know how to answer that. 'Can we have a few minutes, Penny, and before you get worried, this is probably nothing, okay?'

Penny unlocked the front door and held it back for Kyle to push through with her shopping. He set it down on the kitchen table and they went into the lounge.

Penny pointed to two armchairs and they seated themselves. 'What's wrong, Yvonne? It's not the girls, is it? Or my Sean?'

'Please, don't worry. We would just like to talk to your girls, Laurie in particular. We think they might have been in contact with someone we want to speak to.'

Penny folded her arms over her full bosom and frowned. 'My girls don't mix with troublemakers I'll have you know! They're good, hardworking lassies.'

Yvonne wasn't sure how best to explain without terrifying the woman, but after seeing a photomontage on the wall that heavily featured the Gately sisters, she was more certain than ever that their stalker had his eyes on Laurie.

'I know that, and in no way are they in any trouble with us, I promise you. When will they be home, Penny?'

'Adele, any time now, Cindy, around six thirty, and Laurie has a few days off, so she is staying with a friend and I'm not quite sure when she'll be home. Why?' Penny had started to shift about in her chair, obviously getting anxious.

Yvonne took the clearest of the photos from her bag and passed it to Penny.

She stared at it. 'That's my Laurie. What of it?'

'And would you say it was taken here?' asked Kyle.

'Down t'end of terrace, near the playing field. She walks that way to work every day.' She looked hard at Yvonne, 'Now I am worried. What's going on?'

Yvonne returned her gaze. 'We are concerned that she's being watched by someone. We really need to talk to her about it. Can we have her friend's address, please?'

'Watched? You mean, as in followed? Stalked?' Penny's eyes were wide.

'We really don't know at this stage. It could be nothing at all. That's why we need to see her. So, that address, please?'

'I don't know!' Penny said. 'She's nineteen, Yvonne, she comes and goes as she pleases. Her friend's family have a chalet-bungalow, near the beach at Mablethorpe. They've gone abroad, and Kelly asked Laurie to stay with her, that's all I know.'

'Maybe Adele or Cindy will know more?' chanced Kyle.

'They might, but to be honest, my girls aren't as close as they used to be when they were young. Kids grow up and they drift apart as they build new lives for themselves.' She looked ready to cry. 'Is she in danger, Yvonne?'

'I'll be perfectly honest with you, Penny. We are concerned for her safety, but we could have the wrong end of the stick and the photo was simply taken by a friend.'

Kyle nodded in support. 'How about her mobile number? That could save us a lot of worry. Have you got that? Then we can ring her.'

Penny sniffed back a sob, pulled a battered faux-leather mobile case from her pocket and opened it. She scrolled through her contacts, murmuring, 'I never remember any of their numbers. Can't even remember my own half the time. Ah, here it is. Shall I ring her? She won't answer if she doesn't recognise the number.'

'Please,' said Yvonne, 'and tell her we want to speak to her as a matter of urgency, Penny.'

A few moments later, Penny slowly closed the case. 'She's not answering. Now I'm terrified something's happened to her.' She held a hand to her mouth. 'Oh God! My little girl!'

* * *

Rory entered the cottage first. He had requested a few moments alone, and no one ever argued with him over something like that. He might act like the court jester on occasion, but when it came down to it, Professor Rory Wilkinson, Home Office pathologist, was the consummate professional.

Ella was waiting in the wings to photograph the body, but he needed these few minutes to try and understand what had happened, before all hell broke loose.

As only the skull was visible, he was making no guesses as to when this terrible crime had been committed. Being lodged in a confined space would have done many things to a body and he needed the whole person on his mortuary table before he started hypothesising. He looked closer, especially at the teeth, and decided that it was almost certainly a young woman. What bothered him more than anything was whether she was dead or alive when she was pushed down that chimney. He hoped it was just an attempt to conceal a dead body.

Rory stood in the midst of all the rubble and decay, overcome with pity for the poor soul who had been treated so abominably. How terribly sad that she had been left here alone and undiscovered for such a long time. He could visualise her suspended, as if in limbo, waiting to be released.

'Let's get you home again, my dear,' he whispered. 'Your family want you back. Then perhaps you can all find some peace.'

He walked back to the door and called out to Ella. 'You first, dear heart. Work your magic on the body in situ, well, what you can see of it, then, as our gorgeous hunky firemen release this prisoner from her confinement, I want both stills and video footage. That's something that a court will want to see when my friends in CID catch the demon who did this.'

With a nod, Ella Jarvis moved past him into the room. If she was shocked, she didn't show it. Ella was experienced and well trained. She had suffered a serious traumatic reaction to a case in her past but had come back from it stronger than ever. Rory had a great deal of time for her, both as a person and as a bloody good forensic photographer.

When she had finished, he allowed the superintendent to venture inside to see for himself what they were dealing with. Unlike Ella, Cameron Walker certainly did register shock. After a series of explosive epithets — with an apology to Ella — he shook his head and went back out.

Rory could hear him giving very concise instructions to the fire service officer in charge, most of them concerning care and respect for the body.

'Ready in here,' Rory called out, hoping that the dismantling of part of the chimney breast wouldn't cause the wall to collapse, followed by the ivy-covered chimney stack above. If that happened, they would be needing several more body bags and a new pathologist.

It took over half an hour to get her free, and thanks to Bill Thorne's skills as a structural surveyor, and Rory's knowledge of how to handle a corpse causing the least damage, they extracted her intact and without bringing the cottage down around their ears.

Finally the body bag was loaded into the waiting vehicle, and Rory breathed a sigh of relief.

Nikki gave him the thumbs up. 'Nice one, Rory. I'll admit that for a while there, my heart was in my mouth.'

'You were not alone, I promise you.' He looked around for Ella. 'And now I'm going straight back to start work on our charge. I'll keep you updated as to my masterly findings as the story unfolds.' He gave her a polite little bow, beckoned to Ella, and made off in the direction of Dolly, his ancient motor. The pathologist had work to do.

* * *

The old Citroen made its way off along the lanes. A constable hurried up to Nikki and handed her a memo. 'It's from the duty sergeant, ma'am. He said that as you were here . . .'

She read it briefly, frowned and looked at Joseph, 'Aurelia Howard has been left another "gift."'

Joseph let out a low whistle. 'What? With all this police activity on the estate? Just how did he manage that?'

She shrugged, then turned to the constable. 'We'll attend. Tell the sergeant we'll go round and see her straight away.'

There was very little they could do at the crime site until Rory provided some answers, so Nikki thanked Bill Thorne for his help and she and Joseph returned to her car.

A few minutes later, they were sitting in the lounge at Sedgebrook House with all three Howards — Aurelia, Duncan and Richard.

The first thing Nikki noticed was the profound effect of the apparently minor incident on Aurelia. She looked drained of energy, pale enough to cause Nikki to worry about her state of health.

'Can you tell us exactly what happened, Mrs Howard?' asked Joseph gently.

There was a distant look on her face, then she seemed to rally. 'I went out to the greenhouse to pick some tomatoes for lunch, and there it was — this bouquet of flowers.'

Nikki wondered why Aurelia was so alarmed by this. She waited in silence.

'What kind of flowers were they?' Joseph was writing everything down.

'White roses and lavender, tied in a bunch.' Aurelia looked at him, seemingly waiting for a reaction.

'Oh, I see.' Joseph frowned. 'And you believe it's connected to witchcraft because of those specific flowers, Mrs Howard?'

'What do you think, Sergeant Easter?'

Nikki was lost, but there was definitely an understanding between the woman and Joseph.

He turned to Nikki. 'Some kinds of flowers have played a part in witchcraft for hundreds of years, and both roses and lavender are associated with the mystic.'

With a faint smile, Aurelia said, 'He's absolutely right, Detective Inspector. Rose petals are thought to ward off evil, and white roses have been especially revered since the days of ancient Greece. When Achilles slayed Hector at Troy, it was said that white roses sprouted from his blood.' She swallowed. 'When you see the bunch of flowers, you will please take special notice of what they are tied with. I suspect it to be a strand from a scourge.'

Joseph frowned. 'I see.'

'Well, I don't,' said Nikki flatly. This was all getting a bit silly as far as she was concerned.

'Like the athame, it's another thing that's found in a witch's toolbox, boss,' Joseph explained patiently. 'It's said to be an instrument for exercising power over others, and also to stand for the suffering and sacrifice that you are prepared to endure in order to learn.'

Nikki privately thought it was probably just a bit of old rope and Aurelia was allowing her vivid imagination to get the better of her. She decided to keep that to herself for now. 'And you haven't seen anyone around? No callers or delivery people?'

'Since this started, we've been on the alert, Detective,' said Duncan. 'My wife has scarcely set foot outside the house. I cannot think how someone could have got into that greenhouse without us seeing.'

'Perhaps we should take a look at it before we go any further?' Nikki suggested.

A short walk from the main house, the greenhouse was a rather beautiful Victorian structure, a far cry from the little aluminium frame building that Nikki's father had grown his tomatoes in.

She and Joseph looked around. It would indeed be difficult to get across the lawn undetected, but quite possible to skirt around the edges of the garden, close to the shrubbery.

'You probably wouldn't see if you were in the house,' said Joseph, 'but it was risky. Just getting into the garden from the road is tricky.'

They went inside. There, leaning against a row of large pots of tomato plants, they saw the bunch of flowers. Joseph photographed it with his phone, taking a close up of whatever had been used to tie it together.

'I think she's right, although I'm by no means an expert in these things. This is definitely no ordinary binding material,' Joseph said.

'Are you really worried about this, Joseph?' asked Nikki.

'In the light of everything else, yes,' he replied. 'Someone is sending very obscure messages to Mrs Howard. Somehow he, or she, has managed to get past a string of police vehicles and assorted officers to leave this token.'

Nikki lowered her voice, even though no one else was within earshot. 'Could it be Richard? Or the husband? Neither of them would have to worry about police noticing them. Maybe there's something going on within the family that we don't know about.'

'It's possible, but neither of them gives me bad vibes. In fact, I like Richard Howard, and Duncan seems like your typical academic, in a world of his own most of the time.'

Nikki felt the same, but they hardly knew this family and she trusted no one. 'I still think we should look deeper.'

'Naturally.' Joseph touched one of the rose petals. 'Quite fresh. Hasn't been here long, or it would have died in this sunny glasshouse.'

Nikki could smell the lavender. 'It's actually very pretty. It doesn't look threatening at all to me.'

'Aurelia Howard views it differently,' Joseph said soberly, 'and we can't afford to ignore her concerns.'

'I'm not. She looks almost haunted,' Nikki said. 'Do you get the feeling that she knows who is doing this but chooses not to share her suspicions with us?'

They stepped out from the humid interior. 'That, or she really doesn't know and it's really frightening her. Whatever it is, something is affecting her very badly, isn't it?'

'First thing I noticed.' She took his arm and held him back for a moment. 'You know we have to tell them what we've found in Hob's End Copse, don't you?'

He nodded. 'I suggest we do it sooner rather than later. I'm ready if you are?'

They walked back to the house and the waiting Howards.

'We'll be taking the flowers with us when we leave, if that's okay?' Joseph said. 'I just need to get an evidence bag from my car.'

'Get rid of the damned things,' muttered Aurelia, 'and the sooner the better.'

'But first, we need to talk to you all about the cottage in the copse,' said Joseph calmly. 'If we could go back inside?'

Richard was the first to speak when they were seated back in the lounge. 'I gathered from all the activity that something major has happened out there.' He directed his gaze to Nikki. 'What have you discovered, Detective Inspector?'

'I'm afraid I have to tell you that we have found a body concealed inside the derelict cottage.'

Aurelia gasped.

Duncan looked like a rabbit caught in the headlights, frozen in utter disbelief.

Richard just nodded. 'I thought as much when I saw the fire rescue team and a vehicle with blacked-out windows. Was it some tramp or a drug addict that was using the place to sleep in?'

'We can't tell you anything as yet, I'm afraid,' said Nikki. 'There will have to be extensive tests done because the person had been dead for some time.'

Richard stared at her, confused. 'But I was in there when we discovered the cottage. There was no body then. Surely if it had been decomposing, we'd have smelt it?'

'When I said "some time," I meant years, sir,' qualified Nikki. 'And it was concealed, so you would not have seen it.'

'My God! But who on earth would have known about the place?' Richard looked from his mother to his father. 'Did either of you know it was there?'

Duncan and Aurelia shook their heads. 'In all the years I have lived here, we had no idea there was a cottage in that copse. I don't think I ever even set foot in there,' Duncan said.

'It's always been an overgrown wilderness. I even told the boys never to try to play in it, it was simply too dense.' Aurelia looked devastated. 'And now you say someone died there. That's so shocking. Have you any idea who it is?'

Nikki wasn't sharing that information. 'As I said, forensic tests will be carried out, but until then, I'm afraid I can't say anything.'

'Could we ask you to search through any old photographs, or old documents or deeds to this property, to try to discover who owned it, or who lived there?' asked Joseph. 'From some of the contents, it looks like we are going back to the time of the First World War, or even before.'

Duncan Howard suddenly showed some interest. 'Well, we have a lot of family photos. They are stashed away in the attic but Richard will get them down for us, won't you, son?'

Richard nodded. 'Of course. I used to go up there and look through them when I was a kid. I always wondered who all those funny old people were.' He looked at Joseph. 'There are a lot of them, I warn you.'

'And I can source the documentation. I have some filed away, although others are kept by the family solicitor, so it might take a day or so.' Duncan looked apologetic.

'Anything you can lay your hands on will help. We can search too, through public records and registers, but whatever you have will speed things up,' Joseph said.

Richard stood up. 'At least this has made up my mind as to what I'm going to do with the copse. I'm going to raze it to the ground.'

'It will remain a crime scene for a while longer, sir. After that, it will be up to you, but personally I couldn't agree more,' Nikki said. 'Meanwhile, maybe you could rack your brains and try to recall any old stories or local gossip you might have heard about Hob's End Copse. Some of the old timers in the area could well remember something from years back.'

'Goose, the gardener, is a local. His family have lived out here since the year dot,' said Richard. 'He's worth talking to.' He looked at Joseph. 'Would you mind giving me a hand with the boxes of photos, Sergeant? I can pass them down to you.'

'No problem.' Joseph followed Richard out to the hall.

'I'll help too,' said Nikki, and went after them. She wanted a quiet word with the son.

'While we are alone, Richard, I can see that your mother is terribly upset by this mystery gift-leaver. I'd like to reassure you that we are taking it very seriously. The fact that he still managed to get onto the property with the heavy police presence here worries us a lot.'

'She's relieved that Sergeant Easter is here,' Richard said. 'Someone who understands about Wicca and won't make fun of her. That's a big thing to her. So many people ridicule what they don't understand. She's no witch, officers, but she does respect other people's beliefs, and her academic studies have given her an in-depth knowledge of a lot of very strange customs and teachings.'

'I realised that from talking to her,' said Joseph. 'But what puzzles me is what this person's motive is.'

'You and me both.' Richard started to climb the ladder up to the loft. 'And if I get my hands on him . . . sorry, I probably shouldn't go on.'

'We know,' Joseph said with a smile. 'Just keep it within the law.'

'I'll try.' Richard climbed up and disappeared into the attic.

Ten minutes later, they returned to the lounge carrying six large heavy boxes.

'Goodness me!' Duncan exclaimed. 'I feel like a hoarder. Surely it's not all photographs in there, Richard?'

'Every last one, Dad. Must be a hundred years of pictures in these boxes.'

'It's going to be a very long trip down memory lane for someone,' commented Nikki. 'But we'd really appreciate it if you could check for us.'

'It's high time I went through them and sorted out the ones worth keeping, Detective Inspector. It will be less weight on the ceiling joists, at least.' Duncan gazed at the boxes. 'We'll start this evening.'

Richard looked at Nikki. 'If you'll excuse me, I'm off home to fetch some things. I've decided to stay here at Sedgebrook until you find whoever is frightening my mother.'

'Of course.' Nikki glanced at Joseph and they stood up. 'We have to go too, but there will be officers out at the crime site. If you are worried about anything, or see someone suspicious, ring the station and they'll get someone across immediately.'

'I'll get that evidence bag and collect the flowers.' Joseph hurried off to his car.

'Try not to worry too much, Mrs Howard,' said Nikki. She paused at the door and handed Aurelia her personal card, 'Don't hesitate to call me if you need me, okay?'

'I wish all this would end.' Aurelia took the card, looking as if she was about to burst into tears. 'I'm frightened, DI Galena. I know that these incidents seem really petty, but for some reason, they terrify me.'

'We'll do our best to find him for you, I promise.'

Waiting for Joseph to return with the unwanted bouquet, Nikki began to wonder if this mystery person might be connected to the goings on in the deserted cottage. Maybe Aurelia Howard had every right to be afraid.

CHAPTER TEN

It was almost six p.m. by the time they got back to the station. The team was still in the CID room, all waiting to hear about the body and how it had been found.

'Do you think it really is Jennifer, boss?' asked Dave, trying to keep the excitement out of his voice.

'I'm certain of it, but we have to wait for Rory's definitive confirmation.' Nikki was exhausted. The shock of seeing that skull appear from the recesses of the chimney had not yet dissipated. It felt as though it had been a very long day, and she certainly wasn't up to giving the guys the gory details tonight. 'Look, all of you get home now and we'll catch up on everything tomorrow morning.' She turned to Cat. 'Ben is in tonight, isn't he?'

'Yes, boss. Have you got something you'd like him to follow up?'

'I'd like him to find out all he can, from public records and the media, about the Howard family of Sedgebrook House, Jacob's Fen. They are Duncan and Aurelia Howard. Historical stuff as well as up-to-date information. Would you leave him a note to that effect please, Cat?'

Cat grabbed a pen and a memo sheet. 'Anything else?'

'No, that should keep him busy enough. Now, Joseph and I need to make an unannounced call on Mr Patrick Shale, the man who was imprisoned for Jennifer Cowley's murder. We'll do that on the way home, and then we'll fill you in at the morning meeting.' She looked at them apologetically. 'Sorry, but I'm wrung out tonight.'

'Get home, boss,' said Dave. 'Can't Shale wait until tomorrow?'

'I want to see how he reacts to hearing about the discovery of a body, fifteen years after a murder.' Nikki had always wondered about Shale and his continued insistence on his innocence. She knew better than most that there were no guilty men behind bars, they all swore they had either been set up or the law had got it wrong. But Shale had bothered her, as it had so many other officers at the time. It had been proven that he had been infatuated with Jennifer Cowley. He had admitted that he had watched her for months and he had been seen with her several times. But he swore he hadn't killed her. Nikki had never met the man, and now she needed to get a look at him.

'I have to report to Cam, then we'll go straight away, if that's okay with you, Joseph?'

'Ready when you are.'

* * *

'Is the DI still here, Niall?' asked Yvonne.

'Gone to interview Patrick Shale, Vonnie, you just missed her. Can I help?'

'I'm worried about Laurie Gately and almost as concerned about Penny, her mother. She has Adele and Cindy with her, and the husband is due home shortly, but she's in pieces.'

Niall Farrow checked his book. 'I've put out an attention drawn to Laurie. And I've asked the Mablethorpe boys to ring me as soon as they have anything for us. I sent them the photo of Laurie, but as yet there's little more I can do. If only someone knew the name of the girl she'd gone to stay with.'

'Her two sisters only knew the kid's first name — Kelly.' How could a mother let a teenager go off with no address, no contact number and no name for the people she was staying with. Still, Yvonne knew that Penny struggled, and teenagers could be a nightmare, so . . . She sighed. 'Penny is tearing her hair out.'

'And the girl's not answering her phone,' said Niall thoughtfully. 'I wonder if that's a rebellion thing, or whether she can't answer.'

'My thoughts precisely. It's hard not to jump to conclusions, especially when you know what they found at Hob's End.'

'True.' Niall closed his book and stretched. 'I'm off home now, and it's time you went too. Your shift ended an hour ago.' He grinned at her. 'How are you getting on with the newbie?'

'A very different animal to my last protégé, I must say.' Yvonne smiled. 'Not half as gung-ho. But if he turns out to be a fraction of the police officer that you've become, lad, I'll be happy.'

'He's got a great mentor anyway.' He winked at her. 'We had some good times, didn't we, Vonnie?'

She noted the sadness in his voice. He had moved on, but she knew he missed being on the beat, out there in the thick of things with her. 'Oh, we did! And I wouldn't change anything. You were a pain in the arse for a while, but we got you sorted.' She lowered her voice. 'Actually, you were the best crewmate I ever had.'

'Ditto, Vonnie. Now, quit the nostalgia and let's go home before we both start to blubber.'

'Speak for yourself! Blubber indeed,' she said with a catch in her voice. 'See you tomorrow.'

* * *

Nikki and Joseph stared at the home of Patrick Shale. Joseph wasn't sure what he had been expecting — maybe

99

some rundown worker's cottage — but it certainly wasn't this. Calthorpe Lane turned out to be one of those lanes that went nowhere, meandering across the fields before disappearing into some mythical fen hole. There were few houses in Langtoft, but this place had taken a bit of finding. It was a ranch-style bungalow set in immaculately lawned gardens and surrounded by willow trees. A name plate that hung from one of the big trees declared it to be Willow Lodge. Appropriate, if a little unimaginative.

'Not bad,' breathed Nikki. 'Not bad at all.'

'For an ex-con, it's unbelievable,' said a puzzled Joseph. 'How has he managed to keep this going while he's been away all those years?'

'Well, let's ask him, shall we?' Nikki was already getting out of the car.

The bell was answered by a petite woman of about sixty. She looked up at them suspiciously and examined their warrant cards closely. 'He's only been home a matter of weeks and already you are hounding him. What do you want?'

Joseph rallied one of his best smiles. 'Just a few moments of Patrick's time. There has been a development and we badly need to talk to him, Mrs . .?'

'I'm Jane Shale, his mother. This is our home, and you're not welcome here.' Beneath her dark hair the eyes were narrowed and her lips formed a thin, straight line.

So Shale was living with his mother. For some reason, Joseph had him down as a loner. He looked at the angry face. She was being entirely reasonable. He'd served his time, and the police were already knocking on his door.

'Let them in, Mum.' A tall, thin man with a sallow complexion had appeared behind his diminutive mother. 'Maybe they've come to apologise for locking me up for a crime I didn't commit.'

The sadness behind the defiant remark wasn't lost on Joseph. They were going to have an interesting conversation. 'Thank you, sir. We appreciate you listening to us.'

They followed Patrick Shale into a large airy lounge with folding doors that opened onto an ornately paved patio that still maintained its summer colour, teeming with bright red geraniums and pink and mauve petunias. The Shales were obviously not short of money.

Joseph was very aware of the tension in Nikki. Her whole body was saying, *He's a killer, Joseph, cut the nice guy routine*. 'This is actually a courtesy call, Mr Shale,' she said sharply. 'There will be something in the news, either tonight or tomorrow, and we thought we should warn you, in case a media frenzy breaks out.'

The mother stared first at her son, and then Nikki. 'Media? Frenzy? Hasn't he suffered enough?'

Joseph could almost hear Nikki's thoughts . . . *Not a fraction as much as that poor dead kid!* He jumped in before she could air her opinion. 'I'm afraid this is something no one would be able to keep quiet for long, Mrs Shale. A woman's body has been found today and we are awaiting confirmation that it is that of Jennifer Cowley.'

Both their mouths dropped open. Patrick whispered, 'You've found Jennifer?'

He sounded almost reverent, as if Jennifer had been his Holy Grail and the search was finally over. Once again, Joseph was perplexed. He looked more closely at Patrick Shale. He was around thirty-five years old, with lank straight hair of a vaguely rusty-brown colour and pale eyes. His whole demeanour was lethargic, from his way of speaking to his movements, as if his batteries were running down. At a guess, he'd say Shale suffered from anaemia, but it could just be prison pallor.

'We believe so. Forensics will provide the answer very soon.'

'Where did you find her, Detective?'

Again that reverential and worryingly intimate tone. Joseph had an idea that Patrick Shale would be making a pilgrimage to the spot just as soon as he could.

'Are you sure you don't know that already, Patrick?' asked Nikki icily.

'How would I? I didn't kill her.'

But he asserted his innocence with no real fire in his eyes. Joseph wondered what medication he was on.

Jane Shale abruptly stood up, her face still white with shock but her demeanour threatening. 'You've delivered your message. Now go, and leave my son alone.'

'Sit down, Mum . . . please?' Shale looked at them imploringly. 'I have to know where you found her. As you said, it will be all over the papers and the TV in a matter of hours, so why not just tell me now?'

He was right. Joseph glanced at Nikki, who remained silent.

'I've never denied caring about Jennifer, never,' Shale said. 'Have I? That's probably what helped me to get convicted. My solicitor told me to say nothing, but I didn't listen to him. If ever there was a case of *mea culpa* that was it! You have no idea how devastating this has been for me, being accused of killing someone I love.' He swallowed. 'Please tell me where she was found?'

Nikki sighed. 'On Jacob's Fen, in a ruined cottage hidden in in a wood, and that's all I can say until full details are disclosed.' She stood up. 'Now, as your mother rightly said, we've delivered our message. Thank you for your time, Mr Shale.'

Outside in the car, Nikki let out a long breath. 'Bloody hell! What did you make of that?'

'Mixed messages, Nikki,' Joseph said. 'I really want to look at the transcript from the trial, don't you?'

'I certainly do. One minute I'm certain the creepy little perv murdered her, the next I'm wondering if we banged up some lovesick kid and let the real killer walk free.'

Joseph felt the same, although he was leaning towards the latter. 'He was obsessed with her and still is, but he's never denied that. Did you notice how he said how devastated he was about being accused of killing someone "I love," not "loved"?'

'Mmm. After fifteen years, he's still carrying a torch for her. Scary.'

Joseph started the car. 'Let's go home, shall we?'

'Yes please! What a day! And now we've seen Patrick Shale for ourselves, perhaps the transcript will make more sense.' She was about to say something else when her phone rang. 'It's Mum,' she said, with a smile. 'Wonder what she's up to now?'

'We're off tomorrow, Nikki.' Eve's voice resounded through the car's speakers. 'We are setting off around five to beat the morning traffic. I've left the address where we are staying on your answerphone, just in case, but I'll keep my mobile switched on.'

With everything that had happened, Joseph had forgotten that Eve and Wendy were going off on their hunt to find out what really happened to the dead artist, Robert Richmond. He smiled to himself. They would never willingly sit back and take it easy, whatever their ages. Certainly, right now a few grey hairs didn't seem to be slowing them down any!

'Please take care, Mum,' said Nikki, a slight frown tracing a line across her forehead. 'We know what you're like! No risks, no danger, just follow the paper trail that Wendy mentioned, okay?'

'Understood. But honestly, darling, it's a harmless bit of detective work, if you'll forgive the casual reference to your day job. All we are doing is chasing clues to a very old mystery, one that I'm sure only the family cares about. No bad guys this time, just two old ladies ferreting around in parish records and dusty old archives.'

Joseph and Nikki had to chuckle at the thought of Eve and Wendy as "old ladies." Wendy, who still held her pilot's licence, could fly a variety of fixed-wing civilian planes, and Joseph knew she could operate a WWII Spitfire because he'd seen her. And Eve? A law unto herself. Ageless. Fearless. Dauntless but possibly heedless. There could be few less stereotypical "old ladies" than Nikki's mother and her friend.

'Okay, Mum, but try to pamper yourselves a little too. You're being treated to a swanky hotel, make the most of it. I bloody well would. You're traipsing round the Lakes for this family, let them spoil you!'

Joseph loved hearing Nikki talk to her mother. The bond between them was strong, even though they hadn't known each other long. Possibly it emanated from their mutual love of Frank Reid, Nikki's late father.

Nikki ended the call. 'I'll miss her.' She paused, 'even if she does worry the life out of me with all her hare-brained schemes.'

Before he could answer, her tone reverted to the business-like. 'I'd better ring in and see if there's any more news on our missing girl, Laurie Gately, before we try to switch off for the night.'

As he drove, he listened to the update. Mablethorpe police had not managed to locate her. Meanwhile, Ben was checking Laurie's Facebook page to see if he could glean any more info about the friend called Kelly. According to Penny Gately, Laurie's phone was still not being answered and she had sent her two other daughters out, trying to contact other friends of hers and find out where this Kelly lived. Joseph didn't like the way things were going, but he did understand teenagers. Maybe the girl was not accepting her mother's calls because she was angry with her for some reason. Maybe she was kicking back at her mother's interference in her life. Tamsin had blanked him more times than he cared to remember.

Nikki pushed her phone into her bag. 'One thing, Joseph. I hope you agree, but I think we should keep an open mind regarding Shale's guilt for Jennifer's murder and assume we still have a killer out there. It's rare, but there have been miscarriages of justice in the past, so it's not unprecedented.'

'Thank heavens we don't have the death sentence anymore,' said Joseph. 'I wholeheartedly agree. We can't afford to assume the law got it right and ignore the possibility that the real killer is still at large.'

'Good,' said Nikki. 'Well, uniform are doing all they can to find our missing girls, and with Ben beavering away, there's nothing more we can do tonight. I just want to get home now. What's for dinner?'

'Chilli con carne. I had a feeling we'd be late, so I took one out of the freezer before I left.'

'Perfect. Comfort food.'

'All food is comfort food to you, Nikki Galena — as long as *I* cook it.'

'Damn it! You noticed.' She squeezed his leg. 'Better not leave me. I'd starve.'

'Can't have that on my conscience, can I? S'pose I'd better stay, in that case.'

* * *

Night settled over Jacob's Fen. Richard Howard sat down with his parents to eat, thankful for having an understanding partner. Not only did she put up with all the early mornings and late nights, now he had left her and returned to his family for an undetermined length of time.

Ruthie was one of those wonderfully adaptable people who took everything in their stride. You could throw some cataclysmic bombshell at her and she'd weigh it up with a, 'Right, well, in that case, this is what we'll do.' And get on with it. She was the perfect partner for him, so why had they never married? Maybe they just had no need of a certificate to prove their love for each other. Maybe that's just the way it was, so why spoil it?

His mother's whole regime had been thrown off course by the unwanted visitor to her greenhouse. However, she'd managed to cobble together an impromptu supper, so there was good food on the table. His father had opened a bottle of Rioja, saying they all needed a pick-me-up.

He wasn't wrong. Knowing a body had lain hidden on their land, Richard was in turmoil. It seemed as if the very soil had been tainted. He worked hard to get the best produce possible from Sedgebrook Farm, using the best practices to achieve that goal, and now someone had polluted it. He was saddened and very angry.

He should tell his parents what his future plans were for Hob's End Copse and the cottage that sat hunched like some evil goblin in the heart of it. They never objected to any of his suggestions but he told them anyway, out of courtesy. He sometimes wondered how the love of the land could completely bypass a generation, like genes for eye colour. His grandparents had been farmers to the core, but they had wanted Duncan to have a good education, so they saw him through university, thinking he would return to Sedgebrook full of exciting ideas about the running of the estate. How wrong they had been. Duncan left home as soon as he could and went studying fossils in the Vale of Glamorgan, only to return many years later when his father became sick. He did finally settle at Sedgebrook and loved the house, but he employed a farm manager to keep the estate running and went back to his academic career. Fortunately, the farming gene had been passed on to Richard.

'I've spoken to Tamsin Farrow about the copse,' he said. 'She advises felling and clearing all of the non-native trees and replanting with ones that will help the ecology and the environment.' He put his glass down and stared at it for a while. 'In the light of what they have found there today, that cottage will be razed to the ground just as soon as we have the go-ahead.'

His father nodded, but his mother seemed distant, as if she wasn't taking it in.

'Do it, Richard,' said Duncan, 'Best thing all round.'

'Mum? What do you think?'

'Sorry, son? Oh yes, do whatever you think. Your father and I are in complete agreement with whatever you say.' She looked at the food she had scarcely touched and sighed. Then she changed the subject. 'It is very good of Ruthie to be so understanding, Richard. We appreciate you staying, but are you sure she's alright on her own?'

'Ruthie will be fine, Mum. She says she'll cook us dinner tomorrow night and bring it over, to save you worrying about feeding me. She suggested a chicken chasseur with a green salad, if you'd like that?'

'That woman is a saint, boy, you should marry her.' Aurelia gave him a tired smile. 'It's very kind of her to cook, and it'll be absolutely delicious if I know Ruthie. Say thank you, we'd be very grateful.'

That tired smile wasn't lost on Richard. It was unlike his mother, who usually had so much energy. He too had been worried — after all, he had gone to the police about it. But it seemed to have affected his mother differently. He wanted to help but didn't know how. So he changed the subject slightly.

'It's very strange, isn't it? I mean, that neither Dad nor you ever knew of anyone who lived in that cottage. Usually there's someone who knows a bit of old Sedgebrook history. When we were kids, we were into everything, but somehow the copse got overlooked.' He paused. 'Hey, do you think Alex or Jerry might know about it?'

Aurelia shook her head. 'No, I wouldn't think so. I never let any of you boys try to find your way in there. It was far too overgrown to have one of you be snarled up in brambles and get tetanus or something. Anyway, you had acres of farmland and a big garden to play in, and it wasn't as if it was a pretty wood, just a great matted mass of tangled trees and undergrowth.'

Richard vaguely recalled his parents warning him off Hob's End. Still, he thought it worth a long-distance call to his brothers. Alex in particular always did whatever he was told not to, so it stood to reason that forbidding him to go there would mean he tried his best to do just that. Maybe he'd give them a ring after dinner and run it past them. He wasn't close to his brothers, who'd been gone for many years by now, but sometimes he wished they were nearer. He'd always thought that one day he and Jerry would run the farm together. Alex hadn't the slightest interest in the place, but Jerry had always given him the impression that he was happy at Sedgebrook. It had come as a bit of a shock when Jerry decided to go off and live abroad with Alex. Suddenly, Richard had gone from being one of a trio of brothers to being an only child.

Richard's father stood up. 'I'm going to my study. An old colleague of mine is selling off some of his specimen pieces of malachite and I want to see them before he sends them to auction. He's sending some jpegs this evening, so forgive me if I disappear.'

Aurelia smiled at Richard. 'It's his way of getting out of doing the washing up, son. Different excuse every night but same motive.'

Laughing, Richard began to gather up the plates. 'Don't worry. You've got me to help you tonight.'

'I'm glad you're here, Richard, I really am. I'm so concerned about all this.'

It was written all over her face.

'Mum, I've got to ask . . .' He had started, so there was no turning back. 'Is there something you aren't telling us about this person? Because if there is, now's the time to open up, and I promise I'll do all I can to sort whatever's bothering you.'

For a moment he saw a strange look on his mother's face — fear maybe? Or was it anger? Then it was gone, to be replaced by that tired smile.

'You're a good boy. Thanks for your concern, but there's nothing I can tell you. I really don't know who is sending these tokens, I just know it's shaken me to the core.'

Richard sensed that his mother was lying but decided to let it go. He had no idea what was happening, but he did know that something was terribly wrong.

* * *

Carmel Brown switched off the TV and the lounge light. The initial adrenalin rush of her visit to the police station had faded, to be replaced with uncertainty. Would she be able to carry it through?

Carmel checked that all the doors and windows were locked, made a mug of Ovaltine and climbed the stairs to her bedroom. Having been so pleased with her purchase of Honeysuckle Cottage, she was horrified to find that Deacon lived close by. Now the place seemed sullied.

She placed the mug on the bedside cabinet and went to close the curtains. Trying to calm her nervousness, she looked around her at her bedroom, noting its size and shape, the décor. This sometimes helped, but tonight it did nothing to calm her.

Had she done the right thing? Or had she opened a Pandora's box? After ten minutes of this and getting nowhere, she picked up the phone and rang her friend Marian.

Marian Harper's no-nonsense take on the situation was just what she needed to hear. 'You have several things in your favour, Mel, the main one being that the bastard doesn't know that you have moved into the area. On top of that, no one except us — and the police of course — have the slightest idea you are planning to help them. You are doing exactly what you should have done ages ago. A man like that cannot be allowed to victimise innocent women, especially ones in such a vulnerable state. It's despicable.'

'But the whole procedure is going to be not only stressful but degrading. I mean, I'm going to have to stand up in court and tell the world exactly what he did. It's demeaning. God knows what people will think of me.'

'Good Lord, Mel! They'll think you are brave. They'll see a woman who is not afraid to stand up and say, "Enough!"'

What would she do without Marian, without her honesty and friendship? 'You are a rock, a real angel.'

'Stuff and nonsense. I'm just practical. Not only that, I *hate* injustice. Between you and me, when justice fails you, why not turn to vigilantes? Wrongdoers should pay the price, one way or another.'

'Fighting talk, Marian.'

'Sadly, it comes from personal experience. It's old history now, but I'll tell you about it over a glass of wine one evening.' She paused. 'Mel? Would you like me to come and stay for a bit? Just while it is getting underway. Sometimes having someone to talk to and share the load makes a difference.'

Carmel thought this sounded perfect.

'Excellent,' said Marian. 'I'll get a few things together and come round tomorrow after lunch, if that suits?'

'Oh yes, that would be great,' Carmel said, relieved at not to have to face this gruelling task alone. And who better to have by her side than Marian Harper?

Finally, Carmel put out her light, all her former confidence restored.

Perhaps she wouldn't have felt quite so resolute if she had seen the dark car drive slowly through the village, slowing to a crawl as it approached Honeysuckle Cottage. The sole occupant took careful note of the little house, of its hanging baskets and the welcome mat at the front door. After a while it gathered speed, accelerating away from Little Fleeting Village and out into the fen.

CHAPTER ELEVEN

The morning meeting was packed, with standing room only. There was a lot going on and a whole load of stuff to cover. Nikki scanned her notes, half listening to Niall as he listed the reports that had come in overnight.

All had been quiet out at Hob's End Copse, but they had expected that to be the case. The previous owner of the blue tent was hardly likely to pop back for it with an army of coppers there waiting for him.

The officers at Mablethorpe had had no luck in tracing Laurie Gately, and no activity had been picked up from a trace on her phone. Knowing how much youngsters these days relied on their mobiles, this factor was becoming increasingly worrying. Nikki listened, her concern escalating. It was very likely that after a meeting with Cam Walker, the hunt for this girl would have its priority level upgraded.

As soon as Niall had allocated jobs to the various uniformed teams and dismissed them, it was Nikki's turn:

'I'm still waiting on a prelim report from forensics regarding our dead girl, but immediately we hear something regarding her identity, I will inform you.' She glanced at her scribbled notes. 'Now, I know this seems a very insignificant incident to be spending time on when we have so much on our plates right now, but this unknown man or woman who is leaving unwanted and possibly menacing gifts at Sedgebrook House cannot be ignored. Apart from the fact that Aurelia Howard seems particularly disturbed by these occurrences, I want to know how someone can come and go relatively easily when we have half the Fenland Constabulary traipsing about the estate. And in light of what we found in the cottage, namely one dead body and a satchel full of photos of one girl from a cold case and another one now missing, that one-man tent bothers me a great deal. If the two incidents are connected, and I'm certain they are, we could be looking for someone who has committed a crime far more serious than delivering bunches of flowers and witches' knives to old ladies. I want him, or her, found, and quickly.'

'Her?' called a voice from the back of the room.

'Frankly I can't see it being a woman, especially if there is a connection to the satchel of photographs, as that is usually indicative of a male stalker. Even so, open minds, everyone. And while we are talking about open minds, we spoke to Patrick Shale last night, and DS Easter and I both agree that there could be something in his continued insistence that he did not kill Jennifer Cowley. We will be looking deeper into the old case, but while we have the slightest doubt about his guilt, we have to assume there could be another person responsible for her death, and that man could still be free and walking amongst us.'

'Regarding Aurelia Howard's stalker, I've run a check on that witch's knife,' said Joseph, 'and it's not a particularly valuable one. Looks like a Chinese replica of an old design with pagan symbols engraved in it. I haven't found the source, but I'm thinking it was ordered online.'

'From Witchy-Poo dot com?' asked someone sarcastically.

'As it happens, chum,' replied Joseph evenly, 'I'm liaising with a particular company who supply the worldwide Wiccan community with a huge variety of goods, and they are being very helpful indeed.'

'Keep on with that, Joseph,' said Nikki. She looked across to Cat. 'Has Ben left us anything from his night's work looking into the Howard family, Cat?'

Cat stood up. 'Yes, boss. Everything seems completely kosher. All the info they gave us about their jobs and their home is correct. The only ones Ben couldn't get too much on were the two brothers who moved abroad to live and work. They are Jerrard Howard, age forty-one, and Alex Howard, age thirty-seven. They moved to South Africa when Alex landed a job with the Anglo-American Corporation out there. Ben thinks it's something to do with HR, but he's not sure. His brother Jerrard, who is a bit of a computer boffin, took a job with a software company in the same area. Ben's found an address but he's not sure if it's current. He's left a message to check with the Howards this morning.' Cat skimmed down the handwritten notes. 'Nothing suspicious has ever come to our notice about the farm or anyone working there. Lily white, he says, even historically.'

'So what makes Aurelia a target?' Nikki mused.

'Her husband indicated that she could be very outspoken. Maybe she really got under the skin of one of her students at college?' suggested Joseph. 'Some young people don't take criticism well.'

'Nor do some adults,' Nikki couldn't help adding. 'But I suppose she might have upset a student who was perhaps a bit unstable? Maybe we need to look closer at her working life. Even though she is now semi-retired, she might be on committees or still attend certain lectures. Whatever, she seems to have pissed someone off.'

'What about friends and acquaintances?' said Dave. 'Someone in the Howard's social circle? If she's known for speaking her mind, perhaps she's offended one of them?'

'We're clutching at straws, aren't we?' grumbled Nikki.

'But that's what happens when a "normal" member of the public gets targeted,' said Joseph. 'They don't have scores of people out to get them, like some bad guy might have, so you have to look closer to home.'

'Bad guys, or coppers,' muttered Cat. 'There would be a whole string of suspects in the frame if it were one of us.' She pulled a face. 'But as you say, she's just an average family woman.'

'Not quite,' Joseph said. 'She has a degree and a string of letters after her name in a rather obscure subject — psychology, with a specialism in the effects of folklore and superstition on modern society. So maybe not so average. And because of the athame, or witch's knife, the scourge that tied the flowers, and the particularly mystical choice of white roses and lavender, it would appear our man is very aware of her connection to such things, and that she would know their meaning.'

Nikki frowned. 'I get the feeling that could be important, Joseph, but we are going to have to do a whole lot of delving into her personal life to find any suspects, aren't we? And that means someone is going to have to win over the rather tetchy and very frightened Aurelia Howard.' She smiled at him mischievously. 'Someone with patience — and we all know that lets me out instantly — as well as charisma and persuasion and a gentle voice. What about it, Joseph?' She raised her eyebrows.

'Bugger,' he said. 'Me and my bright ideas.'

'Excellent. That's your next job, Detective Sergeant Easter. Now, Cat? Are you and Dave still managing to hold onto the Vernon Deacon inquiry while all this is going on?'

'Yes, boss. We are running a few background checks on Carmel Brown, just to confirm her veracity as a witness, something neither of us doubt but it needs to be done anyway.'

'Absolutely. We want this one to be the star witness. She has to be beyond reproach and then maybe this time we'll nail him.'

'So far all our checks have tallied with what Carmel has told us, boss,' said Dave. 'So it's looking good.'

'And do we have Deacon under observation?' Nikki asked.

'DC Sean Pickford, the new lad, has him under discreet surveillance. It's not twenty-four-seven of course, but at least we'll know if he starts acting out of character or looks like he's preparing to do a runner.' Cat looked determined. 'It's vital he still feels that he's on safe ground, after the last woman to come forward was deemed an unreliable witness. We can't have him finding out about Carmel. She's our *coup de grace*, ma'am, the ace up our sleeve. I want him shitting himself when we slap the cuffs on.'

'Then get those checks completed and go after him as soon as possible. If we hear from forensics that our dead girl from Hob's End is Jennifer Cowley, all hell is going to break loose in Greenborough.' Dismissing visions of the inevitable media invasion, Nikki looked back at her crib sheet. 'Okay. You all know what to do. I'm just off to see the super about Laurie Gately. It's looking bleaker by the hour for that kid.'

Nikki watched them disperse towards their various workstations. She'd like them all working together on one case, but it just wasn't possible right now. And they couldn't turn Deacon over to another team, not when they were so close. No, they'd just have to multitask for a bit. It wasn't the first time, after all.

She glanced at the wall clock, then, with a last look at the whiteboard and its photographs of Jennifer Cowley and her doppelganger Laurie, she hurried off to find Cameron Walker.

* * *

Rory Wilkinson watched his temporary technician prepare to assist with the examination of the Hob's End Girl, as she was being referred to for now. It wasn't the most pleasant of tasks for his assistant's debut performance but it was certainly an interesting one. Rory rather liked the woman — it was that Welsh lilt in her voice.

Erin Rees was no stranger to cadavers that were less than fresh, having embarked on a career in archaeology before changing tack and deciding on forensics. Even so, the Hob's End Girl would be a challenge. Meanwhile, Rory had to remember that Erin was not Spike. He would need to curb his humorous remarks until she knew him a little better if he didn't want to frighten her off on her first day.

'Well, dear Erin, this is a baptism of fire, if ever I saw one. Welcome to my humble abode, chamber of the dead and house of surprises.' He beamed at her from behind his mask.

In the bright light he saw her eyes twinkle. 'Professor, surely this has to be some kind of test? I've read the notes about where she was found, and nothing adds up.'

'I always like to provide something of interest to my newest fledglings. My lovely Spike is often bemused by some of the conundrums I throw his way.'

'He told me. But . . .' Erin stared down the body on the dissecting table and shook her head.

'Ah, now, let me explain.' God, how he loved this bit! The neophyte, gazing up at him open-mouthed, waiting for him to enlighten them with his expertise. 'As you have noted, this dear soul presents with signs of mummification. The skin is thin, and both that and the soft tissues are dry and a brownish black in colour. When we open her up, I'm certain we will find that her internal organs will have decayed into dry, blackish masses.'

'But the conditions are all wrong for mummification. That requires a hot, dry environment with low humidity, not a damp chimney stack in the middle of a wood!' Erin was utterly nonplussed.

He nodded sagely. 'Absolutely correct, but what you are seeing here is a rare forensic case of an atypical precocious mummification that has occurred within specific microclimatic conditions.' He waited for her reaction.

'Good grief! Really?'

'Oh yes. I have to say that in all my years in pathology, I've only heard this mentioned a couple of times and never witnessed it before. You are indeed fortunate to be here. Spike will be pig sick when he hears of it.'

'So how did this occur, Professor?' Erin asked, peering at the strangely darkened skin.

'Well, as far as I can make out, it's the closed environment, the fact that she was tightly wrapped in a sleeping bag, probably to facilitate getting her into the chimney, and the weather at the time of her incarceration. Checking back, if this girl is Jennifer Cowley, then she went missing just prior to a particularly hot, dry spell that lasted for some time. If I'm right — and you will soon find out, dear Erin, that I am rarely, no, *never* wrong — I think this process occurred very soon after her death, maybe over a matter of a few weeks.'

'Amazing!'

'It is, and it's worth looking up the few other documented cases. They are fascinating.' He took a deep breath. 'But right now, we have work to do. Are you ready, my friend? I have an impatient detective inspector chewing her nails to the quick in anticipation of our preliminary report.'

'To be honest, like . . . I can't wait!'

Rory chuckled to himself. Erin was from Cardiff, a city with its own special dialect. She used quirky phrases which she'd explained were a mix of Wenglish, a hybrid of English and Welsh, and Welshisms, things you only hear in Wales.

'Excellent. Then we'll begin.'

* * *

Tamsin finished typing and closed the document. As her printer whirred into life, she began addressing the envelope. After the words, *To Mr Richard Howard,* she stopped, thought for a minute, then added, *By Hand.* She tried to tell herself it was simply a waste of postage when the man was more or less her nearest neighbour, but it was really just an excuse to get back to the Sedgebrook Estate.

She had finally managed to wheedle out of Niall the fact that they had found a body. Tamsin still hadn't got over her amazement that she had stood in that very room, not feet away from the dead girl, and not realised she was there. Now she was even more fascinated, and her chance connection to the investigation was making it almost impossible to concentrate on anything else.

She took the envelope and stood up. 'Fancy a nice walk, Skip?'

As if he would refuse.

The dog bounded off and stood staring at his lead, hanging on the back door. He barked, that single delighted sound that always tugged at her heartstrings. Thank goodness they had taken him in after his owner had died. He was an utter joy to have around — apart from the weight she was losing by walking him.

Outside, the day was still pleasantly warm, cooled a little by a breeze coming from the east. She breathed in the fresh air, noting a hint of perfume from wild camomile drifting across from one of the fields. Along with the clover, it gave off a delicious, subtle scent. It also meant that Richard Howard, who owned this stretch of farmland, was planting clover to improve soil quality and reduce the need for artificial fertilisers. Good for him.

She walked down the empty lane, Skipper bounding ahead, wondering what to say to Niall about her impromptu trip to Sedgebrook House. He wouldn't like it, she knew, so she began inventing plausible excuses . . . "Well, Skip deserves a decent walk, doesn't he?" "We just went in the other direction for a change." "I thought, why go all the way to the post office, when I could deliver it by hand and walk the dog in one go?" She'd stick with that last one. Even if he got mad at her, it wouldn't last for long. It never did.

It didn't take too long to get to the Howards' house. Tamsin was a brisk walker, used to keeping pace with Niall's resolute stride. She supposed his tendency to turn a pleasant stroll into a route march was a copper thing. When she was out walking, she liked to pay attention to small details — an interesting fungus, a new wild chicory plant, whereas Niall focussed on the destination, the quickest route from A to B.

She stopped at the entrance to the estate. From here she could see the dark shadowy cluster of trees rising up from the flat that was Hob's End Copse. The flashing blue lights had gone but there were several vehicles still parked in a nearby field.

Tamsin clipped Skip's lead on and walked up the drive to the house.

At the door, she was assailed by the sound of small dogs yapping. She had forgotten about the dachshunds. She glanced down at Skip, who was waving his tail rather uncertainly.

She hadn't expected Richard to open the door and was surprised when he did.

'Tamsin! Good to see you.' He looked at Skip. 'Maybe I'll come out, if that's okay? The dachshunds can be somewhat noisy and if they catch sight of this handsome chap, there will be no stopping them.' He stepped outside and closed the door. 'I'm in residence for the duration it seems, still working the farm and popping back here to keep an eye on things.' He looked tired and anxious.

'You've got a lot on your plate at the moment,' Tamsin said.

He gave a short laugh. 'I'll say! I don't know what to worry about most. That terrible find at the cottage? The fact that my mother is being harassed by some wicked joker? Or that my work is getting more and more behind by the day?'

'Well, I won't hold you up, Richard. I've just brought my report on Hob's End for you to see.' She took the envelope from her pocket and handed it to him. 'I'll get back now.'

'No, stay for a minute.' He pointed to a seat under a rather beautiful cedar tree. 'If you've got the time, that is?'

He looked so anxious that she couldn't refuse.

With Skip at their feet, they sat on the mossy bench. She waited to hear what he would say.

'I know this is probably an imposition, Tamsin, but I'm in the thick of it here, too close to see things clearly. Could

I run something past you? As an impartial outsider, so to speak, you might make some sense of it.'

Tamsin perked up. 'Of course. Fire away. It's no imposition, I assure you.'

'Well . . .' he hesitated. 'What would you do if you thought someone you loved was keeping something from you?'

The question was unexpected. She had been expecting some juicy detail about the finding of the body. 'Ummm . . .' What *would* she do? 'It would depend on who it was, I guess. If it were Niall, my husband, I'd badger him until he gave in, but he's a pushover where I'm concerned.' She paused. 'Seriously, Richard. Who is it?'

'My mother.' He drew in a long breath. 'She has always been a bit of a dragon, very confident and rather opinionated, but she's gradually become more insular over the last few years and now, well, she's almost a different woman.' The frown deepened. 'Something is eating at her and she won't say what it is. I'm certain it all began to escalate the moment that knife appeared on the doorstep.'

'Is she too frightened to tell you, do you think? Or is it something more prosaic?' Tamsin was intrigued.

He lifted his shoulders. 'I have no idea. The worst thing is she flatly denies having any idea of who's threatening her.'

'And you think she has?'

Richard leaned forward, put his head in his hands and groaned. 'I don't know. Maybe it's just that dreadful find on our land, and this idiot traipsing around our property leaving stupid bloody messages.' He raised his head. She noticed his eyes were red. 'Sorry, Tamsin, it's not your problem. I'm probably just being neurotic!'

'It's okay, honestly.' She touched his arm.

She felt as if she had known Richard for years. From their first meeting, he had felt like an old friend. It happened sometimes. You immediately related to a person, as though you were meeting them again after having spent years apart. It had been the same with her best buddy at university. At their very first meeting, she had taken one look at Elena and felt a flash of recognition, and the girl's expression told her she felt the same. Her grandfather had told her the person was an old soul that you had known in a previous life. She had laughed then, but sometimes she wondered.

Richard apologised again. 'I'm never like this! Ruth, my partner, tells me I don't show enough emotion. Now look at me. I'm a mess!'

'I think it's quite understandable.' She tried to lift his spirits. 'After all, it's not every day a body drops down your chimney.'

For a moment she thought she'd made a terrible mistake in being so flippant. Then he laughed out loud.

'Tamsin Farrow, you are a breath of fresh air.' He let out a long breath. 'And I'm so pleased you agree about clearing that copse. I certainly wasn't looking forward to seeing that staring at me every day. The sooner I get to work on it, the better I'll feel.'

'And in the meantime, would you like me to try and talk to your mother? I'll come back tomorrow without Skip. She might open up more to a complete outsider. It's worth a try, isn't it?'

'Would you? I mean, aren't you busy with work?' Richard looked hopeful.

'I fit work around my life. The people I work for are very flexible, as long as I get the work done.'

'Brilliant! How about ten tomorrow morning? She knows about you anyway, but I'll tell her you're dog mad and you'd like to meet the dachshunds.'

'I'll bring treats.' Tamsin stood up. 'I won't take up any more of your time now. See you tomorrow.'

'Thanks again, see you then,' said Richard, looking more relaxed.

She and Skipper walked back along the lane and past the old hulk of a mill. She would have some explaining to do when Niall got home. Tamsin grinned. Oh well, she had a good few hours to prepare her story, and she'd cook him his favourite pasta dinner. That should do the trick.

CHAPTER TWELVE

Niall poked his head around the door to the CID room. 'They've located Laurie's friend! Her name is Kelly Arthur, and she lives at Sea Breeze, Easthorpe Road. A local car has been dispatched and they are on their way, ma'am. I'll update you as soon as I know more.' Then he was gone.

Nikki was reluctant to get her hopes up. After all, it was just an address they had found, not Laurie Gately herself.

'We've completed our inquiries into Carmel Brown, boss,' said Cat with a sigh of relief. 'She's the real McCoy all right, squeaky clean and everything she's told us checks out.'

'Then go pick up Deacon, now! I could get a call from Rory at any moment, and then I'm going to need every one of us on the Hob's End case.' Nikki had a feeling that events were about to snowball, bringing the press down on their heads in a veritable maelstrom. She looked for Joseph and saw him deep in conversation on the phone in his office. 'Bring him in. Cat, Dave, go arrest the bastard.'

'Oh, with pleasure!'

Seeing Dave's expression, Nikki understood how much this meant to him. It might be the last time he would listen to the caution being read. 'Enjoy yourselves, guys.'

Cat winked at her. 'This one belongs to Dave, boss.'

Nikki hoped it would go smoothly. Cat and Dave had worked together for years before Dave became a civilian interviewing officer, and they had made an excellent team. Well, all things came to an end. At least Cat now had Ben.

'I'll be going to see Mrs Howard tomorrow morning, Nikki.'

Deep in thought, she hadn't noticed Joseph approach her. 'No sooner?'

'She's going to give a lecture this afternoon at Greenborough Uni, so it'll have to be, I'm afraid.' Joseph pulled a face. 'I'm not sure she was too excited at the idea of a cosy, in-depth chat, but she understands the need for it. By the way, don't you think it's odd that Duncan Howard seems to be floating through this major upheaval as if nothing's going on? He answered the phone just now, and he was completely blasé about it.'

'Some men are like that, Joseph.' She rolled her eyes. 'Ignore it and it'll go away, or let the little woman deal with it. One or the other.'

'That's a bit unfair, Detective Inspector.'

'Not really.' She lifted an eyebrow. 'Remember Ron Machin?' Ron was one of the laziest police officers ever to wear the uniform.

Joseph chuckled. 'Ah, the "Olympic Torch."' Ron Machin never went out. 'Okay, I see your point. But Duncan is definitely a little odd. Some academics do get obsessed with their subject, and he is certainly passionate about geology, but he seems almost indifferent to his wife's distress.'

Nikki sucked in air. 'So what could that mean? That he doesn't care? But they've been married for eons, and he seems genuinely fond of her. Or maybe he doesn't take it seriously because he thinks she's overreacting?'

'That's possible,' said Joseph. 'He didn't see the sinister side to that witch's knife and looked totally bemused at the idea of flowers having some ominous message attached to them.'

'Or, what if he knows *exactly* what's going on? Knows she's not in real danger, so can afford to be casual about it?' Nikki said thoughtfully.

'What, doing it himself? I can't see him being so devious, can you? He's an intelligent man, a scholar, a lecturer. Why do something so, well, so petty? It's almost childish.'

Nikki was about to answer when she heard her office phone ringing. She hurried into her office and snatched up the receiver. 'DI Nikki Galena here.'

'And I was *so* hoping it would be Judy Garland!' Rory replied.

'Rory! Be serious! What have you got for us?'

'Just trying to lighten the mood before I drop the bombshell.' He paused for dramatic effect. 'Nikki, you are going to be famous! You have finally found Miss Jennifer Cowley, bless her heart.'

She closed her eyes against the tears that welled up. After fifteen years, Jennifer could finally go home to her family. Her own beloved daughter had died when she was a teenager, but how much worse must be the pain of living for all that time in hope, wondering but never knowing for sure. She swallowed. 'And that's official? No doubts at all?'

'Good old dental records, Nikki. Perfect match. Undeniable. Plus her clothing was still partially intact, and it tallies with what Jennifer was wearing when she disappeared. Add a small silver necklace still around her neck, and I'd say absolutely no doubt at all.'

Nikki thanked Rory and hung up. She looked out of the office, and saw Joseph staring at her. 'It's her,' she called out. 'Joseph! It's Jennifer.'

* * *

The neat little bungalow in Old Fleeting was still just as sickeningly immaculate. 'Will you knock on the door, Daveyboy, or shall I?' Cat asked.

'Ladies first.' Dave grinned. 'Then show him your warrant card, caution him and march him to the car. I'll be drinking in every happy moment.'

It was textbook. Cat recognised him immediately and went straight into the spiel. 'Vernon Deacon. I am arresting you on suspicion of sexual assault. You do not have to . . .' Finishing with, 'And I have here a warrant to search these premises. If you would accompany us to the car now, sir, we are taking you to Greenborough Police Station.'

Deacon said nothing, remaining silent even when the cuffs went on. He merely smirked at her as if to say, *You're wasting your time. You'll never make it stick.*

As they reached the car, two squad cars arrived and four uniformed officers got out, all pulling on blue nitrile gloves. 'All yours, lads,' said Cat. 'Top to bottom please, fingertip search, and don't forget the attic and the garden shed.'

Dave pushed Deacon into the back of the car behind the passenger seat and climbed in beside him. 'Let's go.'

Cat could see his face in the rear-view mirror, still wearing that disdainful smile. Cat smiled back, coldly. *I can't knock that smug grin off your face, slimeball, but I'm certainly going to be around to watch the judge do it. We've got you this time!*

* * *

'The girls aren't there,' Niall said angrily. 'And the chalet bungalows on either side are holiday lets, so no one knows anything about the family. One of the people renting the place next door said his teenage son had commented on two "well-fit birds" going out last night, all dolled up and looking like they were either on a hot date or ready for a film shoot.'

'What time was that?' asked Nikki, finding it hard to concentrate when her head was still filled with thoughts of Jennifer Cowley.

'Around eight thirty, he thought. I'm getting the local guys to check any clubs and pubs in the area that are popular with young people, and we are checking the Greenborough night spots too. We have more nightlife here than that little seaside town.' He passed her a photograph of a tall, willowy girl with long dark hair and prominent, almost Slavic-looking cheekbones. 'This is Kelly Arthur. Every crew has one of these as well as one of Laurie Gately.' He looked at her solemnly. 'We are taking this very seriously.'

'Even more so when I tell you what Rory has just confirmed.' Nikki stared back at him. 'Our body is that of Jennifer Cowley.'

'Oh shit!' He grimaced. 'Sorry, but that's really worrying. If Laurie's picture was in the same satchel as the ones of Jennifer, and your theory that Shale could be innocent is right, there's a good chance her killer is at large, and as Laurie is missing . . .'

'We are all thinking the same thing, Niall.' She looked at her watch. 'Got to go and see the super. He's calling an impromptu meeting. We need a strategy in place to cope with the next few days.'

Niall nodded vehemently. 'I should say we do. I certainly need to have an action plan for the troops. I'll see you there.'

'Joseph! With me, please. Let's break the news to Cam Walker.'

Taking the stairs two at a time, they ran up to the superintendent's office.

'I never expected to see this day, did you?' Joseph asked as they went.

'It's usually some quirk of fate that leads to the final discovery,' Nikki said breathlessly, 'but I certainly never thought it would be us that did the finding.'

With a look at the expressions on their faces, Cam nodded and sat down heavily. 'Positive ID?'

'It's her, Cam.'

He whistled softly. 'And the missing girls?'

'Nothing yet. Although we do have an address. It seems they went out on the town last night and haven't returned.'

Cam Walker shut his eyes. 'Damn!' He looked from one to the other. 'We will have to be very careful how we handle this. But first, what is the situation with the Gately family?'

'We have a FLO with them already. I know it's premature, but I considered it appropriate since we have identified Jennifer.

PC Yvonne Collins is also in attendance until we get some news of Laurie and her friend. She knows Penny and her husband.'

'Good, good. Now, before we do anything else, we have to take this news to the Cowleys. The press and the media are already hovering in the wings. I can't have them telling Jennifer's family before we do. They still live in the Greenborough area, although they moved to a smaller property in one of the villages last year.' He pushed a piece of paper across the desk to Nikki. 'Here's the address. Are you up to this, my friend? I'm happy to go myself if it's a bit much for you, seeing as you were the one to find her, and . . . well,' he smiled sadly, 'your personal history could make it tough on you.'

Nikki smiled at him. 'It's okay, Cam. I'll never stop crying over Hannah, but I've done my crying over Jennifer. I can do it.' She glanced at Joseph. '*We'll* do it. Together. I'll be fine, I promise.'

'If you're sure, you'd better do it now, Nikki, and take a Victim Support Officer with you. The family are going to need a lot of support in the next few weeks, poor souls. Still, it'll be some consolation finally having their daughter back.'

'And they can bury her properly and peacefully at last,' added Joseph, standing up.

'Let me know the minute you are back,' Cam said, 'and I'll call the meeting. Oh, and Nikki, you'll have to put in an appearance at the press conference later today. They are going to want to see the officer in charge who found her.' There was a slight hint of amusement in his voice. Cam knew of her aversion to cameras and the press only too well.

'Actually, she found me,' Nikki said. 'And if anyone should take the praise, it's Joseph's daughter, for discovering the cottage in the first place. I just happened to be there, so no need to mention me by name, Cam.'

'You're not wriggling out of this one, Galena, so don't bother to try. Off you go and break the news to the Cowleys. I'll see you later.'

* * *

127

Nikki and Joseph drove back from their gruelling task, both emotionally drained.

'I'm proud of the way you handled that, Nikki. It was no easy task.' Joseph's voice was full of admiration.

'All part of the job, isn't it?' Nikki sighed. 'The worst part, in my opinion. Still, they took it well, all things considered, although I thought Margaret Cowley was never going to stop crying.'

'And the way they kept thanking us. I felt terrible. How could anyone be so grateful when we'd just taken away all their hope?' Joseph could have cried himself. Margaret had clung to his sleeve, telling him over and over that she could never repay them enough for bringing her little girl home.

'They'll think differently in another few days, when the initial euphoria wears off. Then they will start asking questions and looking for answers. We've been there before, haven't we?' Nikki said.

Joseph nodded. They certainly had. The parents would want to see the place where their daughter had died. They would want to know exactly how she died as well, which wasn't going to be easy to explain. 'Well, whatever, you were brilliant in there, my love.' He decided it was time to steer the conversation into shallower waters. 'I never quite know what to expect from DI Nikki Galena. She never ceases to amaze me. One minute you are giving someone the tongue-lashing of their life, and the next, you open up and reveal a rare glimpse of your softer side. You're a paradox, Nikki Galena, you really are.'

Joseph glanced sideways at her. He had been teasing, but he truly was amazed at the depth of her understanding of human nature. The older she got, the more her sensitivity had developed. When someone was playing her, she was immediately aware of it, and whoever was pushing their luck would find themselves on the sharp end of her tongue. At other times, she had infinite patience to bring out the best in a person.

'Okay, Sigmund. If you've finished analysing me, perhaps we could talk about where the hell we go from here?

Like with two missing teens and a probable killer somewhere out on the Fens?'

Joseph awoke from his reverie. 'Good point. Shall I ring the super and say we are five minutes away? Then he can gather the troops.'

'That's the first sensible thing you've said for several minutes, Sergeant.'

Chuckling, Joseph took his phone from his pocket.

* * *

Superintendent Cameron Walker called for silence and delivered the official news that the body of Jennifer Cowley, missing for over fifteen years, had been found and positively identified. 'As you will all no doubt be aware, this is going to be one of the biggest news stories to come out of the Fens for some time, so expect the media hordes to descend.'

'How much will they be told, sir?' asked a young detective.

'As little as possible to begin with. DI Galena and I will be holding a brief press conference this afternoon — just a simple statement confirming the discovery of a body that we believe to be that of Jennifer Cowley. Other than that, we will be fending off questions with the usual "cannot comment at this time." Our biggest worry at present is the fact that Laurie Gately and her friend Kelly Arthur have been missing since last night. As her mother confirmed that Laurie was the girl in the photographs found with those of Jennifer, we are treating her disappearance as a matter for serious concern.'

'Will the press be made aware of this?' asked a uniformed officer.

'Absolutely not. The photographs found in the satchel at the cottage are not to be spoken of outside this station, is that understood?'

There was a murmur of assent.

'DI Galena?' Cam looked across to her, 'Have forensics lifted anything from that satchel, or the pictures?'

'No, sir, nothing of use to us yet. They suggest there might be a smudged print on one of the buckle straps, and they are going to do further tests on it, but the results from the photos haven't come back yet.'

'And we are no further on with finding who erected that tent in the cottage?'

Again, she answered in the negative, adding, 'We are going back tomorrow to question Mrs Howard again. We think there might be a connection with the person who is threatening her and whoever hid that satchel — as in they might well be one and the same. We are pursuing that line vigorously, sir.'

'Thank you, Nikki.' Cam surveyed the gathered officers. 'You don't need me to tell you that we are in a very difficult situation here. Apart from the hunt for Laurie and her friend, we have to look again into the Jennifer Cowley disappearance. You all know that a man named Patrick Shale has just been released from prison, having served his sentence for her murder. When all the evidence from the site of the crime is in, we may have to reconsider his guilt.' He pulled a face. 'But we'll cross that bridge when we come to it. Meanwhile, get out there and find the two missing girls, as quickly as you can. There will be overtime available, but I expect every officer here to put everything else on hold and do what you have to do to find them. Okay?'

More murmurs of assent, louder this time, followed by the sound of chairs scraping the floor, and the officers filed out.

Nikki turned to her superintendent. 'Cam? Cat and Dave have arrested Vernon Deacon. This time we have a rock-solid witness who is hell bent on making him pay. The clock is ticking on how long we can hold him, so can we leave them with that for the time being? This is the first time we actually have a good chance of making the accusations stick.'

'Yes, of course. We can't let a man like that get away again, but as soon as possible, get them back on the main investigation. We need everyone working at full steam.' He turned away, adding, 'Three o'clock, in the foyer, please, Nikki, for the press statement.'

Nikki grimaced. Perhaps she could suddenly be called away. An emergency of some kind?

Head down, she walked slowly back to her office, busily planning her escape.

CHAPTER THIRTEEN

Silence reigned in Interview Room Four. Cat and Dave looked across the table at the man sitting opposite them. Cat had done the introductions for the tape and was now trying to sum up Vernon Deacon. It was hard to remain impartial in a case like this, but she knew she shouldn't decide he was guilty. Yet.

This one was going to test her, but she was determined to do it by the book. There was no other way. Deacon had a brief sitting next to him who had a reputation for not only being a shit-hot lawyer, but whose only reason for getting up in the morning was to get one over on the police.

After stating what he had been arrested for, she began the interview.

'Mr Deacon, do you admit going to Mrs Brown's home on the evening of February the twelfth, 2019?'

Deacon glanced at his solicitor, who gave a slight nod. 'Yes, I believe I did, although without checking my diary, I can't be sure of the date.'

'And the purpose of your visit, sir?'

'To offer advice and support after the death of her husband.'

Cat looked at him, at his receding grey hair and heavy build. He was an unattractive man, but he did have presence. He sat, ramrod straight. Ex-military, she guessed, and he'd probably been a strong, powerful man when younger. This impression, however, was spoiled by the supercilious smile that played around his full lips.

'Through some organisation? This advice and support?' she asked.

Deacon nodded calmly. 'A local Army Veterans' social club. I've worked with them for years. I advise bereaved members on pensions and how to deal with some of the complicated paperwork that a death in the family generates. There are dozens of members who will testify to the fact that I have been nothing but professional in my approach, and helpful to them.'

'And this is what you were doing at Mrs Carmel Brown's home in Kirk Deeping on the night in question?'

'Exactly.' His expression gave nothing away.

While he spoke, Cat made notes, using the time to formulate her next question. 'And did you at any time, make advances of a sexual nature to Mrs Carmel Brown?'

'I did not.'

'Her allegation is very specific, sir.' She read out loud: '"*After talking for a while about certain benefits that could be due to me because my husband had been in the army until he retired, Mr Deacon suggested I make a cup of tea. He followed me into the kitchen and as I was getting cups from the cupboard, he reached around me and touched my breast. I screamed and he placed a hand over my mouth and told me to calm down. I was terrified and when I looked at him, I saw that he had unzipped his trousers.*"'

'I suggest you stop right there, Detective.' The solicitor gave her a condescending smile, like someone having to contend with an annoying child. 'You have no proof whatsoever that my client behaved inappropriately, other than the word of a hysterical and grieving woman. This is a ridiculous fabrication and a total waste of time.'

'It is your client's right to know exactly what was alleged. I am merely extending him the courtesy of complete disclosure. He can admit or deny it, but he needs to hear exactly of what he is being accused.' With a smile, Cat looked from one to the other of them. 'To continue . . .'

The interview lasted for another fifteen minutes, Deacon flatly denying everything, until Cat called for a break.

Outside the room, she breathed out, long and slow. 'He's as cool as a bloody cucumber, the bastard.'

Dave nodded. 'Makes my skin crawl, just looking at him. The way he makes those poor women out to be neurotic is just horrible.'

'I'm just praying that Carmel is going to be strong enough to take this man on.' She lowered her voice. 'Hopefully then we will have a few surprises for him, things he won't be able to deny or talk his way out of so easily.'

'I think Carmel will come through, Cat, especially now she's told us her friend is coming to stay with her. It means she'll have some support twenty-four seven, not just while we're around. You know, those early hours of the morning when you are all alone and you start to have doubts about everything. A friend will help enormously.'

'That sounds like personal experience, me old mate.'

Dave smiled wryly. 'We've all been there, haven't we?'

'Too often.' She looked at her watch. 'Ready for the next round?'

'Bring it on.'

* * *

At around two that afternoon, Nikki was beginning to think that she might just have to suffer the torment of the press conference after all. She couldn't think of a plausible excuse to offer. Then came a knock on her door that had the sweet sound of repeal. A civilian officer walked in. 'The duty sergeant needs your help, ma'am. Could you spare a few minutes, please?'

Nikki stood up. This had all the makings of a proper excuse. 'Of course. What's the problem?'

On their way to the stairs, the civilian explained. 'He has a woman downstairs who has asked as a matter of urgency to see whoever is dealing with the Deacon case. She seems very upset, ma'am. When he rang DC Cullen, he was told she was interviewing and could be some time, so he wasn't quite sure who to ask.'

'Well, I'll see if I can help.'

In the back office, Sergeant Jones confirmed what the civilian had told her. 'Her name is Mrs Marian Harper, ma'am,' he added, 'and she doesn't seem the panicky type. The thing is, she's concerned about her friend's whereabouts.' He looked at her anxiously. 'That friend is your star witness in the Deacon case.'

'Carmel Brown?'

He nodded. 'Will you talk to her?'

'Where is she, Sergeant?' Nikki asked, her stomach a tight knot.

'She's still in the foyer, ma'am. You could use Interview Room One to get some privacy.'

Nikki went out into the reception area, where Marian Harper was instantly recognisable among the people waiting.

Nikki introduced herself and led the way to the interview room. Marian Harper looked around, obviously taking in the fact that the furniture was bolted to the floor and there was a panic button strip all around the walls, and pulled a face.

'Sorry about the room, Mrs Harper, but we can talk in private here,' Nikki said. 'Please, take a seat. Can I get you a drink?'

'No, I'm fine, thank you. I just need your help.'

Now that she was closer, Nikki noted the carefully made-up face. Marian had looked younger from a distance, but now Nikki saw that she could well be in her seventies, although she had an energy about her that made her seem almost timeless. 'Okay,' she began, 'tell me what's happened.'

'Carmel Brown is my dear friend, and I am going to stay with her until that animal Deacon is safely locked up. She was expecting me at lunchtime today.' She pushed a stray lock of hair behind her ear and chewed on her bottom lip. 'Only when I arrived, she wasn't there. I rang her mobile but it went to voicemail. I left a message and waited outside for about an hour. I looked in the windows, but there was no sign of her.' She looked Nikki in the eyes. 'Normally, I wouldn't have bothered you so soon, but—'

'But you know that your friend is going to testify against Deacon and you are afraid that something has happened to her.'

'If I'm being a fool, then I'm sorry to waste your time, but I'm terrified for her safety. I'm beside myself, Detective Inspector.'

'Well, I can tell you that Deacon is here in custody, but he was only picked up a couple of hours ago. When did you speak to Carmel last, Mrs Harper?'

'Last night. Around eleven thirty, I suppose.'

The knot in Nikki's stomach tightened. She didn't like where this was heading. 'I'm sure Carmel explained everything to you. Do you think it's possible that Deacon found out about her being willing to testify against him?'

'I can't see how, unless he was watching her when she came to the police station.' Marian frowned. 'But this assault happened last year, and at the time he frightened her badly enough to silence her. He's probably forgotten all about her by now. I doubt he even knows she lives in the village. She only moved in a matter of days ago. Why would he be watching her?'

'He could have seen her by chance. It would be very bad luck on her part, but it's possible. Anyway, I'll get someone around to the house and we'll take it from there. I suggest you go home, and we'll contact you as soon as we have some answers for you.' Nikki stood up. 'We'll make enquiries and check the local hospital, Mrs Harper. And try not to worry too much. I'm sure there's a perfectly simple explanation.'

She took a card from her pocket. 'Ring me if she contacts you and I'll do the same, okay?'

Marian Harper took the card with a sigh. 'She was very nervous last night, Inspector, wondering if she was doing the right thing. I managed to convince her that she was, but now I wonder. Maybe she was right to have doubts.'

'She's a brave lady. I have absolutely no doubt that she's doing the right thing. Men like that cannot be allowed to terrorise people. He belongs behind bars, and your friend will help us put him there.' Nikki sounded positive but in her heart she was as uncertain as Marian Harper. Where was Carmel Brown and was she safe?

After she had seen Marian out, Nikki headed for the back office. She wanted a crew sent round to Honeysuckle Cottage straightaway. Halfway there, she stopped, hesitated and pulled out her phone. 'Joseph, come downstairs. I'll meet you in the car park. We're going out.'

* * *

He knew that no one would let him get within a mile of the spot where Jennifer had been found, but he had to try. Jacob's Fen was not a heavily populated area and he would stand out like a sore thumb, but that meant nothing. He needed to be close to her again.

Patrick Shale felt no different now to the way he had when she was alive. She was like a magnet, drawing him closer to her, and he couldn't resist. The last years had been hell. Prison had not only shut him off from the real world, it had shut him off from Jennifer too. Now he was back on the fen, he could at least follow her footsteps, placing his feet where she had walked. He was close to her again, breathing the very air that she had breathed. The feeling was indescribable.

He went to the garage and gazed for a long moment at his Suzuki. Thank goodness he had insisted that his mother have the motorbike serviced regularly while he was away. He hauled it off its stand and pushed his pride and joy out onto the drive.

He had passed the long nights in jail dreaming of zipping himself into his leathers and boots, donning his helmet and taking off across the Fens. He had called to mind every small detail: the sound of the zip as he pulled it up to his chin. The smell of leather. The click of the helmet's visor as he pulled it down across his face. Hours could pass in this way.

Since his release, he had gone out riding every day, although he had the feeling that the police would be keeping a close eye on him in the coming days, so his trips might have to be curtailed.

Patrick ran a hand slowly over the smooth burnished surface of the tank and swung himself onto the bike. His heart was pumping. He was terrified of what the police might do to the place where his girl had been found. If only they didn't desecrate it! He started the bike.

* * *

'You're doing this to get out of that press conference, aren't you?' Joseph barely managed to hide his smile. 'Cam's going to be dusting the ceiling.'

'What? Me? How could you even think such a thing, Joseph Easter? Seriously, I've got a nasty feeling about that woman. She's such a sensible, thoughtful kind of person. I'm sure she wouldn't leave her friend in the lurch.'

'Well, either something's happened to her, like a breakdown or an accident, or . . .'

'Or what, Joseph? She has a mobile phone, why didn't she ring Marian in that case?' The more Nikki thought about it, the more worried she became. 'It's just too much of a coincidence. Deacon gets arrested and the main witness disappears.'

Joseph's voice was even. 'Slow down, Nikki, let's not get ahead of ourselves. She could have forgotten to charge her phone, or, heaven forbid, she could be lying on a hospital trolley somewhere.'

Nikki knew he was right. It had happened before. In fact, quite recently they had found a woman they had believed to have been abducted, unconscious in hospital suffering from concussion. Even so, it just didn't feel right. 'I dread telling Cat and Dave,' she said grimly. 'Without Carmel, that brief will have Deacon out of custody in a flash.'

She parked outside Honeysuckle Cottage and they got out.

As Marian had said, there was no sign of life.

'Let's try the back,' said Joseph, loping off down the drive, which ran alongside the cottage.

Nikki followed him, stopping to peer into a side window. Everything looked neat and tidy. And empty. She was certain Carmel Brown wasn't here.

'All shut up tight,' called Joseph, 'but there's a garage. Let's see if that's locked as well.'

They tugged on the wooden door, but it failed to give. 'There's a door round to the side, Nikki.'

She walked around and found it, surprisingly unlocked. 'No car. That's odd.'

'It makes me feel a bit easier, actually,' said Joseph. 'She must have gone out somewhere.'

'Of her own volition? Or was she made to?'

'That glass-half-empty attitude is beginning to spook me,' Joseph muttered.

Nikki kicked angrily at the gravel and listened as the pebbles skittered across the drive. 'Where is she? I'm going to talk to the neighbours.'

It took a while, but by the time they got back in the car, they had ascertained that there had been a visitor to Honeysuckle Cottage, very early, maybe around six in the morning. The neighbour in the next-door cottage had heard a car pull up and someone knocking on Carmel's door. Unfortunately, he hadn't looked outside to see who was there so early. The neighbour on the other side had told a similar story. That family were early risers, and one of them remembered seeing a dark-coloured Ford Focus parked outside. He reckoned it was only there about fifteen minutes, certainly no longer than that. And, he recalled, it had a damaged wing mirror on the driver's side.

'Do we know what car Deacon drives?' Nikki asked.

'Not off the top of my head, but I can ring in and get someone to do a check.' Joseph put his hand to his pocket.

'Don't bother. Let's call round to Deacon's address and see if uniform have finished the property search. We can check his vehicle at the same time.'

'Okay, and if he does have a Ford, I suggest we see if any cameras caught him on the road early this morning.'

'Totally agree.' Nikki accelerated away, heading for the Old Fleeting housing estate where Deacon lived.

All the roads in the rambling estate of smart houses and bungalows were named after trees. Deacon lived in a cul-de-sac at 14 Hawthorn Close. Two police vehicles were still parked outside. 'That's a relief,' said Nikki. She jumped out of the car. 'Let's take a look in that garage.'

Inside they found a wall rack with carefully labelled key fobs hanging on it. 'Thank you for being so organised, Deacon. It makes our lives easier.' She grabbed the key marked "garage main door" and ran back outside.

They pulled back the doors — to reveal a red Vauxhall Corsa.

'Shit!' she breathed.

'Shit indeed. But at least it wasn't his car that called on Mrs Brown. Not that I'm sure where that leaves us.'

Nikki was about to answer when she saw a woman watching them from the bungalow next door with a sour expression on her face. 'Can I help you?' asked Nikki stonily.

'You should be ashamed of yourselves!' The woman then launched into a tirade against the police for harassing and bullying good upright citizens, while Nikki stood transfixed by the vehemence of the verbal attack.

'He's been kindness itself to me, and to most of the other neighbours along here. It's just horrible the way he's been treated. Horrible.'

When the woman finally ran out of steam, Nikki informed her that they would not be doing their job if they ignored complaints from the public.

The comment was received with a snort of derision. 'Vern would do anything for us and we feel the same about him, so why don't you go and chase real criminals, rather than disturbing a quiet and respectable neighbourhood like this?'

She flounced back into her house and slammed the door. 'Nice woman,' Nikki murmured.

Joseph had been fighting back a smile. 'Your face was a picture. Clearly our man has invested a lot of time and energy in creating the perfect environment to operate from.'

'Inhabited by gullible old dears who have all fallen for his silver tongue.' Nikki was beginning to hate Deacon even more, simply for deceiving decent people. 'Oh well, let's go talk to the search team, although I'm sure they won't have found anything incriminating.'

'Let's just hope that Carmel turns up, or at least gets in touch,' Joseph said.

Nikki sighed. She hated feeling this negative. She glanced at her watch. Well, there was one upside to this calamity. It was four thirty, and the press conference would be well over.

Nikki asked a PC on duty at the house whether they had found anything of use. She responded with a resounding "no."

'This place is more sterile than an operating theatre. He needs help, seriously.' She looked at Nikki, shaking her head in amazement, and solemnly stated, 'He *irons* his underpants.'

Nikki and Joseph both laughed.

'And he's certainly got his money's worth out of a Dymo machine. I've never seen so many labels!' The constable threw up her hands. 'It would be funny if he wasn't suspected of sexual assault.'

A second officer approached them. 'I think we're through here, ma'am. We've taken his bank statements, phone bills and assorted other communications and bills to be examined in detail at the station.' He pointed to an evidence box. 'Nothing untoward, as far as we can see.'

'Okay. It was a long shot anyhow. Men like Deacon rarely leave incriminating evidence lying on the kitchen table. Thanks, guys, you can call it a day.'

The others gathered up their things to leave, but the constable, who was called Bella Crawford, hung back. 'Ma'am, this could be nothing, but he does have a lot of photograph albums. They are all meticulously labelled, with names, dates, locations and so on. There might be something in them worth seeing.'

Nikki glanced at Joseph. 'I think we should take them, don't you?'

He nodded. 'Yes, definitely. If nothing else, they could shed some light on the man himself and his private life,' He paused, 'other than the bit we already know, the part where he molests vulnerable women.'

'Box them up, Bella, do all the paperwork and get them sent up to CID, okay?'

'Will do, ma'am.'

After a last look around, they headed back to the car. 'Let's go and see if there's been any news about Laurie Gately, shall we?' She threw the car keys to Joseph. 'You drive.'

Just catching them, he said, 'Yep, and then you can go and apologise to Cam for leaving him to face the press alone.'

'Ah. Yes, I had, hadn't I? But . . .'

'No buts, Galena! Just do it.'

'Bully.'

'Nikki Galena, you were out of that office like a rat up a drainpipe when you saw a chance to escape, you know you were.' He gave her a reproving look. 'And say sorry nicely.'

Nikki gave an exaggerated sigh.

* * *

Nikki and Joseph returned to find Cat and Dave waiting anxiously. As soon as they walked into the CID room, Dave stood up. 'We've heard the news, boss. Is it true?'

Cat was on tenterhooks. She refused to believe that Carmel would let them down, and she'd never be so stupid as to not let Marian know if she had other plans. 'Is she missing?'

'She's not at home, that's for sure. But her car has gone.' Joseph looked pensive. 'The neighbours say someone called early in the morning. They were driving a dark Ford Focus.'

'Deacon?' asked Dave.

'His car is a red Vauxhall,' answered Nikki, flopping down onto a chair. 'I'm not sure what to think, but I don't like the way this is shaping up.' She looked at Cat. 'How did the interview go?'

Cat grunted. 'It would probably have gone better if that smartass turd of a brief had piped down and stopped sticking his oar in.' She let out a sigh. 'They are working this very cleverly. Deacon isn't denying that he went to Carmel's house, but he says he never touched her. And without Carmel's evidence, we are back to the "her word against his" scenario.'

'Something puzzles me,' Nikki said, head on one side. 'So far that man has had three complaints against him, all coming from women who don't know each other and have no known connection. How does he explain that? Did he say?'

Dave nodded. 'He swears it's all because he turned down a woman's advances to him. He said that this particular woman, whose name his solicitor refused to let him divulge at interview, had pestered him for months. When he turned her down, she became a nuisance, and finally turned threatening. According to him, she now hates him. She contacted several of the women he had "helped," and spun them some convincing story. He said that although they denied knowing each other, in actual fact they were colluding to blacken his name and ruin him.'

'All rather fanciful,' said Joseph, 'but not easy to prove or disprove. Plus, bunny-boilers do exist. We've all seen *Fatal Attraction* and I'm pretty sure the jury will have too.'

Cat made a fist and shook it. 'We need Carmel Brown, or that bastard is going to walk — again.'

143

'And every minute counts,' added Dave. 'Boss? Do you think she might have been abducted?'

'I reckon it's time we took a look inside Honeysuckle Cottage. I didn't see any signs of disturbance through the windows, but I couldn't see into every room.' Nikki turned to Joseph. 'What do you think?'

'Normally I'd say it's too soon but because of the situation, I think you're right. We fear for her safety, so it's time to check it out. Want me to have a word with uniform?'

'Please, Joseph, but ask them to be low key, and do as little damage as possible. I don't want them blowing the bloody doors off.'

Joseph smiled. 'I'll be sure to pass that on, in my best Michael Caine accent.'

For once, Cat failed to smile. The thought of Deacon and his smarmy brief walking out of the station clapping each other on the back and laughing at the police was too much to bear. She recalled the look on Deacon's face when they arrested him. A look that said, "Do what you want, but you won't win."

He had this covered, didn't he? He knew Carmel wouldn't testify. So what had he done to her? And why was her car missing? She closed her eyes tight. She needed to think, and quickly. They could only hold Vernon Deacon in custody for twenty-four hours without charging him, maybe thirty-six if they could get an extension.

While Nikki went back to her office, she turned to Dave. 'We need to act quickly, Davey-boy. Are you prepared to burn the midnight oil?'

'As long as a takeaway is forthcoming at some point, my time is all yours. And if it means keeping Nasty Vernon locked up, I'll even pay for it.' He nodded grimly. 'What do you want me to do?'

'We have to find everything we can about Deacon and his past history, and I mean way back. Has he done anything like this before? Where does he come from? As much as we can, mate.'

'You got it.' Dave was alert, energised. 'I heard the boss say that a whole load of stuff is coming over from Deacon's home, including photo albums. They could help.'

Ben would be in for the night shift, so he could pitch in too. Cat rubbed her eyes. It was going to be a long old night, but they needed to learn a hell of a lot more about Deacon if they were to fathom out what had happened to Carmel Brown. Cat realised that this had become personal. It was as if all those female victims were standing in the shadows behind her, willing her to make him pay. Well, she had no intention of letting them down.

CHAPTER FOURTEEN

Richard Howard was just finishing work for the day and heading back to the house. He was looking forward to Tamsin coming back in the morning. He liked her. Maybe he liked her a bit too much — after all she was married, and to a police sergeant. He kept forgetting about his own serious relationship, and he really did love Ruthie, but . . . well, he could still enjoy the company of a beautiful woman, couldn't he? In any case, it was really good to have someone to talk to who wasn't family.

He parked his vehicle and sat in it for a moment. He had told his mother he'd ring his brothers and ask about the cottage, but she had begged him not to. She was afraid of worrying them when they were so far away, especially Alex, who would be upset if he thought his mother was being threatened and he unable to help her.

Richard frowned. Alex had always been the favourite, and Richard didn't understand why. His younger brother tended to be mercurial, unconventional. Unreliable. You never knew what he would do next. Alex was attracted to anything even mildly supernatural and would have been the first to explore Hob's End Copse.

Richard took out his phone. He had to do it. It wasn't always easy to get through, but he'd give it a try. He'd just say he'd been getting ready to clear the copse and had come across the cottage. No mention of anything sinister. Where was the harm in that?

But the phone howled and whistled, and he ended the call. With a grunt, he keyed in Jerry's number. This time he was successful.

'Hi, Jerry. How's things with you over there in the heat?'

'Hi, Rich! I'm good. And you? Long time no hear.'

'Oh, you know what it's like with the farm, always chasing your tail with something or other. You haven't exactly been communicative yourself.'

'Sorry, bro, but it's the same with me. Don't know where the days go sometimes.'

Although he sounded pleased to hear from him, Jerrard's voice was slightly muffled. 'Bad line? No proper signal?' asked Richard.

'It's not good here. I'm working late this evening to catch up on some problems with one of our systems.'

At this time of year, South Africa was an hour ahead of the UK, so it was around seven. 'Sorry to disturb you. It's just that I made a rather odd discovery this week and I wanted to ask if you knew anything about it.'

There was a delay at Jerry's end, and then his voice came through. 'Sounds intriguing. What kind of discovery?'

'Do you remember Hob's End Copse?'

A moment's silence, then Jerry said, 'Yeah! That big old thicket out on the edge of the eastern field, the one Mum used to forbid us to play in. Why?'

'Well, it needed thinning out, so I called in an ecological advice company to take a look and we found a ruined cottage right in the middle of it!'

'No way! Wouldn't it have been cool if we'd found it when we were kids!'

It was as much a surprise to Jerry as it had been to him, then. Even so, he had to ask. 'So you'd never heard about it before?'

'I never set foot in that wood, Rich. Alex told me it was haunted, which was enough for me. Plus it was too overgrown, even then. We wouldn't have got in. What kind of cottage?'

One with a dead body in it, thought Richard, but he said, 'Really old, maybe from World War One days?'

'That's amazing. So what's going to happen to it?' Jerry asked.

'Oh, it's well dangerous. It'll have to be demolished as soon as possible. The plan is to strip the copse out and replant with native trees in order to keep the grant for the Woodland Payment Scheme.' He paused. 'Anyway, I won't bore you with farm stuff. I just wondered if you'd ever heard any rumours about a hidden cottage somewhere.'

'Can't help you there, bro. It's all news to me.' He sounded rather wistful. 'How are things at home? Mum? Dad?'

'Same old, same old,' Richard lied. 'You know them. In their own worlds most of the time. The farm might just as well not exist.' He exhaled. 'I wish you were here, mate. I'd always thought that maybe . . .'

After a slightly longer silence, his brother spoke more coldly. 'Life takes you on different paths, Rich, and sometimes they're ones that are not quite what you'd hoped for.'

What did he mean? Was Jerrard not happy in South Africa? He'd always given the impression that he'd found his El Dorado. But then they rarely spoke, so perhaps things had changed out there. Richard wondered if he should pursue it but decided not. 'True,' he said noncommittally. 'Er, I tried to ring Alex but I couldn't get through.'

The pause was significantly longer this time.

'I can't get hold of him either at the moment. He's gone after a new job in Limpopo Province, somewhere close to the Zimbabwe border. For heaven's sake don't tell Mum, she'll get really upset. You know how proud she is of her baby and his *important* career in HR.'

So it wasn't just him. Jerry felt it too, the resentment. Alex — Mummy's little star.

'Don't worry, Jerry. Alex can sort out his own problems with Mum. What kind of job? HR again?'

'No, it's tourism. Ever heard of Venda?'

He hadn't.

'It's in the north of the province. They call it the "Land of Legend." It has sacred sites, nature reserves, mountains, forests and a rare inland lake, and it's heaving with traditional culture and original arts and crafts. A lot of people who like "unspoilt" visit the place, even if it is rather dangerous. Anyway, Alex wants to join the team. You know him and his mysticism.'

Given her own interest in legends and myths, Richard privately thought that their mother might actually be pleased to hear about it. Except that Alex would be giving up the security his present job offered. Well, it was Alex's mess, not his, so Alex could sort it. 'I guess he'll contact you when he knows if he's got it or not?'

'I hope so. I hope I don't have to talk to Mum. I've never been good at lying to her.'

'You aren't your brother's keeper, for heaven's sake!' Richard said.

The line became too muffled to hear properly. After a moment or two, it went dead.

Richard ended the call. He had his answer. It seemed that no one at Sedgebrook from his or the previous generation knew about that cottage. But the owner of a blue pop-up tent knew, didn't they? With a shiver, Richard hurried into Sedgebrook House.

* * *

Nikki had made her peace with Cam. He had guessed that she would find more pressing things to do, so he had prepared his statement accordingly.

'I made sure to mention your name several times, so hopefully you can take some of the stream of enquiries that will start to flood in.' He paused, smiling at her smugly. 'By way of atonement, of course.'

'Thanks for that.'

'My pleasure. Now, any update on Laurie Gately?'

'Uniform believe they have a sighting on a CCTV camera here in Greenborough, Cam. They are checking it out now. It's close to a well-known cocktail bar, a favourite of trendy youngsters. The Yellow Umbrella, down Fowlers Alley in the town centre.'

'Not one I know.'

'No reason to, Cam. Very little trouble — bit upmarket for the yobs. Little yellow umbrellas in all their overpriced cocktails, so I'm told. Niall has Yvonne Collins and her new crewmate there now, making enquiries and getting hold of their camera footage from last night. We can but hope.'

'I wish we had more than hope, Nikki. The last sighting, other than what they've seen on CCTV, was almost twenty-four hours ago. That's not good.'

'And her phone is still switched off. What teenager do you know who doesn't check their phone at every damned opportunity?'

Cam nodded. 'They are *always* on the phone. Do we have anything on the friend, this Kelly?'

'Only child, bit of a loner, not many friends other than Laurie, and the parents are abroad.' Nikki pulled a face. 'And she hates social media and doesn't have a Facebook account, which would normally be seen as a good thing but could work against her in this case.'

'No posts as to what she's doing or where she's going. Great.' Cam sighed.

'I'm loath to try and contact the parents, *if* we can find where they are holidaying, just in case the girls have met up with a couple of lads and have sloped off for a bit of nookie.'

'Not that you believe that, do you?' asked Cameron.

'I *want* to, but that's not the same thing. What I don't want to do is frighten anyone unnecessarily.' Nikki had the feeling that was exactly what she would be doing if she didn't find those girls fast.

Cam leaned forward and put his elbows on his desk. 'If you need more help, Nikki, I'll secure it for you. You are juggling the Deacon investigation, the stalker at Sedgebrook House, and the missing Laurie Gately case. You are brilliant, but not a superhero.' He gave her a sideways look. 'Or maybe you are. You are certainly the hero of the hour for finding Jennifer Cowley. You missed out on the accolades because you were, er, how did I put it, "following up leads on another important case." I'll be very surprised if there aren't cameramen waiting for you when you step outside the station. Your picture will be all over the nationals by tomorrow.'

Nikki groaned. 'Oh no! You are kidding me. Aren't you?'

'I'd use the back entrance when you go home and wear a hoodie and dark glasses.' Cam chortled, clearly loving it.

'I hate you, Cameron Walker.'

'I hate you *Superintendent* Cameron Walker if you don't mind.' When they had finished laughing, he said, 'But I meant it about the extra manpower. You just ask, okay?'

'I'll see where all this is going first, Cam, then perhaps we can reconvene and make some plans?'

'Of course. Now, Super Cop, I suggest you get home and grab some shuteye. Tomorrow will be another big day.'

Back in the CID room everyone was still working. Nikki stood with her hands on her hips. 'Hey, guys? Don't any of you have homes to go to?'

'Not tonight, boss.' Cat looked up from her computer. 'There's been no news about Carmel Brown, so Dave, Ben and I are doing a major assault on the life and times of Vernon Deacon. We have to get some dirt on him — anything we can dig up to keep him in that cell until we find Carmel.'

'What did uniform find at Honeysuckle Cottage, do we know yet?' Nikki asked.

'Nada, I'm afraid,' said Dave. 'Nothing disturbed or out of place. Just no Carmel, nor her car.'

'Oh well, we had to check. Have they secured the cottage properly?'

151

'Yes, boss,' Dave assured her. 'Luckily, they managed to open the bathroom window, so no damage done.'

'We should contact Marian Harper and see if she's heard anything.'

'Already have,' said Dave. 'She's beside herself. She's heard nothing at all.'

'What the hell is going on?' Nikki murmured, more to herself than anyone.

'I wish we knew.' Joseph appeared beside her. 'Deacon's brief is screaming that he must be released. It's not going to happen tonight, but I can see us having one almighty fight on our hands tomorrow morning.'

Suddenly Nikki felt totally exhausted, but if the team were staying, she would too.

Joseph seemed to read her thoughts, which happened quite regularly. 'Home for you, DI Galena. You look knackered. And no worrying about these guys either. I've sent out for more food than they deserve, and proper coffee too. They've got it cushy, believe me. *You,* on the other hand, need sleep.'

'Absolutely.' Cat grinned at her. 'The sarge is right. This was my idea, and don't forget, it means I get to spend the evening with my lovely Ben.' She pointed to Dave. 'And Billy No-Mates here just fancied a free meal with friends, didn't you, pops?'

'Beautifully put, Catkin.' Dave gave Nikki an encouraging smile. 'You and the sarge get home, boss. Never fear, we'll not work too late and we'll still be in on time tomorrow.'

Nikki threw up her hands. 'Okay, okay! I'm not arguing this time, but don't get used to it. Night, guys, and thanks.'

Joseph drove them home, while she fought against sleep. All at once, everything seemed to close in on her. But mostly she kept seeing that skull slipping down from the chimney breast.

It had all begun many years ago with the death of Jennifer Cowley, and now Nikki Galena found herself with the task of unravelling an intricate and tangled web. 'Lucky, lucky me,' she whispered, and closed her eyes.

* * *

Out on Jacob's Fen, Tamsin and Niall were sitting on their sofa watching TV. Having initially blown a gasket at the thought of Tamsin talking to Aurelia Howard, Niall calmed down and began to see the possible advantages. Now, after a hearty meal and a glass of beer, he was actively encouraging it.

'You're right. She might well open up to you, Tam, far more than she would to a police officer. And I understand her reluctance to offload onto her son.' He drained his glass. 'I'm looking forward to hearing what she tells you.'

Tamsin breathed a sigh of relief and snuggled up to him. She had expected to get her way, but not quite so easily. 'Another beer, sweetheart?'

Niall sighed contentedly. 'No thanks, not tonight, babe. I need to be on the ball tomorrow. There's so much going on, I don't need a fuzzy head.'

Before she could answer, they heard the sound of an engine in the lane outside their cottage. She looked at the clock. It was after nine thirty. 'You expecting anyone?' she asked.

'No, but whoever it is, they aren't stopping here.' He went to the window and pulled the curtain aside. 'A motorbike. And it's heading towards the Sedgebrook Estate.' He let the curtain drop and shrugged. 'Bit late to be making house calls. But I guess Richard Howard must have friends, or perhaps it's one of his farmworkers needing to talk to him about something. Farming can be a twenty-four-hour game.'

Tamsin wasn't so sure. 'What if it's the stalker, going to deliver another unwanted gift?'

'On a noisy bike? I doubt it. That was one of those off-road bikes, I think. Hard to slip quietly in and out on one of those.' Niall went to the sideboard and took out a pen and a notebook. 'Even so, I'm going upstairs to the landing window. I'll get a good view of the road from there. When he comes back, I'll try to get his licence number.'

'A stakeout from the comfort of your own home. Neat!' Tamsin laughed. 'Shall I bring you a hot drink?'

'We usually have Big Macs and fries on surveillance, but a cup of tea would be good.' He pecked her on the cheek as he went past.

'Want my birdwatching binoculars? They have night vision,' she offered.

'Yes, please. I'll see you up there.' Niall took off up the stairs.

Two cups of tea later, they heard the growl of an engine. Tamsin was sitting on the top stair, notebook in hand, Niall leaning on the windowsill, binoculars trained on the lane.

'Here he comes!' Niall followed the speeding bike through the lenses. 'Ah, shit! The plate is covered in mud. But it's a Suzuki, a DR 650.'

Tamsin wrote it down. 'Well, that's better than nothing. Can't be too many of those tearing around the Fens.'

'Tam? When you see Richard Howard tomorrow, ask him whether he had a late visitor, will you?'

CHAPTER FIFTEEN

Nikki's phone rang. She struggled to extricate herself from the tangle of duvet and Joseph's arms and glanced at the clock. Just after two in the morning.

'Nikki Galena.'

'It's Cat here, ma'am. Look, I'm really sorry to ring you but . . .'

She sounded upset, and Nikki knew that it had to be serious for her to phone at this time of night. 'What's happened, Cat?'

'There was an RTC about an hour ago, on the main road out of Greenborough. One fatality.' Cat's voice was shaky.

Nikki was suddenly wide awake. 'Someone we know?'

'It's Carmel Brown, boss. Killed on impact. Head against the windscreen, or so the paramedics believe.'

'Oh no.' A whole stream of thoughts trickled through her mind. She voiced the first to surface. 'And Deacon is still in custody?'

'Yes, he is.' A long sigh whispered its way down the line. 'He'll be out of here by morning.'

Joseph was now sitting up beside her, listening in.

'Is there any indication of what happened at the RTC?' Nikki asked, glancing anxiously at him.

'Too soon to be sure. The traffic boys said the car overcooked a corner at speed. A foreign eighteen-wheeler lorry was coming the other way, the car clipped him, then hit the concrete stanchion of a pedestrian bridge that spanned the road.'

Nikki frowned. 'If she hit the windscreen, she wasn't wearing a safety belt, was she?'

'She wasn't. Traffic confirmed that was the case.'

Nikki had rarely heard Cat Cullen sound so down. 'Cat? Who is there with you?'

'Ben, ma'am. Dave went home just before this news came in. I wasn't going to ring, but we talked about it, and we thought—'

'You did the right thing, Cat. Now, please go home and try to get some rest. You can't do any more tonight.'

'I guess you're right, boss. Ben says the same. We'd been doing pretty well up until then, built what is shaping up to be a very interesting profile of Deacon, and now our main witness is dead.' Cat sniffed. 'I really liked that woman. She had the guts to stand up and face the bastard, and now look what has happened.'

But what had actually happened? Nikki was imagining all sorts of scenarios. Car crashes have many different causes, mainly driver error, but where had Carmel been? Where was she going? Was she drunk? Angry? Frightened? Sick? Using a mobile phone? Or had it been deliberate, because she couldn't go through with it?

'Are you still there?' Cat asked.

'Yes, just thinking . . .'

'Why? Is that what you are thinking? Why? I can't stop going over it in my head. One thing I do know is that Deacon is to blame. Bottom line, he's responsible, no matter how she died.'

Nikki agreed, but said, 'Get home, Cat. We'll deal with it tomorrow.'

Nikki lay back and looked at Joseph. 'I want to know every bloody detail of that accident. Every skid mark must be measured, no matter how small. The weather, road conditions, every bit of camera footage and the evidence of the lorry driver. This is too damned convenient for Deacon. Somehow . . . somehow that man engineered this.' She closed her eyes and shook her head in exasperation. 'I'm with Cat one hundred percent on this. Vernon Deacon caused Carmel Brown to die, and I'm bloody well going to find out how!'

* * *

Nikki and Joseph were at the station at seven the following morning, bringing their breakfast in brown paper bags. Neither had slept well after the news of Carmel's death, so they had risen early, and despite the late night, all the team were in by eight. The first thing Nikki did was call Cat to her office.

'Are you alright, kid? I know this is a hell of a blow, especially as you've worked so hard to get Deacon put away. We will get him, you know, even if it's not this time.'

'I'm devastated, boss. Honestly, I just feel like running the bastard over! That poor woman was trying to do the right thing, and she paid for it with her life.' Cat could barely sit still for anger.

'If it helps, both Joseph and I completely agree with you. We have no intention of letting this go. If anything, I feel even stronger about it. However, you know the score. Deacon will be bailed this morning, pending further enquiries.'

Cat grimaced. 'I know, boss. But can I stay with the case? We dug up a whole load of stuff last night and alarm bells are beginning to ring. I think there's more to him than meets the eye, something deeper than we have seen up to now.'

'Of course you can. But we can't proceed with anything until we find out what happened to Carmel Brown, and that could take a while. The new CIU team will have to investigate, so we'll need to wait for their report, and also Rory's verdict.' All crashes in the Fenland Constabulary's area that resulted in a fatality were now attended by a specially trained forensic Collision Investigation Unit. Things had changed since her time, when a crash was investigated by a canny copper with a tape measure, a weather report and a good nose for alcohol. 'We'll have to press on with the hunt for Laurie but you keep digging into Deacon's past.'

'Thanks, boss. And Dave?'

'Maybe he can multitask, keep on with you unless I get desperate for his help, okay?'

Cat nodded. 'I appreciate it.'

Nikki frowned. 'What did you mean by there being more to Deacon than meets the eye, Cat?'

'It's more a hunch, but I get the feeling he's some kind of deviant and has been for a very long time. He's constructed this whole facade — big-hearted, good old Vern, the helping hand, the one to turn to in a crisis, which has enabled him to play the victim, the innocent target of a bunny boiler or maybe a whole group of vindictive women, all smarting because he turned down their advances. I mean, really. What a load of cobblers!' She narrowed her eyes. 'The last time I saw her, Carmel told me she had proof of what he did to her. I don't know what that was — she said she needed to think it through before she produced it.' Cat looked exasperated. 'Now I might never know.'

Nikki sat up straight. 'There are only so many ways that you could prove an assault, and as there was no witness it has to be a recording of some sort. A hidden camera? A video? I suggest you make a thorough check of Honeysuckle Cottage, Cat.'

'But she wasn't living there when she was attacked.'

'True, but you'd take your proof with you when you moved, wouldn't you? Keep it safe and hidden, just in case you needed it,' said Nikki. 'It would be of enormous importance to her.'

'You're right, of course, but I wonder why she didn't cough it up when she gave us the statement? I'd be glad to be rid of it.'

'Embarrassment? Guilt? Shame? Take your pick. Think about it, Cat. If something like that happened to you, leaving you feeling soiled, you might think twice before allowing some stranger to see or hear exactly what transpired. That animal might have had dozens of women at his mercy. Why do you think none of them wants to come forward?'

'I know. We've seen it so many times before.' Cat rubbed her eyes. 'But the very one who was brave enough to face the music dies without ever producing her evidence. It sucks.'

'It does, and now we owe it to Carmel to bring this man down, so keep at it.'

Cat stood up. 'Oh, I will, never fear. Now, someone's got to tell Marian Harper. Should I do it?'

'If you would, Cat, and maybe take Dave with you. He can make the tea while you break the news.' Nikki had made this suggestion to give Cat some support. She was very aware that Cat was truly upset about Carmel Brown. It wasn't just that Deacon was once again walking out the front door. Cat had really liked Carmel and probably felt some guilt for pressing her into testifying.

'We'll go immediately after daily orders, boss.'

'Go now and get it over with. There's very little being brought up that you aren't already aware of, and we'll fill you in if anything new transpires from forensics or uniform.'

Nikki watched Cat leave the room. Time to shift her attention to her other case.

As if on cue, the phone rang. 'Nikki, my favourite DI. A word in your shell-like, if I may?'

'Rory! My favourite Home Office pathologist. Of course you may.'

'This is just something by way of an observation, but it might have significance. Then again, it could be nothing . . .'

Nikki was immediately interested. Rory missed very little, and in the past his "observations" had been very useful indeed. 'You have my attention. Come on, don't leave me hanging. Spill the beans.'

There was a tinkling laugh from the other end. 'Well, my trusty Welsh Wonder, Ms Erin Rees, who you have yet to meet and who is doing sterling work in Sweet Spike's absence, has been looking at Jennifer's clothing and belongings and we have a small anomaly.'

'Go on.'

'Two things. The dear girl, who had no doubt been smartly dressed for an evening out, had a stud earring in her right ear, but the left one is missing.' Rory paused. 'Of course, she could have lost it accidentally, but it was not torn off in a struggle because the earlobe is undamaged . . . well, what is left of it. The unusual, no, very rare form of mummification left most areas of her skin desiccated and thin but intact. We have sorted through all the debris in the fireplace and sieved the ash in the tray, but no earring.'

Nikki thought about this. As Rory had said, it could be something, or nothing. Earrings did get easily lost, but . . . 'And the other thing?'

'This is slightly more notable, Nikki. One of her shoes is missing too. We have double-checked every item found and removed from the cottage, but no shoe. It is a kind of fashionable ballet flat, or so fashion-conscious Erin tells me. Now, again this could be explained as in it came off in a struggle prior to getting her to the cottage, but we don't think so.'

'Why is that?' she asked.

'If she had lost it and been forced to walk with one bare foot, or even if she were dragged, I would have expected to find the heels and soles of the foot damaged or at least caked in dirt. The dried skin on her foot is not lacerated or dirty. Plus, and this one comes from my young assistant, the shoes are slip-ons and quite a loose fit. If she lost one fighting off an attacker, she would more likely than not have lost both.' He took a breath. 'Which leads me to this conjecture. I don't need to tell you, Nikki, that among a killer's favourite "souvenirs" of their victims are shoes.'

'Aren't trophies connected more to serial killers, Rory?' Nikki asked. 'We never believed this was anything more than an obsession taken too far.'

'You're right about the serial killers, although some of their choices of trophy are often quite gruesome — eyeballs, fingers, scalps . . .'

'Thank you. I get the picture.'

'Sorry, I forgot about your delicate stomach, except where food is concerned of course, but I digress. If it was an obsession, then he might want a souvenir.'

'Makes sense.' Nikki sucked in air. 'Gives us something to think about, especially if Shale is innocent, as we are coming to believe. If we find another suspect with a nice little ballet pump in his sock drawer, we could be forever indebted to you and your keen eye for detail.'

'Nothing new there then. Oh, and it's a black leather slip-on, low heel, probably because Jennifer was a tall girl, and it has a pretty little gold metal buckle sewn on the front, shaped like a lover's knot. I'll send you a photograph.'

'Thanks, Rory, much appreciated. And call me names if you want, but any idea of how Jennifer died?'

'As if I would be so rude! And, strangely, we do know exactly how she died. The hyoid bone in her throat was broken. We need to get it documented and proven, but it's almost certain that she was strangled.'

Nikki breathed out. 'Well, at least she would have been dead before she was pushed down that chimney. One small mercy, I suppose.'

'Yes indeed. But I must tell you this: because of the risk of collapse, we checked the upper floor with the use of cameras on telescopic poles, and can confirm that she was pushed down into the cavity from the floor above. The old cottage had wide chimney breasts with flues leading to the sitting room where we found her, the kitchen, and also the two upstairs bedrooms. The cottage was already collapsing when the murder occurred, although it was nowhere near as bad as it is now, but part of the outer wall in the main bedroom had already caved in, exposing the chimney flue to the sitting room. They pushed her in, head first, tightly wrapped in a sleeping bag, and hid her from sight with twigs, leaves and other detritus from the encroaching trees and ivy that were invading the upper floor.'

'Phew! Poor kid.' Nikki stopped. 'Rory? You just said "they," not "he."'

'Did I?' He gave a little laugh. 'Not intentional, dear heart, but it would have been difficult getting her up those steep stairs alone. Not impossible, if he was a strong man or capable of a fireman's lift, but I suppose I just imagined it being easier with two. Forget it, Nikki. Slip of the tongue.'

'Okay, but before you ring off, you have an RTC victim with you from a crash last night. Name of Carmel Brown. She's of interest to us.'

'Is she indeed? In what way?'

Nikki said sadly, 'She was our star witness in a sexual assault case.'

'Oh dear, oh dear, that's rather unfortunate. Most of all for the dear lady, of course, but also for you.'

'Can you let me have an interim report as soon as possible after the PM, my friend? I know you are rushed off your feet, but I'd really appreciate it.'

'I can refuse you nothing, Nikki Galena. She is next on my list. Now, as it will soon be standing room only in the refrigeration cabinets if you keep sending me clients, I'd better get a move on. *Ciao*, dear heart.'

'New development?' asked Joseph, placing a sheaf of reports on her desk.

Nikki told him about Rory and his observations.

'I wonder if she was actually killed there — or taken there post-mortem?' he said.

'I have no idea why, but I've got it in my head that she was killed in that cottage. What say you?'

Joseph nodded. 'Me too. Although why would a kid get all dressed up and then go tramping through an overgrown copse, possibly at night? You don't wear nice ballet pumps to go on a cross-country hike. Doesn't make sense to me, but maybe Rory's forensic report will give us some clues.' He straightened up. 'Anyway, as soon as the morning meeting is out of the way, I'm off to sweet-talk Aurelia Howard into hauling a few skeletons out of the family cupboard.'

'Good luck with that one, Joseph, although if anyone can make her talk, it'll be you.'

CHAPTER SIXTEEN

Yvonne Collins had the only piece of new information at daily orders. She and Kyle had spotted Laurie and Kelly on the Yellow Umbrella's CCTV. The two girls seemed to be about to enter the main doors, but then, for some reason they stopped, conferred with each other for a few moments, then moved off down the alley and out of CCTV range.

Joseph pictured the narrow, cobbled lane. He knew it led to a tiny square with a few small shops and some old buildings occupied by solicitors and other non-retail businesses. There was certainly nothing there to attract young people on a night out. All he could think was that they were heading for an adjoining lane that led to the river walk. It was not a route he would be happy to see any daughter of his taking at night. He'd often seen drug dealers hanging around in the vicinity. In fact, he had nicked one himself whilst taking a shortcut one evening. So, where were they heading? There was a small café close to the Black Sluice Gate where kids sometimes hung out. It looked across the river and was, he supposed, a mildly romantic spot, if you were a teenager.

When the meeting was over, he told Yvonne what he suspected.

'I thought the same, Sarge, so I called by, but no one remembers seeing them that evening. They just seem to have walked clean off the radar. Poor Penny is close to a breakdown.'

'I really feel for her.' Joseph knew something about what she was going through, having had some very scary moments with Tamsin in the past. 'Vonnie? I'm assuming Niall is having uniform keep a close watch on Patrick Shale, especially while Laurie is unaccounted for?'

'Oh yes, he's still the number one suspect, but we are doing it as discreetly as possible. His mother is already making waves about us harassing him. As far as we know, he hasn't set foot outside Willow Lodge since you and the DI called on him.'

'Thanks, Yvonne. I'm off to Sedgebrook House to try to wring out of Aurelia Howard just how much she knows about her stalker. We believe she knows something but is keeping it to herself.'

Yvonne turned to go, then stopped. 'You can bet your life it has something to do with a close family member, Sarge. Grill her about her kids and her husband. Ta-ra for now.'

Joseph nodded. Wise woman.

As Joseph drove out over Jacob's Fen, he decided that he would call in on Tamsin on his way home. He slowed down as he approached the entrance to their cottage, but her car wasn't there. Damn. He had been hoping to catch a few minutes with her.

He worried about her living so far out on the fen. He knew they both loved it, were young and fit and both drove, so there was no real cause for concern, but Tamsin was his baby. He would always worry about her as long as they both lived. That's how being a parent was.

'She's a married woman, Joseph Easter! Butt out of their lives and don't worry until there's something to really worry about!' he said to himself.

Empty words. Anyway, at the moment he had Aurelia to think about, and how to get the most information out of her. He would have to turn on the charm, and hope it worked with this intelligent, educated woman. He should be spending his time tracking down Laurie Gately, not chatting about talismans.

He swung into the drive of Sedgebrook House and stopped. Well, at least he now knew where Tamsin had gone. He was staring at her parked car.

He smiled. She just couldn't help herself, could she? She just had to know how the case was progressing. His daughter would actually make a pretty good detective herself.

He parked and got out.

'Dad! Hi!' His daughter hurried out of the house to meet him. She kissed him lightly on the cheek, whispering, 'Call in at home as soon as you've finished here. I need to talk to you urgently.' She raised her voice. 'Must go. Bye, Richard, I'll be in touch about that plan for the new planting. Bye, Dad, sorry to rush off, got another appointment.' Then she was gone, leaving Joseph wondering what was so urgent.

'DS Easter, good morning,' Richard Howard said. 'Mum is waiting for you in the lounge.'

Accepting the outstretched hand, Joseph said, 'Hello, Richard. How are things here?'

'I have no idea, I really haven't.' Howard spread his hands. 'There have been no more unexpected "deliveries" for mother, but we are all on tenterhooks waiting for the next one to arrive. I'm certain this isn't over yet.'

Joseph thought the same but didn't say so. 'I just wish we could get to the bottom of it for you.'

'You and me both,' sighed Richard. 'Mum is edgier than I've ever known her, and my father is doing the ostrich bit to perfection. He now blathers on about rocks and minerals from morning to night. It might be his way of coping, but frankly I could shake him! I just want him to show some interest in what's going on, but no, all we get is the structure of his next thrilling lecture on bloody fossils.'

It was getting to him, that much was clear. It made Joseph wonder even more why Tamsin was so desperate to talk. 'I should go and see your mother, Richard.'

'Of course. Take no notice of me and my complaints. I should be in the office arranging machinery for the next harvest, not standing here bending your ear.' He smiled ruefully. 'You know where the lounge is, Detective. I'm off to the farm. Thanks for coming and for taking such an interest in us.'

Joseph went in and knocked on the lounge door.

'Oh do come in, DS Easter. No need to be so formal.'

'Then it's Joseph, Mrs Howard.' He smiled warmly.

'In which case, please call me Aurelia.' She was seated in a large armchair covered with dog blankets. 'Use the sofa, Joseph, it's less hairy. The dogs seem to prefer the armchairs for some reason.'

He had already noticed that the scattering of dog beds around the room looked fur-free and unused. 'Well, it's their home, isn't it?'

Aurelia beamed at him. 'Our sentiments precisely! But you'd be surprised how many people don't appreciate that.'

Joseph sat down. 'Aurelia, we're trying to build up a bigger picture of you and your family and the Sedgebrook Estate, and we need your help.'

At this, she seemed to withdraw into herself. He pressed on. 'You can appreciate our predicament, Aurelia, I'm sure. A young girl that had been missing for the past fifteen years has been found murdered in a property in your grounds and in that same property we have found evidence that another very similar-looking local girl is being followed, most likely by a dangerous predator. This is as serious as it gets, and that is without your own problem — the worrying messages you have been receiving.' He paused, waiting for her response.

After a while, she said, 'We never even knew about that cottage, Joseph, so how could we know about what you found inside?'

'I believe what you say, but it's very odd that no one here, an old Fenland family that has worked this land for generations, has any memory of the existence of that particular cottage.'

Aurelia exhaled. 'It's probably our fault.' Her face was drawn and her eyes held a pained expression. 'We, that is Duncan and I, should have been more respectful of what we had inherited — this farm and the land itself. But instead, we were, and I'm afraid Duncan still is, interested only in our academic careers.' She drew in a long breath. 'Duncan was an only child. He was expected to carry on farming the land in the family name, but they sent him to university first. It was a mistake. He found a different world and rejected this one.'

This was of little help to the investigation, but there might be a nugget in there somewhere that could be of use. Joseph remained silent, listening.

'I was no help either. When I married Duncan I was delighted to be able to live the rural life while continuing my work at the university. And as for the farm, I gave little thought to how it would be run. Surely, that's what staff were for? I loved the location and the kudos of being a land-owner, but as for farming itself, well, it never even crossed my mind. I was a fool, Joseph, and so was Duncan. Instead of cherishing the special gift we had been given or selling it to someone with a passion for farming and the land, we used managers and hired help and muddled through, making bad decision after bad decision. We lost the old families that you were talking about to other farmers in the area. Why should the workers care about the farm when the owners didn't give a damn? People came and went, and the farm became a mill-stone around our necks, until Richard and Jerrard were old enough to realise what was going on, and stepped in.'

'Richard *and* Jerrard?' Joseph was surprised. 'I thought Jerrard went abroad.'

She nodded. 'He did, but initially he was interested in running the estate. Maybe he just glimpsed a different world, like his father had.'

'When did he go, Aurelia?'

'Oh, years ago. Must have been 2004.'

'Where did they go?' asked Joseph.

'South Africa. Alex, my youngest, was offered a job working for a platinum mining company. I think he saw it as a great adventure. Maybe his excitement led Jerrard to turn away from farming. He is very good with technology, so finding a job was no problem.'

'You must have missed them terribly, Aurelia.'

'And still do. I've visited them a few times, but they no longer come here. They say their home is there now. South Africa is an amazing place for a young man.' There was immense sadness in her voice.

'Either of them marry?'

'Too busy enjoying themselves, or so they say.' She looked at him enquiringly. 'But, Joseph, this can't help with your investigation, can it?'

'We have to find something, possibly in your or your family's past that explains why that girl was found on your property, and also why someone is sending you these cryptic messages.' Joseph stared at her, hard. 'Aurelia, what do you know about those talismans that someone's sending you? Why a witch's knife?'

Was it fear or confusion that he saw pass across her face? 'If I knew, don't you think I'd tell you?'

'Maybe not,' said Joseph, 'if it was about something or someone who scares you or is threatening you.'

'No one is threatening me,' she said tonelessly.

Joseph didn't believe her. Something was frightening her badly. It was time to change tack. 'You and your husband were going to search through all those old photos and deeds for us. We never heard from you, so we gathered nothing came up.'

She seemed to relax very slightly. 'Well, nothing as such . . .' She stood up. 'Duncan lost interest after an hour, but I found these.' From a drawer in the sideboard she took out a couple of old sepia photographs and handed them to Joseph.

Joseph looked closely. In the foreground he made out a group of young men and a couple of old timers with a wagon and a horse, and across the fields, blurred and grainy — the copse. It was smaller, but even then, it was composed of a tight knot of trees and bushes.

'Hob's End Copse,' Aurelia said. 'From the way the farmworkers were dressed, I'd say it was taken in the early 1900s, wouldn't you? But look — no sign of a cottage there, no chimney, no plume of smoke rising up.'

'And no visible means of access — from this angle at least,' mused Joseph. 'Can I take these, Aurelia? I'll return them, but I'd like to get them copied.'

'Of course. And Duncan said to tell you that the deeds make no mention of a property in that location. Even he is mystified. It seems to have been there for generations without ever being discovered.'

Not quite. Someone certainly knew all about it. 'Can I ask you a question?' Joseph said.

The wary look returned, but Joseph ploughed on. 'This is a shot in the dark, but do you think that Hob's End Copse could have had some legend connected to it? I mean, even the name signifies the devil. Could someone, knowing that you are an expert on such matters, be drawing your attention to it or trying to tell you to leave it alone?'

Aurelia frowned. 'As to it having some sort of history attached to it, it's very possible. Do you know about ley lines, Joseph?'

'A little. I know that they are straight lines that criss-cross the globe. They're believed to carry supernatural energy, aren't they? I believe the Great Pyramids are built on one.'

'And a lot of other major structures. Ley lines are said to connect monuments, buildings and landforms in align-ment, and, yes, they have huge spiritual and supernatural significance.' She sat back and crossed her legs, clearly much more comfortable with a subject she had studied. 'I noticed some time ago that Hob's End is on such a line. If you look on an ordnance survey map, you can draw a straight line that connects Rawson's Tower — you know, the old monument over at Seasend — with St Saviour's Church. Hold on, I'll show you.' Aurelia hurried out of the room and came back a few moments later holding a map. She spread it out on the table. 'Look.'

Joseph followed her finger. It traced a direct straight line from the tower to the Seasend church, on to Hob's End Copse, the derelict mill on the edge of the estate, the medieval cross at Dewsbury Dyke and finally Lincoln Cathedral.

'Well, I'm damned! But why the mill? Surely that's not nearly as old as the tower or the churches?'

'Some people deliberately built structures on ley lines to harvest the energy and give it a boost of energy to benefit the health of the occupants.' She gave a little laugh. 'Others avoid them like the plague because of the geopathic stress that they produce. If you pick a negative ley line and not a positive one, it can cause health problems. And not just to humans, but pets and plants as well.'

'You believe in them?' Joseph wasn't being derogatory, he was simply interested.

'Hard not to if you do any in-depth research. Not that I believe in the spooky stuff, but I do think these natural energy lines exist. You can actually see them sometimes, or maybe I should say sense them, like a pattern in the landscape. The most famous is the St Michael Alignment. Look it up, Joseph, you'll be fascinated, there's not just the incredible British one that runs from Hopton in Norfolk to the tip of the Cornish Coast, there's a second St Michael line that takes in Skellig Michael in Ireland, St Michael's Mount, Mont Saint-Michel and through a host of other "Michaels," as far as Israel.'

'I will. You've whetted my appetite,' Joseph said. 'But we are digressing. You really think the copse could have some sort of ancient superstition attached to it?'

'It certainly could. The old Lincolnshire farmers were a very superstitious bunch. Think of the Devil's Holts,' Aurelia said. 'Three trees forming a trinity in the corner of a field.'

'I know about those,' said Joseph. 'They were left there as a playground for the devil, to stop him getting bored and damaging the crops.'

'Exactly, so Hob's End could be significant in the same way.'

'Significant to the person who is sending you warnings?' Joseph asked.

'Maybe.' Aurelia looked uneasy. 'I hadn't considered that.'

'Can I leave you with one request?' He didn't wait for an answer. 'Search your memory for someone you know who is extra superstitious and might want to draw your attention to that copse. Ring me — you have my card — if you think of anyone, no matter how tenuous you think the link might be. Could you do that?'

She nodded. 'I will, Joseph, I promise.'

He stood up. 'Thank you for your time, Aurelia.'

He left her apparently deep in thought. Or did he see a hint of something else on her face?

He drove to Tamsin and Niall's cottage.

'Get the kettle on, Tam, and tell me what's worrying you.' He flopped down on a kitchen chair and watched as his daughter threw teabags into mugs. 'And while you're at it, you can explain what you were really doing at Sedgebrook House.'

Tamsin took the milk from the fridge, grinning to herself. 'Am I that transparent?'

'A pane of glass, kid. Now, confess. It's good for the soul.'

'Richard told me he's worried about his mother. He reckons she's holding something back and as I really did have to deliver our report on the copse, I sort of volunteered to talk to her.' She made the tea and handed him a mug. 'There's something going on in that family, Dad. I'm sure she knows exactly who is sending those weird warnings. And it has something to do with one of Richard's brothers.' She sat down facing him. 'She says she knows her boys inside out, and something has happened to Alex.'

Joseph frowned. 'Like what?'

'According to her, strange things go on in South Africa, bad things, and sometimes people disappear.' Tam looked anxious. 'Richard spoke to Jerrard last night. Apparently he

172

told him that a few weeks ago, Alex said he was going after a new job in Limpopo Province, something to do with tourism, but he didn't want his mother to know. He reckoned she would go apeshit if she knew he was giving up his old job, which had good prospects and a pension, and go somewhere that is pretty unstable.'

Joseph was confused. 'So Richard actually knows where his brother is, but he's letting his mother worry. I don't get it. Why won't he tell her?'

Tamsin sipped her tea. 'Because Jerry can't get hold of Alex. They've been out of contact for days. Richard said he sounded okay about it on the phone, but he got the feeling he was actually worried sick.' She placed her mug on the table. 'Richard thinks something has happened to Alex, but doesn't want to frighten Aurelia, just in case this new job thing is for real and Alex is just partying his way up the Limpopo River.'

'We know zilch about those two brothers, other than that Jerrard seems to have done a sudden about face and gone from wanting to farm here with Richard to following his little brother out to South Africa.'

'Richard never understood why he did that,' said Tamsin. 'He'd always hoped they would run the place together. Alex would never have joined them, he was no good at manual graft and was totally impractical, but Jerry had always been up for it.'

'You've done quite a bit of chatting to Richard Howard, haven't you, Tam? Be careful your husband doesn't get the wrong idea,' Joseph said.

'Oh, heavens, Dad! Niall knows I love him to bits and he also knows what a busybody I am. He'll understand my reasons for poking my nose in.'

'Just tread carefully, love. He might trust *you*, but I'm not sure that he'd trust that rather good-looking, strapping young farmer who is so willing to pour out his heart to a comparative stranger.' Joseph raised his eyebrows.

Tam raised her eyebrows even higher. 'Men! Honestly! Not everyone has an ulterior motive, you know. That poor guy has no one to offload to, and he's sweating bullets over what's happening at Sedgebrook.'

'Just saying . . .'

'Come on, Dad. At least I've got Aurelia to open up about what is worrying her.'

He raised his hands. 'Yes, that was useful, I admit. But what did you mean about the stalker having something to do with the brothers?'

Tamsin lowered her voice, even though only Skipper was listening. 'It was a throwaway comment she made. I casually mentioned how that athame must have frightened her, and she said it did unnerve her a bit, although if Alex had been here, a knife like that would probably have really frightened him. I didn't know whether to push it, so I just asked, casual like, was he into Wicca? She laughed a bit sadly and said he was into anything mystical. Even when he was quite young, he would sit for hours with her while she prepared her notes for her lectures, taking everything in.'

Joseph sighed. 'Lord, how I hate these tenuous links.'

Tamsin shrugged. 'More tea, Dad?'

He shook his head. 'No, I've got to get back. And thanks. I'm not sure what to make of it all, but I'm sure it will help.'

'I'll keep my ear to the ground and pass on anything I hear.' She paused. 'Discreetly, of course, and keeping a respectable distance from the strapping young farmer.'

Joseph pecked her cheek. 'You have been warned. You're a very good-looking young woman, you know. Love you, Tam. See you soon.'

* * *

As soon as her father had left, Tamsin pulled on her walking boots and grabbed Skipper's collar and lead. 'Time for a walk, Fur-face!'

When they reached the gate, Skipper pulled to the right, which was the usual direction they took, but Tamsin led him the other way. 'Not today, chum, we're going sleuthing. You can call me Miss Marple, and you are . . .' The dog tilted his head to the side, looking up at her. 'I think you'd better be Scooby Doo and if you're good, you get a Scooby treat when we get home. Deal?'

Skipper waved his tail, clearly recognising the word "treat."

'Okay, partner, here's the mission. Last night a motorbike came this way. Your dad and I saw it. It came back thirty minutes later, but when I asked Richard if anyone on a bike had called at Sedgebrook House, he said no. So, where does this road go, other than to the Howards' place?'

Skipper tried to look intelligent, but had no answer, so Tam told him. 'Nowhere, that's where. So we have a mystery, don't we?'

They walked for over half a mile, until, as they were passing the old deserted windmill, Tamsin saw tyre tracks. Motorcycle tracks. 'Come on, Skip,' she said, 'Let's see where he went.'

They walked cautiously along the drive leading up to the mill, following the trail.

The mill itself was little more than a brooding circular hunk of old, much weathered brickwork and decaying woodwork. Even so, the door, though faded and mildewed, seemed solid enough.

Tamsin shivered. They could see it silhouetted from their bedroom window at home, and she had always found it a bit intimidating. There was something about it that disturbed her, a kind of stark desolation. Now, standing beneath it, she felt distinctly uncomfortable. Even Skipper drew closer to her. 'Don't think we'll hang around here, Skip, do you? Let's check it out quickly, and split, huh?'

The tracks ended at the side of the mill, in a spot that was hidden from the lane. She could see the imprint of the bike's stand where he had parked it. There were boot marks too, not particularly clear, but nevertheless a deep heelprint and part of an unusually patterned sole. 'So you walked from here,' mused Tamsin. 'But where to? Did you go to the house, the farm or Hob's End Copse?'

It had to be one of the three, and whichever one he had visited, it would not have been by invitation. Tamsin and Skipper made their way back to the lane.

As they walked back to their cottage, she took out her phone. Time to ring Niall.

CHAPTER SEVENTEEN

Joseph arrived back in the CID room to see Superintendent Cam Walker coming out of Nikki's office. He wore a grave, preoccupied expression. Poor Cam. What he must be having to contend with.

'Joseph! My office, please,' Nikki called.

Joseph hurried over. 'Cam looked pretty anxious.'

'He wants us both upstairs ASAP, so we'll go straight there. He said he wants a situation report, all cases, and all associated leads.' Nikki looked as tense as the super. 'He's being hounded by the press for more details about Jennifer Cowley. He thinks it's time to release pictures of our two missing girls but there could be massive repercussions if we do. Let's go.'

Joseph followed her out of the office and up the stairs. 'Repercussions?'

Nikki stopped and turned to him. 'A girl who's the image of Jennifer Cowley goes missing in the first few weeks of Patrick Shale's release from prison. There could be a witch hunt.'

'Understandably so, but if Shale was innocent of Jennifer's murder . . .' He groaned. 'Huge repercussions.'

'Exactly.'

They walked the rest of the way in silence.

'Come in, you two, and sit down.' Cam looked slightly more relaxed. 'We'll find a way through this mire, I'm sure, but I need to be completely in the picture, and time is not on our side.' He gave them a weary smile. 'So, in a nutshell, all you have, please.'

'I'll tell you this first because Joseph doesn't know about it either,' said Nikki, with a glance at him. 'It came in while you were visiting Aurelia Howard. Laurie and Kelly were spotted talking to a man outside the café at the Black Sluice on the night they disappeared. Yvonne Collins and Kyle Adams found someone who was in there that night and noticed them out of the window. They never entered the café and the witness suspected they went off with that same man.'

'Did they get a description?' asked Cam.

'Medium build, age around thirty or just over, trendy dresser. According to the witness, he was wearing a long dark coat, designer jeans and a kind of trilby hat.' She shook her head. 'That description doesn't fit anyone known to us, including Shale.'

'And that's the last sighting we have?' Cam pulled a face. 'Doesn't sound good at all, does it? And it puts me fair and square between the devil and the deep blue sea. I need to get the public behind us, looking for those girls, but I can't afford them putting two and two together and taking the law into their own hands. The Gately girls are well known and well liked here in Greenborough. I can visualise a lynch mob heading for Patrick Shale's doorstep, can't you?'

Joseph could, and it wasn't a pleasant picture. 'What if we spirit Shale away for the duration of this case? Or at least until the media have had a field day with it?'

'A safe house would also put him under our supervision, Cam,' added Nikki. 'So if he did happen to be guilty, we would have him where we wanted him.'

Cam nodded slowly. 'It's a possibility. I'd have to clear it with my chief, but it might be the only way to ensure his safety and keep a close eye on him at the same time.' He scribbled a few notes on a pad. 'So, what else?'

'It's nothing concrete,' Joseph looked from Cam to Nikki, 'but I've spent some time this morning with Aurelia Howard and so, incidentally, did my daughter, Tamsin.' He rolled his eyes. 'There on a completely bona fide mission regarding woodland maintenance, or so she assures me, but in any case she found out more than me. It appears that Mrs Howard is terrified for the safety of one of her sons. His name is Alex, and he's suddenly gone off the radar, somewhere in South Africa.'

'And this is connected in some way to the stalker, you think?' asked Cameron.

'I have no idea,' Joseph said. 'But she is one very frightened woman. Added to what we found in the cottage in the copse, I'm getting more and more uneasy about this whole strange family affair.'

'Me too,' added Nikki. 'Joseph, do you think Aurelia is still holding something back?'

'Without a doubt. I just have no idea what it is or whether it's relevant to the main enquiry. All I do know is that we can't afford to ignore one single piece of information, no matter how insignificant or unrelated it seems.' Joseph folded his arms. 'She told me lots of stuff about the copse being on a geopathic energy line and the possibility of Hob's End being connected to old superstitions, so maybe it is related to the objects left by the stalker.' He shrugged. 'Who knows?'

'Mumbo bloody jumbo,' grunted Nikki. 'Whatever happened to good old straightforward?'

Cam cast Joseph an amused smile and nodded towards Nikki. 'No grey areas there, are there?'

Joseph grinned. 'Absolutely none, Cam.'

'I am still in the room, you know!'

'Sorry.' Cam laughed. 'We are just delighted by your black-and-white take on matters. Keeps our feet on the ground and stops us getting too fanciful.'

'Hope you heard that, Joseph,' muttered Nikki. 'Now, back to the *facts*. Remember what they are?'

Joseph looked down at his feet. 'Consider me duly chastised.'

'Carmel Brown. Cam, you heard she was killed in an RTC last night?'

'Dreadful business. I read the report from traffic.'

'Well, we are waiting on the pathologist's findings, but several things bother us, apart from the obvious one of her being our main witness in the Deacon case. One, she wasn't wearing a seat belt. Two, the driver's airbag did not inflate, and, three, she was driving at speed, not something she normally does according to her closest friend.' Nikki leaned forward. 'Now Cat tells me that Carmel stated she had hard evidence that Deacon assaulted her.'

Cam frowned. 'What kind of evidence?'

Nikki grimaced. 'That died with her, Cam, although Cat and Dave will move heaven and earth to find it.'

'So you think he's in some way to blame for the crash, Nikki?'

'Without a doubt. But how the hell he did it while he was here in custody is another question.'

Cam sighed. 'You know he has Worthington as a brief, don't you? And you know how he works.'

'Sadly, yes, but if we can find whatever that evidence was, we are happy to take on a supercilious git like Worthington any day.'

'I admit it would be nice to see him lose for once, but . . .' Cameron stared at the pile of reports on his desk. 'You know we have to prioritise our missing girls, so all extra help will go in that direction. I'm happy for Cat and Dave to continue for a while, but you guys need to focus back on Laurie and Kelly.'

Nikki and Joseph nodded. 'Of course, Cam,' she said. 'We are going to go over the court transcript of the Jennifer Cowley trial again and the arresting officers' reports. We need to be clear in our minds about Patrick Shale's guilt.'

'Or innocence,' added Joseph sombrely. 'We are still in two minds.'

'Mmm, and meanwhile I have to formulate a way of getting the public to support the search for our two missing girls without rousing a horde of vigilantes, all baying for Shale's blood. I'm putting a car outside on obbo, and I'm seriously considering your suggestion of a safe house.' He gave them a half smile. 'But that's my problem. You two go and do your thing. Just keep me updated, okay?'

They made their way back downstairs, where Joseph began to sort through the court transcripts while Nikki went to find Cat. She was concerned about her and the guilt she was feeling about having persuaded Carmel Brown to testify against Deacon. It was understandable for Cat to be upset over Carmel's death, but Nikki didn't want it to escalate into a major issue. Carmel had made her choice. If she hadn't wanted to take it further, then no matter how much Cat cajoled her, she would have refused.

She found Cat, head down, working at her computer. There was a hard glint of concentration in her eyes.

'You okay, Cat?' Nikki asked.

'Just doubly determined to get this bastard one way or another, boss.' She looked up from her screen. 'Actually, I was just about to ask if Dave and I could go back to Honeysuckle Cottage. Carmel's friend, Marian, has said she will help us in any way she can, and she came up with something interesting.'

Nikki perched on the edge of Cat's desk. 'Like what?

'Marian told us that, knowing she was going to be staying with Carmel for a while, she had offered to help her with the unpacking. Remember, Carmel had only very recently moved in? Well, apparently Carmel jumped at the offer, saying there was masses still to do. She went on to say, *"Actually, there's something important I want to show you. I never thought I would, but now the case is going forward, I think perhaps I ought to."* Marian reckoned she sounded very serious, kind of anxious, but she didn't say any more about it.'

'So you're thinking it's still packed away in an unopened box?' asked Nikki.

'Like you said before, boss, if it is concrete evidence, it would be very important to her. It's going to be somewhere in Honeysuckle Cottage, isn't it? And we'll find it, even if we have to take every damned box to pieces.'

Cat seemed to be showing signs of becoming obsessed with nailing Deacon. Nikki hoped this wasn't going to affect the way she conducted the investigation. She glanced across at Dave, who gave her an almost imperceptible wink. He knew Cat of old. That wink told Nikki not to worry, he'd keep her on the straight and narrow.

'Okay, but have a word with Niall and take a uniformed officer with you, someone who can get you in and then secure the place again. Her house keys were on the same fob as her car keys, according to the evidence log, and they haven't been documented yet, so you will need to get in the way uniform did earlier. And keep in touch, Cat. If you find something, I want to know.'

'You got it, boss.' Cat stood up. 'Ready Davey-boy?'

Dave closed the photo album that he had been engrossed in, and sat for a moment, looking thoughtful.

'Something bothering you, Dave?' asked Nikki.

'I, er, I think I need to go over this one again when we get back. Something about this particular book is bothering me.' He placed it on the top of a pile of similar-looking albums and stuck a Post-it on it. 'Okay, Catkin, I'm right with you.'

Nikki went over to Joseph's tiny office and stuck her head in the door. 'Bring those transcripts to my office, Joseph. The desk there is bigger.'

'So is everyone else's. Not to mention their offices.' He gathered up the thick folders. 'This'll be no five-minute job. The trial ran for over a month.'

'Then we'd better be selective. I'm very interested in his responses when he was questioned about his feelings for Jennifer, but not so much in the alibis and the like. We can deal with those later. I want to get a feel for Patrick Shale — besotted, lovelorn young man, or callous killer?' She closed the door to her office. 'Ready?'

'As I'll ever be.' He opened one of the folders. 'But,' he looked at her with a grin, 'not before I get us two very large coffees.'

* * *

Marian Hammond made yet another pot of tea. She felt numb, and at the same time was burning with anger. She was no stranger to grief, having lost almost everyone she truly held dear. Now her dear friend Carmel had joined the list. It felt like the last straw.

She went into her conservatory and sat down, looking out over the garden. The herbaceous border and the mass of terracotta pots that she had religiously planted were full of late summer colour, but it had suddenly lost its vibrancy. The care she took of her garden suddenly felt rather pointless. Marian liked her own company, and was content to live alone, but she also valued her close friends highly. Carmel had been the dearest, and her loss was going to take some getting over. She sighed. If she ever did.

She sat sipping her tea, suddenly overwhelmed with hate. She hated the man who had brought about Carmel's death.

She frowned, lost in thought. Even if Carmel had taken her own life, evil Vernon Deacon would have caused it. But she knew Carmel — she was incapable of running over even an animal on the road, so she would never have endangered another life by heading straight for a lorry. She could have been distracted by thoughts of Deacon, Marian supposed, but that didn't seem likely either. Carmel had been a good driver, and careful. She wasn't one to take risks or act the fool behind the wheel.

'Where were you going, my friend?' Marian whispered to herself. 'Where had you been?' She closed her eyes for a moment. 'And what did you want me to see that was so important?' Marian brushed away a tear and sniffed. No time for that now. She had an important job to do — if she could only make it work. It had to. Carmel Brown must not have died for nothing.

CHAPTER EIGHTEEN

After two solid hours spent studying the court transcripts, the phone call came as a relief. 'Cat. How goes it?' Nikki said.

Cat sounded excited. 'We are on the right track, boss. We haven't found what we're looking for yet, but we do know that something exists. Dave found an android tablet packed away in one of the removal boxes. When he switched it on it wasn't even password protected.'

'She lived alone. Maybe she didn't see the need,' said Nikki.

'That's what we thought, especially as it mainly had games on it, but then Dave found a journal.' Cat paused. 'It's a bit harrowing, boss, knowing that she's dead, but we think she used it as a safety valve — you know, like therapy. She wrote all her feelings out and, believe me, what that beast of a man did had damaged her pretty badly.'

'She described it?'

'Not his actions. It was more about her reaction to what happened.'

'That doesn't constitute proof. The prosecution would say that she could have made it up.' Nikki waited, hoping for more.

'Exactly, boss, and she says as much herself. Just before this outpouring comes to an end, roughly three months ago, she states that she is leaving the home where this abuse took place and is looking forward to a new beginning. Then she says, and I quote, "*Even though it is abhorrent to me, I am glad that I kept my little piece of insurance, just in case I ever find the strength to go to the police.*"

Nikki sat up. 'Then keep looking, Cat. Deacon has been released, as we knew he would be, so if you want to see him back in custody, you *have* to find the "insurance" she was talking about.'

'Will do, ma'am. Just keeping you updated.'

Nikki rang off and relayed Cat's piece of news to Joseph.

Joseph closed a file and stretched. 'Let's hope it wasn't so abhorrent to her that she destroyed it before starting her new, sadly very short, life in Little Fleeting.'

'I doubt it.' She was about to say more when the desk phone shrilled out. 'DI Galena.'

'Still no Judy Garland? How disappointing.'

'Hello, Titania, what can I do for you?'

'Rats, she recognised me. Oh well, better press on. I've just heard from the forensic workshop. Our people have been sifting through the wreckage of your poor woman's car, and thus far two things have come to light. First, the airbag didn't inflate because the sensor wiring had been severed. Now, don't jump to conclusions, this can be due to a variety of causes, such as a manufacturing defect, or they could have been installed in a vulnerable position, or they could simply have been severed in the crash. Number two — and this is far more serious — they suspect a steering failure caused the accident. There was almost no fluid in the power-steering system. After a manoeuvre like a sharp turn or one that required effort, she would have been unable to return the wheel to the straight-ahead position. Bang, crunch!'

Since it would be some time before the full official crash report landed on her desk, Nikki hadn't thought much about it, but even so, this news took her by surprise. In her heart, she had believed that Carmel had been so upset by the impending police interview that she had lost concentration, and it would all come down to driver error. Now there were questions of a different kind. 'How long do you think it will take before they know if the steering had been damaged in the collision, or whether it had been tampered with, Rory?'

'A few more days, I suspect, and of course it's more complicated than that. There could have been manufacturing faults, mechanical failures, a damaged hose or a degraded seal. It was not a new car either. If the power-steering fluid level is low, it reduces the amount of hydraulic fluid pressure the pump can create. That can make the pump work much harder and therefore wear out faster. It's not cut and dried, dear heart, but I thought you should know that at least she didn't deliberately drive herself to Valhalla.'

After the call had ended, Nikki tried to sum up her thoughts. It had always seemed too much of a coincidence that Carmel, their main witness, had suddenly acted out of character by ignoring her appointment with her best friend, and finished up dead. But even so, the accident could easily have been caused by stress. Maybe Carmel Brown had not been the strong woman they believed her to be.

'A waiting game, yet again,' said Joseph softly, interrupting her reverie.

She nodded. 'As usual. The suspicions flood your mind, and you have to hold them in check until you have hard evidence.' She grunted. 'And we all know about my patience, don't we? I'm famous for it.'

'*In*famous, more like,' said Joseph with a wry smile.

Nikki stuck out her tongue. 'Alright, alright.' She paused, serious again. 'I wonder if she was a methodical woman.' She picked up her mobile from the desk and called Cat. 'Going through Carmel's things, does she strike you as neat and tidy? What about her paperwork — her bills, bank statements and the like?'

Cat didn't hesitate. 'Yes, ma'am, she was. Not obsessively, but she filed them all in labelled plastic wallets.'

'Have you seen anything for her car? A finance agreement? Service records?'

'Just a mo, boss.'

Nikki heard the rustle of papers.

'Yes, a Renault Clio,' said Cat, 'bought from a local dealership almost three years ago.'

'I need to know if it was serviced regularly, and if so, who by.' Nikki picked up a pen and waited.

Another rustle of papers. 'Regular as clockwork, boss, and she stuck to the dealer she bought it from — Campbell Crowe, High Broadgate, Greenborough.'

Nikki thanked her and ended the call. 'Just one more small indication of foul play.' She looked at the files strewn across her desk. 'And while we wait, back to Patrick Shale. Any thoughts so far?'

'The evidence is pretty damning — it had to be for them to get a conviction, even without a body. The whole thing smacks of obsession, and you and I have seen that it continues. For Shale, that girl is a kind of saint, even though she's dead. Does that mean he killed her? Would he destroy the object of his desires and fantasies? And would he desecrate her dead body by shoving it head first down a chimney? It doesn't equate.'

'Suppose it was a case of *if I can't have her, no one will?*'

'Possib—'

He was silenced by a loud knock on the door, followed by the entrance of a uniformed officer saying, 'DI Galena! Can you come? There is someone in reception needs to talk to you urgently, ma'am.'

Nikki was already on her feet. 'Who is it?'

'Kelly Arthur, ma'am.'

Wide-eyed, she looked at Joseph. His chair rocked as he stood. 'On our way!'

* * *

Kelly sat at the table in the interview room. She was pale and drawn, and dressed more appropriately for a Friday night at the Blue Lagoon Bar than a mid-week workday.

'I came as soon as I heard!' she blurted out when they entered. 'Have you found her? Have you found Laurie?'

She was tearful, almost hysterical. 'Not yet, Kelly,' Joseph said softly. 'Hopefully, you'll be able to help us out.'

'I don't know where she went!' Kelly cried.

'Hey! It's all right. Just try to stay calm,' Joseph said. 'Now, you want to help or you wouldn't be here, so why don't you tell us what happened from the very beginning — when Laurie and you went out that evening.'

Kelly sat hunched forward, rubbing her hands together as if she were cold. She swallowed. 'We went to the Magpie to have a few drinks. When we got there, we met a couple of mates who said they were going to a club in Greenborough and did we want to go too?' She sniffed again. 'We had enough money for a cab back, so we said yes.'

'And you went to the Yellow Umbrella?' asked Nikki.

Kelly pulled a face. 'Yeah, but we never went in. Laurie saw an old boyfriend of hers in there with his new bit of stuff, and refused to go in. I thought she was being stupid, and I told her so. The Yellow U is a really cool place and there are always some well-fit blokes hanging out there.'

'So you had an argument?' asked Nikki.

'Not exactly. I just got the hump, so we decided to go to the café bar down by the Black Sluice Gate, have a coffee, then go back and see if her ex had moved on somewhere else.' Kelly stared at the table, 'But we didn't go in there either.'

'What happened, Kelly?' Whatever she said from now on was new territory for them. Laurie had not been seen from that point onwards.

'We were about to go in when this man called out to us. Laurie knew him, but I didn't.'

'Did she introduce him, Kelly?' asked Joseph.

'She called him Rob. He was much older than us, but I think he fancied her.' She pouted. 'Every bloke with a pulse fancies Laurie, so no surprises there.'

Sensing Nikki's impatience, Joseph said, 'And you went off with him?'

Kelly looked away. 'Yes, we did. He told us he was going to a party with his girlfriend but they'd had a row and she'd stormed off. He wondered if we'd like to go with him.' She hung her head. 'He said there was plenty of drinks and food, so we said alright, we'd go.'

'Where did he take you? I assume it was in his car?' asked Nikki.

'No, we walked, but it wasn't a part of Greenborough I know. I live in Mablethorpe, so I was lost.'

Joseph cursed inwardly. No address. But at least they had a vague idea of where to look. 'And was there a party?' he asked gently. He'd seen kids lured that way before, promised drinks and fun, only to find themselves victims of some pervert.

'Oh yes, and it was pretty cool. Bit upmarket for me, but I met this gorgeous guy . . .' She smiled, but it faded quickly. 'We went off together. I should never have left Laurie. But she said she was enjoying herself, and this Rob bloke promised to drop her home later. She had a spare key, so . . .' her eyes filled again, 'so I left her there.' Kelly began to cry in earnest now. 'Where is she?'

Joseph couldn't help sighing. This was not good.

'Did she say anything at all about this Rob? Anything that could help us identify him?' said Nikki urgently.

'No — well, I don't think so.' Kelly accepted a tissue from Joseph and wiped her eyes. 'She might have mentioned something to do with a newspaper but I'm not sure.'

'As in he was a journalist? A photographer? Or maybe he worked in the print side?' Nikki said.

'I don't know!' Kelly sniffed.

'Kelly, where did you go after you left the party?' asked Joseph.

'Back to Simon's pad. His parents were away, like mine, and he had the house to himself. I stayed the night and the next day.' She couldn't help smiling. 'Like I said, he was gorgeous.'

'And you didn't worry about Laurie?' Joseph felt like shaking her. She'd swanned off to some strange guy's home to have sex with him, leaving her best friend with a bunch of strangers, some of whom were apparently a lot older than her. What had these kids been thinking? They were nineteen, for heaven's sake!

'We've done it before, you know.' She looked superior. 'We aren't children. We can look after ourselves, and we like to have fun.'

Joseph bit back his retort. 'Did you try to ring her?'

'Of course, but her phone was turned off so I thought she'd scored and didn't want to be disturbed.' The bravado faded. 'But she's never turned it back on, and she never went back to my house either, so . . .' She swallowed. 'Has that man taken her?'

'We are concerned for her safety, Kelly,' said Nikki gravely. 'We do not know where she is any more than you do.' She leaned forward, elbows on the table. 'Kelly, do you think that if we took you back to the Black Sluice Gate café, you could find the house where that party was?'

Kelly looked doubtful. 'I could try, I suppose, but as I said, I don't know Greenborough well.'

Joseph looked at Nikki, then back to Kelly. 'Excuse us for a moment. Would you like a drink while we go and make some arrangements?'

'A black coffee, please, no sugar.'

Outside the room, Nikki asked one of the civilian staff to get Kelly's drink, and they went back to the front office.

'I was thinking about getting Yvonne and her new crew-mate to go with her,' Joseph said. 'They know this town better than any of us. With Vonnie helping, we have the best chance of finding it, don't you think?'

She nodded. 'Let's ask Niall if he can spare her.' She grinned at him. 'No, let's *tell* Niall he has to spare her. He won't refuse his father-in-law.'

Niall looked pleased to see them. 'I've got something for you,' he said immediately. 'Tamsin and I heard a motorbike last night, going in the direction of Sedgebrook House and return-ing a while later. We now know that no one visited the house or the farm. This morning, Tamsin was walking the dog when she found motorcycle tyre tracks at the old mill. He obviously parked there and walked to wherever he was going.'

'Aurelia's mystery stalker?' asked Joseph.

'Who knows? But I doubt it. This is the first time we've heard a bike heading out that way. I thought it was someone interested in Hob's End Copse, but no one on duty out there saw a soul, so I'm puzzled.'

'Is Tamsin doing her Secret Squirrel act again and padding round the Fens alone?' Joseph said.

'Oh, she's been told, I promise you,' said Niall with feeling. 'But you know Tamsin. Once she gets an idea in her head, you can't stop her.'

Joseph smiled. 'Do your best, son. Now, can you spare Yvonne? We have a job for her.'

'Sure. She came back in for a break around ten minutes ago. I'll call her.'

'Ask her to join us in Interview Room Four, please, Niall,' said Nikki. 'We need to use her as a Greenborough tour guide.'

'No one better, ma'am. I'll send her down to you.'

As they walked back along the corridor to the interrogation rooms, Joseph said, 'I don't like the sound of this Rob bloke, do you?'

'Not one bit,' muttered Nikki. '*Considerably older.* So what's some adult male doing picking up a teenager off the street? Only one reason I can think of, and it stinks.'

'Kelly looks a lot older than nineteen, so I'm guessing Laurie does too. Still . . .' Joseph sighed. 'Oh, Nikki, they are playing such dangerous games! Apart from the casual sex with random partners and all that can lead to, they have no idea who these men are, or what they might be capable of.'

Nikki turned to him, her expression sombre. 'Well, it looks as though Laurie might have found out the hard way, doesn't it?'

Joseph had no answer.

CHAPTER NINETEEN

Cam stood in the doorway to Nikki's office, shaking his head. 'He's refused protection. Patrick Shale will not hear of going into a safe house, and he doesn't want to see uniforms anywhere near his home. He was adamant, and his mother was bloody rude.'

'Yeah, I've met her.' Nikki pulled a face. 'Saves us some money, I suppose, but it also makes life a whole lot more difficult.'

Cam came in and sank down into a chair. 'I cannot believe that no one apart from us has found out where he lives. Well, someone's going to unearth him soon, and then . . . We all know what can happen when people start taking the law into their own hands.'

'Has he clocked the crew on obo?' asked Nikki.

'He didn't mention them, and they are a discreet distance down his lane, but like it or not, they're staying put. Plus, we need to search that house. I'm sending two of our most "diplomatic" officers to just do a walk-through. They won't turn the place upside down, just make sure there's nowhere a girl could be concealed. The Shales will object, but we'll have a warrant. Above all, we have an obligation to the public. Until we find Laurie, he's going to be watched, day and night.'

'According to the obo boys he's not stepped outside the house and has had only one visitor; a "surprise" visit from his probation officer. Even though he's served his time, his supervision plan requires contact once a week, but he's a rum one alright.' She pointed to the piles of paperwork. 'Joseph and I have been going over the trial, looking for anything indicating his possible innocence that hasn't been noticed before.'

'Any joy? Any opinions?'

She shook her head. 'Face value? Guilty as hell, and nothing screams out for closer inspection. But even so, we still aren't convinced.'

'Then it's open minds, and I'll keep up the surveillance.' Cam stood up. 'Better get on, but at least we have one of the missing girls safe. That's something to be thankful for.'

'I'll let you know how Yvonne gets on with the hunt for the party venue. Joseph's gone with them. He's all fired up about these youngsters' morals and the dangers of waltzing off with strange men.'

'Bit different to my day,' Cam mused. 'It used to take me a month to ask a girl to go to the pictures with me, and she would take another week to decide!'

'Oh bless!' Nikki laughed. 'I can't see that at all.'

'You better believe it. Ask my wife.' Cameron winked and closed her door behind him.

* * *

As the end of their shift approached, Cat and Dave returned to the office. Dave was carrying the phone in an evidence bag.

'Anything else turn up?' asked Nikki.

'Not yet, boss, but just before we left we found a whole load more boxes in her attic. We'll hit those first thing tomorrow morning, if that's alright with you?' asked Cat.

Nikki said it was. 'You were late last night, get home now and re-charge. I've asked uniform to put a watch on Carmel's cottage, so if there is anything, it'll be going nowhere.'

Cat yawned. 'I think I need a bit of a rest. It's all been a whirlwind since I heard Carmel was dead. A night's sleep might clear my head.'

'You too, Dave. An early night won't do you any harm either.' Nikki smiled at him.

'Just one thing.' Dave peeled the Post-it from the photo album and waved it at her. 'Need to go over this again. Something was calling to me, something I missed.'

If he didn't check it out, it would bug him all night, Nikki knew, so she nodded. 'Just don't make it another late one. For one thing, Joseph isn't here tonight to order fine dining.'

Dave grinned. 'It's alright. I've promised myself fish and chips this evening, and it won't take long I'm sure. It was just this particular album. None of the others had anything in them that stood out even slightly.'

Nikki heard her phone and pulled it from her pocket. She stared at the unknown number. 'DI Galena.'

'It's my mother, Inspector. She's had another, er, gift. Can you come, please?'

Richard Howard sounded really shaken. 'Okay, Richard, what is . . . ? Oh, never mind, I'm on my way.' She turned to Dave. 'If you are still here when Joseph gets back, tell him I've gone out to Sedgebrook House.'

'More trouble?'

'Sounds that way.'

Dave threw her a worried glance. 'Take care, boss. Everything seems to be centred in that place.'

Just as she was getting into her car, she saw Joseph arrive back with Yvonne. 'Any luck?'

Joseph nodded. 'We found it, but no one's at home. Young Kyle is waiting there, and he'll ring in when the owners arrive. Neighbour said they work out of town. Where are you off to?'

'Sedgebrook House. Aurelia has had another present.'

'Hold on, I'll come with you.' Joseph sprinted across and hopped into the car. 'Yvonne is taking Kelly to an aunt and uncle's place for tonight. It's not a good idea for her to be alone at home right now.'

Nikki pulled out of the car park into a sea of cameras and mikes. Swearing softly, she drove slowly through the mêlée, trying to ignore the faces pressed to the window, until she could accelerate away. 'Don't you just love all this? It would happen right now, wouldn't it, when we are run off our feet with all these cases. Richard Howard sounded well upset. No messing around, just a direct "can you come, please?"'

'It must be getting them down, waiting for the next thing to happen.' He paused. 'I just don't get how this person seems to come and go unnoticed.'

'Me neither. We've checked all the people who go there regularly, like the gardener, the cleaner and so on, but none of them seems likely to be involved. There are no neighbours, so . . .' Nikki shrugged.

'Is it time to bring uniform in to do observation, Nikki?' Joseph asked.

She groaned. 'With our overstretched budget? A missing girl *and* a media-fest going on in town? No chance — well, not unless something serious happens.'

When they pulled into the drive, Richard Howard was waiting for them. He looked haggard, older than his years. 'Mother is beside herself this time, officers, and understandably so.'

'You'd better show us, Richard.' Nikki was feeling more than a little apprehensive.

'Come round the back of the house.'

They rounded a corner, walking alongside a well-tended herbaceous border, and arrived at a beautifully laid-out patio area. Goose clearly knew what he was doing.

'There.' Richard pointed to a door that opened out into the garden.

Nikki's hand flew to her mouth.

The lifeless remains of a massive rook had been nailed to the door. It hung upside down, its wings outstretched, a trail of blood dripping from its beak and staining the painted woodwork.

Nikki turned away. 'Deal with it, Joseph! Just deal with it!'

She was aware of the two men staring at her, but she couldn't help herself. Dead birds. The one thing she couldn't handle. She even struggled with live ones if they came too close. At a distance, birds were fine — she even put out food for them — but any closer and she went to pieces. As for dead ones, then panic set in.

'Sorry,' muttered Richard. 'Maybe I should have told you.'

'Not your fault,' she murmured through gritted teeth. 'I never gave you the chance.' Keeping her eyes averted from that door, she said, 'It's a phobia. Can't help it.'

'Could you get me a refuse sack, Richard?' Joseph asked. 'And, Nikki, go back to the front of the house. Richard can let us in that way.'

He joined her after a few minutes. 'All sorted. I've photographed it in situ and bagged it. Goose the gardener has put it in his shed for now. Like it or not, it's evidence.'

Nikki made a retching noise. 'Well, it's not travelling back to the station in my car.'

'Don't worry.' He smiled at her. 'You okay now? I knew you didn't like them, but I didn't realise just how much they affected you.'

'Since childhood. Something happened . . .' Nikki shuddered but didn't continue. 'Sorry. I just can't hack them.' Taking a deep breath, she said, 'Okay, let's go talk to the family.'

'Yes, but be prepared. It wasn't so much the bird that upset Aurelia. Richard told me there was something else left as well. The family is shocked to the core.' Joseph ushered Nikki towards the open front door. 'Come on, they'll explain.'

Back in the now familiar sitting room, they found Duncan, Aurelia and Richard. The silence in the room was ominous.

'I believe something else was left. Can you tell us what that was?' asked Nikki, looking from one to the other.

Duncan waved a hand vaguely at Richard. 'You tell them, son.'

'We found this attached to the bird's claw, Detectives.' Richard pointed to a small object that was sitting in an evidence bag on a coffee table in the centre of the room.

Nikki and Joseph went over and looked at it. It was a heavy silver ring, a Celtic Knot design with polished trims on either side of the inner Celtic braid. It was well worn, but still solid.

'You recognise it?' asked Joseph.

Aurelia stifled a sob. Duncan nodded mutely.

Richard said, 'It belongs to my brother, Alex. He never takes it off.'

* * *

Dave carefully examined each photograph. These ones were older, possibly dating back twenty years, judging by the clothes and hairstyles. Deacon had written names or initials under each picture, and some short descriptions but, oddly, there were no dates, unlike the older books.

He turned a page and saw what he'd been looking for.

'Gotcha!' he said out loud. He gently removed the picture from beneath the transparent cover. Needing to see it more clearly, he scanned it. He enlarged the image on his computer, then printed it off.

'Well, I'm blowed! Hello, Todd. I wonder what you're doing here?'

Dave sat down and stared at the enlarged photograph. It showed three young men sitting on the grass in front of a large house — or was it a hotel? A school? The three of them wore smiles — smug, knowing, as if they shared a secret. Dave took a look at the album. Under the empty square the photo had occupied were the letters, TR, GL, and HS at PH.

TR was Todd Ridler. Dave had arrested this young man some sixteen or seventeen years ago, for committing sexual offences against minors. He had no idea who the others were, or what or where was PH.

He swung his chair round and searched for Todd Ridler on his computer, finding that he had been in and out of prison ever since Dave had banged him up all those years ago. Now he was on the register of sex offenders. Dave puffed out his cheeks. Why had Deacon taken a picture of this young pervert? He wasn't a friend, was he? Dave stared more closely at the house and decided that indeed it wasn't someone's residence. This was some kind of home, or institution. He looked again at Todd Ridler's record. Time spent at Penhaligon Hall Rehabilitation Centre. Dave did a search for Penhaligon Hall. Now closed, it had run rehabilitation courses for young people with problems.

But where did Deacon fit in? He couldn't have been a patient there, he was too old. A visitor maybe? Surely he hadn't worked there.

Deacon's sexual misdemeanours hadn't come on overnight. He had probably always been that way. So what the hell was he doing with these young people?

Dave slipped the photo back into the album and as he did, he saw another one. Three young men again, but different ones this time, and the setting was a park with a boating lake. Dave looked at the initials. PS, AH and JCS.

'Shit!' He pulled the picture from the album and scanned it. Could it be? He looked closer. PS? Could that be Patrick Shale? Dave found Shale's record and looked closely at the mugshot. It was Shale, without a doubt.

Dave's head span. Deacon knew the man who had been convicted of Jennifer Cowley's murder. What did that mean?

Dave paged through the photograph album. With very few exceptions, all the people in these pictures were young men. He swallowed hard. He needed to know a lot more about Deacon's background and exactly what he'd done after he left the army. As far as he knew, no one had ever looked deeply into the man's early history. At the first trial the defence had concentrated on his impeccable reputation and his volunteer and charity work. With a string of professionals all ready to sing his praises, little attention had been paid to his other activities.

Dave thought about it. This was a proper lead to something even darker in Deacon's past. Had he been grooming these vulnerable young people? If he had, it looked as though he had been remarkably successful. A killer and a sexual predator had passed through his hands, and that was just two among a whole host of the young faces that were staring back at him from this old photo album.

'Evening, old-timer.' Ben came in and placed a large Tupperware box of food on his desk. 'How goes it? Shouldn't you be going home?'

Dave didn't answer. He was still trying to get his head around what he had found.

'You're not having a heart attack, are you?' asked Ben suspiciously. 'You've gone a very funny colour.'

'So will you when I tell you what I just discovered.'

Ben listened, his expression growing increasingly horrified with every word. He stared at the picture, and then at the mugshot of Shale. 'It's him alright, isn't it?'

Dave nodded. 'Ben? Could you dig into Deacon's past tonight? See if you can rake up anything about what he did when he hit civvy street?'

'Of course. I'll go through the lot. This is big, man! Well done you for spotting that Todd bloke, and then Shale!' He took another look at the image, then stopped speaking.

'Ben?'

'Jesus! I hope I'm wrong on this . . .' He rubbed his forehead. 'Look at this, Dave.' He pointed to the photo with Shale in it. 'See the young guy next to him? I've been researching the Howard family for the boss, and I swear that teenager is Alex Howard.'

Dave traced the carefully written initials, AH. 'This is going too fast for me. Are you sure?'

Ben scurried over to his desk. After a few minutes of swearing at his computer, which was slow to boot up, Dave heard the hum of a printer.

'Check this out.' He thrust the printout at Dave. 'The Howard brothers, in their teens. Look at the one in the middle. Wouldn't you say that was the guy in Deacon's snap?'

Dave compared them. 'It's Alex Howard, Ben. I'm sure of it.'

* * *

Kyle had not yet developed a means to combat the boredom officers inevitably suffered during long hours of waiting. He didn't even have a car to sit in. After two hours, his back and feet were aching and his mind had gone numb. Then he saw a likely looking couple walking towards him and his hopes rose.

'Mr and Mrs Canter?' He held out his warrant card. 'PC Kyle Adams. Could I have a word, please?'

The woman glanced anxiously at the man, but they led the way up to their door. Kyle followed them inside the plush residence, a three-storey house that overlooked a waterway.

'In here.' Andrew Canter indicated a very elegant lounge. 'Do sit. I'll just take my coat off and I'll be with you.'

'I won't keep you long, sir. It's regarding someone who came to a party at this address the night before last.' Kyle already had his pocketbook out. It was his first time out alone and he was keen to impress Yvonne.

Canter returned from the hall and sat down opposite Kyle. He was in his early forties, Kyle guessed, with a full head of dark brown wavy hair and a slightly weathered face that clearly didn't come from hard graft on the land. More likely the tan came from tropical holidays or time on the piste. He was impeccably dressed.

'There was a man at this party whom we believe to be called Rob. Long dark coat and a trilby hat? Could you give us his full name and an address if you have it?' Kyle asked.

Andrew Canter frowned. 'Can't place him, I'm afraid. Hold on a moment, Claire might know him.' He stood up again and went to the door. 'Claire! Have you got a moment, sweetheart?'

Mrs Canter listened to the question and smiled. 'Of course. That would be Robin. He turned up with two young models on his arm.' She looked at her husband. 'Darling, you remember them, surely? One was a brunette and the other a blonde.'

'Oh yes. Very striking, the pair of them. And if I remember rightly, my nephew Simon soon absconded with the brunette. I just didn't see who brought them. Who's Robin, Claire? I don't think I've met him.'

His wife rolled her eyes. 'You and he talked for ages about the best places to ski this year.'

'Oh, him. Didn't catch his name.'

Kyle watched and listened. Obviously Rob wasn't a regular visitor to this posh des res, but at least Mrs Canter had confirmed that he had arrived with Kelly and Laurie. That was a start. 'Mrs Canter, can you tell me anything about Robin?' he asked.

'Not really, Officer. He turned up at a party we had a couple of weeks ago, with a work friend of mine. I'd never met him before, but he seemed pleasant enough.' Her smile faded. 'He's not in trouble, is he?'

Kyle decided on discretion. 'We want to talk to him, that's all. He might have seen someone we are anxious to find. I wonder if I could have the name and address of the woman he accompanied to the previous party?'

Her expression changed. 'Well, her name is Helen, but she's off on holiday at the moment. Somewhere exotic, but I have no idea where exactly. She loves the sun.'

'Phone number?' Kyle asked.

She looked vague. 'I don't think I have it. We always just chat while we are at work.'

'So, did Robin leave with the blonde girl, Mrs Canter?'

Claire Canter shrugged. 'Must have done, I suppose. We didn't see her after he'd gone.'

Like the rest of the world. These people obviously hadn't seen the evening news, or they would no doubt have recognised the photos of Laurie that were prominent across all the channels.

'It would have been polite to thank us, I would have thought,' she added tersely. 'Young people these days. I don't know.'

'Did you notice if they stayed together while they were here?' Kyle asked. 'Did she seem to know him well? As in, did she seem comfortable with him?'

'Oh yes. In fact I got the feeling they were already an item,' said Claire Canter thoughtfully. 'They seemed quite close — you know, laughing and joking, heads together. Then again, she had a fair bit to drink. Maybe she was just a bit tipsy.'

Seeing he was going to get nothing more from them, Kyle said, 'So you know very little about this Robin?'

The couple looked at each other. 'I'm afraid not,' said Andrew Canter. 'Look here, he's obviously done something serious, can't you just tell us what it is?'

Well, they were going to find out soon enough. 'The young woman that came to your party, the blonde one, is missing,' Kyle said. 'Her name is Laurie Gately, she is only nineteen and we are concerned for her safety.'

Claire Canter gasped. 'Oh no! Nineteen, you say? We thought she was much older than that. Oh my God, this is terrible.'

'Do you have parties often?' asked Kyle.

'We are very sociable people, Officer. We have a get-together every couple of weeks, I suppose.' Canter frowned, 'Why do you ask? There's no law against it, is there?'

Kyle smiled. 'Oh no, sir, not that I know of. I was just thinking that I can't remember the last party I went to, and you mentioned two in as many weeks.'

Again, husband and wife exchanged that rather furtive glance, but said nothing.

'I'm going to need a list of names of your guests, and we will be interviewing them in due course. If you could prepare this for me I'll call back in the morning.' Kyle stood up. 'Thank you for your help. Would you ring us if you should either see or hear anything of Robin?' He handed them a card. 'We are very concerned about Laurie.'

'Of course, of course.' Canter said. 'We hope you find her soon.'

Outside, Kyle decided to walk the twenty minutes back to the station instead of calling for a car. Parties every two weeks? Blimey, they must be loaded!

CHAPTER TWENTY

When Nikki and Joseph finally got back to the station, they were surprised to see Dave still there. He stood up the moment they came in the door.

'You had your orders to go home, Dave Harris! It's after eight.' Nikki looked at his expression and raised her eyebrows.

'Ben and I have some pretty worrying news.' Dave picked up a small sheaf of printouts from his desk and held them out. 'Take a look at these, boss.'

They stared at the images. 'Jesus!' Nikki glanced at Joseph, wide-eyed. 'Alex Howard again. That's twice he's turned up in as many hours.'

Leaving Joseph to explain to Dave what they had found out about Alex Howard, Nikki went over to Ben's desk.

'Evening, boss,' he said. 'I'm trying to put together Deacon's history from when he left the forces, and whether he was actually employed at that rehab centre.' He picked up a memo. 'Back when those pictures were taken, it treated young people with different mental health issues, especially teens with complex sexual behaviour problems.'

'I have a horrible feeling you are going to find Deacon either on their staff or listed as a volunteer worker there.'

'Me too.' Ben shook his head. 'I'm guessing we have only touched the surface of what he's been up to over the years.'

'It was a bit foolish of him to have kept that photo album, wasn't it? It could well turn out to be our key to opening doors that Deacon would prefer to keep locked.' She looked at Ben. 'I know there's only so much you can do in a night, but I have another job for you too.'

'Throw it my way. I'll do what I can.'

'Alex Howard. I'm getting very concerned about that man.' Nikki pulled up a chair and sat next to Ben. 'I'm not one hundred percent sure he's still in South Africa. Would you get hold of the passenger lists of flights out of South Africa to the UK for the last three weeks? It's a long shot, but as he's still out of contact, I have to wonder if he isn't here in Greenborough. And now you've found him in a picture taken by Deacon, the alarms are ringing all over.' She paused. 'I think it's time to bring in the South African Police Service. Richard Howard is going to speak to his brother Jerrard and give us the name of the province to contact — apparently they all have their own provincial commissioners.' She went on to tell him about the Celtic ring.

'And they swear he never takes it off?'

'Aurelia is adamant. It's quite an expensive ring, a twenty-first birthday present from her. She said she'd never seen him without it.'

Ben frowned. 'So why give it back? And in such a ghoulish manner?'

Nikki had a brief flashback to the rook hanging on the door. Then that blended into a vision of Jennifer, also dead and hung upside down. She dismissed them. 'Indeed. And why return the present?'

'Because you've fallen out with someone, or you no longer love them?'

'Or to hurt them,' added Nikki.

'Very true. So is it Alex sending those messages to her? And where is he? No one has seen him. He just comes and goes like a spectre.'

'Well, if anyone knows the layout of that farm, it will be a person who has lived and grown up there, especially as an inquisitive child.' Nikki was beginning to come around to the belief that this whole scenario had been orchestrated by the youngest son of the Howard family. But what about the murdered girl?

Joseph joined them. 'I've sent Dave off, but he says he calling in on someone called Todd Ridler on the way home. The guy is under curfew apparently, so he should be in. He's going to question him about Vernon Deacon and his connection to the Penhaligon House Rehab Centre. He'll ring us when he gets home.'

'I have a feeling that with or without Carmel Brown's insurance policy, this time next year, Deacon will be looking at the world from behind bars.' Nikki hoped fervently that that would be the case.

'Leave it with me, boss,' Ben said. 'I'll do all I can tonight.'

Nikki patted his shoulder. 'Good man.'

Joseph followed her to her office, 'Nikki, I know we should be going home, but I'm wondering if we should go back out to Sedgebrook House again. What do you think? I'm absolutely certain Aurelia Howard knows exactly what is going on and I think it's time to lean on her.'

'That's not something I would have expected to hear from you, Joseph,' Nikki said. 'She was in bits over that ring. Do you think putting pressure on her is wise? Or kind, for that matter?'

'I think it's the perfect time to exert a little pressure. And I'll bet you anything you like that we get some answers.'

'I'm not convinced, Joseph, I really am not.' She hesitated, holding up Deacon's picture of Alex Howard sitting beside Patrick Shale. 'Okay, we'll go. But don't push too hard, or I'll pull the plug. Understood?'

This was a complete reversal of roles for them. Nikki wasn't normally the one playing good cop.

'Understood. I've no intention of using thumbscrews, you know, just some authoritative Easter persuasion.' He smiled innocently at her. 'I promise.'

'All I can say is you'd better have something decent planned for supper. Let's get this over with. I'm starving!'

* * *

In the early evening, just as the daylight was beginning to steal away from the village, Marian walked slowly through the close. She knew that Doris Butters would be out watering her flowerpots before it got fully dark. Doris wasn't the kind of woman Marian had time for normally, but right now she was an important strand in a web that Marian was about to spin.

'You've had a wonderful display of colour this year, haven't you? I admire them every time I walk past.'

Despite her surprise at being spoken to by Marian Harper, Doris visibly swelled with pride.

'I have, haven't I, dear? I love my geraniums and petunias.'

'That's obvious. Grown with care. It always makes a difference.' Marian smiled benignly at her. 'I really should make more of an effort, but,' she heaved a dramatic sigh, 'I don't know, since my husband passed away I don't have much enthusiasm for anything, especially gardening. That was his domain.'

Doris beamed at her, eager to know more. 'You poor thing! I had no idea about your hubby. Was it long ago you lost him?'

'It was very sudden, I'm afraid, totally unexpected, just before I moved here. In fact, that's why I came to the close. I was downsizing.' The lies were flowing smoothly, and luckily Doris was living up to her reputation as a nosey parker.

'Well, I've seen you walk down the close, of course, but you've always seemed so, well, private. And I *never* like to pry.' She looked hopefully at Marian. 'If you ever fancy a chat, you know where I am, dear. Anytime.'

'It's my fault, Mrs Butters. I don't mean to be standoffish. To be honest, I'm lost without my husband.' God, what garbage she was coming out with! 'I'd love a chat sometime.'

'Why not now, dear? The kettle's on.' She gave a little tinkling laugh. 'The kettle's always on in my house!'

Result! Marian smiled. 'Well, that would be lovely, if it's not too much trouble.'

Inside, the bungalow was Doris Butters to a tee and everything that Marian loathed. Knick-knacks cluttered every surface, with houseplants filling the few remaining gaps on the windowsills and occasional tables. The walls were hung with embroidered pictures of kittens and puppies, along with a collection of plates showing country cottages. And endless photos of snotty-nosed children.

Marian removed a multicoloured, migraine-inducing crocheted cushion from a chair and sat down.

'Won't be a mo, duck. Tea's brewing.' Doris bustled in and sat down opposite her. 'Did I see the police down at your place earlier?'

Thanks for the cue, Doris! 'Mmm,' said Marian. 'Asking about that poor Mr Deacon. I never met him to speak to, so I couldn't tell them anything, other than that he seems a charming man, and he's always helping out down the close.'

She turned a wide-eyed, innocent face to her hostess.

'He is indeed! He's a wonderful, giving person. Whoever started that terrible witch hunt against him should be ashamed of themselves. I hate to think what the poor soul must be suffering!' Doris shook her head, her iron-grey permed curls remaining motionless. 'Criminal, I call it! He's the most caring neighbour I've ever had.'

'Oh, that's so reassuring when you live on your own, isn't it?'

Doris went off to pour the tea. Marian took a deep breath and closed her eyes for a minute. God, this was bloody painful, but it had to be done.

A few minutes later, sipping weak tea from a cup decorated with kittens, Marian said, 'Doris, I heard that Mr Deacon was very good with financial problems such as probate and the like. I had been going to ask him to give me some advice about a few problems I've run into regarding my late husband's affairs, but with all this happening, I haven't dared approach him.'

Doris put down her cup and saucer. 'I'm sure he'd be happy to help you, me duck. Take his mind off this nastiness. He was brilliant with my friend Enid. Saved her a whole lot of money.'

'Oh no, I really don't think I could impose on him.' Marian paused. 'But then again, I suppose it might be nice for him to think that his neighbours are supporting him through all his troubles?'

'My thoughts precisely! Tell you what, would you like me to have a word with him for you? Seeing that I know him so well.' Doris smiled warmly at her. 'It would be no trouble, dear, and I could check up and see if he's alright at the same time.'

'If you think so, Doris, I'd be ever so grateful.' Marian drained her cup. 'And thank you for the tea. You've been so kind, but I'd better get home. It's getting dark and these days I'm a bit nervous in the dark.' She stood up, aching to be out of this ghastly little room.

With many effusive thanks, Marian made her escape. My God, Deacon had really done a number on Doris Butters! The bastard had achieved little short of sainthood in that woman's eyes! Anyway, that was Phase One done with, and it had gone pretty well. Phase Two would take off when Vernon Deacon knocked on her door.

She let herself in, put the light on, and went into the kitchen. She needed a drink. On the cupboard shelf next to the bottle of Scotch whiskey were two glasses. The second was to have been for Carmel when she came to visit. Only she never made it.

Marian poured herself a good-sized measure and swallowed deeply. She wanted desperately to cry for her dead friend but refused to allow herself the luxury of tears. That would come later, when her plan was successfully completed.

* * *

Richard Howard opened the door to them. 'Oh, Detectives. I didn't expect you back tonight. Is there a problem?'

'We just need a few words with your mother, Richard. If we may?' Joseph was already in the hall.

'Sure. She's still in the lounge. She's hardly spoken a word to Dad or me since you left. I rang Jerrard, by the way. There's still no news of Alex. Jerrard offered to come home, but I said he should stay until we know more. I hope I did the right thing?'

'I think so. For now, at least,' answered Nikki.

'He told me to tell you to contact the Limpopo police. That's where he went last and since then, no sign.' Richard led them back into the lounge, where Aurelia still sat, stiff and unmoving, in a high-backed armchair beside the fireplace. Joseph thought she looked rather regal, in a sad, Miss Havisham kind of way.

'I thought you'd be back,' she said quietly. She waved a hand absently, indicating that they should sit down, and looked up at Richard. 'Son, I wonder if you would mind leaving us for a few minutes.'

Richard opened his mouth to protest, and then left the room, closing the door behind him.

'He'll find out soon enough.' Aurelia's voice was stronger now, decisive.

'It's Alex, isn't it?' Joseph said.

'It's always been Alex, from the day he was born. He was different to Richard and Jerrard in every possible way. There was something about him — beautiful and yet terrible. Strange thing to say about your own child, but there it is.' She looked past them into the distance. 'He didn't seem to abide by the same rules as the rest of us. He always went his own way.'

'Is that why you sent him away, Aurelia?' Joseph asked gently.

'You know why I sent him away.' She stood up. 'Wait here.'

As the door closed behind her, Nikki half stood. 'Should I go after her?'

'No. She'll be back. She needs to finally speak about what she's been keeping to herself all these years.'

After what seemed like an age but was probably just a few minutes, Aurelia returned, carrying a small canvas handbag that had tropical flowers printed on it. She sat back down, staring at the bag, while they waited. Then, slowly, deliberately, she opened it up. 'This is why I sent him away.' She reached in, took something out and held it towards them.

It was a single black slip-on shoe, with a buckle in the shape of a lover's knot.

She then produced a yellowing newspaper clipping. 'It describes what Jennifer Cowley was wearing when she disappeared. It says here, "black slip-on pumps with a distinctive buckle." I found it under his bed in a box where he kept his treasures. You know, boys' things — an old coin, a special fishing fly, a piece of quartz, a school certificate.'

Neither Joseph nor Nikki spoke while they absorbed this revelation. So Patrick Shale had been innocent all along? If Alex had the missing shoe, he had to have been with her when she died. Was he the killer then? Is that what his mother was saying?

'You believed your son had killed Jennifer, so you sent him to South Africa?' Joseph needed to get it absolutely clear.

'He denied it but he'd had obsessions over girls before, and I knew of other rather disturbing aspects of his dealings with women. He told me once that he wanted to marry Jennifer Cowley, that no other girl would do, and I became concerned about how infatuated with the girl he had become.' She stared at the black shoe in her hands. 'When I found this after she had gone missing, I knew I had to protect my child, get him to safety. But I didn't want him to . . . to do anything like this again, so I sent Jerrard to watch over him.'

'You do understand what you are saying to us, don't you, Mrs Howard?' said Nikki. 'You deliberately withheld evidence, in fact you failed to hand over something vital. Your silence allowed an innocent man to spend fifteen years in prison for a crime you believed your son to have committed. You have perverted the course of justice.'

'That would be how you would construe it, yes. I saw it as protecting my boy.'

'And what about your other child, Jerrard?' asked Joseph incredulously. 'He'd done nothing wrong, and yet you condemned him to live as a jailer, watching his brother every minute of the day. That's monstrous!'

'He went willingly, taking a large sum of money. It was a new start for both of them. I had contacts, relatives in South Africa. I secured two excellent jobs for them and they made a good life there. They would tell you that themselves.'

'And now Alex is back. That wasn't part of your master plan, was it?' asked Nikki.

She sounded old suddenly, her voice faltered. 'I don't know why he's back, and I don't know why he didn't just come straight to me.' Suddenly she was weeping. She wailed, 'He has no need to threaten me! I still love him, I always did. I always will.'

There was no condoning what she had done, but looking at her now, Joseph was also overcome by the depth of this woman's love for her child. He asked himself if he would go to such lengths for Tamsin.

But there was no time for conjecture. 'We will have to ask you to come with us to the station. You do understand that, don't you, Aurelia?' he said.

She nodded mutely, and then looked at them, her expression beseeching. 'You have to find my son, detectives. You have to.'

'We will.' Nikki's voice sounded strained. 'But right now, we need to ask you a few questions. Did Alex know Patrick Shale? Were they friends?'

'Who? The man who went to prison?' Aurelia thought for a moment. 'No. He never mentioned anyone of that name.'

'How about a man named Deacon?' continued Nikki.

This time she nodded. 'There was someone called Deacon who used to run a youth club of some sort in Greenborough. It was a place kids could go to and get information about things that worried them but that they were too embarrassed to talk to their parents or teachers about. I think his name was Vincent, or possibly Victor.'

'Vernon,' said Nikki flatly. 'Vernon Deacon.'

'That's right. Vern, they called him. Why?'

Ignoring the question, Joseph retrieved a copy of Deacon's photo from his pocket and took it over to Aurelia. 'This is Alex, right?'

Aurelia stared at it, nodded. 'Yes, that's my lad. He used to row on that lake. It was close to the old Greenborough Lido. The lido has gone now, but the lake is still used for boating.' She peered closer. 'I don't know who the others are though. I'm sure they weren't close friends of his or I'd recognise them.' She handed it back. 'I don't understand. Who took that picture?'

'Vernon Deacon, we think,' Joseph said.

'And this bothers you?'

'We think he groomed vulnerable and impressionable young men,' Joseph stated.

'Alex was not vulnerable. And far from easily influenced!' She gave a short laugh. 'He did what he wanted, not what others expected of him.'

'But he went to South Africa when you told him to,' snapped back Nikki.

'He had no choice. He knew what the alternative was.'

A silence fell. There was no going back from Aurelia's revelation.

'Aurelia, did your husband know about this?' Nikki asked. 'Did Richard, or anyone else, know what you'd done?'

'No, it has always been a private affair, my personal skeleton in the cupboard. I swore both Jerrard and Alex to silence. It should have died with me. My husband knows nothing about it. He lives in his own world, as I'm sure you have realised by now. As for Richard, well, he was naturally upset with Jerry. He had counted on working with him on the farm and felt that his brother had run out on him.' She shrugged. 'As it happened, that played into my hands, because it meant he wasn't always on the phone to his brother.'

Joseph was amazed at how single-minded she had been, determined to protect her youngest son above all else, even at the expense of alienating the other boys and her husband. Not to mention the pain she had helped prolong for the dead girl's parents. Then something rang alarm bells. Just now, she had said that Alex had denied killing Jennifer. His mother had seen the shoe, recalled his history and decided that he was lying. But what if he had just found that shoe? There was no hard and fast evidence to prove that Alex had been the murderer, and yet still his mother had hastened him out of the country. That was some major step for something that was unproven. Maybe some of his "issues" with women and sexuality were more serious than she had cared to mention.

Nikki stood up. 'Mrs Howard, I need to speak with my colleague alone for a few minutes. I'm sure I don't need to remind you not to leave the house. If you would excuse us?'

'Don't worry,' Aurelia said. 'I'm going nowhere, and I'm fully aware I will be arrested. I'll be here when you get back.'

CHAPTER TWENTY-ONE

Outside, Joseph and Nikki stared at each other. Nikki let out a low whistle. 'Phew! I didn't expect that.'

Joseph leaned against the side of their vehicle. 'Me neither, though I did suspect that it might be Alex who was leaving those tokens. As soon as Richard told us that no one could get in touch with him, I wondered if he'd sneaked home.'

'Can you *believe* that woman?' Nikki's voice rose. 'Where is her moral sense, for God's sake? She had no compunction at letting another young man take the rap for something her son did, costing him fifteen years of his life. Not to mention adding to the agony of the poor girl's parents not knowing the final resting place of their daughter. It beggars belief!'

'We have to arrest her,' Joseph said, 'but I'm going to suggest we give her until the morning. It's getting late and it's going to be complicated. We'll probably have to get the Director of Public Prosecutions involved, and heaven knows where that will lead.'

'I was thinking the same thing.' Nikki shook her head. 'What a mess! But you're right, she won't do a runner. She didn't have to fess up like she did, and if her missing baby is skulking around here somewhere, she's not going anywhere before she finds him.'

'I feel sorry for Richard,' Joseph said. 'This is going to come as a hell of a shock to him.'

'All those years of thinking his brother had opted for the good life in the sun when he'd been bloody shanghaied!' Nikki added.

'And by his own mother!' Joseph massaged his temples. 'My head hurts.'

'Not surprising. Oh, Joseph, we need to talk this through. I've got questions popping up everywhere.'

'Time to call it a day, I think. Let's go and let her know what is going to happen, take that bloody shoe and stuff it in an evidence bag—'

'Fifteen years too late, but that's fine,' Nikki rolled her eyes.

'And maybe we'd better get Duncan and Richard in and put them in the picture.'

Nikki scratched her head. 'So what do we do? Throw the bombshell in the air and run for cover?'

'Something like that.' He pulled a face. 'There won't be much sleep for anyone in Sedgebrook House tonight, will there?'

'Come on then, let's get it done,' said Nikki, 'or there'll be even less in Cloud Cottage Farm.'

When they got back to the lounge, they were surprised to see both father and son sitting anxiously on one of the sofas. Aurelia was still in her high-backed armchair.

'I was waiting for you, Detectives, before I talked to Duncan and my son. I wasn't sure if we would be going directly to Greenborough Police Station.' Aurelia was perfectly calm, apparently resigned to the situation.

'We have a little discretion here, Mrs Howard.' Nikki sat down on the other sofa. 'We've agreed that rather than arrest you now, you may present yourself at the station at ten a.m. tomorrow. We think it would be better all round.'

'Arrest?' Aghast, Richard looked at his father. 'Do *you* know what this is about?'

He only had to look at Duncan's face to see the answer to that question.

'You can't arrest my wife! What on earth are you thinking?' Duncan's expression was one of utter confusion.

Joseph went and sat beside Nikki. 'Aurelia, would you like me to explain?' he asked.

'Yes, damned well explain this tomfoolery!' Duncan seemed to have suddenly awoken from his stupor.

'As I said before, detectives, this is my affair. I'll be the one to tell my family.' She took a deep breath. 'Fifteen years ago, I did a rather foolish thing. Now, it is time to pay for it.'

'Foolish thing? What foolish thing?' Duncan stared at her.

'Please, darling, don't interrupt. Just listen,' Aurelia said. 'Understand this. These officers will be arresting me for perverting the course of justice, and they are absolutely correct to do so. This is not some terrible mistake. I committed a crime, and now I must face the music.'

Joseph sat back a little, and watched the reactions of Richard and Duncan, as Aurelia, in an even tone, explained exactly what she had done, and why.

The silence when she had finished was interminable.

Finally, Duncan said, 'Our son? He committed . . . ?' He swallowed hard, unable to continue.

'We don't know that for certain, sir,' said Nikki. 'But there's a strong possibility that that is the case.'

'And Jerry?' Richard's voice cracked with emotion. 'You sent Jerry away too — to babysit a murderer?'

Richard seemed to accept without question the fact that Alex had been capable of such an act. His outrage was reserved entirely for the fact of Jerrard's banishment. Joseph found this interesting.

'Yesterday, he said to me, "Life takes you on paths that are not quite what you hoped for."' Richard choked back a sob. 'Now I know what he meant.'

'I'm sorry,' Aurelia said.

'Sorry?' Richard shouted. 'Sorry? Do you think that means anything?'

Joseph tensed, ready to intervene.

Then Nikki said, 'Richard. Your mother volunteered this information. We knocked on your door tonight, knowing nothing about it. She's had the courage to confess to what she did. None of us can know how she felt when she discovered this terrible thing. I've no doubt she would have done exactly the same for you, or Jerrard, if the circumstances were different. What she did was wrong, there's no question about that, but at the time she was thinking only of her child.'

Richard looked at his mother coldly. 'I doubt very much that she would have done it for Jerry, or me. No one but her precious Alex is worth that much.'

His mother looked at him, an enormous tenderness in her eyes. 'Oh, my darling. If only you knew! All that attention I showered on Alex, all the extra time I took with him, everything you believed to be affection and favouritism, was simply because I was afraid to let him out of my sight. I was petrified of what he was capable of, and what he might do next.' Tears filled her eyes. 'Richard, you may have believed he was a free spirit, a one-off, a daredevil, but there was more to him. There was something terribly wrong with your brother. Yes, he had a wonderful side — inquisitive, full of wonder at nature and the people he came in contact with — but he also had another, darker side. That was why I kept him close. I loved you and Jerry just as dearly, but Alex was my responsibility. I brought him into the world, and it was up to me to try and protect him from himself.'

She sat back, looking utterly drained.

'Why didn't you ever tell me?' croaked Duncan. 'You carried this whole thing on your own shoulders. Why? Am I such a dreadful husband that you thought you couldn't share it with me?'

'You're a gentle soul, my darling Duncan, and precious to me. I decided it was my cross to bear, not yours, and certainly not Richard's. He was our one hope for the future.'

'And Jerry?' Richard's voice had lost all its anger. Now he sounded more like a child himself.

'Jerrard saw some things once, bad things involving Alex, so after Jennifer Cowley went missing and I found the shoe, I decided to tell him everything. For the sake of the family and for the Sedgebrook Estate, which we both knew you have always loved, Jerry agreed to go abroad with Alex. It broke his heart to leave you, son, and to know that you would hate him for it, but he went through with it anyway, rather than see Alex go to prison for life.'

Nikki and Joseph stayed just long enough to explain to the family what would happen now. Aurelia would be arrested and a complex process set in motion, as this pertained to an old, closed case in which a judgement had been served. Aurelia would then be sent home on bail.

When they finally rose to leave, the family were all sitting together on one couch, Richard on one side of his mother, Duncan on the other. Joseph closed the door softly and they let themselves out.

'That was a nice speech, DI Galena, considering you had previously decided she had no morals.' He unlocked the car and climbed in. 'It defused Richard's anger a treat.'

'I had a few moments to think about just how far I'd have been prepared to go to protect Hannah,' Nikki said. 'I still think Aurelia made an appalling decision, but I do kind of understand. Anyway, I'm in no position to judge. I would willingly have swung for the man who harmed my girl.'

Joseph nodded. 'I had the same thoughts about Tamsin, but the law is the law. All I know is that it's going to be hellishly complicated.'

'Just what we need.' About to say more, Nikki was interrupted by her phone ringing. 'Dave? How did your meeting go?'

'As you can imagine, Todd was not exactly delighted to find me on his doorstep, but we had a pretty interesting chat.'

'Anything that helps us with Deacon?'

'Indirectly. No way would he stand up in court, but he's given me some names, dates and addresses that could prove useful. He admitted, unofficially, to spending time with Deacon, and told me that young men came and went at Deacon's "club" all the time.'

'Nothing actually damning?' she asked.

'Not yet, but he mentioned someone that could be very useful indeed. Ever heard of a man called Georgie Lawson?'

'I have,' said Joseph, who was listening in on loud-speaker. 'He wrote a book, didn't he? After doing a spell inside.'

'That's him, Sarge. His books were all over the place at one point — the ex-con who made good.'

'And he had a connection to Deacon too?' asked Nikki.

'He certainly did, but I very much doubt our Vernon got a mention in his book. Deacon is a dirty secret, even among old lags.'

Joseph could almost see Dave's smug smile. 'I have an idea you know this Georgie rather well, Davey-boy. Am I right?'

'Oh yes, Sarge, certainly well enough to get some real evidence from him if I play my cards right.'

'Well, then I suggest you shuffle your deck and run a few practice hands before you go to bed, and tackle your literary pal first thing tomorrow,' said Nikki.

'How did you get on, boss?' Dave asked.

'I wouldn't know where to start, my friend. We'll fill you in at the morning meeting, okay? Now, switch off for the night, Dave. You are supposed to be winding down ready for the big goodbye, you know, not working back-to-back shifts.'

'If it means pinning something credible on Deacon, I'd work twenty-four seven. Plenty of time for R&R when the time comes. Night, boss.' He ended the call.

Nikki put her head back and closed her eyes. 'We are going to miss that man.'

'We certainly are. Though I have a feeling we'll see plenty of Dave Harris in the future.' After all, Dave was family. He wasn't just going to disappear overnight.

'I cannot wait to know what luck Ben has had with South African Airways.' Nikki spoke softly, her eyes still shut. 'Because if Alex is here and delivering gifts to his mother, he might also have abducted Laurie Gately.'

'One scary thought, considering what his mother said about his unusual sexual tendencies.' They would have to question Aurelia further on that tomorrow.

Nikki sat up, opened her eyes and yawned. 'I so need a clear head, and right now it's full of Fenland fog.'

'Then I suggest we eat, have a large glass of wine and brain-storm what we've got. After that, we'll see what the morning brings.'

There was a silence. Nikki looked at Joseph. 'Only one glass?'

* * *

Richard Howard went out into the garden to phone Jerrard. 'It's time to come home, Jerry. Everything is out in the open now. I know the whole story. We believe that Alex is here in England.' He hardly knew where to start. 'Oh, there's been such a lot happening here that you don't know about, bro. And the worst thing is that Mum is going to be arrested tomorrow.'

Jerrard gasped. 'Why? Because she spirited Alex away? They've finally found out?'

'She told them, Jerry.'

There was a long pause, then a sigh. 'It had to happen one day, I guess.'

'Come home, please? We need you.'

'Richie, I can't.' There was another sigh. 'I had already made up my mind to come — I phoned the airlines, checked flight times, then I went to check my passport. It's missing, Rich. It's gone. Now I can't get home until I sort a replacement.'

'Gone? Surely you've just misplaced it?'

'I keep it in my desk, with all my important official papers. I never move it. It's been taken alright.'

'Did Alex keep his in the same place? Is his still there?' asked Richard anxiously.

'He took it with him, along with other documents, when he travelled to Limpopo. You don't travel any distance out here without formal identification. But, Rich, what do you mean you think he's in England?'

Richard told him what had happened, and about the items mysteriously appearing at Sedgebrook House.

'God, that does sound like Alex, doesn't it? He is still into all that mystical stuff. I think that's why he wanted to go to that particular area of Limpopo, it's full of legend and ancient history. But why would he do such a thing, Richie? He's been on an even keel for years now — no trouble, no odd behaviour at all. And why Mother? After what she did to protect him, why cause her pain?'

'I don't know, Jerry, but then I'm beginning to think I no longer know much at all about this family.'

'Hang on in there, brother. I'll get home as soon as I can sort out some travel documents, okay? I promise.'

'Okay, and I'll keep you posted on what happens here, especially with Mum.'

'Give her my love, Rich, and Dad too. Tell her to be strong. I'll talk to them soon.'

After he had ended the call, Richard sat silently in the darkness, on the seat where he had so recently sat with Tamsin. It seemed like eons ago now. If only she were here, she might be able to make sense of this mess. This only served to make him feel guilty. He should be thinking of Ruthie, not another man's wife. He had had to tell Ruthie not to bring dinner tonight, and she was obviously disappointed.

He looked up, searching for stars, but the sky was black. He would get no answers there. How quickly things could change, how fast the clouds massed where a short time ago it had been light. Before tonight, his biggest worry had been finding an alternative to using pesticides. If only he could push those clouds away.

CHAPTER TWENTY-TWO

Before the morning meeting got under way, Nikki had a visit from Yvonne Collins.

'Ma'am, last night a man came into the station saying he'd seen the late news and the appeal for anyone who'd seen Laurie Gately to come forward.'

Nikki put down her notes. 'And?'

'His name is Robin Faber, ma'am, and he admitted to meeting Laurie and her friend outside the Black Sluice café and taking them on to a party.'

'Sit down, Vonnie, and tell me everything he said.'

Yvonne took a seat. 'I think he's legit, ma'am. He said he knew her from a Saturday job she'd had when she was younger. He's given us full details and Kyle is checking it out right now. The thing is, she didn't leave with him. He said he had a message from his girlfriend apologising for the row they'd had and asking him to go home. He showed the message to the officer who spoke to him, and the time fits. He said he went to look for Laurie and explain, but someone told him she'd already left.'

Nikki frowned. 'If his story checks out, that's another lead down the pan.'

'Not quite. He mentioned a woman at the party that I'd had some dealings with not long ago, and who owed me

224

a favour. I rang her and had a word. She recognised Laurie's description and recalled that although she spent quite a bit of time with Robin, there was another man who'd shown considerable interest in her. She thinks they left at around the same time. She's going to try and find out who he is, though finding the name of someone at that kind of gathering won't be easy.' Yvonne smiled. 'Young Kyle couldn't understand why Andrew and Claire Canter had so many parties.'

'How is that relevant?' Nikki asked.

'They told him they were very sociable.' Her grin widened. 'Bless him, he had no idea that most of these parties are full-on sex romps. The one the other night was a kind of meet-and-greet evening for couples who were new to the scene.'

Nikki smiled. 'I assume you put him right about that?'

Yvonne laughed. 'The bright red cheeks clashed a treat with his hair!'

'Let me know if you come up with a name, won't you? Maybe you could call Kelly Arthur. See if she remembers seeing Laurie talking to a stranger before she buggered off with a stranger of her own.' Nikki shook her head.

Yvonne nodded. 'I'll do that. Now I'd better get back and see how my little neophyte is getting on with Robin Faber's alibi.'

At least "Rob" had been identified, but it meant that Nikki had run up against yet another dead end. For some reason, she felt certain that they would draw a blank on this other man who had been interested in Laurie. Somehow, she knew that the unknown man had taken Laurie, and that he was Alex Howard.

Nikki glanced at the clock. She'd been hoping for one more piece of information before she took daily orders, but time was running out. Above all, she wanted to know if Alex had indeed left South Africa, and if so, whether he'd been heading for England.

Last night Ben had contacted the Limpopo police and now they were waiting for a call from them. He had also requested the passenger lists for flights out of South Africa to the UK — though of course Alex might not have flown direct. This morning Joseph, assisted by two other detectives, had taken over where Ben had left off.

Another reason that she was so desperate for this news was that Aurelia Howard would be with them soon, and Nikki wanted to be able to give her solid proof that her son was back in England.

Cameron Walker strode into her office and closed the door. 'I've just read your message about the Howard woman. It's not good news, is it?'

'Absolutely not, Cam. We will be arresting her this morning, then all we can do is interview her, gather every bit of information that we can, log our reports and pass it up the chain.' She gave him an apologetic smile. 'Sorry about that. It's messy, and the DPP will need to be informed. We will have to follow strict protocol with a case as complicated as this.'

'So the man who paid the price might indeed be as innocent as he's always sworn he was? It doesn't bear thinking about, does it?' Cam went to the window and looked out. 'I'd be interested to see this Aurelia Howard.'

'Interview Room One, ten thirty. You are welcome to listen in, although I must say I won't enjoy making the arrest. I'd much prefer to be slapping cuffs on the bastard who abducted Laurie Gately.' She paused. 'Or, talking of bastards, Vernon Deacon. Only this time I'd make damned sure he never saw his neat little bungalow again.'

'Amen to that.' Cam's brows knotted. 'It beats me how that man's name has cropped up in the Howard enquiry. I've been going over that ever since I read your report this morning. We want him for going after older women, so what the hell was he doing grooming boys with sexual issues? The two don't go together, do they?'

'That's what Joseph and I said. I've left a message for Laura Archer to give us a ring or better still, drop in and give us her professional opinion.'

'Good move, and do please tell me what she says. It's really bugging me.' He checked his watch. 'It's almost nine. I'd better let you take the morning meeting.'

Nikki stood up. 'I'll come and find you when Aurelia gets here. I don't think she'll strike you as some criminal mastermind, more just a mother who put her sick son before everything else.'

Cam grunted. 'Including another man's freedom and closure for grieving parents.'

'I think she saw that as collateral damage, although we'll know more after the interview.' She picked up her notes. 'See you later.'

* * *

While Nikki addressed a roomful of police officers, Vernon Deacon was walking purposefully towards a smart Victorian-style new build at the far end of the cul-de-sac.

He had been watching Marian Harper ever since she moved in. She was everything he admired in a woman — good posture, smartly dressed, beautifully cut hair and immaculate makeup. She had still retained her looks well into her seventies. As soon as he saw her, he had been reminded of . . . He pushed the thought away.

He took several deep breaths. This was risky. No way could he try anything on with a woman who lived in such close proximity to him, nor would he dare to act inappropriately so soon after being released from police questioning. But her invitation had drawn him in like a moth to a flame. For once, that old gasbag of a neighbour, Doris, had something of interest to say, amidst her usual simpering platitudes — Marian Harper wanted to see him. She was fully with the rest of the close in believing him to be a terribly wronged soul and to prove it, she wondered if he could spare her a few moments of his time to give her the benefit of his financial wisdom. He was entering dangerous territory here.

He stared at the pavement, counting his steps, clearing his mind. He must think of the coming meeting as something to be relished, savoured long after he returned home. What games his mind would play as night fell! What dreams he would have!

But now he must forget all that and play the kindly and helpful Vernon Deacon that the gullible residents of Hawthorne Close perceived him to be. He painted on a benign smile, strode up the garden path and rang the doorbell.

* * *

Just as Nikki was drawing the meeting to a close, Joseph saw a young detective waving a memo at him from the other side of the room. It stated that Vernon Deacon had been one of a team of volunteers working with teens and young adults at Penhaligon House and another unit that was now defunct due to cuts, called the Wesley Centre. For several years prior to the closures he had been active as a well-respected mentor and general assistant. This was some seventeen years back. Joseph thought hard. The perfect environment for a predator operating under the guise of a big-hearted do-gooder. Now they needed to know more about the youth club that he had apparently run in Greenborough. Maybe Mrs Howard would be able to throw more light on that. Joseph's priority was tracking the movements of Alex Howard, but he was currently waiting for vital calls from South Africa, so he was temporarily unoccupied.

As the officers all dispersed, he heard his office phone ringing and went to take the call. Five minutes later, he was staring at the hurriedly written notes he had scribbled. Nikki needed to see this. Limpopo Police had just confirmed that although Alex Howard had been expected in Venda, he had failed to turn up and was not answering any calls or texts. No one had seen him in the area after that. It was another indication that he could have returned to the Fens. All they needed now were those passenger lists.

Nikki put her head round his door. 'Joseph, Aurelia's here, and Richard is with her. I'm just going to the super's office, so I'll see you downstairs in ten. Okay?'

He murmured an affirmative, then had a thought. According to Richard Howard, Jerrard had said that Alex had driven up for his interview. So where was his car? He found a map of the Limpopo Province on the computer and looked for Venda. The nearest official airport was Polokwane. So, if Alex had decided to fly home, that might be the place to start.

Joseph jumped up and hurried downstairs to where Richard and Aurelia sat waiting. He greeted them and told them that he would be with them in five minutes, but meanwhile, would Richard be able to find the vehicle registration number of Alex's car for them? He could track it officially, but that would take time.

Richard immediately took out his mobile. 'Jerrard should know. They often swap vehicles. His is more a city car and Alex has a pickup truck, something they call a *bakkie* out there.' He stared at the phone. 'No signal.'

'Try outside the front doors,' suggested Joseph. 'We do have black spots in the building.'

A few minutes later, Richard hurried back inside. 'I've got it.'

Joseph scribbled the number in his detective's notebook, thanked Richard and ran back upstairs to his office. There, he sent off a message to the Limpopo police, asking them if they would check the long stay car park at the airport for Alex's red Toyota Hilux and get back to him as soon as.

'Dave! Can you watch my messages for me?' he called out.

'Sure, Sarge. No problem.' Dave called back.

'Anything from South Africa about Alex Howard, come down to Interview Room One, okay?'

'Wilco'

Downstairs again, he took a deep breath and went inside the interview room. This was one arrest he wasn't looking forward to witnessing.

* * *

From the kitchen window, Tamsin saw Niall draw up outside. He had rung ahead and told her to put the kettle on. His officers were being pulled out of Hob's End Copse today and he wanted to oversee the boarding up of what was left of the cottage.

Usually the wheels of evidence retrieval turned very slowly, but due to the dangerous condition of the site and its impending demolition, it was hoped that everything that could be collected by forensics had already been gathered.

'Trumpton say it has to come down immediately,' said Niall, gratefully accepting a mug of tea. 'But in case we get any ghouls out here trying to nick a slate from the roof of the Cottage of Death, it has to be made as safe as possible.'

'It's on the Howards' land, so it's down to them, surely?' Tamsin sipped her own drink.

'Most likely, but meantime we can't risk someone getting in and injuring themselves. That place is a death trap.'

'In more ways than one,' said Tamsin darkly.

'Listen, sweetheart, besides seeing your lovely face, I had another reason for calling in.' Niall looked uncommonly serious.

'Then cut the flannel and tell me,' Tamsin said.

'There are going to be officers out here checking all the places a man can hide. That includes the old mill, as well as the various barns, sheds and stores. We have reason to believe that Laurie's abductor could be in this area.' His gaze became almost beseeching. 'He is dangerous, Tamsin, especially to women. So, no more traipsing off alone, and Skipper is not protection enough. Okay?' He paused. 'And no more visits to Sedgebrook House. It's probably the worst place you could go right now. I mean it, Tam, stay away.'

'I understand, Niall. Luckily, I have work booked for the next two days, so I won't even be here. I can take Skip with me, so no worries, I've got the picture.' She leaned forward and lightly touched his face. 'I'll hang up my magnifying glass and deerstalker, I promise.'

He covered her hand with his. 'I couldn't cope if anything happened to you.'

'Ditto, my dear. And you must take care too. Just because you wear a uniform doesn't mean it will protect you from some psycho.'

'True, but it helps to have a radio, handcuffs, an asp and big boots.' He laughed and kissed her. 'I'd better push on and get this cottage sorted. I love you, Tam.'

And then he was walking back to the car.

She waved him off, then sat back down to finish her tea. 'Well, Skip, it looks like we've been relegated to the sidelines, but it was fun playing detective, wasn't it?'

The dog looked up at her, his tail wagging. She rubbed his ears. 'Now I get what my dad and my lovely husband love about being police officers.' In another place and another time . . .' She gave a little laugh. 'Nah. Two coppers in one family is plenty. I'll just stick to looking after our planet and leave catching the bad guys to them.'

CHAPTER TWENTY-THREE

The interview with Aurelia Howard had lasted for over two hours. They learnt a lot about Alex, very little of it good. Joseph was left with the feeling that years of denying his true self, being constantly watched by his brother and threatened by his mother, had probably done him no favours. Alex should have had professional help as soon as his unacceptable behaviour had been noticed. Instead of protecting him and covering up, he should have been given proper counselling. Alex must have been a pressure cooker, boiling with pent-up emotions. Now the lid was off.

Aurelia was now on her way home with Richard. They had charged her, and then bailed her with the condition that she remain at Sedgebrook House and surrender her passport. She would have to attend her hearing at the magistrate's court and hopefully be bailed again until her trial began.

Dave jumped up immediately Joseph and Nikki walked into the CID room. 'I just rang downstairs and they said you were on the way up, Sarge. SAP have just contacted you. You were right. They've located Alex Howard's vehicle in the airport car park at Polokwane. It's been there for at least three weeks.'

Joseph thanked him and went to his office, Nikki following.

'Every little bit of new info is telling us that he's left Africa, isn't it?' he said.

'I wonder why the brother didn't sound the alarm, especially to Aurelia, when he lost touch with his ward,' Nikki said.

'Sick to death of his job as minder and scared shitless of what mother would say, I should think. And initially he was in contact with Alex, who was telling him what a great place it was and how he hoped he'd get the job.'

Nikki eased herself into the only other chair in the tiny room. 'Do you really believe that someone with a serious problem regarding young women, someone who was capable of intense obsessions and possibly murder, could abstain for fifteen years?'

'It's possible, although improbable. Serial killers have been known to kill, then stop, sometimes for very long periods of time, and during that time carry on what appear to be perfectly normal lives, until some trigger sets them off on another killing spree. Maybe Laura Archer can shine some light on that point. She's due here after lunch.'

'Good. I like Laura, and we can certainly do with a psychologist's take on it all. She'll no doubt have a field day with the Howard family.' Nikki smiled grimly. 'But I'm glad Richard came with his mother today. Aurelia might be a tough cookie, but it's no picnic being charged.'

'It's tough on us too, when it's not some hardened criminal or scumbag that deserves everything he gets. Seeing her sitting there taking it on the chin was kind of bizarre.' Joseph hadn't enjoyed the procedure any more than Nikki. But as he'd said before, the law is the law and you cannot take it into your own hands. 'I keep having to remind myself that she condemned a man to fifteen years in a Cat B prison and Jennifer's parents to more hell.'

Nikki nodded. 'And if dear Alex is back in this country, he's certainly not repaying the debt in a very nice manner.'

'It will be interesting to see what the other brother, Jerrard, has to say when he gets home. Richard said he's desperately trying to arrange something. He's reported the theft of his passport and got a case number, but the process of getting a new one isn't simple. Luckily he still has evidence of his citizenship, but it won't be sorted in a couple of days.'

'Couldn't have happened at a worse time.' Nikki paused and frowned, 'I wonder if Alex took Jerrard's passport, to make sure he couldn't follow him if he suspected something?'

'It's certainly possible,' replied Joseph. 'And if that was the case it worked, because it's certainly curtailed Jerrard coming back to England,'

Nikki stood up. 'I'm going to look for Yvonne and see if there's any more news about the man who was lusting after Laurie at the party. With every hour that passes, the hopes of finding her alive are fading. I don't know what else we can do. We have officers all over the town, talking to her friends, neighbours and people in general, searching unoccupied buildings, and there's a whole team out on Jacob's Fen looking for that girl, or the man who took her.'

'Yes. Niall told me he's taking all the officers away from Hob's End Copse and boarding the place up, prior to its demolition. He's sent them out on a search of the countryside. If it is Alex, he could be hiding close to his old home at Sedgebrook.'

'Then why the hell haven't we found him?'

Nikki took a call and smiled. 'Mum! How are you doing?' She pressed loudspeaker so that Joseph could hear.

'Oh, my darling, we are having the most exciting time! This detective work is quite addictive, isn't it?'

Joseph grinned. It was a breath of fresh air to hear Eve's obvious delight flooding down the phone.

'Any results yet?' Nikki asked.

'Far too early for that, sweetheart, but we are on the trail all right! Our missing artist was certainly here, at least for a short time. Tomorrow we are going to see a woman who claims to have one of his paintings. It was apparently given to her great grandmother by Robert himself. Exciting stuff, huh?'

Nikki winked at him and walked away towards her office, still talking to her mother. It was good to see her smile again.

Joseph saw that another passenger list had arrived. He exhaled. It was boring stuff, but it had to be done. If they knew an exact date it would help, but at least he could now work on flights after the date when Alex's car had been checked into the airport car park. Ten minutes into checking, his own phone rang.

'Sergeant Easter! We need you to come out to Sedgebrook again!' It was Richard Howard, and he sounded almost panic-stricken.

'Calm down, Richard. Tell me what's occurred.'

'We got home and I made Mum a cup of tea. A few minutes later, I went back to the car for something and there had been another present left on the doorstep.' He took a shaky breath. 'I haven't touched it.'

'Right, we'll be on our way, but meantime Sergeant Farrow is out at Hob's End. I'll divert him directly across to you, so expect him. And, Richard, you did well not to touch it. Just make sure it stays that way. It's evidence.' He suddenly thought of Nikki after seeing their last nasty surprise. 'Oh, and it's not another dead bird, is it?'

'No, nothing like that. Well, it doesn't look like one. I'm not sure what to make of it, to be honest.'

'No matter, I'm leaving now.' Joseph ended the call and rang Niall and told him what had happened. Then he hurried to Nikki's office.

'Sod it! Rory is just on his way over to see me, ETA five minutes,' she said.

'Don't worry, I'll go. You stay here and see Rory. Niall's already en route. I'll meet him there.'

'Okay, but ring me and tell me what it is this time — er, unless it's a . . .' She grimaced.

'It's not, I checked. But I'll ring anyway. Speak soon.'

* * *

235

Phase Two complete, Marian Harper sat quietly in her conservatory, rested her head back on the cushioned willow seat and allowed herself to relax. It had gone much better than she had hoped and, oddly, she had found it easy once she was into her role.

Vernon Deacon was a consummate liar and a very good actor. He was a player, she could see that. But unlike the women he had preyed on before, she knew exactly what he was all about, and she had a purpose. He might be a player, but Marian Harper was a better one, as Mr Deacon would find out to his cost. Or that was the plan.

Marian closed her eyes and calculated the next phase. This part would be far more complex and risky, but it was a step closer to the finishing blow or, as she liked to think of it, the kiss of death.

She chuckled to herself. With luck and a fair wind, Phase Three could begin in a matter of hours. So she would rest for a while, gather her mental strength, and prepare herself for his next visit. No matter when he decided to return, she would be ready for him.

* * *

Rory backed into her office carrying three coffees from the deli around the corner, balanced precariously on top of a white cardboard box.

'No Joseph?' he said, looking around.

'Called out,' Nikki replied

'Maybe that's for the best when you see what's in this box.' He passed her a coffee and opened it up. 'Naughty but nice, just like me. Enjoy!'

Nestled inside, sat three enormous cream cakes. 'Oh, I say! I see what you mean about Joseph. Which one is mine?'

'You choose, and you can have the spare one for emergency rations.'

'I'll have the Belgian chocolate éclair, please.'

'Well, I'm a sucker for a fresh cream meringue, so that's worked out nicely.'

After a few moments of silent munching, Nikki wiped her mouth. 'I hope this isn't a literal sweetener. Are you preparing me for bad news?'

'Partly.' Rory licked icing sugar from his lips. 'I've been talking to the lads from the Collision Investigation Unit. It's their impression that Carmel Brown's car was indeed tampered with. They are not finished yet, but it's pretty certain that's what their report will show, so I thought I'd give you advance warning. I'm afraid you have another crime on your hands.'

Nikki chewed reflectively. 'It will be hard to pin on anyone, especially as the number one suspect was enjoying our hospitality when the incident occurred.'

'I would suggest he used a hired help, wouldn't you?' Rory smiled benevolently at her. 'I mean, far be it from me to teach a grandmother to suck eggs, but why not ask around the low life of Greenborough? See if anyone's heard about a lucrative little job being offered a few nights ago.'

'Oh I will, never fear. We did have a dark-coloured Ford Focus spotted at her house the night before. Maybe that's when the damage was done.' She sipped her coffee. 'My goodness, this is sublime.'

'Don't you still have your secret coffeemaker hidden away somewhere?'

It was the team's pride and joy, fiercely protected from the rank and file. 'Cat's taken it home to give it a clean and an overhaul. We are making do with vending machine rubbish at present.' She took another mouthful, savouring it like a vintage wine. 'And? What else do you have for me, Prof?'

'Well, you don't need me to tell you that the shoe you sent last night is an exact match for the one belonging to Jennifer Cowley. It's hers, no doubt about it.'

As he said, they knew that already, but it was good to have it officially confirmed.

'Finally, the fingerprints on the photos from that satchel. We have isolated four separate sets of prints, and one of them clearly belongs to Patrick Shale. It would appear that whoever took the pictures shared them with friends, none of whom appear in police records. Plus, we examined that partial fingerprint found on the satchel but it's not one of Patrick Shale's — we have his prints on file from when he was first arrested. This one too is not on the database, but it does match a set of prints on the pictures themselves, so it's someone who hasn't had their fingerprints taken before. A tad irritating to be sure but if you find another suspect, we'll have something to compare, so it's not all bad news.'

'We might just be doing that, Rory — if we can only find him.'

'You have someone in mind, other than Shale?' Rory asked.

Nikki gave him a brief resumé of the situation in the Howard family, especially Aurelia's drastic action.

Rory nodded. 'Ah, the lioness and her cub. Protecting him at all cost.'

'Despite what he did.'

'*Because* of what he did, Nikki. All the more reason to protect him, in that case.' He closed the box with the remaining cream cake and pushed it towards her. 'Hide it from Joseph, or you'll be in trouble.'

'Are you sure about this one, Rory?'

'All yours, dear heart.' He stood up. 'Now I should go. I'm sorry to add another murder to your workload.'

Nikki stashed the box in the bottom drawer of her desk. 'We are gradually building up a very interesting file on Vernon Deacon. I would be happy to add to the list of his possible crimes.'

'Oh, and by the way, that disgusting piece of "evidence" that Joseph kindly gifted me with, namely, one deceased *Corvus frugilegus*, was not killed with the intention of decorating Mrs Howard's front door. It was roadkill. Most likely your suspect came across it and said to himself, "Oh perfect! I'll hang that on Mummy's knocker — er, door.'"

Nikki winced, both at the thought of the dead rook and Rory's dreadful pun.

* * *

Joseph arrived at the Sedgebrook Estate to find Niall deep in conversation with Richard Howard. They both looked up at his approach.

'I haven't opened it, sir,' said Niall, 'although I have photographed it on my phone.'

Joseph stared down at what looked like a hastily wrapped present. At least it wasn't another rook — too small. He had looked up the rook or crow and found the bird to be generally associated with the black arts. It was believed to represent the Trickster, a figure signifying devious behaviour, manipulation and mischief.

And now this.

The three men stared down at the brown paper parcel — oddly shaped, roughly wrapped but tied with a rather beautiful wide silk ribbon.

'It's no incendiary device, at least,' said Niall. 'It's been handled quite carelessly by the look of it.'

'The sender obviously isn't used to wrapping gifts. And I agree, it's not a parcel bomb.' Joseph looked at the two other men. 'Even so, I'm going to ask you to leave me to open this.'

Niall made to object, then saw Joseph's expression. He was thinking of Tamsin.

Niall and Richard moved a safe distance away. Joseph knelt down and gently touched the parcel, aware of the significance of the green ribbon that bound it. Such ribbons were used for hand-fasting, a pagan ritual used instead of or as well as the exchange of rings in a marriage ceremony. The ribbon gently bound the couple's hands together — literally "tying the knot."

239

He untied the bow, unwound the ribbon and opened up the wrapping, revealing a woman's shoe packed with three small plastic bags. He removed the bags and examined them.

'All clear!' he called out.

Richard and Niall hurried over to his side.

Richard understood immediately. 'Someone is reminding us about what Mother did when she found that dead girl's shoe!'

'What is in those bags?' asked Niall. 'Drugs?'

'No, it's salt,' Joseph said, but didn't smile.

'Salt? Why?' Niall said.

'White Dead Sea salt, pink Himalayan rock salt and black Hawaiian sea salt. They are all part of a Wiccan altar kit.' Joseph stared at the little packets. 'They represent earth energies, I think, and are supposed to be cleansing. But what our friend means by them, I have no idea.' He looked up to see Niall thumbing through his pocketbook, a look of consternation on his face.

After a few moments he read something to himself, then stared at the shoe. 'Kelly Arthur gave Vonnie a list of what Laurie was wearing when she went missing, sir. The shoes sound very much like this.'

Joseph had guessed as much the moment he opened that parcel. His chest tightened. If it was Laurie's shoe, had it been taken from her dead body? He took out his phone and photographed it. 'I have to go and see Kelly Arthur. We need to know for certain, and she'll be able to tell us.' He stood up. 'Niall, can I leave you to bag and tag this and get it to Seized Property for forensics to collect?'

'Of course. I'll be taking some men from Hob's End to keep obo on this place until we find whoever's doing this. I've arranged for a two-man crew to be here around the clock, just as soon as I close down the cottage. That should put a stop to his comings and goings.' He turned to Richard. 'And if you need help for any reason, they'll be right outside.'

Richard nodded and mumbled his thanks. He was beginning to look worryingly overstressed.

Joseph left the two men and hurried back to the car, where he rang Nikki to tell her of their find and his intention to visit Kelly.

'Forget that, Joseph. I was just going to ring you. We've had a development. First, text the photograph of that shoe to Yvonne. She and Kyle are bringing Kelly Arthur back to the station to see if she can tell us more about Laurie and her social life. They can show her the shoe.'

Nikki sounded tense. 'Okay,' Joseph said, 'doing that now. So, what's occurred?'

'The name Howard is listed on a South African Airways flight from Polokwane to Johannesburg, and then a Virgin Atlantic flight from O.R. Tambo International Airport at Joburg to London Heathrow. He travelled just over three weeks ago.'

'He *is* here!' breathed Joseph.

'But . . .' She seemed to hesitate.

'But what?' he asked impatiently.

'I want you to go back and ask Richard a question, Joseph. This is important.'

'Okay. What?'

'Ask him if Jerrard and Alex look alike, and what the dates on their passports are. Listen, Joseph, the Howard listed on the flight back here was *Jerrard* Howard! We think Alex stole his brother's passport and has been travelling under his name.'

'I'll go and ask him now. I'll ring you back.' Joseph sprinted back to the house.

Richard looked slightly puzzled. 'Well, yes, you can tell they are brothers. When they were kids they deliberately wore their hair differently and made sure not to wear the same type of clothes. Even though there was more than three years between them, they looked remarkably similar.' He gave a small laugh. 'Nothing like me. I was the odd one out. I took after Father, while they favoured our mother.'

Joseph asked about the passports, but Richard had no idea of their dates of issue. He did recall the complicated bureaucratic procedure their relocation to South Africa entailed.

'Mother was born in South Africa and she still has relatives there. That helped. Foreigners can purchase property there and are subject to the same laws as nationals. Mother financed the purchase of a small property for them. Back then, a decent medium-sized home cost in the region of seventy thousand pounds.' Richard didn't seem put out by her generosity. 'I know there was a whole lot of legal stuff relating to Immigration, as well as acquiring permanent resident status, visas, work permits and the like, but Mother would have to explain all that to you. As to their passports, I have no idea. Shall I ring Jerrard?'

'That would help. If you could do that now.' Joseph paused. 'Richard, do you think Alex could impersonate Jerrard well enough to fool the airport authorities?'

'I haven't seen either of them for years, so I can't answer that, Detective Sergeant. All I can say is that when they were younger, they could have accomplished that easily if they wore their hair the same way.'

Joseph went and stood a little apart and rang the station.

'I think it's a possibility, Nikki. Richard said they looked very similar, only their hair was different. He's on the phone now, asking his brother about the passports.'

'Hair can be easily changed, can't it? So we can be pretty certain that we have one very disturbed member of the Howard family in our midst. Wait and see what the other brother says about the passports, then get back here.'

Joseph ended the call and walked back to where Richard was still talking to his brother. 'Could I have a word with him?' he mouthed.

Richard nodded and handed the phone to Joseph, who introduced himself. 'Knowing what your brother has just told you, do you think it's possible that Alex could have used your passport to get out of the country?'

The voice on the other end was clear and Joseph noted the acquired South African twang. Jerrard Howard sounded pretty wrung out. 'I can do better than that, Officer. I'll text a fairly recent photo to Rich's phone. It's just a selfie of the two of us. We do that occasionally for Mother.'

Was there a slight coolness when he mentioned his mother? 'That would be really helpful, thank you.' Joseph handed the phone back and they waited.

Niall had collected the shoe, the ribbon and packaging and the bags of salt, and placed them in individual evidence bags.

While he filled out the paperwork attached to each bag, they heard Richard's phone buzz. He looked rather sadly at the message and handed the phone to Joseph.

At first he wasn't sure about the likeness. He looked closer. Alex had a mop of shaggy dark hair, worn in a casual tousled style. Jerrard's was short and clean cut. It made them look very different. Joseph handed the phone back, asking Richard to forward the message to him.

As soon as it arrived, he phoned a colleague at the station. 'Spooky? Could you do me a favour if I text you a photo?' Spooky could do anything. She'd have no trouble transposing Jerrard's haircut onto the image of Alex.

'I have to get straight back to the office, son,' he said to Niall. 'I'd take the evidence bags for you, so that you can finish off whatever you were doing in Hob's End Copse, but since you packed them, you'll have to sign for them.'

'No worries,' Niall said. 'I'll follow you back to the station and call in on Hob's End Copse on my way home. I just need to get back before dark, to check that they've done a good job on the cottage. Leaving it unattended worries me a bit.'

His words briefly transported Joseph back to their last case. Niall was right to be concerned.

Richard had been looking at a weather app on his phone. 'Another summer storm is forecast for tonight. Early evening until almost dawn, by the look of it.'

'Might save on a few demolition bills,' muttered Niall. 'The fire officer said a hearty push could cause it to collapse, so a full-blown storm could flatten it.'

'And all my crops,' added Richard morosely. 'Many more of these torrential downpours and there will be little wheat left to harvest, let alone the potatoes rotting in the waterlogged ground.' He looked dejected. 'Not the best year for the Sedgebrook Estate.'

And it hadn't ended yet.

'I must go,' Joseph said. 'And don't forget what Niall said — there will be a car out here. If anything worries you, call them in, okay?'

Richard nodded. 'We will. My father should be home late this afternoon. He's been at the college all day, probably just keeping away from everything. He doesn't do stress and he's hopelessly impractical.' He hesitated. 'Not that he doesn't love my mother, he adores her. He just can't get his head around it all, especially that Alex might have murdered that lovely girl.' For a moment, Richard looked totally lost.

Joseph squeezed his arm. 'Hang on in there, Richard. We'll get to the bottom of it all, I promise.'

'And my mother? What on earth is going to happen to her?'

'That I can't tell you,' said Joseph gently. 'It will all come down to the outcome of this investigation. Alex told her he didn't do it. Maybe he's telling the truth. Maybe he simply found that shoe. And maybe Laurie Gately's disappearance has nothing whatsoever to do with him. There are a lot of unanswered questions, which is why we have to find him.'

'And he could be a murderer, which is even harder to consider. Sure, he was wild and played by his own rules, but a killer? A sexual predator? Why did I never get the slightest hint that something was terribly wrong with him?'

Joseph grimaced. 'Probably because of your mother's watchful eye. She never allowed you to see it.' He glanced at Niall, who was looking anxiously at his watch.

'We have to go.'

'Thanks for coming out, I appreciate it.' He turned and walked slowly towards the front door, still stained with the blood of the dead bird.

CHAPTER TWENTY-FOUR

Cat had spent the day staring at a computer screen. Her head was aching, but she swallowed a couple of paracetamols and pressed on. So far, she had identified five men, all of whom had criminal records for some variety of unacceptable sexual behaviour and all had featured in the photographs taken by Vernon Deacon.

'Coincidence, my arse,' she muttered, and picked up the phone. 'Ralph Smith? Ah, Mr Smith, this is Detective Constable Cat Cullen from Greenborough CID. I was wondering if you could spare me a few minutes of your time . . . ?'

A couple of minutes later, she replaced the receiver, a broad grin spread across her face. 'Halle-bloody-luja! Finally! A taker!'

Dave raised an eyebrow.

'I've found someone who's prepared to talk!'

'About?' Dave asked.

'The youth club that Deacon ran.' She stood up and took her jacket from the back of her chair, 'I'm off to Cleveland Road, Dave.'

'Want me to come with you?'

Cat shook her head. 'Nah. Just in case he chickens out. At least we won't both be wasting our time.' She placed a note on his desk. 'This is where I'll be if the boss asks — number seventy-seven, talking to Ralph Smith, whose brother was put away for assault and attempted rape a good few years back. More importantly, he's a former member of Deacon's band of merry perverts.'

'You are doing better than me then. I had a great lead with Georgie Lawson, the best-selling ex-con writer, only to find he's out of the country, on some tropical island spending the royalties from his book deal. Good luck, Catkin.'

* * *

Dave turned back to his screen and sighed. Once upon a time, you found things out by pounding the pavements, talking to people and following leads. You didn't spend your time staring at a screen. Back in the day, coppers suffered from flat feet, fallen arches and policeman's heel from all the walking they did. Now they risked getting piles from too much sitting.

He looked up at the wall clock. Almost four o'clock, time for the afternoon meeting. Then he remembered the new directive. There were to be no more regular meetings unless a major incident made it necessary, and they could be called at any time. Everything was computerised and easily accessible to them all, no matter when their shift started. No more gathering around for briefings, officers were updated at the click of a mouse. Things were changing, even out here in the Fens.

In an hour his shift was due to end. Another day would have passed without finding Laurie Gately. It was looking very bleak for the poor kid. He rallied himself. 'Another hot drink, Harris, and press on. You have very little time left here, so make it count.'

The sarge hurried in, acknowledging Dave with a brief wave, and made for Nikki Galena's office. From the look on his face, something important had occurred. Oh well, they'd tell him when they were ready.

Dave got himself a cup of tea from the machine and settled back to his search. Everyone seemed to believe that Shale had been wrongly convicted. He was beginning to feel that way himself, but he did wonder. Miscarriages of justice on that scale were rare, and Shale was certainly an obsessive, possibly a very dangerous one. To get a verdict of guilty without a body requires very particular circumstantial evidence, which had all been produced at the trial. Dave would have liked to meet Shale face to face and make up his own mind about him.

Dave was trawling back through old history, hunting for minutiae, tiny connections between names considered to be of interest in the matters of Jennifer's death, Laurie's disappearance and the pervert, Vernon Deacon. So far, those damning photos were the only thing connecting any of them, with Deacon the one common denominator. Dave laid out several of the photographs on his desk, wondering how many of those young lads had been infected by Deacon in some way. He looked back at his monitor screen. He was accessing the "old boys" site of a preparatory school just outside Greenborough, where Shale had been sent as a child and had stayed until he was thirteen. Dave was waiting for a list of the pupils. Meanwhile, he thought he would do a little informal ferreting.

It was one of those sites for people trying to find old school friends that they'd lost touch with. People posted photos of themselves, their classmates, sports days or other school functions. Dave wasn't sure what he was looking for, mostly he was just passing time. He found himself looking at a picture of five boys, arms draped around each other's shoulders, the one in the centre holding a rugby ball. Underneath were their names. Dave leaned forward. Screwed up his eyes. It wasn't seeing Patrick Shale that had rung the alarm bells — after all, he knew that Shale had been a pupil there. It was the name Alex Howard that caught his attention. They were school pals? Frowning, he pulled Deacon's photograph towards him. Shale, Howard and another boy at a boating lake. He looked closer and saw that the third boy was in the rugby team too. They were clearly friends. Alex Howard's mother had denied that he knew Shale. How could that be, if they were at school together? And who was boy number three?

Dave printed off the picture, picked up the original photo and stood up. This was one for the boss.

* * *

It was just before five when the doorbell rang.

Marian Harper took a deep breath. *Courage. This is for Carmel.*

She forced a smile onto her face, opened the door and invited him in.

Legs crossed, she sat on the sofa and listened closely to the information he was giving her about probate and bereavement allowance. He certainly knew his stuff. She could tell because she'd settled her own probate months ago and, being an intelligent woman, had sorted the rest as well, with the help of her family solicitor and the government website on death and benefits.

She had chosen her clothes with care, her hair was immaculate and she wore a hint of expensive perfume, just enough to be noticed.

After a suitable interval, she offered him tea and, as expected, he said that would be lovely. He didn't follow her to the kitchen, but she hadn't expected it of him so soon. She returned to the lounge and handed him a bone china cup, her hand lightly brushing his as she did so. She smiled inwardly. Yes, that was definitely a tremor.

She sat back down. 'I can't tell you how much I appreciate your help, Mr Deacon. It's a minefield, people thrusting information at you and at such a terribly traumatic time. It's hard to take everything in, especially when you are feeling so low, and so desperately lonely.' She shook her head sadly and gave a little sigh, supposedly trying to pull herself together.

'Doris tells me you were a military man yourself, Mr Deacon? I thought as much of course. You can always tell.'

'Twenty-two years, Mrs Harper. Royal Artillery.'

She looked at him admiringly, wanting to throw up. Army indeed. 'The army certainly knows how to make a man.' Then, without allowing him time to reply, she added, 'And now you are here, and being such a welcome support, a rock to your neighbours. It's very commendable.'

'It's nothing. I've always tried to help where I can. Military widows have a special place in my heart. They deserve far more support than they receive, so . . .' He smiled at her and gave a little deprecating shrug. 'Anything I can do, just ask.'

Oh, I can think of plenty of things, thought Marian maliciously. 'I will, thank you.'

He placed his cup on the table between them, looked her in the eyes, and said, 'No, it's me who should be thanking you, for approaching me despite the slanders you must have heard about me. I honestly felt like just shutting myself away from everything and everybody, but you've made me realise that I have to tough it out. I've done nothing wrong, so why should I stop being the man I've always been?'

'Oh, I do so agree! It's unbelievable how devious and unkind some people can be!' She looked coyly at him. 'Well, you are always welcome here, Mr Deacon.'

'Vernon. Please call me Vernon.'

'And I'm Marian.'

He left ten minutes later but Marian knew he would be back.

* * *

Cat stood outside 77 Cleveland Road. It was a semi-detached with a single garage, solidly built but in need of a little TLC. Since she and Ben had started house hunting, she had begun to view all properties from the perspective of a potential buyer. 'Concentrate, Cullen!' she told herself. She had been wool-gathering, pondering their eternal dilemma — shall we, shan't we?

'Mr Ralph Smith? DC Cat Cullen. Is this a good time?'

Ralph Smith was a tall, thin man whose rather birdlike air reminded her of a heron.

He led her through to his sitting room. She wasn't sure what she had been expecting but it wasn't this. It was as if she had wandered onto the set of a Poirot film. She gazed around, noting the uplighters, a striking fantail mirror and the vintage patterned wallpaper. The man was obviously very keen on Art Deco. 'It's beautiful,' she said.

'Glad you like it. It's a passion of mine.' He looked around. 'It's a little overpowering for some people, and of course this house is no palace, but I love it.'

'That's what counts, sir. And for the record, I think it's stunning.' She accepted a seat and took out her notebook. 'I appreciate your talking to me, sir. I'm very anxious to find out everything I can about a man named Vernon Deacon and a youth club that he used to run.'

'Vern's Place, that's what they called it,' he said coldly. 'My brother used to go there regularly.' He puffed out his cheeks. 'Look, this is a bit difficult for me . . . I was just about to make some tea, can I interest you in a cup?'

Cat nodded, trying to hide her impatience. She mustn't rush him. He was the only person willing to talk, so she must make sure to go carefully. 'Thanks. Milk, no sugar, please.'

Even the mug was a Clarice Cliff design. Cat was almost afraid to touch it, in case it was an original. Her mother, bless her, had a milk jug and sugar bowl in a similar design. Never used — they were too good for that — just displayed behind the glass of a china cabinet. Memories of her mother flooded her mind and again, Cat had to push away unwanted thoughts. The milk jug and sugar bowl belonged to the mother of her childhood, before her nervous breakdown, as they called them back then. Cat rarely saw even a glimpse of that person now . . .

'Tell me about your brother, sir.'

'It's a short story, Detective, but a painful one. Hughie was younger than me and from a very early age he showed signs of an, er, inappropriate interest in girls. My parents chose to ignore it, and in fact I became the one in the wrong because I refused to let it go. They accused me of bullying him. If someone had listened to me, well, who knows?'

'Where is he now, sir?'

'He's dead, Detective, one on the long list of prisoners that have killed themselves in custody. Do you know, there were 325 recorded deaths in 2018, an increase of ten percent on the year before, and I expect it's gone up again this year.'

This was news to her, both Hughie's death and the figures. 'I'm so very sorry, sir. I thought he was still incarcerated.'

'It happened quite recently, so perhaps the records haven't been updated yet. No matter. If there's anything I can tell you that might stop another young man going down that road, I will be glad to help.'

There was immense sadness in the man's voice. 'It's that youth club we are interested in, and some of the boys who frequented it.'

'I went there once, after Hughie told me about this amazing guy who really understood the kind of problems teenage boys had.' He took a mouthful of tea. 'The thing was, I loved my brother, despite what my parents thought. I looked out for him and tried to guide him as best I could, but I was only two years older than him.' He sighed. 'Anyway, I went to the club to check it out, and it seemed kosher. Table tennis, pool table, soft drinks and tea, crisps, chocolate bars, all very harmless. But after a month or two, Hughie seemed to get rather more secretive, tight-lipped, refusing to answer my questions. I decided to follow him one night and found out that he was not going to the club at all, he was going to this Vern-bloke's home. That worried me so I challenged him on it. He told me to fuck off and get out of his life.' He paused, apologetic. 'Sorry about the language, but those were his words.'

'I've heard worse,' said Cat with a grin. 'I've said worse, if truth be told.'

'I suppose you have.' He gave her a faint smile in return. 'I made enquiries, but as I said, Hughie had clammed up on me. I was only a teenager myself, so I didn't know how to go about finding out what was going on. I just knew that this Vern had a little group of favourites that he took especial interest in.'

'You suspected he was grooming them for sex?' asked Cat.

'Initially, but in fact it wasn't that at all. All teenagers are obsessed with sex to some degree, but Hughie had taken it to another level. And it was getting worse. He tried to keep me out of his room, but I got in anyway. I won't go into detail but, believe me, he was utterly fanatical about women.'

'So what conclusion did you come to?'

'That good old Vern was cultivating their fantasies. I think he was deliberately encouraging their excessive behaviour and getting a kick out of it. All I know was my brother got worse, and he took his fantasies into the real world.' He stared at her. 'Even though I have no proof, I continue to believe that Vernon Deacon was responsible for my brother assaulting and trying to rape a teenage girl, and also for his subsequent death.'

Cat drew the conversation to a close. She needed help with this, it was too complex for her. She'd heard the boss say that Laura Archer, the force psychologist, was calling in at the station later in the afternoon. Maybe, if she got a move on, Laura'd still be there. Cat left the Poirot house, as she now thought of it, with a distinctly unpleasant taste in her mouth.

* * *

By six o'clock, well after the end of the shift, there were people crammed into Nikki's office — too many to seat them all. 'Okay, guys, everyone out to the CID room. Let's give ourselves a bit of space, shall we?' They all gathered in front of the whiteboards.

She scratched her head and looked up at the three boards. 'Things seem to have escalated over the afternoon and I, for one, need to sort it all out in my overloaded brain.' The first board contained what they had on Deacon, the second dealt with the discovery of Jennifer Cowley and the third the disappearance of Laurie Gately. 'It seems to me that Jennifer's death and Laurie going missing have always been interconnected, with Deacon being a completely separate case. Now, we are finding odd pieces of information that relate to all three.' She paused. 'We actually need a fourth board — only we don't have one — that's dedicated to Aurelia Howard and the goings-on at Sedgebrook House. That,' she looked around, 'is central to everything.'

She picked up a marker pen and went to the largest of the boards. She proceeded to draw a line across it, dividing it in two, and drew a circle in the centre of the blank half. This, she labelled, *Sedgebrook*. In a silence broken only by the squeak of the felt pen, she drew a series of lines and arrows radiating from the circle to all their other enquiries. Finally, she stood back and looked at the blank faces around her.

'I see you're all as confused as I am. Joseph, could you give a brief summary of what we know to date?'

Joseph stood up, flipped open his notebook and cleared his throat. 'Right. A previously undiscovered cottage is found at the heart of a place called Hob's End Copse on the Sedgebrook Estate. Concealed inside is a satchel containing photographs of Jennifer Cowley and Laurie Gately. Further investigation produces the body of Jennifer. The man convicted of her murder, Patrick Shale, is now out of jail and still insisting on his innocence. Meanwhile, various threatening items that we believe to be directed at Mrs Aurelia Howard are being left on the doorstep of Sedgebrook House.' He drew a breath.

'A case running in tandem with this is that of Vernon Deacon, a man who allegedly preys on bereaved widows, mainly from military families, in the guise of giving a helping hand concerning their wills, benefits and the like. Our main witness against him dies in an RTC in what have now been confirmed as suspicious circumstances — her car was tampered with. Further investigation into Deacon's background reveals certain unorthodox behaviours involving vulnerable and disturbed youths. Photos found at his place of residence show an affiliation between Deacon, Patrick Shale and also Aurelia Howard's youngest son, Alex, who has since disappeared from South Africa, where he now lives. We believe that he stole his brother Jerrard's passport and has travelled back to London Heathrow under the brother's name.'

Joseph picked up two sheets of paper from the desk and held one of them up. 'A recent selfie taken by Jerrard showing him and his brother Alex together.' He passed this round and held up the second image. 'And this is Spooky's computer-generated likeness of Alex with the same haircut as Jerrard.'

Nikki was pretty sure that Alex, as Jerrard, could have walked through passport control with no trouble at all.

Joseph continued. 'Aurelia Howard then made a shocking confession. Fifteen years ago, she found a woman's shoe in her son Alex's room. It matched the description of the single shoe worn by Jennifer Cowley when her body was discovered. She also admitted that she knew he had dangerous tendencies with regard to young women, and she believed he had killed the girl. He denied this to her, but nevertheless she spirited him and his brother Jerrard — who was to act as a minder — out of the country to South Africa, where she had relatives. We believe he is now back in the UK, harbouring a grudge against his mother for sending him away. We are also concerned that if he did kill Jennifer, he might be the man Laurie went off with after a party. She has not been seen since.' He flopped back down. 'I *think* that's it.'

Nikki nodded. 'We now have something from Cat and Dave to add to all this.' She looked towards Cat. 'You first.'

'After he came out of the army, Deacon ran a youth club for boys. It gained a reputation for being a place where kids could go to offload their problems. I've spoken to a relative of one of these boys, and he believes that Deacon was actively encouraging these kids to explore their fantasies — all for his own enjoyment. He allegedly gathered a core group of kids that he took back to his home — God knows what for, but I intend to find out.'

'Dave?' said Nikki. 'Your story, please.'

Following Cat's lead, he launched straight in. 'It has been noted that Aurelia swore that Alex did not know anyone called Patrick Shale.' He held up his printout of the rugby team photo. 'Proof they were at school together.' He held up the second picture. 'And these two youngsters, plus a third boy also seen in the rugby picture, photographed at a boating lake by Vernon Deacon. They were all in their teens.'

'Now for the hypothesis,' Nikki said. 'This all leads us to suspect that Deacon was deliberately hunting down confused and disturbed boys and adolescents and, not helping them, but influencing them, even inciting them to take their abnormal desires to the next level. He knew Shale, who was obsessed with Jennifer. He knew Alex Howard, whose mother has told us had an aggressive sexual interest in young women, and especially Jennifer. Did Deacon provoke one of them to commit murder?'

There was a low intake of breath.

'Nasty thought, but Deacon's a nasty piece of work.' She turned to Laura Archer, who had been listening to all this with interest. 'Now we need your help, Laura.'

'Happy to, but in what way?'

'We don't understand Vernon Deacon,' Nikki said bluntly. 'Nothing gels. He's a pervert who preys on older women, some of them old enough to be his mother. Why would he also have an interest in cultivating young men, encouraging them to become predators who assault girls?'

Laura said nothing for a few minutes. 'Sometimes human beings don't conform to the stereotypes. They act out of character, threads get interwoven and complicated patterns emerge. I think you might have partly hit the nail on the head when you mentioned Alex's mother. He could have a mother fixation, hence his desire for older women.'

'An Oedipus complex?' asked Joseph.

'I'd need to know more of his family history to say for sure, such as what his relationships within the family unit were like. The Oedipus complex, as described by Sigmund Freud, illustrates a psychological phenomenon, that of small boys' adoration of the mother and the unconscious wish to destroy their rival, the father. It's something that can happen in the course of a boy's growth and development, and is generally worked through until the father becomes a role model, after which the child transfers his desire for his mother to a desire for other women. Although nowadays there is quite a lot of scepticism about Freud's theories, they do contain some truth. If there's a lack of resolution at that point, then problems may begin.'

'So we are thinking he was damaged from childhood?' asked Dave.

'Most likely, Dave. It would be very useful to know more about his immediate family history.' Laura looked over to Cat. 'Did you say he was in the military?'

Cat nodded. 'British army.'

'It would be very interesting to know if there were any "incidents" mentioned in his record, any worrying behaviour.'

'Tough one to follow up, Laura,' Nikki interjected. 'The military are notoriously tight-lipped when it comes to revealing information about their personnel.'

'I might be able to pull a few strings, if we are really desperate,' said Joseph, sounding hesitant. 'I do still have a few contacts left, even if I don't keep in regular touch with them, and Vinnie Silver, my old army mate, is still friendly with some of the guys. It's possible he could make some unofficial enquiries.'

'We'll take you up on that as a last resort, Joseph, but let's see what we can discover from this end first.' Nikki was aware that Joseph harboured bad memories of the army and she didn't want him to have to stir them up again.

'Maybe that's not quite so important right now,' mused Laura. 'Like you, without more evidence I can only make a guess, but I'm pretty sure Deacon is hunting for a mother substitute. I suspect that as a child he harboured an intense desire to take his father's place in the matrimonial bed and now he's searching to realise that with other older women. Or . . .' she frowned, 'and this isn't a nice thought, but possibly his family were incestuous and as a young boy he was heavily involved.'

'Now he wants more of what he perceived to be the norm?' asked Joseph.

'Exactly. Now, put yourself in his shoes for a moment. As you are growing up, you suddenly realise that the kids you know don't do these things, and your family is different from other families. Where do you go to talk it through? Who can you tell? Your teacher? I don't think so! A priest? God forbid! Maybe your father or mother has warned you never to speak of it outside the family. You become anxious, and it festers inside you. Then you grow older. You see your schoolmates all pairing up and talking dirty about girls, but you don't get it. You have desires too, but they are not the same as theirs. You begin to realise that you are not the same as other men. So, what do you do?'

'Hide away.' Dave said. 'Take a job that means you work alone, like a night-watchman or something. You live alone and fantasise about your perfect woman — a woman like your mother.'

'Yes, that's one way a man might deal with it, but don't forget, every night those desires are crowding in on you, festering slowly in your mind. That's a dangerous way of being,' said Laura.

Cat frowned. 'I think he might try to prove that he's normal, on the surface at least, by being one of the lads. Maybe he'd take on a heavily male-dominated career, like the army. All that exercise, the emphasis on physical fitness and the lack of time to ruminate could quell those feelings, hold them at bay.'

'Nicely put, Cat.' Laura nodded. 'Put up a macho front for long enough, and you might just begin to believe that it's the real you. I think maybe you're right, and that's how Deacon lasted so long in the army. Don't forget, too, that back then, women hadn't been incorporated, so there'd be no temptation to seek out an older woman.'

'Then he's back on civvy street,' said Nikki, taking up the thread. 'Surrounded by women — older women — and the longings return. I get all that, but why the kids? Why those disturbed boys?'

'Suppose,' Joseph said thoughtfully, 'that initially he really wanted to help them. He was damaged himself so he knew what they were suffering. They may have had different problems to him but they were still psychosexual. Maybe he remembered how he felt — helpless, and with no one to turn to. Maybe he genuinely wanted to give them somewhere to go where they could talk without fear of censure.'

Again Laura nodded. 'That's very possible. Somehow, in spending so much time with young men brimming over with testosterone and dark fantasies, he got lost. Maybe he began to wonder if society was wrong to vilify people with "different" attitudes to sex. It wasn't his fault that he was the way he was, and maybe he felt the same about those kids.'

'So, rather than point them in the direction of psycho-logical help or counselling, he encouraged them to just be themselves. Act out their fantasies,' said Dave. 'Maybe he saw it as freeing them.'

Nikki sighed loudly. 'I know it's all we've got, but I think we are speculating too much, because there's a damn good chance the scumbag could simply be a depraved, twisted devi-ant with an incurably warped mind who groomed and manip-ulated vulnerable kids who should've had professional help.'

Smiling, Laura threw up her hands. 'Yes, that's a real possibility. He could well be filled with frustration and hate for the whole world and used this little band of easily moulded kids to get a little of his own back.'

'I'm backing that notion,' said Nikki firmly. 'We already know for sure that he's a controlling and devious bastard from the way he's treated those poor bereaved women.'

'*And* from the look on his ugly mug when he was questioned under caution,' added Cat fiercely. 'Supercilious git! He's evil, I know it.'

'And maybe he found a way to permanently dispose of the most dangerous one of them all,' added Yvonne, contributing for the first time. 'If Carmel Brown's car was tampered with, as the forensic crash boys confirm, he's capable of anything.'

Nikki stretched. 'Look, everyone, it's getting late, there's a storm on the way and I need you all here bright and early tomorrow. I suggest we take all of this home with us and sleep on it.' She looked at Laura. 'Have you got a few minutes to spare tomorrow? I badly need to talk to you about Aurelia Howard and her sons, but any more of this psychological stuff tonight and my head will explode.'

'No problem. I'm over here anyway, sitting in on some boring meeting with your ACC about restructuring the assessments for new officers.'

'Sounds riveting.'

Laura rolled her eyes. Nikki smiled to herself. At one time she had been certain that Joseph would fall for those model good looks, the blonde hair and those cornflower blue eyes. How could he not? But apparently Joseph preferred his women to be fiery tempered and distinctly lacking in cover-girl beauty. No accounting for men. Soon after Nikki's burst of insecurity, Laura became the live-in partner of the handsome DI Jackman of Saltern-le-Fen. So now Nikki could simply admire her beauty. 'Thanks, Laura. See you tomorrow, then.'

'Ma'am?'

Yvonne and Kyle were waiting to speak to her, Kyle looking not a little awed at having been present at a CID meeting, albeit an impromptu one.

'That photograph of the shoe that we showed to Kelly Arthur?' Yvonne said. 'She identified it positively as being the same brand and size as the ones that that Laurie was wearing the night she disappeared.'

It was no more than Nikki had already thought, but it felt as if another nail had been hammered into Laurie Gateley's coffin. 'Where is she, Yvonne? How could a sensible girl walk off with a strange man? Where's he taken her?'

'I wish to God I knew, ma'am, but as for sensible, these youngsters are all about excitement and pleasure. They seem to have lost all sense of danger.' Yvonne shook her head. 'I'm just praying that Laurie hasn't found that out the hard way.'

Joseph joined them. 'Sorry to interrupt but, Nikki, I was wondering how you feel about a quick unannounced visit to Patrick Shale on the way home? I thought he might like to see an old photograph of his younger self, taken by the delectable Mr Deacon.'

'Good idea. I'll be very interested to hear what Shale has to say about that man's influence in his early life — if his mother lets us over the doorstep, that is.' Nikki glanced at the clock. 'And a fish and chip supper? There's a wicked chippie in the next village from there.'

'I'm all for that tonight. Shall we go?'

CHAPTER TWENTY-FIVE

Joseph pulled up behind a patrol car that was sitting in a layby in Calthorpe Lane. PCs Ernie Bass and Peter Marsh got out and came over to them.

'Any activity at Willow Lodge, lads?' Joseph asked.

'Nothing, Sarge,' Peter answered. 'Must be the most boring obo I've ever been on. This really is the back of beyond.' Peter was a muscular copper with a shaven head. Nevertheless, Peter Marsh was widely known to be the softest touch in the division. Despite his size and somewhat intimidating appearance, animals, kids and old people seemed to gravitate towards him and his messroom nickname was Marshmallow.

Ernie, his crewmate, was the complete opposite. Unlike Peter, Ernie was skinny, almost emaciated looking, with fine, wispy hair, sharp features and a reputation for being tough as old boots. 'Evening, Sarge.' He looked into the car. 'Evening, ma'am. I've got the log here, but there's precious little on it.' He handed a clipboard to Joseph.

Ernie was right. The only visitors the entire day had been the postman, an Ocado delivery and a window cleaner's van. No one had left Willow Lodge, not even briefly. The only person to actually come and go in the lane had been the owner of a small property a few hundred yards further on, and even he had made only two trips that day.

'I still can't fathom how come none of the press have traced him,' Joseph said.

'They will,' said Ernie grimly. 'Then things are likely to be a whole lot livelier round here.'

'Apparently his mother house-swapped with her step-brother while Patrick was banged up,' said Peter. 'I did a bit of sleuthing myself the other night. This house isn't even in the Shales's name. I don't know any more than that, but my sister lives close to where they lived before and knows the stepbrother quite well. I've asked her to dig the dirt when she sees him next. Might help with something, don't you think?'

Joseph grinned. 'Knowledge is power, Peter. You never know, a trivial bit of info can sometimes turn out to be invaluable.'

'We'd better get moving, Joseph,' said Nikki.

Joseph knew exactly what she was thinking — crispy battered haddock, mushy peas and chunky chips.

'Keep up the good work, lads, we are just making a house call.'

'I'll log you in, Sarge.' Ernie raised an eyebrow. 'It'll pass a few seconds.'

Joseph pulled out of the layby and drove on to Willow Lodge. This time Patrick Shale answered the door, and although he didn't look pleased to see them, he at least invited them in.

'Mother has a migraine. It's the stress.' Shale looked at them accusingly.

'Sorry to hear that, Patrick,' said Joseph evenly. 'We won't keep you long.' He reached into his jacket pocket and took out the copy of Deacon's photograph. 'We are hoping that you might be able to help us.' He unfolded the piece of paper and handed it to Shale. 'The man who took this picture — what can you tell us about him?'

Shale took the image and stared at it for some time. 'Where did you get this?' It was almost a hiss.

'I see you recognise it,' said Nikki, wryly. 'Perhaps it's a good thing your mother's not here right now.'

Shale kept staring at the photograph.

Joseph could almost hear him turning over in his mind what to say to them.

'His name is Vernon Deacon, isn't it?' Nikki prompted.

Shale nodded dumbly.

'Did you ever go to Vern's Place? The youth club,' Joseph enquired. 'Or did you meet him through Alex Howard?'

Shale started at the mention of Alex's name. 'I don't know anyone called Howard.'

'You've got a short memory, Patrick. You went to school with him. You and he were in the same rugby team.' Joseph produced the second picture. 'You look friendly enough to me.'

Shale looked down. 'Oh, him. I'd forgotten him. He wasn't in my form, we just happened to be in the same team, that's all.'

'And many years later you were photographed sitting in the park by the boating lake with him. So frankly, Patrick,' Nikki gave him a knowing smile, 'it's either early onset dementia or you're lying. And I know which one I'd bet on.'

'He wasn't my friend! We just crossed paths because of Deacon, that's all.' He sank down into a chair, waving a hand at the sofa.

Joseph decided to try a different tack. 'Patrick, a lot is coming to light about this man Deacon, and we are starting to believe that he is a very dangerous individual. We are here to talk to you simply because we found this picture, and a lot of others, in his home. This is nothing to do with what you may or may not have done later — it's entirely about Vernon Deacon.'

Nikki added, 'Yes, Patrick, guilty or innocent, we believe that Deacon may have influenced your subsequent actions in some way. Would you tell us about him?'

Patrick Shale got up and made sure that the lounge door was firmly shut. Back in his seat, he closed his eyes and took a

263

couple of deep breaths. 'I did go to the boys' club. I had issues that I desperately wanted to talk to someone about, and a friend suggested Vern's Place.' He swallowed hard. 'You have to appreciate that I was young and terribly confused about my sexual feelings. Vern listened. He didn't judge and he never patronised or criticised. For once, I didn't feel like a freak, not so alone.' He let out a long sigh. 'I thought we were friends. He invited me and a few others to go to his house, have a drink with him, and talk out our problems.' He gave a staccato laugh. 'God, we were a messed-up bunch!'

'He never came on to you in any way, did he?' asked Nikki softly.

'No way! We'd have been out of that door like rats up a drainpipe, all of us. None of us was like that, not the boys and not Vern. He had hang-ups of his own, we all knew that, even if he never talked about them. He showed far too much empathy, he understood our fears too well. He had to have been there himself to make sense of what we were going through.'

'Do you think he was actually trying to help you?' asked Joseph.

'To begin with, yes. Then, over the months, it began to change. Well, hindsight is a wonderful thing, isn't it? Now I can see that he was feeding off us. He was revelling in our fantasies and, fuck, we had fantasies! Every goddamned one of us was screwed up and Vern delved into every nasty, dirty little thought in our heads. I thought about him a lot when I was in prison. I hadn't understood it at the time, but he was like a leech, drawing all the badness to the surface and drinking it in.'

'I'm sorry to ask this,' said Joseph seriously, 'but did he encourage you to act out these fantasies, Patrick?'

There was a long silence, then Shale whispered, 'Yes.'

At last! Then the elation faded. Shale would never testify against Deacon. Joseph was sure of that.

'And Alex Howard?' asked Nikki. 'Do you think he feels the same about Deacon?'

'We lost touch long ago. None of us wanted to meet again and dredge all that up. I have no idea where Alex's life took him. Maybe he found ways to cope with his problems. Maybe he grew out of them, though I doubt that very much. He was as messed up as I was.' He looked directly at Nikki. 'I don't know and I don't care.'

Nikki returned his gaze. 'I'm going to ask you a hypothetical question, Patrick. If, and I only say if, you were wrongly convicted, do you think Alex Howard would have been capable of murdering Jennifer Cowley?'

'By the time Deacon had finished with us?' He gave a bitter laugh. 'Of course he would! We all were. Of the five who were his favourites, every last one of us was ready and willing to show our true colours. By the time we left his house of an evening, we were so hyped up that no pretty young woman would have been safe on the streets. It had to happen one day.'

'Why didn't you mention this at the trial?' asked Joseph

'Come on! Think about it. We were victims. He had us believing all sorts of crap. I was terrified when the real world came down on my head. I was little more than a kid, and a maladjusted one at that.' He stared at his feet. 'Anyway, Deacon had disappeared by then. One day, the club just didn't open, and he was gone.'

'He's back now, Patrick. Not in Greenborough town, but he's around.' Joseph waited for Patrick's reaction.

Several emotions crossed his face, fear being the dominant one. Then Joseph saw anger.

'We are watching him, Patrick, very carefully. We will find a way of stopping him.'

'You can try.' Shale sounded unconvinced. 'But he's a mind-bender.'

Joseph had no intention of sharing any details about Deacon's latest category of victim. All he said was, 'He's changed his MO but he's still a danger to life. He's in our sights, I promise you.'

'If he burned in hell, it wouldn't be enough,' Shale snarled. 'He's pure evil.'

And that from a convicted murderer. Joseph glanced at Nikki and saw the tiny lift of her eyebrow. She too was thinking that it was high time they got Deacon off the streets. He might be older now, but it seemed that he was still a high-risk predator. Joseph recalled the brave woman who had attempted to take him down — Carmel Brown, his last victim.

Shale must have read his mind, because he suddenly said, 'You really must be worried about Deacon to spend all this time on him when you should be out looking for your missing girl. I assume that's why — against our wishes I might add — there is a police car permanently parked down the lane. You still think I've got her ensconced in the airing cupboard? Your officers have already searched the house — that's why mother's in the state she's in — but feel free to double-check.'

'That car is there for your sake as much as ours,' Nikki chipped in tersely. 'It would be better for everyone if you were miles from here. The press are pretty tenacious, you know. I shouldn't think it will be long before you have them ringing your doorbell day and night and stuffing their fluffy mikes through your letterbox.'

Shale didn't answer. Joseph decided that they had got all they came for. 'We'll leave you now, Patrick. We appreciate what you've told us.' He and Nikki stood up.

At the door, Shale said, 'I meant what I said about Deacon being evil. Be careful of him, Sergeant. I don't know what game he's up to now, but people will get hurt, you can be sure of that.'

'They already have been,' Joseph answered soberly, and he and Nikki turned away.

* * *

By the time Niall had signed in the evidence bags and checked into the office to make sure everything was running smoothly, it was growing dark, but not the dark of an early nightfall — dark, ominous storm clouds had gathered above the horizon.

He set off for his last job of the day, ensuring that the boarding up of Hob's End cottage was complete and that the remaining crew were transferred across to Sedgebrook House.

On his way there, he rang Tamsin. 'I could be pretty late, sweetheart. Hope I'm not spoiling dinner?'

Tamsin laughed. 'I've learnt my lesson from past ruined dinners, my darling. I've got us something that won't spoil, don't worry. Just try to get back before the storm breaks — they're warning of thunderstorms and torrential rain for this area. I've already taken Skip for his evening stroll, and then it'll be batten down the hatches.'

'I'll do my best. I'm heading out of Greenborough as we speak.'

He looked at the clock on the dashboard. He needed to get a wriggle on. There were already distant lightning flashes out towards the Wash, and a low rumble of thunder could be heard. Niall put his foot down.

Just as he was approaching Jacob's Fen, his phone rang. 'Sarge! It's Tim out at Hob's End. What's your ETA here?'

'Three minutes. I'm almost there. Is there a problem?'

'Depends how you view my missus going into early labour!' Tim said. 'I promised I'd be there for the birth but we've not quite finished here.'

Niall parked next to the other police car. As soon as he got out, Tim and his crewmate Jilly ran towards him. 'Can we go, Sarge? There's just one door to finish boarding up, then that's the whole place secured.' He looked at him imploringly. 'It's my first kid.'

Niall smiled at him. 'Bugger off, the two of you. I'll finish up here.'

'We've left the boards, nails and the tools by the door. Thanks, Sarge. I'll buy you a pint next week to wet the baby's head.'

Niall grinned. 'Just the one?' As he spoke, there was a loud crack of thunder. 'Jilly, contact the duty sergeant and make sure he knows I want a crew sent out to Sedgebrook House, since you guys won't be able to cover the evening shift.'

'Got it, Sarge.'

Niall pulled on his boots, checked he had a torch and hurried off into the copse.

First, he made sure that what they had done was fully secure, and soon saw that Tim's mind had obviously been elsewhere. Methodically, Niall went over every join, making fast the loose boards and driving home nails.

It was gloomy in the heart of the copse, and creepy. Niall told himself that his sense of foreboding was probably down to knowing that a murder had taken place here. Even so, the sooner he finished the better.

A thin drizzle had started to fall, penetrating the dense foliage and soaking through his clothes. Finally, he reached the last door. He stood looking back at the old cottage. Someone had lived here, it had been their home, and now it was nothing but a death trap and the site of a murder. What a sad end for the old place.

He couldn't resist taking one last look inside before it was sealed up forever.

He pushed open the door, switched on his torch and looked around. The kitchen table was still there, in the centre of the kitchen. It had probably sat in that same place for a century. Overcome with nostalgia, Niall stood and gazed around, lost in thought.

A deafening clap of thunder brought him back to reality. He had work to do, a home to get back to.

He bent down to pick up a piece of timber and something struck him from behind, so hard that he was propelled through the door and into the cottage. Before he could gather himself, he was hit again.

He was vaguely aware of a figure standing over him, holding a length of wood in both hands like a baseball bat. He reached for his radio emergency button, but his hand was knocked away. He felt his bones crack.

Holding one arm up to deflect the blows, he staggered to his feet, hoping to get a grip on his baton and at least try to fight back. With a body slam, his assailant sent him crashing backwards into one of the internal walls.

Through his cry of pain and the growing storm, Niall heard another more ominous rumble. Masonry was crashing around him, battering him and knocking him back to the floor. The cottage was collapsing, falling in on itself, with him inside. With a loud crack, a massive piece of one of the roof struts slid through a gaping hole in the ceiling and fell across his legs.

For a merciful few moments, Niall blacked out.

He came to in darkness and almost unbearable agony. His cry for help emerged as a whisper. His radio was gone. Then he heard it, and knew he was finished. A hammer. Someone was finishing his job, sealing up the cottage, and he was inside.

CHAPTER TWENTY-SIX

Richard Howard pushed the front door shut with his elbow and, cursing, pulled off his rain-sodden jacket. His mother had been distraught because she couldn't find one of the dachshunds so he had been out in the storm hunting for the little dog. When he'd been out long enough to get soaked to the skin, he heard his mother calling from an upstairs window that Rheinhardt had been hiding from the thunder beneath her bed.

Bloody brilliant! Now he would have to go and change.

His evening had not gone well. Ruthie was fretting, increasingly anxious about him staying so long out on Jacob's Fen. His father had phoned and said he was going to stay the night at the college because he was concerned about possible flooding on the roads. His mother was a nervous wreck over the situation with Alex and, as far as Richard could see, the promised police presence was missing too.

Peeling off his wet clothes, he wondered if he should ring DS Easter. The detective had assured him they would have support at Sedgebrook, and he would probably be furious to know that it hadn't materialised. Ironically, it was this that stopped Richard ringing. Maybe there was a genuine reason, and he didn't want to cause some poor bobby to get a dressing down for something that was beyond his control. Given the storm conditions, they were probably overwhelmed with traffic accidents.

He gazed out of the window at the rain-lashed garden and the trees whipping this way and that. The wind was picking up speed with every passing hour. The gale must have reached number nine on the Beaufort scale — *a strong to severe gale, of forty-seven to fifty-four miles per hour. Land conditions, slight structural damage (chimney pots and slates removed).* And it was still building up. He just hoped it wouldn't reach eleven or twelve — *widespread damage* and, finally, *devastation.* He shuddered. Maybe it was all for the best that some poor coppers were not sitting outside in this.

He sat on his bed and towelled his hair dry. He still struggled to absorb the news that Alex had possibly stolen Jerry's passport and come home secretly. What on earth was going on? No matter how hard he tried, he could not imagine Alex having the kind of deep psychiatric problems that had been suggested. Could his mother have been wrong? Alex could have chanced upon that shoe, picked it up after the real murderer dropped it as he dragged the girl towards the copse. Why not? Was his brother out there somewhere on the fen in this terrible storm? So many questions.

Richard pulled on dry clothes and went downstairs to find his mother. He wasn't surprised to find her sitting in the kitchen surrounded by her precious little 'Daksies'. Neither was he surprised to realise that there was no supper prepared. 'I'm going to make an omelette, Mum. I'll make you one too.' It wasn't a question. He whipped up the eggs, speaking softly to her, trying to coax her into talking about Alex, and the things she believed he had been responsible for.

But Aurelia just shook her head. 'Best you don't know, son, not until it's all over.'

'I'm not a kid, Mum. I need to understand.'

'You will, I promise.'

And that was all she'd say.

Finding that the toaster was broken, he recalled his father saying he'd pick up another one at the supermarket close to the college. Richard sighed. Another little thing his father was supposed to have done. He put the slices of bread under the grill.

They ate in silence, listening to the storm and Helmut's whimpers. Richard looked outside, but there was still no sign of a police car in the drive, so he went to his room to ring Ruthie, dismissing her worries about him being in such a remote place, alone with a mother who was the target of some unknown person's twisted hatred. Instead, he voiced his concern for Ruthie's safety, and even tried to joke about the mixed-up family she had got herself involved with.

He hated being apart from her, but after he ended the call, he found himself worrying about Tamsin. She, too, could be out on the fen alone.

He tried to relax, telling himself that was little to fear tonight. No one would be wandering around in this weather. They were all safe.

Maybe he would not have felt like that if he had known that, allowing for the depth of the wall between his bed and the crawl space that ran under the eaves of this part of the house, he was probably around twelve inches away from his brother, and a silent girl.

* * *

Tamsin was really worried now. This was her third call to Niall, and still there was no answer. She looked down at Skipper, who seemed to sense her anxiety and was sticking close to her. 'I shouldn't worry, should I, Fur-face? It's happened before — diverted to an emergency, no time to answer a call. But . . .'

But. Tamsin felt edgier than she could ever remember having been before. She stared out of the window, desperate to see headlights, but there were only shadows. It wasn't yet night, but it could well have been.

Just as she was about to ring off, her call was answered.

'Darling! Are you okay? I'm getting pretty worried, you know.'

There was a noise at the other end of the line, but she couldn't make out the words. A really bad signal? No, it didn't sound like that. 'Niall?'

The noise came again, and her blood ran cold.

'Tam?' The voice was little more than a croak. 'Help me . . .'

'Niall! Where are you? What's happened?' She tried not to panic, but she was already losing the fight.

'Hob's End Cot—'

There was a clattering sound, and the line went dead.

She knew instantly that she would be wasting her time trying again. Instead, she called the station, shouting to the receptionist, 'Officer down! Sergeant Niall Farrow in serious trouble at Hob's End Copse, Jacob's Fen! Call an ambulance and get help to him, now! And, please, for God's sake hurry!'

Tamsin knew that Niall had been out there closing up the crime site. There would be no officers left out there by now. The station was a good distance away, and even if someone happened to be in the area, there was no one closer than she was, and her husband was hurt.

She grabbed the battery-powered storm lantern that they kept by the door in case of power cuts, jammed her feet into her walking boots, cursing as she did, and pulled on a weatherproof jacket. Snatching up her phone and the car keys, she ran out into the driving rain.

She opened the car door and there was Skipper, already in the passenger seat. She hadn't meant him to follow her, but he was a reassuring presence. She hurtled out onto the lane, scattering mud and grass in her wake.

She drove on, admonishing herself to be careful. She would be no help to Niall if she finished up in a ditch. It was hard to see the road through the driving rain. Squinting through the windscreen, she suddenly thought of her father. She fumbled about for her phone and called him. When he started to tell her on no account to go into that dangerous old building, she ended the call. If Niall was there, in need of help, then that was where she was going.

Another thought struck her. Of course! There was another person close by, someone who would help. Richard Howard. Thankfully, he answered and she blurted out what had happened. Without a moment's hesitation, he said, 'I'll just check on Mum, and then I'll be there.'

The drive took only minutes, but on opening the car door she was knocked sideways by the force of the gale. Somehow, she and her dog fought their way to the path leading into the copse.

Inside, Tamsin ran, her lantern swinging wildly, sending shards of light dancing through the wildly thrashing trees. She screamed out his name, but the howling wind snatched the word from her lips.

When she reached the cottage she stopped abruptly, shocked to see how much damage had occurred since she had been here last. Was Niall inside? He could be lying somewhere, injured by falling masonry. While she hesitated, Skipper dashed forward and raced around to the back entrance.

Something told her to follow him. She rounded the corner and found him digging furiously at the base of the back door. She raised the lantern and, to her horror, saw the door was not just closed, it had been boarded up.

There was no way in. She stood, frozen in panic, and then she noticed the kitchen window. It too had been nailed down, but a recent collapse of the brickwork had torn some of the boards away and left the window frame hanging drunkenly at an angle. Tamsin peered in. Barely discernible among the shadows, Niall lay beneath a mass of debris. He wasn't moving. She called out that help was on its way, but there was no sign that he had heard her.

In desperation, she grasped one of the boards and pulled, hoping to make a hole big enough to allow her to squeeze through, but with a piercing squeal, part of the frame slipped down and blocked the gap completely. When she touched it, she realised that the whole wall area was ready to collapse. She dare not take that risk.

It was the door or nothing. Only that way could she drag him out.

She stared at it hopelessly, and then she saw it. A big hammer someone had left lying just beside the step.

She seized hold of it, set down the lantern and using the claw, started to prise the nails and boards from the frame. The job had been done badly, more of a token gesture than a serious attempt to keep anyone out. In no time at all, she had released enough boards to rip the rest away and open the door.

Through the chaos inside, she could see her husband. He was lying still, partly covered with bricks, plaster and some branches and leaves that must have blown in from the collapsed roof.

'Niall! I'm here, I'm here!' She picked her way across the rubble towards him, mindful that a sudden rash move could cause more masonry to fall.

She knelt beside him, feeling the side of his neck for a pulse. Nothing. She gave a sob, moved her shaking finger a little, and found it, thready and weak, but he was alive.

She could hear an ominous groaning coming from the building that seemed to grow louder with every gust of wind. She had to get him out.

'Come on, Tamsin,' she muttered. Everything depended on what she did now.

The first problem was a massive spar that was lying across his legs. She took a deep breath, grasped one end and lifted, groaning with the effort. It was old, solid wood that had supported the building through generations, but she found the strength from somewhere. With a final almighty heave, she had his legs free. But the creaking of the building told her she had very little time to spare.

There was a lot of blood seeping through his uniform trousers. One leg was obviously broken, and his hand appeared to be deformed, the fingers sticking out at impossible angles. 'Later. Think about that later,' she whispered to herself. 'First, get him out. Somehow . . .'

Tamsin pulled the leather belt from her jeans and splinted the broken leg tightly to the one that seemed undamaged. Niall gave a low moan. Tears streamed down her face. 'This will hurt, my darling, but I have to get you out of here, so grit your teeth and try to forgive me.'

She moved round behind him and managed to get her arms underneath his shoulders. She heaved at him until he was half sitting up. He shouted in pain, but she knew she must ignore that. Very, very slowly, she managed to ease him from the rubble. When he was just about clear of it, her strength failed and she was forced to lay him down again. Then Skipper was there, his teeth at the shoulder of Niall's uniform jacket. He dug his heels in and began to drag his master backward. Seeing this, she redoubled her efforts, took the other shoulder and bit by bit they edged him towards the door.

Suddenly, she was not alone. 'Tamsin! It's okay. I've got him!'

The dark shape of Richard Howard stood towering above her. She released her grip and sank to the floor. A picture flashed into her head of the young farmer lifting hay-bales as if they were made of tissue paper. In seconds, he was pulling Niall out through the door.

She staggered to her feet and followed him out. It was almost a relief to feel the rain lash against her skin, washing away the dust and grime.

'We have to get him as far away from here as we dare!' Richard shouted above the noise of the storm. 'But I can't lift him right up, because of that broken leg. Can you support his legs, while I take the weight of his body?'

Together they inched Niall away from the cottage and around to the pathway, lying him down in the most sheltered spot they could find. Almost instantaneously, Tamsin heard another sound, a strange rushing noise, followed by a dull whump.

'It's gone!' Richard shouted.

The chimney stack had finally fallen, having ripped itself clear of the ivy that had held it in position for so long, and had crashed directly into what was left of the cottage.

Tamsin looked back the way they had come. Despite the rain, a great rolling cloud of dust and debris was powering towards them. She threw herself across Niall's body to shield him and felt Richard's weight on top of her. Then they were coughing and choking, wiping the dust and dirt from their filthy faces.

'If ever there was a case of "just in time,"' rasped Richard, 'that was it.'

'If you hadn't arrived when you did . . .'

'And if you hadn't already got him as far as you did,' he added. 'I don't know how you did it!'

'With Skip's help, would you believe.' The dog was lying pressed against Niall, and she saw her husband's good hand come up and jerkily grasp the dog's fur.

'Tamsin! Tamsin!'

Torchlight, bobbing and weaving towards them along the path, and the flashing cobalt blue of the emergency services, blurred in the rain.

Nikki came out of the darkness, and dropped to her knees beside Niall, checking his pulse and then throwing a thick car blanket over him. And then Joseph was holding her, clasped tightly in his arms. No one spoke for a long time.

Suddenly they were surrounded by paramedics and police officers carrying powerful torches. 'Okay, we've got him!' One of the medics seemed to be addressing her. 'What can you tell me?'

She wiped tears from her eyes and, through chattering teeth and spasms of shivering, she explained what had happened and how they'd got him out.

They were joined by a doctor, scrambled from the Greenborough A&E Department. Everyone stood back and watched the ambulance technicians gently place Niall on a spinal board, ready to be carried to the ambulance. Protected from the storm by a large tarpaulin, the doctor and the medical team carried out a hasty assessment.

After what seemed like forever, the doctor told them he was stable enough to move. 'He was briefly conscious,' the doctor said. 'Is one of you called Joseph?'

Her father moved closer. 'Joseph Easter.'

'He kept saying, *Tell Joseph . . . attacked.* 'Just that, nothing else.'

'Attacked?' Joseph looked aghast. 'So it wasn't an accident?'

'I'd say not, although it's difficult to ascertain out here. He has certain injuries that appear to be the result of deliberate blows with a heavy object.' The doctor looked around. 'Sorry, but we really need to get him out of this weather and into hospital.' He glanced at Tamsin. 'You too, I think. We can take you as well.'

'I'll go with Niall, Dad,' she told her father. 'But first I have to tell you that someone boarded up the door with my Niall inside. He left him to die and made sure he couldn't be rescued easily.' Her voice broke. 'Someone tried to kill him.'

Then she was wrapped in a foil blanket and, supported by a strong arm around her, ushered away to safety.

CHAPTER TWENTY-SEVEN

Deep in thought, Vernon Deacon made his way down the close. For the first time, he sensed he had lost control of a situation. He thought he could read people. It was why he was so successful. He always knew when someone was lying, and that people often didn't say what they meant. But for once in his life he was baffled and didn't know what to think.

The fact was that Marian was everything he'd ever dreamed of. It was as if he had idolised some impossibly beautiful movie star for years and come home one evening to find her lying naked on his couch, waiting for him.

He kicked at a loose pebble. If it seems too good to be true, it probably is, he said to himself. But here he was, drawn to her end of the close. She didn't know he was coming, he'd made the decision just minutes ago. He wanted to see her reaction when he reappeared unexpectedly. Maybe then he'd be able to see what she was about.

He reached her garden path and almost faltered, almost turned around and went home. But he went on.

Before he was halfway to her door, it opened. She didn't appear, but he knew she was waiting just inside.

Suddenly he was a little boy again, climbing to the top of the stairs and seeing his mother's bedroom door slowly open, and a hand beckon him inside.

Deacon swallowed. His mother had been a dangerous woman. Probably Marian Harper was dangerous too.

He walked on, went inside and closed the door behind him.

* * *

'I'm going to the hospital, Nikki. I'll follow the ambulance.' Like all of them, Joseph was drenched to the skin. 'I'll put Skipper in my car. He'll be safe with me.'

'Why don't you stop off at the house first, Sergeant? I can find you a dry sweater and you can borrow one of Dad's wax jackets.' Richard was trying to brush wet brick dust from his hair with his hands.

'I'll be okay, thanks all the same.' He stared at Richard. 'What actually happened here?'

Richard told him all he knew. 'But I have no idea who could have been out here in this terrible weather, or why. And why hurt Sergeant Farrow? He was just trying to make the place safe, that's all.'

Nikki, her hair plastered to her head, said, 'Sorry to say this, but I can only think it was Alex, your brother.'

Richard had already wondered about this, but again that brother thing kicked into play. 'He would have no reason to hurt the sergeant, and why should he be here at all? It has to be someone else.'

'We hope so,' said Joseph grimly. 'In any case, I have a lot to thank you for, Richard. If you hadn't got here so quickly I might have lost my daughter and my son-in-law tonight.' He put his hand on Richard's shoulder and squeezed. His voice faltered. 'I don't know what to say to you. I'm indebted to you forever.'

Richard smiled weakly at him. 'Anything I did was nothing. Tamsin did all the heroic stuff. I'll never know how she prised all those boards off that door or managed to lift that roof spar off him. She's amazing.' He shook his head and gave an incredulous laugh. 'When I walked in, there she was, her and her dog, desperately dragging Niall to safety while that blasted, ill-fated cottage was falling to bits around their ears. I'll never forget that sight as long as I live. You have one hell of a brave woman for a daughter, Sergeant Easter.'

They stared at each other for a moment, until Joseph released his grip. 'I have, haven't I? Stubborn as a bloody mule!'

Richard was in danger of caring too much for that brave woman but knew it would be a huge mistake to try and get closer. Tamsin loved Niall Farrow, that was evident.

'Well, for once, Joseph, you can thank your lucky stars that she is so stubborn,' said DI Galena soberly.

The three of them looked back to the pile of rubble that had once been a cottage. The only part recognisable was a small portion of the kitchen. Richard said, 'Oh well, it's just a case of clearing the site now. No demolition team required,'

'This place really isn't lucky, is it?' said Joseph. 'Your mother told me it was built on a ley line. If it was a bad energy ley line, it would attract negativity.'

'My mother and her eccentric beliefs! I—' He stopped. 'Oh my God! I've left Mother alone!'

'Joseph! Go to the hospital!' DI Galena said. 'Be with your family. I'll take a couple of uniforms and go with Richard. Go on. Off with you!'

Joseph hesitated, took a step towards her and then nodded. 'Take care, Nikki. I mean it.' He called Skipper and hurried away.

Richard almost smiled. He'd seen the look that passed between the two detectives. They were more than just work colleagues. Anyhow, it was none of his business. He had to get home.

* * *

Nikki looked around and saw two older PCs watching the ambulance leave with their sergeant inside.

'Rob! Lennie! With me! We need to check out Sedgebrook House. Get in your patrol car, boys, and follow me as fast as you can!'

In minutes, they were turning into the drive of the big old farmhouse. Nikki leapt from her vehicle and crunched across the soaked gravel. Richard was already inside and calling for his mother. No answer came.

They ran from room to room, but it seemed that the only occupants of the house were the three little dachshunds, all safely shut in the kitchen.

'Where is she?' Richard was almost hysterical. 'Oh, what have I done? I should never have left her!'

'Richard, you've just saved two lives,' Nikki said calmly. 'Now, think. Maybe your mother was frightened by the storm and went looking for somewhere she felt safe.'

'Mother is fascinated by storms, Inspector, not frightened. And I can't think of a single reason why she would go out in this deluge.' His eyes widened. 'She's been taken!'

'We can't know that.' Nikki tried to keep her tone reasonable. 'Is her car still here?'

Richard frowned. 'I don't know. She keeps it in the garage. It's her pride and joy.'

Nikki was slightly surprised. Aurelia Howard didn't look like the kind of woman to be enamoured of an inanimate tin box, but then Aurelia was full of surprises.

'I'll go and look.' Richard hurried from the room.

When he was out of earshot, Nikki called to her officers. 'Go over this place from top to bottom, lads. Attics, cupboards, everything. If you don't find anything, start on the sheds, any other outbuildings, the lot.'

They nodded and moved off. 'We'll start at the top and work down,' called back Lennie.

Richard returned, looking even more perplexed. 'It's gone! But where would she go? And why not leave a note for me? She'd know I'd be distraught, what with all the bad stuff going on here.'

Nikki could think of a whole string of reasons, the main one being that she had had no time, or no choice, if she had left under duress. 'Your father? Where is he?'

'At college. He was staying there tonight as the roads are so bad.'

'Could he have rung her? Would she go and collect him?'

'Maybe. She has no qualms about driving in bad weather, though she wouldn't like getting the car dirty.'

'What is this precious car, for heaven's sake?' asked Nikki.

'A Jaguar XJ-S. It was her father's.'

'Ah, I see.' Nikki had done the same thing herself, kept her dad's old car — two of them to be precise. 'Well, the first thing is to contact your father and, without frightening the hell out of him, find out if she's with him. Worst case scenario is that he's unwell and she rushed off forgetting to leave a note.'

Clearly unconvinced, Richard made the call. It was soon ended. 'Did you say there was a Plan B?'

'He's heard nothing?' Nikki asked.

'Nothing at all. He's on his way home, decided to brave the weather.'

'To be honest, Richard, I'm glad. You need some support here.' Events were taking an increasingly sinister turn, and Nikki was worried. 'I know you say your father isn't the most practical person, but you need someone here with you. It works both ways — he's going to need you too, until we find out what's happened.' Nikki rang the station and asked uniform to check all cameras for sightings of the distinctive Jaguar. After that she rang Ben, who was still doing the graveyard shift, and briefed him on the situation, asking him to liaise with uniform and telling him to be ready to join her if necessary. As for Joseph, well, there were times, even in their job, when family came first.

When she'd finished, she said to Richard, 'We need to take a deep breath, and assess the situation. The first thing

283

that strikes me is that there is no mess, no sign of a struggle and as far as I can tell, not a thing is out of place.'

'I know.' Richard sounded totally baffled. 'Even the dogs are all in their beds, with their nightlight plugged in.'

'Which indicates that your mother went of her own volition.' Nikki's mind was beginning to tick over again. 'And I'm betting that she wouldn't let anyone else drive that car.'

'No way,' Richard said. 'She could be pretty unyielding about that. I'd love to drive that beauty, but I've never even been allowed behind the steering wheel.'

'Ma'am?' PC Lennie Jewel stood in the doorway. 'There's something you should see.'

She followed him up the stairs, Richard immediately behind her.

PC Rob Curtis was standing in one of the bedrooms in front of a low door.

'What's that?' asked Nikki.

'The crawl space.' Richard stared at the open door. 'But it's been locked for years. It runs right along this side of the house, under the eaves. We used it for storage to save going up to the loft, and we played in there when we were kids — you know, a secret place to hide from Mum. But squirrels got in and did a lot of damage so Father put poison down and locked it up.'

'Well, someone's unlocked one of the doors,' said Lennie. 'Not this one — the key was still in the lock on this side, but there are two other doors that I can see.' He glanced at Richard. 'And you've had more than squirrels in there recently.' He stood aside for Nikki to see.

'Well, I'm . . .' Nikki took Lennie's torch and shone the beam inside. She saw a sleeping bag, similar to the one from the cottage, blankets, pillows, plastic water bottles and a cardboard box full of biscuits and chocolate bars. 'I think we now know where our elusive mystery man has been hiding — right here in your own home!'

'But . . .' Richard, peering over her shoulder, exclaimed, 'my old room, the one I'm staying in now, is right next to the crawl space, and I haven't heard a thing!'

'Yes, but how often are you in it?' Nikki asked. 'Just to sleep, and change your clothes?'

'True, and I've been late to bed and up early because of the farm, and old houses do creak and groan. Even so . . .' He swallowed. 'It has to be my brother, doesn't it? No one but Alex would know about this place.'

Nikki agreed. 'Richard, how often is the house actually empty?'

'Until the last few days, when Mum has been in most of the time, quite a lot. I'm not here in the daytime, Dad spends his days at the college, or out on field trips, and Mum came and went quite a bit too — shopping, doing research at the college — oh, and working in the garden with Goose.'

Nikki noticed a number of other objects that she was pretty certain had been purloined from the kitchen and one of the bathrooms. There were china plates, a fork and a spoon, a hand towel and a can of deodorant. She pictured a figure slipping out of his hiding place and roaming the house, taking the various items that he needed. 'How many toilets in Sedgebrook House, Richard?' She hadn't noticed any bad smells or bagged up waste material.

He frowned, then said, 'One downstairs, one in the family bathroom, and there are two en-suites, one in the master bedroom where my parents sleep, and another in the guest bedroom. Why?'

'And you are using?'

'The family bathroom. Why?'

'I suggest your uninvited guest has been using the facilities, probably in the guest bedroom.'

He shook his head. 'Unbelievable. So where does this leave us regarding Mother? He's not here now, is he?'

'I think they have to be together, Richard. I would guess that she went willingly, since there's nothing to indicate the contrary.'

'But what for?'

Nikki was asking herself the same question. 'It's no good making endless guesses, we'll never get anywhere. I'm relying on technology to find her car and, depending on what sort of camera picks her up, hopefully see how many occupants it has.' She turned back to her two waiting officers. 'Shut this up again, lads, and stay in situ. I'm calling a SOCO.'

There had to be fingerprints here. They already had that partial print found on the satchel and prints all over the pictures of Jennifer and Laurie. Supposing they matched? She shivered. There would be DNA too, and if it matched that of the family members, then there would be no doubt that Alex Howard had finally come home. He had been twisted and possibly dangerous before he left. What would he be like now?

* * *

Joseph sat in the family waiting room outside A&E, his arm around his daughter's shoulders. After she had been checked over for injuries and had some superficial cuts and bruises tended to, the enormity of what had happened hit her like a runaway truck. She had laid her head against his chest and shivered and sobbed until exhaustion overcame her.

Joseph began to realise how much he had missed by being a soldier on active service in the years when his child was growing up. It was something he would always regret.

One of the nurses was addressing them. 'You can come in now if you would like to. He is conscious, but sleepy from the drugs. Don't expect too much from him yet.'

They followed him into the resus room. All Joseph could think of was that the boy was still alive. They would cope with the rest in good time.

In the room with Niall, they found a baby-faced doctor in a deep purple tunic. 'Mrs Farrow, I'm one of the Emergency Department consultants. We'll be taking him to theatre shortly to sort that leg. It's a compound fracture with a considerable amount of debris in the wound. They will attend to his hand at the same time.' He smiled at her kindly. 'It looks worse than it is, honestly. There are some small fractures, but it's the finger dislocation that makes it look so awful. Is he left or right-handed?'

'Right,' said Tamsin shakily.

'At least it's his left hand that suffered the damage.'

'Is he . . . ? Well, is he okay, apart from the two injuries you mentioned?' asked Joseph. 'He took one hell of a beating, and that's without a building falling on him.'

'He's a tough young man. The scans showed no internal bleeding and no brain or spinal damage, just concussion and very heavy bruising. The worst problem was the shock, and the fact that he was soaking wet. It was not easy to keep him stable, but he's good to go to surgery now.'

Reassured, Joseph left them together and went off to find a drinks machine. He bought himself and Tamsin a hot chocolate and by the time he got back, Niall was being wheeled out to theatre.

Tamsin took her drink greedily. 'I know it's hot in here, but I'm frozen!'

'It's the shock, sweetheart. Let's go back to the relatives' room.'

The place was empty, and after they had sat for a while in silence, sipping their drinks, he said, 'Are you up to telling me everything that happened, Tam? If it's too soon, just say, but we have to try to fathom out what the hell is going on at Sedgebrook, and find whoever hurt Niall.'

Signs of the old Tamsin were already beginning to return. She told him all she knew, but it was little more than what he had already gathered. Joseph was keen to get back out there and join the hunt for the maniac who had tried to kill Niall, but he couldn't leave his daughter. He settled back in his chair to wait for news. It was going to be a long night.

CHAPTER TWENTY-EIGHT

'We've picked up the Jag, ma'am,' said the PC who had been checking traffic cameras.

Nikki's hopes rose, only to be dashed again.

'But now it's gone off the radar completely. Sorry, but we've lost it. We think it took off into the fen villages south of Greenborough, and cameras are few and far between out there. We'll keep vigilant, ma'am. We have cars out that way and everyone's been alerted.'

'Well, there aren't too many XJ-Ss on the road, so keep trying. Any indication of how many people in the car?'

'The camera showed a woman driver, that's all we know.'

Nikki ended the call. It had answered nothing. Hell, she wished Joseph were here! She had grown accustomed to bouncing everything off him, listening to his take on whatever situation they were dealing with. Right now she felt as if she'd been cut adrift, and she was worried sick about Niall. Over the years, he and Tamsin had become her surrogate children. They couldn't even begin to fill the chasm left by the loss of Hannah but having them there certainly helped.

She went to look for Richard and found him wandering aimlessly from room to room, as if, rather half-heartedly, he was looking for clues. 'We have a bit of an impasse until forensics get here.' She looked out of a window and saw more police cars now parked in the drive. 'We have officers all around the house and in the grounds, in case your lodger comes back. We have no proof that he was the person who attempted to kill Sergeant Farrow, so we have to consider that a different killer could be at large and we need to keep you safe.'

He didn't seem to hear. 'Can I go and get a shower, Inspector?'

Nikki had rarely seen a man look more bedraggled and dejected. 'Of course you can. I'll wait here and see your father when he arrives. You need to get some dry clothes on.'

'You look pretty damp yourself, Inspector. Mother might have a sweater that would more or less fit, though you're much slimmer than her.'

'I'm fine, Richard. Sort yourself out. My Gore-Tex kept the worst off me.'

She watched him go. He had been a hero to go into that building and get Niall out and didn't deserve to then come home and find his mother gone.

Nikki went down to the kitchen where the three dachshunds greeted her vociferously. 'It's okay, guys, relax. No one's leaving you.' She sat down at the kitchen table. She needed to ring Joseph and find out how Niall was.

He answered immediately. 'Badly fractured leg and damage to his left hand, but he was lucky, Nikki, so lucky. No internal damage, no head injury. He's in theatre now.'

'And Tamsin?'

'Cuts and bruises, nothing more. And shock of course. She's worried about Skip being left in the car for too long, so she's gone down there now to sit with him for a while.' He laughed. 'Skipper is fine of course, having a nice sleep on my back seat, all wrapped in my tartan car rug and a thermal foil blanket. I took him out for a toilet break a little while back and he hopped back in and nestled down straightaway. It's as if he knows his master is safe now and he can stand down.'

'I reckon a couple of people and a certain canine should be up for a civilian award for bravery,' Nikki said.

289

Joseph's voice dropped to a whisper. 'Oh, Nikki. I keep thinking about what could have happened in that cottage. It makes my blood run cold.'

'But it didn't, Joseph, did it? They are safe, a bit battered maybe, but alive.' She yearned to hold him. 'Right, let me fill you in on what we found when we got to Sedgebrook.'

She gave him the whole story, from finding that Aurelia had disappeared to the mysterious inhabitant of the crawl space.

'Nikki, this is just a supposition, but what if Aurelia knew Alex was there all along? What if she was hiding him? She said herself that he was her responsibility, and she'd protected him before. That would explain the undisturbed house. Maybe he didn't steal those things, maybe she gave them to him?'

Nikki smiled. His mind was working again. She had her Joseph back.

'It's a thought, isn't it? After all, Duncan and Richard were out a lot,' she said. 'Hell, he could have showered and everything. That's a real possibility. And when Richard ran off to help Tamsin, she knew it was getting too dangerous to keep him there, so she put him in the car and took him away.' She paused. 'But I wonder. Could she really have fooled us so successfully? She was so convincing when she confessed to sending her sons away.'

'She fooled her husband and her other son for years, Nikki. You and I, two complete strangers, would have been a pushover.'

'Well, that's given me something to think about. By the way, I think you should bring Tamsin back to Cloud Cottage Farm with you. Get her off Jacob's Fen, it's far too dangerous for her to be there alone.'

'I was going to say the same thing, but are you okay with Skipper coming too?'

She looked down at one of the little dachshunds that had somehow crept up onto her lap. 'Why wouldn't I be? He's welcome. He is a hero, after all.'

'Thanks, Nikki, that's perfect. I appreciate it.'

'Not sure when I'll make it home, I'm waiting on forensics at present.' Nikki tickled the little dachshund's silky ears. 'Poor Richard looks like shit. No way can I walk out before his father gets back. Then I have to go back to the station and tie up with Ben. It could be a late night for both of us.'

Joseph lowered his voice. 'Please go carefully out there, Nikki. I love you, and I couldn't bear to think—'

'Stop right there, buster! I love you too, Joseph Easter, and don't worry, there'll be no heroics from me tonight. All I want to do is get home to you guys.'

As she ended the call, she saw headlights pull around the side of the house and head towards the garage area. Not a Jaguar, this was an Audi. Duncan Howard climbed out, turned his collar up against the rain, and hurried towards the back door.

'DI Galena! I came as quickly as I could, but the roads!' He threw his hands up. 'Flash flooding everywhere.' He tore off his wet jacket. 'Any news of Aurelia?'

'Not yet, sir, although she was seen driving her XJ-S just south of Greenborough.'

'But where on earth was she going?' he murmured.

'I was hoping you might be able to help us there, sir,' said Nikki. 'Is there anywhere in one of the villages that she might go? A close friend, maybe?'

'Oh dear. I'm afraid I don't know much about Aurelia's friends or colleagues, but she's never mentioned anyone in those villages.'

Nikki gave up. He would be no help at all. If it didn't concern lumps of rock or million-year-old fossils, Duncan Howard would be oblivious to its existence.

While they waited for Richard to return, she told Duncan about the crawl space. As she had expected, he was totally at a loss as to what to say. Then she said, 'I hate to ask this, sir, but do you think it's possible that your wife hid your son Alex in the crawl space?'

'No, of course not!' He went slightly red in the face. 'I thought we believed that he meant her harm with all those Wiccan messages, or threats, or whatever they were? Why would she help him?'

'If she happened to find him in the house or the garden and she talked to him, she might have convinced him that she only had his well-being at heart, and so he let her conceal him from us — I mean the police.' It sounded a bit weak, even to her, but they were clutching at straws.

Instead of answering, Duncan Howard opened a cupboard door and took out a brandy bottle and a glass. 'I'm supposing you won't join me?'

Nikki was beginning to feel both the chill from getting so wet earlier, and the shock of seeing their lovely Niall bleeding on that muddy ground. 'You suppose wrong, sir, but just a tiny snifter. It might help warm me up a bit, thank you.'

Duncan reached for another glass and poured her a measure. 'I cannot tell you how sorry I am that my family has caused so much trouble.' He shook his head sadly. 'I must say I don't understand any of it.'

Nikki believed him. It would be hard to make sense of all the secrets and lies that had been fed to him over the years — years he had spent like the proverbial ostrich, head buried deep in the sand. Now the sand had blown away, and Duncan Howard was going to have to open his eyes to what was going on in his family.

'Dad, I'm glad you're home.' Richard stood in the doorway, looking almost overcome with emotion. 'I'm so sorry, Dad. I should never have left her, but—'

'If he hadn't, sir,' Nikki cut in, 'two lives might have been lost. Two young people who happen to be very dear to me. Your son was very brave tonight.'

Unexpectedly, Duncan went to his son and hugged him. 'It's not your fault, son, none of it.'

Duncan was right. Richard was the only one of this troubled family that functioned normally. He worked hard, cared about the land and, unlike the rest of the family, seemed

292

open and honest. Yet he had been made to suffer the distress of watching those closest to him disintegrate.

* * *

At close to nine o'clock, Nikki was surprised and delighted to see a familiar lime green Citroen Dolly draw up outside the house. She hurried out to meet the pathologist and was pleasantly surprised to receive a hug.

'My dear friend! What a day you've had! How are young Niall and the lovely Tamsin, bless them?'

Nikki told him what Joseph had said, and how brave Tamsin had been.

'Ah, you see, it's the lioness and her cub at work again, isn't it? Seeing her beloved injured and helpless like that gave her strength she would not normally possess. Okay, as a scientist I know it's adrenalin, but even so, it takes some doing to lift a roof spar.'

Nikki said, 'Prof, you shouldn't have come out in person. I don't even have a body for you. This is a SOCO's job, not one for an eminent Home Office pathologist.'

'*And* his trusty technician. May I introduce Cardiff Erin!'

Erin climbed out of the passenger side of the little car, exclaiming, 'Are these old bangers actually legal, Inspector Galena? Ain't gonna lie to you, I've never been so shaken up in all my life!'

'Cardinal error number one, Erin Rees! You never, *ever* criticise my Dolly!'

She rolled her eyes. 'As if.'

Nikki felt a little of the strain melt away. This was just what she needed.

'Now, regarding the absence of a body, it's a shame but there you are. We can't have it all. Tonight is a one-off. First,' Rory peered at her over the top of his glasses, 'after hearing what happened to our Sergeant Farrow, we've come as friends to offer you our support. Second, my darling David is away visiting an ailing relative, so I only have a cold bed to look forward to, and, thirdly, there were no SOCOs available.'

'And poor Erin here?' asked Nikki.

Erin pulled a face. 'Apparently, for the duration of my time as Spike's stooge, I have to pledge to be available to work at any time — as long as I'm still breathing, that is.'

Rory was lucky with his young acolytes. After all, working with him had to come as rather a shock to a young intern. He was about as far from the stereotype pathologist as you could get and not everyone would be comfortable with his very particular style.

'Before I forget, Nikki, we are pretty sure that Jennifer Cowley was killed somewhere else and taken to the cottage. We found fibres embedded in what remained of her clothing, and they are definitely from the rough carpet they have in the boots of older model cars. She was transported, I'm certain of it.' He looked around for Erin. 'Now lead on to the crawl space. I can hardly wait to see what I am able to dredge up from my memory about basic evidence retrieval. I'm usually the one barking orders, not grovelling around on hands and knees with a pair of tweezers in person.' He grinned at her. 'Come, Erin. Back to our roots!'

It took around two hours to collect all they needed. Nikki filled the time gleaning more information from Duncan and Richard about the family. She also checked in with Ben, who had nothing new for her, and with Joseph, who was now on his way from Tamsin's place to Cloud Cottage Farm.

She was almost out on her feet by the time Rory finally brought his sample boxes and equipment down the stairs.

'Anything stand out, Rory?' she asked.

'One very important fact, actually.' He paused and for the first time since he arrived, looked almost serious. 'There were *two* people camping in that narrow little space — one male and one very definitely female.'

'What?' Nikki's exhaustion vanished.

Rory held up a plastic screwtop container. 'One very long blonde hair found in the sleeping bag.'

'Oh my God! Laurie has very long blonde hair!'

'In that case, I need something of hers from her home so I can check for a match. Interesting, isn't it?'

Questions were crashing around in Nikki's head. *He brought her here? But how? And why didn't anyone see or hear something? Surely he couldn't have kept her drugged all the time? Unless she couldn't make a noise because she was dead? But surely his mother wouldn't have gone so far as to help him dispose of a body, for God's sake! Think, Galena, this doesn't make sense!*

'I see confusion upon your countenance, divine.' Rory smiled sympathetically. 'Since we won't get a match until tomorrow, I suggest you go home and rest those little grey cells before they implode.'

Having waved Rory and Erin off, Nikki went back inside. 'You will have officers here, inside and outside the house, Mr Howard, and I can only apologise that they didn't come any sooner. I don't know why the crew didn't turn up but I'll find out, I promise.' She pulled on her Gore-Tex jacket. 'Please don't go anywhere near the crawl space, or the guest en-suite. Forensics will be back again tomorrow, so we've taped the doors closed for now. Anything you hear, either from Mrs Howard, or anyone else for that matter, tell the officers on duty here, okay? They will report it in for you.' She looked at the little dogs, all curled up in their comfy beds, and wished she was doing the same. 'I'll see you in the morning. Please try to get some rest. I know that's easier said than done, but do try.'

Finally, she was able to head home to Cloud Cottage Farm. There was nowhere else she would rather be going.

CHAPTER TWENTY-NINE

On the day after the storm, the sun rose in a glorious burst of colour. Joseph looked out to the horizon, into a breath-taking riot of scarlet, vermillion and flame orange, which melted into a purple and pink sky boiling with layers of dense cloud. High above the drama, a clear wash of blue sky heralded a beautiful day to come. 'Looks like an apology, doesn't it?' he said.

'It'll take more than a sky to lift my spirits,' grumbled Nikki.

'Well, I see it as a new day. Just think, those two kids might never have seen all this if things had taken a slightly different turn.'

'You can say that again, Dad.' Looking upwards, Tamsin clipped on Skipper's lead. 'It is breath-taking. What's more, Niall had a good night, all things considered, and the surgeons are happy with the way the op went. Today is going to be full of positive things.'

'Let's hope that extends into our day too,' said Nikki. 'We could do with some positive answers for a start.'

Joseph opened the back of his car and ushered Skipper inside. 'I'll take Tamsin, and we'll see you at the factory.'

'Sure, see you later.'

They drove off down the lane. 'Are you really okay with this, Dad?' Tamsin asked. 'I could easily go home, you know. There's nothing wrong with me, and I'm not worried about being there alone.'

'Sorry, Tam. Let's play this our way until we find out who tried to kill Niall, okay? Come in with me, and once I know what I'm doing today, I'll drop you at the hospital. Neither Nikki nor I want you anywhere near the Sedgebrook Estate until whatever's going on there is sorted out.' He nudged her. 'Humour your old dad?'

She nudged him back. 'If I must.'

They drove on in comfortable silence. After a while, Tamsin said, 'I should find some way to say thank you to Richard Howard. If he hadn't arrived when he did, Dad . . . well, I was drained. I wouldn't have had the strength to get Niall out. Richard was a life saver, literally.'

'We'll think of something, don't worry.' He frowned. The best thing he could do for Richard would be to find his brother and get his mother back, but that was easier said than done. He wondered if there had been any developments overnight, though he doubted it. Someone would have rung them. Where in hell's name had Aurelia gone?

Tamsin brought him back to the present. 'What shall we do about Skip today, Dad?'

'Well, the guys in the back office will definitely want him. Someone is always there and Sheila, our office manager, is crazy about dogs. She'll adore him.'

She squeezed his arm. 'Sounds like it's all worked out. I do appreciate it, honestly. As soon as I'm back from the hospital, I'll take him for a walk.'

Joseph smiled back. 'You just concentrate on your husband, sweetheart. I should think Niall's officers will be happy to take Skip out.'

'You're a great bunch, Dad, all of you.' Her voice faltered. 'I got it wrong, you know. All the years I spent thinking about the police force in such a negative way. I can't believe what a blinkered, ignorant idiot I was. After what happened yesterday, I woke up in the night and thought, I could have died and never told Dad how sorry I was.'

Joseph was lost for words. He dreaded spoiling this moment, the biggest milestone in their whole relationship.

Tamsin saved him. 'Say nothing, Dad. It doesn't need any justifying. I simply wanted you to know that I'm proud to be part of a police family, and deeply ashamed of my old attitudes.'

'I love you, Tam.'

'And I love you too, Dad. Right. Now the slushy bit's over, we can get on with our day.'

He nodded. 'Did you pick up the lunch box I left for you?'

'In my bag. Now don't fuss. I'm hospital visiting, not trekking through Nepal.'

What a daughter. Joseph hoped his pride wouldn't cause his heart to burst.

* * *

Nikki was just taking her jacket off when Cat Cullen rushed up to her.

'Boss! Have you heard?'

'Heard what?' Nikki said.

'Deacon! He's back in the Custody Suite! And this time he's going nowhere!' Cat's eyes were sparkling with excitement.

'Okay, okay. Grab me a coffee and come into the office. I want to know exactly what has happened.' Maybe Tamsin had been right. Having Deacon in custody was definitely a positive. 'Nice way to start the day,' she muttered.

On her desk lay Ben's report on the night shift, but before she could open it, Cat was back, setting down a coffee in front of her.

'From the beginning, Cat. And take it easy.'

Cat perched on the edge of her seat. 'Last night — must have been around midnight — I got a call from Ben asking if

I could come in. A woman had walked into the station asking if we had a Haven Suite, or the equivalent.'

'She'd been raped?' In the Fenlands Constabulary this facility was called the SHASA suite, an acronym for Support and Help after Sexual Assault. It was a referral centre for those who had suffered sexual violence or abuse. It was situated at Greenborough Hospital, but they did have what they called a "comfort room" at the station. It was a comfortable and less formal place, where women, and men, could give evidence with some privacy.

'She claimed to have been seriously sexually assaulted. Apparently the man had attempted to rape her, but she'd fought him off.'

'And this man is Deacon?'

'Absolutely. Then she went into shock, was in a terrible state for a while, and finally said she wanted to talk to me, and only me.' Cat stared at Nikki. 'Naturally, I came over here and — guess what — the woman was Marian Harper.'

After her initial surprise, Nikki wondered where this was going. 'Really?'

'Really.' Cat leaned closer, her elbows resting on Nikki's desk. 'She was still wearing the clothes she'd had on when he attacked her. She had purposely not showered, although she said that was the one thing she really wanted to do, and she swore we would find DNA forensic evidence, his semen, on her. That's why she wanted the Haven Suite. She was insisting on a full examination and that she wanted him arrested.'

'Cat? Isn't this just a bit, how can I put it, coincidental? The same man that attacks and possibly kills your best friend then attacks you?' Nikki stared into her coffee. 'She really knew the procedure, didn't she?'

Cat nodded slowly. 'That's what I thought at first, boss. But now listen to the story she gave me. She had been chatting to one of the residents of Hawthorne Close, Vernon Deacon's next-door neighbour, a Mrs Doris Butters.'

'I met her, a great fan of Deacon's. She insists we are harassing an innocent man.'

'That's her. Marian said Doris had tried to convince her that the police were wrong about the man. His friends in the Close were making a stand and demonstrating their support for him. Marian thought this might be a chance to get a look at the man for herself. She pretended to be convinced, and told Doris that she needed advice on pensions, as her husband had passed away and she wasn't sure about what was available to her. Doris sent Deacon to talk to her.' Cat paused. 'Doris will verify this, by the way. Well, he made three trips to her home. She said that on the first visit he was charming, and very knowledgeable about financial matters and pensions. So too was he on the second visit. So much so that she began to wonder whether the neighbours might not be right, and that Carmel, in her grief, had somehow mis-read his kindness. However, on the third visit — which was last night — he made advances to her, which she adamantly rejected. He then proceeded to assault her. She swears that she thought she could handle him, that she was just trying to get a glimpse of the real Deacon, and whether or not he was capable of hurting Carmel. Well, it backfired on her, badly.'

'I don't believe it,' Nikki exclaimed. 'Never in a month of Sundays would Marian Harper convince herself that her gullible neighbours might be right about Deacon!'

'We have a sworn statement to the contrary,' Cat said. 'Anyway, I then drove her to the hospital, where they called in a special forensics nurse and a trained health worker and we talked further. She was traumatised, boss. She really had believed that she would pick up on any warning signs, but there were none. She said it was like Jekyll and Hyde. Suddenly, he moved in on her.' Cat puffed out her cheeks. 'Her description of what he did is in her statement, and it doesn't make pleasant reading.'

'What did she do, Cat, immediately after this alleged attack?'

'She said he threatened her with all manner of conse-quences if she told anyone what had happened. He said he had very influential friends, even some in the police, and she would be labelled a liar and a troublemaker.' Cat raised an eyebrow. 'Sound familiar?'

All too familiar. Nikki merely nodded.

'Anyway she made sure he was out of sight, then ran next door and told them what had happened. They could see the state she was in, so they offered to take her to the hospital or the police station. She thanked them but said she was so ashamed and embarrassed that she would rather go by herself. And she came here.'

Nikki looked at Cat shrewdly. 'I get the feeling there's a lot more to this, isn't there?'

'Oh, there is. Two things, maybe three. Number one, Deacon was brought in. He rang his solicitor, Mr Supercilious Git Worthington, if you recall him? And, joy of joys, he listened to Vernon's spiel and declined to represent him! The long and short of it was, no way could he get away with using the same defence again. That brief doesn't like backing losers, so Vernon Deacon was ditched. He's accepted the duty solicitor.'

Nikki was starting to see why Cat was sounding so confident that things were working in their favour. In the past, Deacon had relied on Worthington, who knew him well, to get him off. The duty brief would be nowhere near as clued up as her predecessor.

'Wait for it, boss, the best is yet to come. This morning we will be paying a visit to Doris Butters, who will undoubtedly furnish us with a most vital piece of evidence.'

'Get on with it, Cat, and tell me!'

'In a conversation with Marian Harper, and in an attempt to convince her of just how much she liked and trusted Deacon, Doris said, and I quote, *'I would hardly lend dear Mr Deacon my car if I didn't trust him completely, would I?'*

Nikki sat up straight. 'Don't tell me — early morning on the day that Carmel went missing!'

Cat nodded. 'Doris said that he came to see her late one evening and told her that his car wouldn't start. He said he had some urgent paperwork to get to someone a few villages away. They had to be there very early, as the woman was catching an early train to London for a meeting with her solicitor. So, she loaned him her dark blue Ford Focus, a car that Marian believes has a damaged wing mirror.'

'Yes!' Nikki punched the air. 'So, he did know where she lived, and he paid her a call.'

'And then she disappeared. I know it's not enough, but it's another nail in his coffin, isn't it?'

'Oh yes, it sure is.' Her smile faded. 'Can I ask you something, Cat? Strictly between you and me?'

Cat nodded.

'Do you believe Marian Harper's story?'

Cat blinked, all innocent. 'Of course! It's a sworn statement. She's a respectable woman. Why wouldn't I?'

'Because it's a load of bollocks, and you know it.'

Cat gave a low chuckle. 'Yup. I'm pretty sure our Marian has set one humdinger of a honeytrap, but I'm damned if I'm going to try to prove it.' She looked at Nikki eagerly. 'And, whatever, she's bought us some time, hasn't she? He's back in our tender loving care and we are learning new things about his shady past with every hour that passes. I say hats off to Marian. I'm going to use this time as productively as possible. Oh, and I can't wait for his interview this morning. And,' she added, 'the forensic results on Marian. I forgot to tell you, the nurse even believed there were latent fingerprints near her throat. Notoriously difficult to lift, but it's possible.' She stood up. 'I must get moving but before I go, how's Niall?'

'Surgery on his leg went well. We'll know more later today, after Tamsin's seen him.'

'Poor guy,' Cat absentmindedly touched a faint scar that ran down the side of her face. 'I feel for him.'

Cat had been attacked some years ago, and they had feared for her life too. 'I'm sure you do, Cat,' Nikki said, 'more than most.'

'He'll survive. I did, and so will he. He'll be back in no time.'

After she'd gone, Nikki mulled over what Marian Harper had — possibly — orchestrated. Honeytraps, with no support or backup, are one of the most dangerous games to play. *You must really care about your friend, Marian. But if you pull this off, we really will have to have a heart to heart one day.*

'Talking to yourself again?' Joseph was at the doorway, grinning.

'Of course not. I'm talking to my imaginary friend.'

'Well, I wondered if you are free for a campfire meeting? You can bring your friend if you like.'

'As she seems to be talking more sense than anyone, I might just do that. Give us five minutes to read this report from Ben, and we'll be there.'

Joseph backed out, shaking his head. 'No great mind has ever existed without a touch of madness, according to Aristotle.'

'Bugger off, Easter. And take your mate Aristotle with you.'

CHAPTER THIRTY

Cat returned to her workstation and went over Marian Harper's statement again. It was quite shocking, and pretty damning. Deacon's defence had always fallen back on the old "my word against hers," with no supporting evidence, but this time Cat had a feeling there would be evidence, a lot of it. Then he would claim that what had occurred had been consensual, but again she was pretty sure that Marian would be able to convince a jury otherwise. Add that to all the past complaints against Deacon, plus the absence of his old brief, and she could see him sinking slowly into the mire.

She thought back to the previous night and recalled a particularly meaningful look that Marian had given her at one point. Cat had the ability to figure out people very well and she knew she was being asked to let Marian run with this, no matter what. In return, she had given Marian the slightest of nods, affirming an unspoken pact between them.

She knew it was not enough to know that Vernon Deacon had been driving a dark Ford Focus, the same kind of car that had been seen at Honeysuckle Cottage on the morning Carmel disappeared. But it gave her another lead to follow up, and had delivered her some precious time in which to find hard evidence that Deacon was connected to

Carmel's death. Marian was risking everything for her friend, and now it was Cat's turn to put everything she had into helping Marian Harper.

* * *

'Cat? What time is Deacon's interview?' Nikki called across the room.

'Brief will be here at ten thirty, boss.'

'Okay, then come over here and listen in on the camp-fire meeting. I need you to be abreast of what's happening with us, then you can get back to Deacon. Dave will have to alternate between the two investigations, but let him in on this morning's interview as it was his baby from the out-set, even if I need to steal him back afterwards. If DC Sean Pickford is free, use him as well.'

'Understood. Where is Dave, by the way?'

'Seeing if we can pinch Yvonne and Kyle. I need some additional bodies today.' She looked towards the door. 'Ah, right on time, and it looks like he was successful.'

Vonnie and her new crewmate followed Dave in.

When everyone was seated Nikki said, 'Okay, everyone. This won't take long but you need to be updated on last night's incidents, and we need a discussion on how to pro-ceed.' She looked at Joseph. 'Would you please give every-one a brief situation report on what happened to Sergeant Farrow?'

Joseph did so, adding, 'Forensics have the hammer that was used to nail up the door, but we suspect any prints left by the assailant will have been obliterated by Tamsin's, since she used the same tool to rip away the boarding. We will be talking to Niall today to see if he might have caught a glimpse of his attacker. Again it's very doubtful, due to the lack of light in the cottage and the injuries he sustained.'

Nikki thanked him. 'Now, when I arrived at Sedgebrook House, we discovered that Aurelia Howard had vanished, taking her very distinctive car. On examining the house we

305

found a crawl space and evidence that a person or possibly persons unknown had been hiding there. We have reason to believe that this was Alex Howard, possibly with Laurie Gately, although we need forensics to confirm that. We have a strand of blonde hair found in the crawl space, and some items from her home to match it to.' She glanced down at her notes. 'I'm very interested in the time scale here. If we suspect that Alex was the person who attempted to kill Niall, did he have the time to carry out the attack, get back to Sedgebrook House, organise his mother, and maybe an abductee, put the dogs away and take the car?' She pulled a face. 'Frankly I don't think he would have had a hope in hell, but we need to check it carefully. Joseph? What time did we arrive at Hob's End?'

'Around nine forty-five, I think.'

'And Richard Howard had only arrived about another quarter of an hour before we did. Mmm . . . Tamsin thought that she must have spent twenty minutes trying to free Niall from the rubble and drag him towards the door. She had spoken to Niall ten minutes prior to her driving to Hob's End, so let's say five more minutes.'

'But we don't know if Niall had been unconscious, do we? Or how long for,' Joseph added.

'Okay, okay, we can't be accurate but I just need a reference to either put Alex in the frame or look elsewhere.'

'Then let's stick all the times we *do* know into the pot, and see what we come up with,' said Dave.

They spent the next ten minutes listing times of phone calls, distances travelled, arrivals and departures, finally coming up with a rough figure.

'One hour, or thereabouts,' said Nikki, 'to do all the things I mentioned earlier and, remember, he had no car. He would have had to walk or run back to Sedgebrook House in a raging storm.'

'Highly improbable,' said Joseph.

'But not impossible,' added Kyle quietly, 'if he's a fit bloke.'

'And if the mother was working with him, she could have sorted the dogs and got the car out ready for his return. I say it's possible,' said Cat.

Nikki held her hands up. 'Not the answer I wanted to hear, but okay, that places Alex back in the frame. So, moving on. That car. It's a Jaguar XJ-S, deep red, in other words a bloody statement piece of automobile history. A vintage classic. People notice it. So where the hell did it go?'

Yvonne said, 'The duty sergeant has officers out in the three fen villages nearest to where it was caught on camera. They are asking locals and other drivers if they saw it last night.'

'It has to be garaged or hidden somewhere,' said Dave. 'It would have been picked up again if it had returned to a main road. You don't use a car like that if you want to go anywhere undetected, do you?'

'No way. Which makes me think they had no choice.' Nikki recalled that Duncan was at the college, Richard had taken his 4x4 to help Tamsin, so there was only Aurelia's car left at the house.

'Which of the villages are they looking at?' asked Joseph.

'Fentoft, Eaton Eaudyke and Eaton Mere,' said Yvonne. 'The main road forks and leads to those three. After that, there's nothing but farmland, the marsh and the river.' She shrugged. 'Sounds simple enough to get out there and ask questions, but those three villages straggle for miles and miles — a few houses here, a few more half a mile away. Half of the lanes aren't even marked. It's a nightmare to find an address if you are looking for one.'

'And then there are farms, barns, sheds and stables,' added Kyle. 'Hundreds of places to hide a car.'

'They had to be going somewhere in particular,' mused Nikki. 'All those barns and sheds belong to people. You wouldn't just drive into one at random. I think we need to get hold of someone who knows Aurelia's friends better than her husband does. Maybe she has an address or phone book somewhere. Joseph, check that out with the Howards.'

Joseph nodded. 'Will do.'

'I think you should go out to Jacob's Fen when you've taken Tamsin to the hospital. Maybe Richard knows more about his mother than Duncan does. I'm sure she had a definite destination in mind when she drove off last night.' She narrowed her eyes. 'Which could mean that she phoned ahead to whoever she was going to, telling them to expect her. Check the home phone logs, Joseph, and look for calls made between nine and ten o'clock, give or take.'

'Good point. Actually, could I get away now and sort Tamsin out? Then I'll go on to Sedgebrook.'

'Yes. I think we're done here anyway. And, Cat, are you okay with interviewing Deacon this time?' Knowing what Cat felt about Carmel Brown, Nikki wasn't sure if putting her in a small room with Carmel's possible killer was a wise move.

'I'm good, ma'am. And I know what you're thinking, but just knowing that we might be on the verge of taking him down for something even worse than sexual assault means I'll hold it together.' She gave Nikki a cheeky smile. 'And I'm hardly going to cock up Poirot's final case, am I?' She nodded towards Dave.

Nikki grinned. 'I forgot about that. Oh well, the very best of luck. Take Poirot with you and get yourselves ready.'

She turned to Yvonne and Kyle. 'Would you two take a trip over to see Professor Rory Wilkinson for me? Ask him for whatever he has for us, anything at all — on Laurie Gately, Vernon Deacon, the Howards or Niall's attacker. Even the smallest thing might help.'

Nikki went back to her office and the overnight report from Ben. The third young man in Deacon's pictures had been identified as Josh Caley-Smithers, and Ben was pretty certain he had been one of Deacon's special boys at the youth club known as Vern's Place. He'd checked as far as he could and he was sure the man was still in the area. Not in Greenborough itself, but somewhere not too far away, and indications were that he had been a close friend of Patrick Shale.

Nikki had nothing to do until she either got some forensics back, or Joseph returned from Sedgebrook, which could be a while. 'Okay, Patrick Shale,' she muttered, 'maybe I'll drop by and ask why you forgot to mention an old friend who was one of Vern's nasty little gang.' There was an outside chance that if Josh Hyphen Whassaname had overcome his teenage problems and made a decent life for himself, he might be prepared to testify against Deacon. That would really make her day a positive one!

'I'm going out for half an hour, Sheila,' she told her office manager. 'I'll be at Patrick Shale's place, so ring my mobile if I'm needed urgently.'

For a while they had been without Sheila Robbins, due to a health problem, and now she was back, Nikki realised how much she had been missed. Sheila was a rock, one of those sensible, unflappable people who can field several calls at once, keeping all the plates spinning without breaking a sweat.

There was little traffic on the roads, and soon Nikki was drawing up behind the ubiquitous patrol car. Yet again it was PCs Ernie Bass and Peter Marsh who had drawn the short straw.

'Hello, Inspector.' Peter stretched and yawned. 'Welcome back to limbo.'

'Still no action, lads?'

'If you told me they'd moved out while we weren't looking, I'd believe you,' grumbled Ernie.

'Any news on the sarge, ma'am?' asked Peter Marsh.

'Not recently, but we know the operation on his leg was successful, and his fingers are now all pointing in the same direction, which is a definite improvement on before.'

'He's a damned good skipper, so God help whoever did that to him if we get our hands on the bastard.'

'I feel the same way.' She looked across towards Willow Lodge. 'Oh well. I have a few questions for Mr Shale, but I won't be long.'

'No DS Easter?' Ernie said rather anxiously. 'Perhaps Pete or me should go in with you?'

'Thank you, Ernie but I'll be okay. If I'm not out in fifteen minutes, you can always come and get me.'

She drove on down the lane and into the driveway. As usual, Shale's car was standing outside the front door. From the leaves covering the roof and bonnet, it was clear that it hadn't moved in days.

Shale answered the door, looking furious. 'I think Mother's right about you harassing me.'

'Not you, Patrick. I have a few more questions about your old buddy Deacon.'

'Deacon's no buddy of mine,' he growled.

'Do we have to talk on the doorstep, Patrick?'

Without a word he turned his back and marched into the lounge.

'No mother again? How's her migraine?' Nikki enquired.

'Worse, thanks to all this fiasco. Her bad ones sometimes last for days. But what do you care about that? Just ask your questions and leave me alone.'

Nikki sat down, while Shale paced the room restlessly. 'Why didn't you mention Josh when I showed you those photographs on my last visit? He was with you in both pictures, and he was a close friend, but you didn't mention him at all. Now I want to know more about him — where he lives for one thing.'

Various emotions fought for dominance on Patrick's face. 'You seem to forget that I've been incarcerated at Her Majesty's pleasure for a decade and a half, so forgive me for not being totally up to date on the whereabouts of my old school chums.'

Nikki thought he did sarcasm rather well. 'You might have remained in touch. There are such things as visiting orders, telephones and pen and paper.'

The anger seemed to dissipate, and Patrick sagged. 'I wanted to keep Josh out of this. He got help, the right kind, and he tried to get help for me, but by then Deacon was in my blood and I was having none of it.' He sighed. 'Josh is married with two kids and a stable job. Now do you see why I didn't mention him?'

'I did wonder if that was the case. But I have to speak to him, Patrick. I'll be discreet, I promise. Do you have his address?'

'He lives in Holbeck. I honestly don't have an address, but I know he dropped the double-barrelled surname. He's now plain Josh Smithers and runs a garden maintenance and landscaping business there. I think it's called Father Earth, or something droll like that.'

'I appreciate that, Patrick. Thank you.' She stood up, looking hard at the thin, pale man. 'I have to take Deacon down. He's out of control, and he's dangerous.'

'He was always dangerous, Inspector.'

Before she could stop herself, Nikki said, 'Would you testify against him?'

'You're joking!'

'No, I'm desperate. I need to put an end to his vile and dangerous games. He can't go on ruining people's lives.'

But a shutter had come down. 'I think it's time you left, Inspector.'

Nikki let herself out.

She stopped at the patrol car again. 'Mother has a migraine and Shale is so pale he looks as if he died in the night. They've battened down the hatches.'

'Oh well, another boring shift for us. Even the neighbour who comes and goes never stops for a chat. Certainly never thinks to offer us a cuppa, miserable bugger.'

'The joys of being on obo. Have fun, guys.'

Back at the station, Cat and Dave had suspended the interview so that Deacon could talk to his solicitor and they could grab a coffee.

Cat waved to Nikki. 'If it wasn't so bloody serious, it would be funny.'

Dave nodded furiously. 'This Deacon is a very different bloke to the one who was in here last time. He's outraged, spitting tacks and swearing it was consensual, but even the brief seems to think that his continual protestations of being some vindictive women's innocent victim is wearing thin.'

'He's rattled, boss, and very angry.' Cat was suddenly serious. 'We need to gather enough evidence to make sure he doesn't get out on bail again. If not, I would not want to be Marian Harper.'

Dave added, 'I get the feeling that whatever went on between them triggered something in Deacon. He's acting as if he's been betrayed, if you get my meaning. I think she hurt him.'

'As in, he really liked Marian? That she wasn't just prey?' Nikki asked.

Cat sniffed. 'I'm no shrink, boss, but I'd say it's even deeper than that. Why don't you go into the viewing room and see for yourself? We're just finishing our drinks and then we'll be going back in.'

'Maybe I'll do that. So, let me get this straight, he's not denying they had a "sexual encounter," shall we say, but he's saying she consented to it?'

'Yes, but it's different to last time. Then, he was arrogant, supercilious, disparaging about the women involved — he was putting on this injured air and making them out be unreliable and flaky witnesses. Dave's right. It's like two different people. Last time he was in control, and he and his pompous brief knew he would walk. This time he's fighting, and he knows it could be a losing battle.'

'Do you want us to talk to him about the Ford Focus, boss?' asked Dave, throwing his paper cup in a nearby bin.

'No, leave that for now. Just concentrate on Marian Harper's allegation.'

Before Dave could answer, the duty sergeant approached. 'DI Galena, sorry to interrupt but you have a visitor wants to speak to you and DS Easter immediately.'

Nikki began to remonstrate. Didn't he know that *no one* waltzed in and demanded to see her like that?

Knowing his DI of old, the sergeant threw her an amused smile. 'This one is different. She arrived in a red Jag, with half the county's traffic cars on her tail.'

'Aurelia Howard!'

'The very same.'

Nikki pulled out her mobile. 'Joseph! Get yourself back here, fast!'

CHAPTER THIRTY-ONE

Nikki would have preferred to speak to Aurelia in her office, but she decided on an interview room. This needed recording. She led her into the room and asked a constable to get them both a hot drink.

'We are waiting for DS Easter, Mrs Howard. He will be here very shortly. He was with your son, Richard, and I told him not to say that you are here until we have spoken to you. Frankly, I think your family's patience is just about exhausted by now.'

Aurelia gave her a rueful smile. 'Wait until you hear what I have to tell you before you judge me, Inspector Galena. As I see it, I had very little choice.'

Okay, fair enough. It was not Nikki's place to make judgements before she had all the facts. 'I'm sorry. But seeing them so distraught last night — well, it was very upsetting.'

'There was no time for niceties. And they will understand when they hear what has happened.'

Nikki wasn't so sure.

Not long afterwards, she heard Joseph's familiar tread outside in the corridor. He came in and sat down, as surprised as Nikki had been to see Aurelia.

Nikki switched on the tape and went through the introductory rigmarole. She sat back and regarded Aurelia. 'Where did you go when you left Sedgebrook House last night, Mrs Howard? It's not very sensible to do a disappearing act when you are on bail, is it?'

'Yes, yes, all that can come later, Detectives. The first thing I have to tell you is that Laurie Gately is safe and well. She is being looked after by someone who would never hurt her. Never.'

'Are you talking about your son Alex, Mrs Howard?' asked Nikki.

Aurelia closed her eyes for a moment. 'My son wants to speak to you in person.'

'Then why isn't he here with you?' Joseph asked gently.

'Because he is terrified. He is in a very dangerous situation. It relates to events that happened a very long time ago, but which have resurfaced. Lives are at stake, Detectives.' She shook her head. 'It sounds as though I'm being melodramatic but believe me, I'm not. It's real and very frightening.'

Nikki took a deep breath. It looked as though she was going to have to allow Aurelia to explain in her own way, without any prompting from them. 'Okay, what do you want from us?'

'To come with me and talk to my son. Then you must take Laurie to a place of safety. Someone wants to hurt her, and if he finds her, he will do just that. And then he'll kill her.'

'Surely, if you know who this dangerous man is, it would be better for us to just pick him up and arrest him?' Joseph said reasonably.

Aurelia gave a harsh laugh. 'It would be, if we knew who he was.' She drummed her fingers on the table. 'Look, my son knows more than I do. Please come with me? Just the pair of you. I've told him you are decent people who will listen and not jump to wrong conclusions. Will you talk to him?'

Nikki looked at Joseph. They both knew that it was irregular, but then so was the whole case. If, when they got

315

there, they felt uneasy, they could arrest both mother and son and be done with it. Joseph gave her a slight nod. 'Interview terminated at ten fifty-five hours.'

* * *

Further down the corridor, Cat was wishing that the boss had been able to watch them interview Deacon. During the break, he had flown into a rage and dismissed the duty solicitor. While he sought out one that could do a decent job, he said, he would defend himself.

Following that, he had resorted to silence, or the occasional, 'No comment.'

He was unravelling, but even so, she couldn't afford to drop her guard for an instant. He was like an animal backed into a corner, fighting for his life. After yet another lengthy silence, she suspended the interview.

As she and Dave made their way back to the CID room, she saw Yvonne go in ahead of them.

'Any forensics that could help me with Deacon, Vonnie?' she called out.

Yvonne handed her a sheet of paper. 'Just a prelim report, more by way of a heads up than anything else.'

There was a message for her in Rory's elegant script. *Hang onto him tightly, dear Cat! The forensic nurse at the SHASA Centre took enough swabs to keep us in business for days, but I prioritised the DNA samples, and they match Deacon. As far as whodunnit is concerned, case closed, but of course you will have to prove that she wasn't a willing participant. I'm afraid the rest of the results will take a few days. Sayonara sweetie-pie. Rory*

She passed the message to Dave. 'It's another step forward, but we've still got some work to do, and I can hear that clock ticking.'

'The boss handed me this before she dashed off. Told me to do a very diplomatic interview — you, know eggshells and kid gloves and all that.'

Cat squinted at the name. 'Josh Smithers? Who's he?'

'One of Deacon's special boys, but apparently he's the one that got away and made good.'

Cat understood. They needed a witness to stand up and be counted, someone brave enough to tell the truth about what Deacon did to a group of vulnerable and impressionable kids. 'Do this one alone, Dave. You have a lovely way with you. I'd probably yell at him.'

'No problem.' He gave her a mock salute. 'See you later. Holbeck, here I come.'

* * *

They took Joseph's vehicle, leaving the Jaguar in the car park, surrounded by drooling police officers.

It was a bizarre journey. A million questions crowded in on them, but, other than Aurelia giving directions, no one spoke.

Aurelia had made it clear that it was her son's story to tell. Only when he was done with his story would she give them her own.

All Nikki wanted was to see Laurie Gately safe and unharmed. Then they could direct all their energies towards apprehending whoever had tried to kill Niall Farrow. As they had suspected, Aurelia was directing them to the small village of Eaton Eaudyke. They were now into territory that Nikki barely knew and she began to feel slightly uneasy. These small hamlet-like clusters of houses and cottages were scattered across miles of empty farmland criss-crossed with tracks that ran nowhere. Though only a few miles from Greenborough, it was another world.

'At the junction by that pumping station, turn right along the towpath to the drain.'

Nikki stared down the long straight waterway and wondered where on earth it led. Joseph pulled onto the track that ran alongside the drain. Ahead of them they could see a few scattered buildings, often surrounded by trees, walls and high fences that acted as wind breaks. It was hard to know if these were residences, farmhouses or barns. He drove slowly. The uneven surface of the dirt road crunched beneath his tyres.

'Bet your XJ-S liked this,' muttered Nikki.'

'It wouldn't have been my first choice, no, but it was certainly the safest for my son — and for Laurie.' Aurelia looked out of the window. 'It's the next property along. It has wrought-iron gates. Sound your horn and someone will open them.'

'What is this place?' asked Nikki.

Unexpectedly, it was Joseph who answered. 'It's a retreat.'

'Well, well!' Aurelia said. 'You are full of surprises, Detective Easter.'

'Isn't he just! How on earth do you know that?' Nikki asked.

'That case I told you about involving a Wiccan woman? She used to come here. She recommended I try it too. If I remember rightly, it's a healing sanctuary.'

Nikki wondered briefly if Joseph had ever actually stayed here. It wouldn't have surprised her.

'Some friends of mine run it,' said Aurelia. 'I met them years ago, when I was studying pagan beliefs, and we have remained close ever since. As soon as I told them my family was in terrible trouble, they offered to help.'

'I should have thought of this place before. I knew Eaton Eaudyke rang a bell, but I couldn't place it,' murmured Joseph, pulling into an open area in front of two high gates. He sounded the horn.

Nikki saw a large sign that read "Spring Haven Retreat." The gates opened silently and Joseph slowly drove inside.

The main house was a rambling old property with verandas and gables, rather like an American Colonial style house, definitely not your typical Fenland residence. It was surrounded by a scattering of chalets, cabins, yurts and covered outdoor areas, all set in a large natural garden filled with trees, ponds and flowerbeds.

The beauty of the place impressed even prosaic Nikki. 'Who'd have thought?' she whispered.

Seeing a car park behind a walled area, Joseph pulled in and turned off the engine. They got out slowly, looking around them.

'They are waiting for us,' Aurelia was already hurrying towards the house, and they followed her up the steps and in through a pair of lovely stained-glass double doors.

Two people, both tall and willowy, were standing inside, apparently ready to welcome them in.

Aurelia hugged them and turned back to Nikki and Joseph. 'My dear friends, Desmond and Brianna.'

Joseph held out his hand. 'DS Joseph Easter. Very pleased to meet you. And this is Detective Inspector Nikki Galena.'

Nikki was a little surprised by how ordinary they looked. She hadn't quite expected black capes and pointy hats but she also hadn't expected cotton sweaters, check shirts and jeans.

'Is everything alright here?' Aurelia asked them.

'They are in the quiet room. Maybe you'd like to join them. No one will interrupt you.' Brianna smiled at Nikki. 'I'm sure you'd like some tea?'

Nikki said she would, hoping it wouldn't turn out to be some herbal concoction made of twigs and other stuff gathered from the forest floor.

'This way,' said Aurelia. 'Now you'll get your answers, DI Galena.'

Nikki drew in a deep breath and followed Aurelia into the room.

The first thing she saw was a teenager with long blonde hair, her features straight off the CID room's whiteboard.

'Laurie?' That single word contained a wealth of emotion, mostly relief. 'You have no idea how pleased we are to see you.' It was all Nikki could do not to take the girl into her arms. 'Are you alright? Not harmed in any way?'

'I'm fine, honestly.' Laurie glanced at the only other occupant of the room. 'You can thank him for my being here. If he hadn't found me, you might have been dragging my body from the marsh.'

Nikki and Joseph looked at the man, who was indeed very much like the passport photo. It had to be . . .

Aurelia went across and put her arm through his. 'Detectives, please meet my son — Jerrard.'

Neither Nikki nor Joseph spoke for a moment. Jerrard?

'Yes.' He looked at them with a rather sheepish grin. 'When Richard checks his monthly phone bill, he'll find that all his calls to me in, er, South Africa are charged as local. Including the one when I spoke to you, Sergeant Easter. I apologise for the deception.'

'I think we need to talk, don't you?' said Joseph grimly.

A separate area of the room contained six soft chairs arranged in a semi-circle. They sat down and looked at each other in silence for a few moments.

'We had been expecting to meet Alex. It's a bit of a surprise to see you here, Jerrard,' said Joseph. 'Is he here too? Or did you come alone?'

Jerry reached for his mother, who was sitting beside him, and gently touched her hand. 'Detectives, Alex is dead. He was murdered in Venda.'

Nikki exhaled. 'We need to hear the whole story, Jerrard. From the beginning.'

Proceedings were briefly interrupted while Brianna came in with a tray of tea. 'Anything you need, just call me.' She left, closing the door softly behind her.

When they each had a cup, they sat back and looked towards Jerrard.

Nikki noted that he had a rugged outdoorsy complexion and had acquired a slight South African accent. He looked nothing like Richard but closely resembled his mother.

'I hardly know where to start. I guess Mother will have told you the reason why we went to South Africa, so I'll take up the story from there.' He stared at the floor for a while. 'At first it was very difficult, we were both all over the place. Alex was still declaring he was innocent of Jennifer's murder, swearing that Mother had got it wrong. I hated her then.' He looked at her apologetically. 'Sorry, but even though I had agreed to go, in my heart I bitterly resented having been taken away from the farm and from Richard. Still, after a while we kind of settled. We had good jobs and we both took up crewing for a local yacht owner in our spare time. Alex even started doing extreme sports, like fly-boarding and skydiving, which really helped him with his other problems.' He looked from Nikki to Joseph. 'You know about those?'

Nikki nodded.

'It must have taken three years for him to trust me enough to begin talking to me, and it took forever to get him to tell me what really happened with Jennifer Cowley. Even then, he didn't tell me everything. That's why I'm in the situation I'm in now.' Jerrard bit at the side of his thumb and looked rather sadly at his mother. 'He didn't kill her. Mum got it wrong, understandably so. Nevertheless, he *was* involved, so maybe it was all for the best that he went away.'

Nikki wondered if he was saying that to make his mother feel better.

'He told me that ever since he was a boy, he had known that he had an abnormal interest in girls and their, er, anatomy.' He glanced across to Laurie. 'Sorry, but this has to be said. I hope it doesn't embarrass you.'

Laurie smiled at him. 'I'm not very old, but I'm no virgin either.'

Having heard about the antics of Laurie's best friend Kelly, Nikki could well believe it.

'He told me that when he was a teenager, he was frightened that he would go too far one day and he started to avoid being around pretty girls. Then he joined a boys' club.'

'Vern's Place.' Joseph's tone was hard. 'Run by Vernon Deacon, a supposed philanthropist and volunteer helper of boys with sexual problems.'

'The same. And that was when things started to go horribly wrong. He wouldn't tell me exactly what happened at that time, only that there were five boys who Deacon chose to "befriend." Alex was one of them.'

'Did he give you any names?' asked Nikki.

'No. But he said there was one who was far worse than the others. Vern used to spend an awful lot of time with him. I got the impression that he showed them videos — pornography, and other bad stuff from what we now call the Dark Web. Things disturbed boys should never be watching. Then he used to set them dares.' He sighed. 'Teenage boys can be very competitive, and Alex was no exception, apparently. He said that the one thing Vern liked most was getting them to take selfies performing obscene acts. He had an old-style camera phone. Alex told me that while he was out looking to set up one of Vern's dares, he met Jennifer, and for the first time he felt differently about a girl. He really liked her, and although he still had some of the old urges, he never did anything out of line with her. He became quite infatuated, almost to the point of stalking her, but he never made it obvious. He was scared of asking her out, in case his problem reared its ugly head again.' Jerrard stopped and drank some tea.

Nikki was growing impatient.

'Thing was,' said Jerrard, 'he wasn't the only one of the group who fancied Jennifer, two others did as well. And one of his rivals was not as "noble" as Alex. One of them was keen to show his hero Vern exactly what he was capable of, and things got terribly out of hand. This boy got carried away and finished up strangling Jennifer. When he realised that she was dead, he wrapped her in a duvet and put her in his car. Not knowing what to do with her, he rang Alex, saying he had a "bit of bother" and needed some help. When my brother got there, the boy threatened him, saying that if he didn't help him dispose of the body, he'd send his parents some indecent photos that he had of Alex. He also reminded Alex that he had admitted to being obsessed with Jennifer and had taken secret photos of her, and he would make sure the police knew about it.' He hung his head. 'Alex helped him, not knowing what else to do. He had always known about the Hob's End cottage, and they took her there. As they hid her body, he saw the other boy take an earring and put it in his pocket, saying it was "a souvenir of pretty Jennifer." That was when Alex made his second stupid mistake.'

'He took her shoe, as a memento of the girl he cared about,' said Joseph gravely.

'He did — the idiot! Still, he was little more than a kid, and he was terrified of being exposed as a pervert, or even a killer.' He looked across to his mother. 'And so we were rushed off to South Africa, courtesy of Mother.'

Aurelia, who had been silent throughout this exposition, admitted that she already knew from Jerrard that she had made a mistake in believing her youngest child was a murderer. However, she was not sorry to have sent him away. 'At least I spared him being a suspect. I doubt the boy that killed that girl really had photos of Alex. There wasn't the technology back then, and those young men could not have afforded camera phones of their own. I expect they just used that beast Deacon's.'

'And in retrospect,' said Jerrard, 'Alex said he was always very careful not to show Jennifer too much attention. If he'd been thinking more clearly, he would have known that the threats were empty ones.'

'You do stupid things when you are frightened,' said Joseph. 'And as you say, he was little older than a messed-up teenager.'

Jerrard finished his tea, gathering his thoughts before he went on with his story. What followed was pathetically ironic. 'Earlier this year, Alex met a woman and they fell in love. Her name was Sarah, and to start with she was the best thing that could have happened to Alex. He told her everything about his teenage troubles, including having been an accessory to murder.'

'To start with?' Nikki wondered what was coming next.

'Sarah convinced him that he should return to the UK and tell the authorities everything he knew, especially regarding Vernon Deacon and how he had groomed a killer. She said that for Jennifer's family's sake, he should tell them about Hob's End Copse. She believed that he would never free himself of guilt if he didn't make a clean breast of everything. He told her he would consider it. We talked it over, but I couldn't make up my mind. Should he or shouldn't he? Although I had never really forgiven her for sending me away, I didn't want to get Mother into trouble. Then, out of the blue, Sarah contracted a fatal virus and was dead within a couple of weeks.'

'Oh my God, how terrible for him!' Laurie said.

'How I wish he'd felt able to talk to me about her,' said Aurelia forlornly.

'How could we?' Jerrard sounded bitter. 'The moment you heard he was involved with a woman, you would have been certain it would all start again. Don't forget, you believed that he had harmed Jennifer.'

'Oh God,' she breathed. 'What kind of mother was I?' No one answered.

'As you can imagine, Alex was devastated. He told me that in respect to her memory, the least he could do was follow her wishes, go home and take everything he knew to the police. It became a kind of crusade.' He suddenly stopped. 'At this point you should know that there is a letter, which I believe he sent to his solicitor. It needs to be found, and sooner rather than later.' He drew in a breath. 'Anyway, he then made yet another mistake, and this time it turned out to be a fatal one.' He sighed. 'He told someone else of his intentions.'

'Who?' asked Nikki, unable to contain her impatience.

'The problem is, Inspector, I don't know.' Jerrard stared at her. 'I always knew that someone had kept in touch with him, not on a regular basis but maybe once every couple of months. He said it was an old friend who had turned his own life around and was happy to hear that Alex had done the same.'

'That indicates it was one of Vern's victims, doesn't it?' said Joseph.

'Yes, that's what I always thought,' said Jerrard. 'I believed the man to be a true friend, but I now think he was just keeping tabs on Alex, to make certain he never told the truth.'

'It was the killer then?' suggested Nikki. 'But surely, Alex would never have dreamt of keeping in touch with him?'

Jerrard nodded. 'That's why I think Alex never knew it was the killer he was communicating with. I reckon the devious bastard pretended to be one of the other "special boys."'

That was possible, but Nikki had one big question. 'Jerrard? All through this, you've never mentioned the fact that a man was convicted of Jennifer Cowley's murder. Your brother must have known that Patrick Shale was found guilty. What did he say about that? After all, he *knew* the killer! He'd helped him hide the body! If it was Shale, wouldn't he have admitted it?'

Jerrard let out a long, loud sigh. 'That was one of the things Alex would never share with me. The only comment he ever made about Shale's incarceration was, "Be thankful that at least it wasn't me."'

Joseph went over to the window. Staring out, he said, 'That rather points to the fact that he knew Shale was innocent, doesn't it, Jerrard?'

'I never really knew, and he never spoke about it again.'

'Then the threats began?' said Joseph, turning back to look at Jerrard.

'Terrible threats, and this is where Laurie comes in. Alex received a photograph on his mobile phone, with the message, 'Look what I've found!'

Laurie turned slightly pale.

'Then there was another one, with a different photo of Laurie, that said, "Would you like history to repeat itself? It's up to you."' Jerrard shifted uncomfortably in his chair. 'It escalated. Alex was warned that if he dared to speak, his whole family would be annihilated and Sedgebrook burned to the ground with its occupants trapped inside. And I can't repeat what he proposed would happen to Laurie, not in front of her.'

'I can't believe that someone was creeping around taking pictures of me all that time! I don't think I'll ever want to go anywhere alone again.' Laurie shuddered at the thought. 'Even here where I'm safe, I can't sleep.'

'Neither can I,' added Jerrard darkly, 'and I know I won't until that man is caught and locked away, hopefully to rot for what he's done.'

Joseph lowered his voice. 'I know this is hell for you, Jerrard, but, please, finish the story. Then we can get out there and find him.'

Jerrard squeezed his eyes shut for a moment. 'Because of the threats, Alex said he would do as he was told, but we hatched a plan. He and Sarah had planned on getting jobs up in Venda but he'd put that on hold when she died. We agreed he should go up there and lie low for a while. I'd keep my head down until I heard from him, then I'd travel to England and find a way to tell the authorities about the danger this unknown girl was in.' He took a deep breath. 'But he disappeared soon after his first interview. I drove up there, went to the place he'd rented for a month and found his body. He'd been stabbed to death. We never knew, but for all the talk of a land of legend, there is a lot of corruption in that area. Bad things happen there.'

Aurelia put her hands over her eyes.

'Then I got a text message. It said, *The same conditions apply to you as to your brother. Go to the police, speak a word of this to anyone, and your family will fry and a beautiful young woman will die in agony.*' I was in turmoil wondering what to do. His eyes filled with tears. 'I did what I believed was the only thing I could do. I took his ring and his ID and left him there. Then I told my work and everyone I could think of that I was sick and needed time to recover, and that my brother was looking after me. The next day, I got a plane home. All I could think about was saving my family and finding the girl in the picture and getting her to safety.'

'Why on earth didn't you come to us?' Nikki exclaimed.

'Time! Think about it! He had her in his sights. He's a psycho and a murderer. Any moment that urge could have got too much for him, and this beautiful girl would have been dead.' He looked almost accusingly at Nikki. 'For a start, you would have thought I was mad, a time waster. For heaven's sake, a man had already been convicted of that crime. And even if you had slightly believed me, how long would it have taken to check everything out and then start making enquiries? Don't you see? There just wasn't the time!'

'How did you find her?' asked Joseph.

'I recognised the old cricket pavilion in the photo because I'd played there as a kid. So I went there, waited until I saw her walking home from work and followed her. Once I had her address, I just needed a way to get to talk to her so as not to frighten her, but then she disappeared.'

'When I went to Kelly's in Mablethorpe,' Laurie said.

'I was desperate. I walked the streets at night, checking out bars and clubs and pubs, and then one night I actually saw Laurie with a friend. I knew I had to act at once or I could lose her again.'

'You followed her to the party?' asked Nikki. 'So you were the one she left with.'

He nodded. 'Nobody seemed to even notice that I'd gate-crashed. They were a weird bunch.'

Laurie added, 'I'm afraid I'm a bit of a naughty girl sometimes, or I was. But not anymore.'

'When I had got Laurie well away from the party — I'd even hired a car — I told her everything. I think it was showing her the photos, and that old press picture of Jennifer, that did it, wasn't it?'

'And reading that text and knowing that your brother was dead.' Laurie looked at Nikki. 'I went willingly, Inspector. I knew my family would be beside themselves, but they'd get over it once they knew I was safe. Jerrard's family were the ones in danger.'

'So you went on the run,' Joseph said, 'hiding in the old cottage in a blue pop-up tent.'

'No way!' Jerrard said. 'I wouldn't go near that cottage, not when I knew there was a body hidden there. And I certainly never had a tent. I took the hire car back and bought a rucksack and a load of provisions. We pretended to be foreign workers and hitched a lift in a lorry to the outskirts of Jacob's Fen, and then we walked the rest of the way to Sedgebrook. My only thought was to get home. My family was in danger and I needed to be as close to them as I could get. I remembered hiding in the crawl space as a kid, and that my parents' room was on the other side of the house. I didn't know Richard would be staying in his old room, of course, but luckily he was rarely there. We hid in the old mill for a day or so, and then one of the farm barns, and we finally got into Sedgebrook House itself while Dad was out and Mum was gardening.' Jerrard pulled a face. 'Now I'd found Laurie, I didn't know what to do next. I was a mess. It was Laurie that held it together.' Tears started to run down his cheeks. 'It was purgatory being in that house, so close to my family but too scared to reach out to them and tell them what was happening. And all the while knowing there was a murderer out there, a man who would be eaten up with rage at Laurie's disappearance. She was amazing.'

'Just practical,' said Laurie. 'I kept my phone switched off, and I got into the house when everyone was asleep, or out, or busy in the garden, and steal small amounts of food. I'd also make sure Jerrard's phone was charged up. He was desperate that Aurelia, and the killer of course, believed that he was still in South Africa. Hence all the lies he told Richard about poor Alex supposedly going missing. The worst thing was the police that were crawling all over the estate. Not only did it make life almost impossible for us, the murderer might have believed that Richard had called them in and carried out his threat against the family.'

Jerrard had gathered himself again. 'We needed a plan but I still wasn't thinking straight. I thought I would wait until the family was all together and then I'd walk right in and tell them everything. Then I'd call the police. I mean, you were there every bloody day, would the killer have known any different?'

Laurie turned to him. 'But we didn't dare. Even though I'm pretty sure everyone in the neighbourhood knew about Richard wanting to clear the copse, and about the discovery of that mysterious cottage. That sort of thing spreads like wildfire in the Fens. And the killer had no idea you were even in this country. Jerrard, we simply did what we thought was best at the time, for everybody, and it can't have been that bad, because we are here now and still alive.'

'Did *you* leave all those bloody silly witchy things?' blurted out Nikki suddenly. 'Why on earth leave threats on the doorstep? What was that all about?'

'In retrospect, I don't think they were threats, Inspector,' said Aurelia. 'They were messages. Nothing more. Jerrard was trying to tell me something, but I misread it.'

Nikki's patience was really wearing thin. Just how sodding often was Aurelia Howard going to confuse the issue and lie to them? She had supposedly been worried sick about that pagan crap on the doorstep, and now she was saying they were just messages? 'Explain, please! But quickly. We do have a murderer to find, and a sergeant who's been badly injured. I need to get on, instead of trying to unpick all the knots you've tied us up in!'

Aurelia looked startled, then shamefaced. 'Alex was very interested in Wicca and the occult in general. When he was young, we used to play a game in which he would send me cryptic messages and tokens, and I'd have to decipher their meanings and reply. We haven't talked about this yet, there hasn't been time, but I'm guessing that Jerrard found the box with Alex's witch tools. Maybe they were stored away in the crawl space?'

He nodded slowly. 'I should tell you — and this is something I've never told anyone, even Laurie. Maybe I never really acknowledged it to myself, but I still harboured bitterness towards you, Mother. I never wished you real harm, but I took great delight in leaving those messages. I know now that it was wrong, even childish, but I hoped you would feel scared and confused, just like I had all those years ago.'

Laurie took up the narrative again. Nikki was struck by how sensible and grownup she was, and also by her obvious fondness for Jerrard.

'Well, I could hardly blame you. Which is why I helped. We found books on the meanings of different objects, including that bouquet with the scourge. We crept into the garden one night and picked the roses and lavender for that. Please understand, there was never any harm intended. Jerrard wanted to try to communicate with his mother in a way that Duncan and Richard wouldn't understand, and so he used Alex's old games.'

'And the roadkill? Surely, you couldn't call that harmless,' Nikki said disgustedly.

'Actually, crows are associated with life,' said Aurelia. 'Often with good luck and prophecy. They are intelligent birds, and not all about death and ill-omen. The next message was Laurie's shoe and the salt — salt being something that is placed in a witch's bottle for protection. I should have realised they were trying to tell me that Laurie was alive and being protected.'

'Frankly, all it did was throw a bloody great confusing spanner in the works,' Nikki said. 'And when she saw that Celtic ring, Aurelia might have been led to believe that Alex was here and alive, not stone-cold dead in Africa.'

Joseph flashed her a warning look. Too late — she was furious with Jerrard. He had handled the whole thing badly. If he'd only come directly to her . . . She stopped herself. Then what, exactly? How many times had she decided some nutter had a screw loose and should be booked for wasting police time? And how long would it have taken to put something official in motion? Certainly not just a matter of days, which was all it took for Jerrard to find Laurie and get her away. The anger subsided.

'We have a lot of work to do on this,' she said to Joseph. 'And we have to be very careful how we proceed. We need to get back as soon as possible.'

'Let them tell us about the night Niall was attacked and Aurelia whisked them away, then, yes we should go,' Joseph said. 'But we need to hear this.'

'Just before Richard got that call from Tamsin Farrow,' Aurelia said, 'I bumped into Laurie coming out of the guest bedroom, and their days of hiding were over. I was overjoyed to see Jerrard, and heartbroken to hear about Alex. They told me briefly of the trouble they were in, and I mentioned that Richard had dashed off to Hob's End because there seemed to have been some kind of incident, and I hoped it wasn't connected to them in some way.'

'We knew immediately that there was a chance that we were all in danger, and I told Mother about the killer's threats. She offered to get us away, knowing that Richard would naturally involve the police, and in half an hour we were on the road.' Jerrard shrugged. 'And that is it. Now, finally, we are in your hands.'

'Thank God you are,' Joseph said. 'Now, if DI Galena agrees, I think you should stay here while we sort out an action plan. Would your friends agree to keep them a little longer?'

'Without a doubt,' said Aurelia. 'If the DI is alright with that? And I'll stay with them. There is still a lot to talk about.'

Nikki had never seen a more remote or perfect place to hide. 'I'll arrange for two plain clothes protection officers to come out here immediately. They can pose as guests.' She turned to Laurie. 'Now, I need to speak to your mother and father. They are suffering far more than you think. They have to be told you're safe, but they must tell *no one* other than immediate family just yet. No arguments. We do this our way now, understand?'

Laurie nodded. 'I'm sorry. Mum and me haven't been getting on very well recently. I thought she wouldn't care that much. I've gone off before and not said where I'm going.'

'Your mum is in pieces, and if you're ever a mother yourself one day, you'll understand why. Lecture over. Come, Joseph. We need a serious talk.'

CHAPTER THIRTY-TWO

Joseph waited while Nikki arranged for the two protection officers to be dispatched to the retreat. He was going over those photos from Deacon's album in his mind, trying to visualise the boys.

One of the youngsters in those pictures had grown up to become their killer. But which one? Patrick Shale, Alex Howard and Josh Smithers were known to be the principal boys in Deacon's secret little club. Alex was dead, so it had to be Shale or Smithers. Or did it? There were three other boys from the rehab centre, one being Todd Ridler, but he was on a curfew and wore a location tag. Cat had found another, but he had committed suicide in prison. The other one had yet to be identified.

Nikki ended the call. 'That's sorted, they'll be here within the hour, both in civvies, but armed.'

'Not sure that will go down too well in a healing retreat, but this is an unusual situation,' said Joseph.

'It will be a damned sight more effective than chanting spells over them,' Nikki grumbled. 'Now, do we wait until the armed officers arrive, or go back now?'

'Let's talk our options through, then get back. I reckon here is about as safe as anywhere for them, don't you?'

Nikki rubbed her eyes. 'Definitely. Hell, I was so sure it was Alex we were looking for. Wrong again.'

'Well, let's not be wrong about the killer. It has to be Shale or this guy Josh Smithers. And let's face it, Shale and Mummy are practically hermits. We need to go talk to Mr Smithers — or Father Earth, as he calls his business.'

'Yes, I've got his addr—' She stopped. 'Oh shit! Cat and Dave! I gave them his address before we left. What if I've sent them into the lion's den?'

'Ring them, now,' Joseph urged.

She found Cat's number and they waited, hardly daring to breathe.

'Boss, hi! How's it going?' Cat's voice rang out through the loudspeaker.

They looked at each other and smiled.

'We've got a lot to tell you, Cat, but first, what's your opinion of Josh Smithers?' Nikki asked.

'Still waiting for Dave to get back. He went on his own while I tied up with Deacon.'

Nikki looked at Joseph. 'How long has he been gone?'

'He went the same time as you, boss. He's certainly taking his time, I must say.'

Nikki ended the call and fumbled for Dave's number in her contacts.

The phone rang and rang, echoing around the car. A chill seeped into his bones. 'Can you remember that address, Nikki?'

'Yes, Saltmash Corner, Holbeck. Smithers runs his business from there. It's called Father Earth Landscaping and Gardening.'

Joseph was already pulling out of the gates before she finished speaking. 'Fifteen minutes from town? We can do it in ten from here.'

'Oh, Joseph, I'll never forgive myself if anything's happened to our Dave.' Nikki's voice shook.

'Come on, there's a dozen reasons why he could be held up, let's not jump to conclusions. If you think about it, we've been pretty wrong about most things this week.'

It took just under ten minutes before Joseph was screeching to a halt in the parking area next to the bungalow. They saw a few vehicles, mainly vans and pickup trucks bearing the nursery logo, but no people seemed to be around.

'Look! His car's still here.' Nikki pointed to Dave's old Suzuki on the opposite side of the car park. 'He must still be in—' She stopped mid-sentence, pointing.

Joseph saw the familiar figure of Dave Harris lying sprawled on the ground. He ran over and dropped to his knees beside him. 'Come on, mate! Open your eyes. Can you talk to me?'

'Has he been attacked, Joseph?' Nikki said. 'Has he? Because if he bloody has—'

'Call an ambulance, Nikki. Now!'

'It's on its way!' someone called out from behind them.

Joseph looked up to see a man running towards them carrying a couple of blankets. 'He was just leaving. I think it's a heart attack.'

'Josh Smithers?' asked Joseph.

'Yes.' The man knelt down and covered Dave with the blankets. 'He's worse than he was. Do you officers know CPR?'

Wordlessly, Joseph pulled the blankets away from Dave's chest and ripped his shirt open. He placed the heel of one hand on Dave's sternum and began the chest compressions. It seemed to take for ever before he heard the sirens. His muscles were cramping but he kept it up until a paramedic gently pulled him away and took over.

Finally they had Dave wired up and stretchered. 'We're taking him to Greenborough General. Does anyone want to follow us?'

Nikki reached out and took Joseph's arm. 'I'll ring in and make sure someone gets there straightaway. We have other business, Joseph.'

He was about to object but saw the steely glare in her eyes. 'You look after him, you hear? He's one of the best.'

'We've got him, Sergeant. We have a cardiac team waiting for us.'

Then the ambulance was pulling out of the yard.

'Can I get you both a hot drink? You look pretty shaken.' Josh Smithers pointed towards the bungalow. 'My wife's inside, so the kettle will be on.'

'We have to go, but thank you,' said Nikki. 'And thank you for calling 999 so quickly.'

'I hope he pulls through. He was a nice man.' Smithers hesitated. 'When you see him, tell him I'll do as he asked, okay?'

Joseph looked at him. 'Deacon?'

'Tell him, yes, I'll testify.'

Joseph clasped his arm. 'Thank you, Josh. Believe me, if anything will pull him through, it'll be hearing that.'

* * *

Back in the car, Nikki had regained her composure and was back in control. Dave had not been attacked, thank heavens, plus his last interview had mostly likely been the one that would seal Vernon Deacon's fate. He had scored a winning shot by convincing Josh Smithers to testify against Deacon. Now he was in safe hands and being blue-lighted to a waiting cardiac unit. It was their turn to do their bit.

'We both know who our killer is, but *I* know how he found the freedom to do it. Now put your foot down, stick a siren on and get us to Calthorpe Lane as fast as this heap of junk will take us!'

On their way, she asked for a call to be sent to the patrol car on observation outside Willow Lodge. 'Tell them not to let anyone in or out of that lane, and especially not the neighbour!' She turned to Joseph. 'It's been bugging me since the last time I spoke to Ernie and Peter. This neighbour has been going backwards and forwards for days, and never once has he shown any interest in the police car camped on his doorstep. What's the most natural thing to do as you drive past?'

'Ask what's going on?'

'Exactly. Maybe even offer them a cuppa, for heaven's sake. At the very least you'd talk to them, wouldn't you? But this guy, head down, can't wait to get past them.'

'It was Shale?'

'Bet you a three-course meal at Mario's it was.'

'You are that certain, huh?'

'Yep. But just pray he's in when we get there.'

This time they drove straight up to the house, Nikki calling out of the window for the uniformed crew to follow them. 'Block the road with your car, and one of you stay there in case the neighbour tries to make a run for it. The other one, with us!'

They rang and knocked on the door. Joseph delivered a couple of bone-jarring kicks at the lock, which groaned and creaked but held firm. Then Peter was by their side holding an enforcer. 'Stand back, Sarge!'

The door flew inwards after a single blow.

'Police! Stay where you are!'

They ran from room to room, until Peter cried out from upstairs, 'DI Galena! In here!'

They found Jane Shale lying fully clothed on her bed, surrounded by packets of tablets, dozens of foil sheets, all empty of their contents. It looked very much like suicide, but Nikki wasn't making any assumptions, not when a man like Shale was involved. 'Twice she wasn't around when I called. He said she had a migraine but by the state of her, I think she was already dead.' She sighed. 'Another guest for Rory's chiller cabinet.'

They checked the rest of the house but found nothing. 'Time to hit the neighbour's pad, Joseph. Let's go. Peter, you stay here, radio in and tell them what we've found. Tell them we have a body, very much life extinct, and we need forensics. And I want them to put out an attention drawn for Patrick Shale, but to be aware, he's likely to be very dangerous.'

It was quite a trek to the next property so they drove. 'This place isn't lived in,' Nikki stated. The curtains were dirty and the paintwork weathered. As expected, no one answered the door.

'Broken window around the side,' called out Ernie. 'Shall I do the honours, ma'am?'

'Go for it.'

There was a crash followed by a few choice swear words, and shortly after, Ernie was unlocking the door from the inside. 'Stinks like a bloody midden in here, ma'am. Hold yer nose.'

'Oh fuck,' she groaned, stepping inside. 'I'd know that smell anywhere.' She clamped her hand over her face. 'Two out of two properties with dead residents in them. This certainly won't do the house prices in Calthorpe Lane any good. Must be an estate agent's nightmare.'

Joseph was watching her, a faint smile on his face. She knew what that look meant. She was herself again — whatever that was.

'Okay, guys, let's find him.'

Ten minutes later, they were outside, breathing in great gulps of fresh air. 'Well, that one could hardly be considered a suicide, could it?' Joseph said.

'Shale must have really needed that route in and out, mustn't he? I think he probably killed the poor old guy shortly after he came out of prison.' They had checked the back of the cottage and found a rough track, edged with scrubby trees and elders, that connected Willow Lodge with this cottage, and was probably only ever used once a year when the ditches were cleared out. By the tyre marks in the mud left after the storm, it appeared that Shale had ridden an off-road bike down here, dressed himself in the neighbour's clothes and wide-brimmed wax hat and come and gone as he pleased.

'So where has he gone?' breathed Joseph.

Where, indeed? Before she could answer, she heard the sound of approaching two-tones. 'We need to get back to base — one, to find out how Dave is, and, two, to try and fathom out what Shale's next move will be. He's no home to return to now, and I'm guessing he has an agenda, a dangerous one. We just need to know what that is.' She turned to Ernie. 'Will you organise getting the crime scene set up, please?'

'Yes, ma'am. It'll be a pleasure to actually *do* something for a change. I'm pig-bloody-sick, I can tell you. For days, I've been letting that little shit drive right past us.' He shook his head. 'The messroom are going to have a field day with this alright.'

* * *

When they arrived back in the CID room, they were surprised to find Ben Radley at his workstation.

'Cat rang me, ma'am.' He looked worried but remarkably alert, considering he had just completed five consecutive nights on the graveyard shift. 'I've had a sleep, so I said I'd cover for her while she went to the hospital to see Dave. She won't stay long, she just needed to see him and let him know she was there for him. Hope you're okay with that?'

'Of course. If we didn't have a murderer on the loose, we'd all be there.'

Ben stood up. 'What would you like me to do, boss?'

'And me too.' Cameron Walker strode into the room. 'And young DC Sean Pickford — he can join you for the duration. You are short on staff, Nikki, so make use of us, okay?'

Well, she was hardly going to refuse. 'Brilliant! But first I'll fill you all in on what we have just learned about Alex and Jerrard Howard.'

It took a while, for there was a lot to explain. Finally, she said, 'Now, we need to decide where Shale is likely to go and what his endgame is. He's burnt his bridges — he has no home or family to run to, no secret cottage anymore and to our knowledge, no friends. So where does he go?'

'He finds a place to hide, to lie low and plan his next and what might be his final move,' said Joseph. 'It depends what his motivation is, and what he wants to achieve.'

'Or he could cut and run,' suggested Ben. 'If he planned to abduct Laurie, someone got to her first, so that's out. Alex is dead and his mother is out of the picture. Sedgebrook is heaving with police, so burning it down is not an option. With odds like that against him, he could well have decided it was time to do a runner.'

'Why do I believe he has unfinished business here?' asked Nikki, more to herself than to the others.

'I agree with you,' said Cameron. 'What is most worrying is that he has no qualms at all about who he kills. The neighbour, possibly his mother . . . no one's life is sacred to him.'

'And don't forget my Niall,' added Joseph. 'Brutally attacked and shut inside a collapsing building. How callous is this guy?'

Nobody answered. They didn't need to.

Nikki closed her eyes, thinking hard. 'Right, he's out of control. There's a chance he's just run off, but I very much doubt that. Because of what he's done in the past, we have to assume that he still has someone in his sights. Who would be important enough to stay here and chance being caught for? Who does he hate enough to risk everything in order to kill them?'

There was a long silence, then Joseph said, 'Vernon Deacon. The man that encouraged him on a path that led to murder.'

'Deacon has a record for being brought in but always let out again in a very short space of time,' said the new member of their team. 'Mightn't he go underground and wait, hoping that Deacon'll be either freed or bailed?'

'Valid point, lad,' said Cameron. 'Deacon has never stayed with us long. That smart-arsed brief has always got him out, sometimes within a matter of hours.'

'Shale has no idea that Deacon is really in the shit this time,' Nikki mused. 'I wonder if he would dare keep tabs on the police station?'

'More likely to watch Deacon's home,' Ben said. 'Not so risky.'

Nikki nodded. 'That's a real possibility. I must say that if the super wasn't standing here, it would almost be worth letting the bastard out and using him as bait.'

Cameron smiled. 'If he wasn't such a dangerous man, the super might even be tempted to agree with you. But, for Marian Harper's sake, he stays.'

'Thought you'd say that.' Nikki returned the smile. 'But apart from Deacon, who else do we think might be on Shale's hit list?'

'Would he still try to find Laurie Gately?' suggested Ben. 'Because if he did, he'd also kill the guy who got there before him — Jerrard Howard.'

'They have two of our most experienced protection officers with them, Ben, both armed, in a place that few people know even exists. I personally would not look for a runaway girl in a retreat for stressed-out witches.'

There was a ripple of laughter. Yvonne and Kyle entered, Yvonne carrying several reports. 'That's everything from forensics so far, ma'am. And Professor Wilkinson said to thank you profusely for producing a three-week-old corpse just as he was about to have his lunch.'

'Nonsense. He's got a cast-iron stomach. Have a seat, you two. We're trying to work out who Patrick Shale's next victim will be. Any suggestions?'

'Let me think on that,' said Yvonne, pulling up a chair.

'You know, I keep thinking of what a silver-tongued liar Shale is,' said Joseph. 'The lies he told us when we first visited him. All those protestations of innocence, those crocodile tears when we said Jennifer had finally been found. He was practically begging to be told where she'd been found when he knew all along. God, he had me completely and utterly fooled!'

'You weren't alone, Joseph. I believed him too,' Nikki said. 'I was almost convinced there had been a miscarriage of justice. How could two experienced and hardened detectives have been taken in so easily?'

'Make that three,' declared Cameron.

'To my mind there's one other person he might hate.' Joseph looked at Nikki. 'When we spoke to him about Jennifer and told him about where she had been found, I got the feeling he was about to rush over there to be at that same spot, to somehow share his grief — you know, like when people hang around a place where someone they love has died, maybe in a car crash, and they leave flowers?'

'Like being at the scene of their death will make you closer to them?' said Nikki. 'Yes, I think you mentioned something about his being obsessed and probably making Hob's End Copse a sort of shrine.'

'Well, what if it always was?' Joseph went on. 'What if it's always been a hallowed place to him, ever since he and Alex took her body there? What if he dreamed about it while he was banged up? And what if it was the first place he went when he got out of prison? That tent was most likely his. He stayed in the cottage to be close to his dead love.'

Nikki narrowed her eyes. 'It was Shale who cleared the path to the cottage. He liked to spend time there. He admitted that he was obsessed with Jennifer, and I believe he was speaking the truth for once. He wanted to be close to her.'

'And someone is planning to take his sacred place away from him, clearing the site and stripping back the copse. Now wouldn't he maybe hate that person very much?' Joseph's words hung in the air. 'It wouldn't matter to him if it were just a pile of stones, as long as it was still there, like a memorial cairn.'

'Richard! Richard Howard!' Nikki felt a stab of concern. 'Of course, that's who he wants to kill. Either in the hopes of stopping the destruction of the copse or maybe just as payback. We need to contact the officers that are watching Sedgebrook House. They have to keep Richard where they can see him, and I'm thinking an armed unit too. Super?'

Cameron was already on his way out of the room. 'I'll see how quickly I can muster one.'

'Okay, everyone, I want you all in stab-proof vests, and we'll get out to Hob's End.' She called across to Sheila, the office manager, 'When Cat gets back, please let her know what is occurring but tell her to stay put, just in case I need a liaison officer here at base.'

Sheila stuck up her thumb. 'Good luck!'

Nikki turned to Joseph. 'It all started at Hob's End, and it looks like it might just end there too.'

'Ma'am? I'm sorry to say this but,' Yvonne's face was creased with concern, 'if Shale has been hanging around Jacob's Fen for the past few weeks, talking to the locals, having a drink in the pub, listening to gossip, there's someone else he might not be too pleased with. The person who advised Richard to cull that copse. Tamsin, ma'am.'

Nikki swallowed and looked at Joseph. Yvonne was right. 'Ring her at the hospital, Joseph. Niall has officers watching him. I'll get the duty sergeant to make sure they watch her too.'

'I'll go and tell him, shall I?' asked Yvonne.

'Yes, please. Tell him what we suspect, and then get out to the vehicles. We don't have time to hang around.'

Nikki noticed Joseph's drawn expression.

'No signal, Nikki. I can't get hold of her.'

'Then go, Joseph. The hospital is ten minutes away. See her for yourself, talk to the officers there, then, when you are happy about her, drive out to the Sedgebrook Estate. I've got this, okay?'

Joseph looked utterly torn, and her heart went out to him.

'Do I have to pull rank, Sergeant? Just go!'

Everyone else had left the room, which was lucky, as Joseph leaned in close and kissed her cheek. 'I love you.'

Then he grabbed his jacket and car keys and ran.

CHAPTER THIRTY-THREE

Late afternoon with the sun, still warm, sinking slowly towards the horizon should have been a time of tranquil beauty. Instead, it felt menacing, full of unknown dangers. Hob's End Copse was a fat green wart, a blemish on the face of the farmland.

DC Sean Pickford and PC Kyle Adams had gone with Cameron Walker to Sedgebrook House to await the firearms unit, while Nikki commandeered Ben and Yvonne to accompany her to the copse.

On the drive there she had been horrified to receive a call from Joseph saying he was unable to locate his daughter. She drove on with a sinking heart until a second call came, full of apologies for frightening her. He had just seen Tamsin coming out of the ladies' toilets. It was funny and terrifying at the same time. Sometimes Nikki thought that you might do better in this job if you were a person with no family and no loved ones to worry about.

Nikki parked close to the track that led to the now ruined cottage, and as she got out, another squad car drew up beside her. Four officers got out and all looked to her for instruction. She recognised them as having been on duty at the crime scene when she first found Jennifer's body.

'You guys all know this spot, don't you?' she said.

'Too well, ma'am, thank you. Spooky bloody place,' said one of the younger constables.

He was right. Nothing good had happened here. Joseph had talked of negative energy ley lines and how they can affect their surroundings and naturally, being Nikki Galena, she had mocked his superstitious beliefs. Right now, she was wondering if she'd been right to laugh at him. There was something malignant about this innocent-looking cluster of overgrown trees and bushes. On closer inspection, she noticed that many of the trees were twisted and stunted. Their fallen leaves, damp after the summer storm, were clagged and rotting with mould.

She sniffed. This was not the attitude she needed right now. 'So you are aware that there is only one path in. It's perfectly accessible now, but be careful. The storm broke branches and toppled some of the weaker trees, so it's a bit of a mess in there.' She hoped she was not leading her small army into danger. 'Silent approach, all phones on mute please, and when we reach the cottage, we split into two groups, one going left, the other right, and we'll meet at the back of the old place. Keep your eyes peeled. We are looking for anywhere in that ruin that could possibly conceal Patrick Shale. If you see him, or anything suspicious, stop and raise your hand. Do not approach him. He doesn't care who he hurts or kills. Is that understood?'

There was a murmur of assent.

'Then let's go.'

Before they could move off, another car drew in behind them and came to a halt. A young female PC jumped out. 'DI Galena, the superintendent sent me. Richard Howard was not at the house when he arrived. Someone said he'd gone to the estate office to sort out some problem or other, but he's not there either, and the super said to say that an off-road motorbike was found behind one of the barns close to the farm office.'

Nikki let out a groan. 'Oh, sod it! Sod it!' This was exactly what they were here to try to prevent. 'Stand down

for a moment, everyone, but for heaven's sake be vigilant.'
She hurried to her car and rang Cameron.

'Have your guys checked the house, sir? Is it clear?'

'Top to bottom, Nikki, he's not inside. They are checking the grounds now.'

'I need that armed unit, sir. If Shale has taken Richard,
he'll bring him here and nowhere else. It's the core of his
whole world. Hob's End is where he will kill him, I *know* it.'

'They are coming, but they'll be a while. They were on
the other side of the county dealing with another incident.
I'm on my way. Hold off going into that wilderness until
I'm with you.'

'Understood, sir.'

Nikki went back to her officers and told them of the
change of plan.

Ben looked at her thoughtfully. 'What if I went in alone,
as a scout? Not all the way to the cottage, but keeping to the
undergrowth, just to see if there's anything untoward going
on. It would give us, or the firearms unit, an idea of where
to concentrate on.'

'I think I'd be better suited to that job, don't you?'

She hadn't heard Joseph's car draw up. He'd left it a
little further away and walked to where they were gathered.

'Special forces, remember? We did recce rather well.'

There was no doubt he was the man for the job.

'No disrespect, Ben, but you've just been relegated by
Action Man here.' She tried to keep it light, but the cottage
in Hob's End Copse was the last place she wanted him to be
going. 'Okay, Joseph. Sounds like a plan to me. I'll defer to
your expert knowledge this time.' She looked into his eyes hoping he would see the message in hers. 'But no heroics, Sergeant.'

His lips moved almost imperceptibly, and she knew he
had understood.

Nikki spent the next ten minutes in hell, and then suddenly Joseph was beside her.

'He's in there. He's found a way through the rubble. It
looks as though he's cleared some of the debris and reached

346

a corner of the kitchen that is fairly undamaged. I got as close as I dared and I heard voices. He's not alone, Nikki.' He looked at her anxiously. 'I think we are going to have to leave this one to the commander of the firearms unit. It's a matter of freeing a hostage, and in such tight conditions,' he sucked in air, 'it doesn't look good.'

'When the ARV arrives, will you liaise with them?'

'Of course. I'm hoping they'll have a Tactical Rifle Officer with them. Our one hope will be to find a suitable observation point for a marksman. That's if he has a gun, of course, and we have no evidence he's ever used one.'

'What if he's not armed, Joseph?' she asked.

'He used a knife to kill his neighbour. If he is threatening another life, then we are duty bound to try to stop him. But the first thing will be an appraisal of the situation, then negotiation — if that's possible and doesn't pose a threat to his hostage. Then they must decide if he's posing an *immediate threat to life*, and if he is, it will be down to them to decide whether to use a standard incapacitating shot, or a head shot — a kill shot.' He touched her arm. 'It's what they are trained for, Nikki, I'm just going to brief them with a situation report. I don't know what is going on in there, it's down to them to find out and handle it accordingly.'

Nikki was desperately afraid for Richard. He was a farmer. He loved the land and worked hard, trying to do his best for his farm, his soil, his crops and the environment. And for that, he was now being terrorised by a twisted man who wanted him dead. Richard was no fighter, she was certain. Sure, he was strong, but not in combat. 'I'm wondering how Shale overpowered him,' she said to Joseph. 'Shale was thin and pasty-looking when we saw him, wiry maybe, and possibly with a sort of core strength, but Richard is tall and very well-built.'

'Probably took him by surprise, stunned him, tied him up and frog-marched him here, especially if he had a weapon. Or maybe threatened someone else to make him cooperate.'

Nikki had done enough talking. She wanted to act, to do something about the situation. 'Joseph, I don't think we have the time to wait for this armed backup. If Shale is out of control, he could attack Richard at any moment, and if he is tied up, there's no way he can defend himself. I'm going to make a judgement call. I think we have to make a move now, before it's too late.'

'That won't be easy, Nikki, and it's extremely risky. We have no idea what kind of weapon he has, or just how volatile he is, or how much danger Richard is in.' He breathed out with a harsh sound. 'But I'm with you regarding the time we're wasting. Let's see what we've got at our disposal and work out a plan of action.'

Nikki beckoned to the others. 'We're not going to wait for the ARV. I believe that would be putting Shale's captive at risk. We are going to have to sort this out ourselves.' She turned to Joseph. 'Do you think you could get any closer than you did before? Maybe you could get us a clearer picture of how to take Shale down, and also to ascertain whether he is armed.'

Joseph nodded. 'I'll try.'

'Right. Now, are any of you Taser trained?' She ran her eyes over the uniformed officers, searching for the holster with the bright yellow Taser in it.

PC Billy Johns raised his hand. 'Yes, ma'am, and I'm trialling the new Taserx2.'

'Ah, right, that's excellent.' Nikki had seen the new "two shot" Taser in use. It could fire two charges without the need to change the cartridge, so its user had a second chance to stop whoever was posing a threat to the public. 'That's good. Then, depending on what news Joseph brings back, you could be taking the lead, okay?'

Billy nodded furiously, eyes sparkling. 'Yes, ma'am.'

'Okay, Joseph. Then we'll waste no time in getting straight in there. Time really isn't on Richard's side.' Joseph made his way back into the copse, while the remaining officers looked to Nikki for instructions.

'Right, I'm just going to ring the super and tell him what we intend to do. He should be here soon but if we get a green

348

light from Joseph, I want to go in straightaway, so you guys check your equipment belts and prepare yourselves.'

Cameron sounded dubious. 'The ARV's ETA is approximately fifteen minutes. I'd rather you waited, but if you feel it puts that young man's life at risk, I'm going to have to let you do what you see fit. I got held up sorting things out here, but now we have officers both inside and outside Sedgebrook House, so I'm coming straight across to join you. We haven't told Duncan Howard about his son yet. I don't want to frighten him. I think it's best we wait until we have an outcome.'

Nikki agreed, thanked him and rang off. Then she heard a car draw up and park close to hers. She decided to go and stop whoever it was before they accidentally wandered into an active operation.

'Sorry, sir, but this area of out of—' She stopped, rooted to the spot, as Richard Howard stepped out of the car.

'What's happened?' he asked anxiously.

'Richard? But we thought . . .' She exhaled loudly. 'Where on earth have you been?'

'Sorry, but we had a bit of an emergency with one of the pieces of hired machinery. I took a quad bike out to check it over before ringing the company we'd hired it from. I'm still trying to keep this place running, even though the family's in tatters.' He looked puzzled. 'What on earth is going on? Why are all these vehicles here again?'

Not knowing whether to laugh or cry, Nikki said, 'Because we believed a killer had abducted you from the estate office.'

'Jesus!' He scratched his head. 'I did say I was going there, but I didn't think to ring again when I went out. This is my fault, I'm so sorry.'

So who was in that ruined building with Shale? 'Sorry, but I have to get back to my officers. I need to tell them you are okay. Stay here, Richard. Don't go anywhere, whatever happens. My superintendent is on his way. When he gets here, please tell him what's happened.'

Nikki turned and hurried back to the waiting officers.

'Guys, that man standing by my car is Richard Howard. Now we need to know who the hell is in that cottage with Patrick Shale.' As she spoke, Joseph emerged from the copse, looking somewhat puzzled.

As soon as he was within earshot, she blurted out, 'Richard is here!'

'That answers a lot,' he said, 'because I'm damn sure the hostage is female. I think she's gagged — I could only hear Shale's voice, and he definitely sounds as if he is talking to a woman.' He shook his head. 'Thing is, the way he was speaking — well, it wasn't threatening at all. In fact he sounded like he was comforting her.'

Nothing made sense. Nikki tried to think who it could be. Aurelia and Laurie were under protection, miles away. Shale's mother was dead. Tamsin was being watched by police officers at Greenborough Hospital. There *were* no more women connected to the case. 'Do you think he's armed?'

'No way of knowing, but somehow I don't think so. I could just about see him, and there was certainly no weapon in view.'

'So, Joseph, with all your previous military experience, I could use a suggestion on how we should tackle him.'

'Well, we have to give him warning of our intentions. And I suggest you be the one to do that. Try to talk to him. Shale knows you, he might just listen.'

'Fat chance! I'm not the most diplomatic of negotiators, Joseph. In fact, I failed the course.' She threw him a rueful glance. 'Although I expect that's no surprise to you.'

His smile said it was no surprise at all.

'So, what if it fails?' she asked.

'We take him by force. We can only get in one at a time, so, if it were down to me, I'd say I go first and see how the land lies. I'd want the officer with the Taser right behind me in case he acts up. Hopefully, that will be that. Then you get straight in next and take care of his prisoner — whoever she is.'

The thought of Joseph going in first terrified Nikki but thanks to his army training, he was by far the best equipped for a situation like this.

She told the others what they were going to do, and they moved silently towards the cottage, Nikki marvelling at how quiet a bunch of flat-foot coppers could be when it was called for. When they reached the ruined building, they spread out, keeping low and out of sight. Joseph and Billy edged closer to where Shale had cleared a way inside. When Joseph was as close as he dared go, he beckoned her forward.

Nikki took a deep breath, prayed that Shale didn't have a gun, and walked across the yard. She stopped a few metres from the entrance and called out, 'Police! Patrick Shale! It's DI Nikki Galena, Patrick. Will you please step out of the building? I want to talk to you. We won't hurt you, Patrick. We just need to talk, okay?'

'Go away! Please! Just go away!'

Nikki tried to remember all the things she'd learnt about negotiating a hostage situation, but soon realised she'd just have to wing it. Active listening, gauge the state of mind of the subject, remain patient, calm and stable, oh right! The only technique she was going to use was to engage in dialogue. At least he wasn't harming his captive while he was talking to her.

'I can't do that, Patrick. I can't leave you here, you must realise that. This old cottage is far too dangerous. I need to know that you are safe and unhurt. *Are* you hurt, Patrick?'

'Leave me alone! I'm not hurt, so please, go!'

The voice sounded muffled. Had he been crying? There was no venom in his words, just desolation.

'We found your mum, Patrick. I'm so very sorry. You must be so sad. Why don't you just come out and we can talk about it? I won't hurt you. There are no guns out here, you are quite safe. Come outside, so I can see for myself that you're alright.'

'I don't want to talk about my mother. She left me. She took the easy way out. I survived fifteen years in jail and never

351

once attempted to kill myself — for her sake. And what does she do . . . ?' His voice cracked. 'Just go away!'

'I can't, Patrick, not until I know you are out of that cottage. It could collapse again at any moment, so, please, just walk out.'

'Inspector, I don't need help, I don't need saving. I don't care if the cottage falls on us. We just want to be alone.'

We? Whoever it was, it sounded more like someone he loved than a person he wanted to kill.

'You are both in terrible danger in that cottage. It's my duty to help you, both of you. If you don't come out, I'm going to have to come in.'

'No!'

She saw Joseph tense, ready to go in. She shook her head and mouthed, 'Wait.'

'It's over, isn't it?' His voice shook with emotion.

'Yes, Patrick, it is.'

'I'll come out.'

'That's good. Come out very slowly, and be careful. As I said, that last remaining part of the building is on the point of collapse. Come out and walk towards me, okay?'

Very slowly, Patrick Shale, completely unarmed, scrambled over the rubble and walked towards her. Moments later he was face down on the ground being handcuffed by Billy and Joseph.

Two other officers appeared and took him back down the path to a waiting police car. As he passed her, Shale said, 'I didn't kill anyone. I'm innocent.'

'He was crying,' said Nikki in a low voice. 'Sobbing.' She shook herself. 'The captive! Let's get in there.'

She led the way, closely followed by Joseph. 'Police! You are safe now! Don't be frightened, we've got you!'

No response. It was very dark inside, but Nikki could just make out a figure sitting in a battered old wooden carver chair. She slid and scrambled over the rubble, calling out, 'You're safe now, we'll soon get you ou— Oh! Oh, Joseph!'

Nikki let out a cry and put her hands to her mouth. 'Not again! Oh, please! Not again!'

In front of her, tied to the chair and wrapped tightly in some sort of thick cloth, was another skeleton. All she could see, emerging from the strange, grubby cocoon, was a skull — a skull with clumps of dirty blonde hair still attached to it.

'It's okay. Come on, let me get you out of here.' Joseph had his arms around her and was steering her away from the nightmare sight.

* * *

Once again, Hob's End Copse was a circus of blue lights and emergency vehicles. Nikki sat on the tailgate of a police car wrapped in a foil blanket. Despite the warmth of the evening, she couldn't stop shivering. She had no idea where Joseph had got it from, but she found herself gratefully sipping from a small hip flask of brandy.

'Who is she, Joseph?' she asked, trying to quell the tremor in her voice.

He drew in a long breath. 'At a guess, I'd say Jennifer wasn't the first to die. And from the way she was wrapped, I suspect there were two bodies in that chimney stack, and that only one was dislodged when the storm brought part of it down. The chimney was completely blocked with leaves and twigs, so forensics' cameras missed it. That poor soul was probably buried in all the debris.'

'And he's still saying he's innocent.'

'Deluding himself. That, or he's playing with us. But he's guilty alright.' He put his arm around her. 'I'll be very interested to read the letter that Alex Howard sent to his solicitor, won't you? That should give us some answers.' He looked at her. 'Feeling better?'

'No. Both Laurie and Jerrard said they couldn't sleep, well, you can add me to the list. I'm getting heartily sick of bloody nasty surprises.'

'Anyway, I was most impressed by your negotiating skills. You should have passed that course with flying colours.' He gave her a little squeeze. 'Seriously, well done for getting him out unharmed.'

'I was shit scared and flying, as always, by the seat of my pants.'

'Worked a treat.'

They sat for a few moments, quiet in the midst of the bustle of activity. 'I'm glad Cameron is here and has taken command. I couldn't organise a piss-up in a brewery right now.' She sat up. 'Oh! Can you ring Cat and get an update on Dave and Niall?'

'Already done. Dave's having all sorts of tests, but so far they think it's unstable angina. He might be referred to a specialist cardiac hospital, but he's back in the land of the living, which is the main thing. Apparently he told Cat to tell you he's sorry for letting you down.'

'Silly old sod! I hope she told him about his resounding success with Josh Smithers.' Nikki smiled.

'She did, and apparently more and more incriminating stuff is starting to come in about Deacon, so this time he will definitely not be returning to his own little bed in Hawthorne Close.'

'Hu-bloody-rah!'

Joseph beamed at her. Nikki was back to her old self.

TWO WEEKS LATER

Monks Lantern, Beech Lacey.

Nikki and Joseph took a rare day off. They spent it at Monks Lantern with Nikki's mother and Wendy. One of the most relaxing days they'd had for a long, long time. After lunch, they sat out in the garden, enjoying a glass of wine in the late summer sunshine.

'So did you enjoy playing detectives?' said Joseph.

Wendy cast a quick glance at Eve, who said, 'Well, it's ongoing, actually.'

'Oh. That sounds ominous,' said Nikki, in mock horror. 'Spill the beans, you two.'

'We made a lot of headway and discovered far more than Robert Richmond expected us to, but just before we left the Lake District we had a note from a relative of the woman who had been given an original painting. She indicated that there was some sort of foul play involved in his disappearance.' Eve's eyes lit up. 'She's coming to Lincoln next month for a conference.'

'So we are going to meet up,' continued Wendy. 'And, hopefully, take it from there.'

Nikki looked at Joseph. 'They're like a pair of terriers, aren't they?'

Joseph grinned. 'Once they get their teeth into something . . . But you enjoyed it?'

'Oh yes!' they said in unison, then laughed.

'We are thinking of taking jobs as researchers for a firm of heir-hunters. We've discovered that we're pretty good at tracing old records.' Eve looked rather proud of herself.

'Well, it sounds a little safer than all your previous jobs,' said Nikki.

'Unlike yours,' Eve said, suddenly becoming serious. 'You've had a rotten time over the last few weeks. Which reminds me, how are your two lovely colleagues getting along?'

'Dave is at home now, being watched over by two mother hens, in the form of Cat and Ben. Apparently he was about to move house, but he's postponed that for a while until he's stronger. The owner of Old Cressy Hall, where he was taking a cottage, has been brilliant, he's holding the cottage for as long as Dave wants.' Nikki sighed. 'We miss him already. It doesn't seem right without him in the office.'

'And Niall is driving Tamsin nuts,' laughed Joseph. 'He's the world's worst patient! He's got half a ton of metalwork in his leg, plus one hand all strapped up, and he wants to get back to work!'

'Dedication. Don't knock it, Joseph. You'd be the same,' declared Eve, standing up. 'Would you two excuse us for a while? We're going to prepare tonight's meal, so we can have the rest of the afternoon with you.'

After they had gone inside, Nikki leaned back and stretched out her legs. 'I'd almost forgotten how to relax.'

Joseph took a mouthful of wine. 'There are still things about that case that I can't get my head around.'

'Me too,' Nikki said, 'but at least Deacon is out of circulation.'

Joseph raised his glass. 'I'll drink to that. Hats off to Cat and Dave. They took on that whole case and nailed it!'

'I think finding Carmel Brown's "bit of security" in the shape of her old phone in one of the unpacked removal boxes was the catalyst, then the rest slotted into place,' Nikki said. When Carmel had been attacked by Deacon, her phone had been lying on the kitchen work top. She had managed to hit the video button, and although the footage showed nothing but the kitchen ceiling, the soundtrack was enough to damn him. Rory had used forensic voice analysis software to compare it to Deacon's interview tape. It was a perfect match. Add to that Marian Harper's determination to nail him, and Deacon hadn't a hope in hell. And that wasn't the end of it. One of Rory's SOCOs managed to lift a fingerprint from Carmel's garage door, which placed him at the scene. Cat went through the search history on his laptop and found a site explaining steering malfunctions in Renaults.

'And after that guy Josh Smithers finally came forward, a whole load of others found the courage to do the same.' Joseph stared out over the garden. 'I think this case will get bigger and bigger now the press are running with it. There will be others, maybe a lot of them.'

'I don't think our Dave realised exactly how massive his last case would become, do you?' Nikki raised her glass. 'To Dave, and let's hope Deacon never walks free!'

'I'll drink to that!' They touched glasses. 'And what will that mysterious letter from Alex Howard reveal, I wonder? More graphic and incriminating evidence against good old Vern, I hope.'

Two days earlier, Nikki had received a message from a South African solicitor notifying her that a document was being forwarded by courier to the officer in charge of the Jennifer Cowley investigation. It was from Alex Howard, whose body had recently been found by the local police.

Nikki was suddenly apprehensive. Jerrard Howard's story had never sat well with her, and after they'd found the second body in the cottage, more doubts had set in.

'We'll know tomorrow.' Nikki gazed into her wine.

'I wonder if he'll mention the second body?' Joseph asked. 'Rory believes she was killed not long before Jennifer, but we have no reports of missing persons that fit her description. He says he's going to proceed with forensic facial reconstruction from the skeletal remains.'

'I hope we find out who she was,' said Nikki. 'It's so sad when some poor soul remains unidentified and no one claims them.'

Joseph closed his eyes and turned his face to the sun. 'Let's leave all that until tomorrow, shall we?'

Nikki agreed, but she knew she would have no peace until all the questions were answered.

* * *

Hawthorne Close, Old Fleeting.

Marian Harper opened her door and was delighted to see that her visitor was DC Cat Cullen.

'This is an unofficial call, Marian. Can I come in?'

Marian opened the door wide. 'Of course.' She had been hoping the young detective would stop by.

Once they were seated in the conservatory, Cat said, 'I've come for two reasons. The first is to tell you, strictly off the record, that we now have enough evidence against Vernon Deacon that if you chose to not go through with the trial, he would still be convicted on other serious charges. It will be harrowing for you, and I wanted you to know that you don't have to put yourself through it if you don't feel up to it. Your evidence could be given in camera, or you could walk away. He will still go down.'

Marian smiled at Cat's obvious discomfort. 'Rest assured, my friend, I will relish taking this on. I owe it to Carmel, as a testament to her courage, and I will *not* let her down.' She reached across and patted the young woman's hand. 'And now I'm going to make this a little easier for you. I'll tell you a secret, but it stays right here and won't ever be spoken of again.'

Cat understood perfectly.

'I married young, and my husband was killed in an accident in our second year of marriage. Circumstances found me struggling to get by. Like a lot of girls back then, I looked for an alternative means of survival. I was lucky to be taken on by a very exclusive agency. It catered for a clientele that demanded absolute discretion — and I mean absolute. I'll say no more about it, only that my name will never come up as being associated in any way with that kind of profession.' She sat back, speaking softly, as if to herself. 'It was there that I met my second husband, a military man, a widower and very well-respected. It was love on both sides, no question about it, and my life became decent and proper again. It was a good marriage but beset by loss and sadness. I won't bore you with the details. The main point of this story is that due to my earlier career, I understand men very well. I instinctively know what they want, and why they want it.' She gave Cat a knowing smile. 'I'll say no more, other than sometimes in this life, no matter how clever you think you are, you come up against another person who knows the game better than you. *C'est la vie*, Detective.'

Cat tilted her head to one side. 'Then I can stop worrying about you, Marian?'

'Oh yes, my dear, you certainly can.'

* * *

The following day. Greenborough Police Station.

Nikki and Joseph sat in Cameron's office and prepared to open the sealed envelope, couriered to them from South Africa.

'I'm assured by Alex's solicitor that this is a perfectly legal document, correctly signed, and that his signature was witnessed by two people of good standing.' He looked from one to the other. 'Ready?'

'Been ready for days! Thought it would never get here,' said Nikki impatiently.

359

'Okay.' Cameron opened the sealed envelope and extracted several handwritten sheets of paper. He drew in a breath and began to read . . .

To whom it may concern,

I am writing this for two reasons, the first because my life is in danger, and secondly, to fulfil a promise.

Examination of the derelict cottage at Hob's End Copse, Jacob's Fen, will reveal two bodies. You may or may not know this already. One is Jennifer Cowley, and the other a young prostitute that I only ever knew as "Lucinda." Patrick and I had "shared" her. They both died as a result of the actions of two very sick young men who had been goaded into it by a man named Vernon Deacon. I "confessed" some of this to my brother, Jerrard Howard, but what I told him is only partially true. My friend Patrick Shale was guilty of killing Jennifer, but prior to that, I omitted to tell Jerrard that I had asphyxiated Lucinda. Patrick helped me to conceal Lucinda's body and, later, I helped him with Jennifer. We swore that we would never speak of what we had done and would continue to declare our innocence whatever happened. Even if one of us was arrested, the other would still not disclose the fact of the second death. Initially we kept that promise to each other, but prison changed Patrick, and I believe he came to hate me, because I was free and he was paying the price. I do not know for sure how he came to hear that I was going to confess to what happened, but I suspect I had been fooled for years by letters from a man I believed to be an old friend. I now suspect it was Patrick all along. I'm sure that you will have been told by my brother about the threats that began at that time. If not, contact him and he will explain. I tried hard, for Jerrard's sake, as I knew he was in exile because of me, and for years, I fought the terrible longings that sometimes almost overpowered me. Then, when I finally escaped Jerrard's watchful gaze and came to wonderful Venda, to my shame, I lapsed. Now a certain girl's father is looking for me and I know what the outcome will be. I almost welcome it. I never meant to hurt her so badly, but I did, and I'm not sure I want to live with the guilt anymore.

My mother, at huge expense to herself, both financially and emotionally, offered me a second chance, but it seems I wasn't strong enough to fight my nature and I apologise with every fibre of my being. I love my family and I'm deeply ashamed at bringing such heartache and shame down on them.

Regarding the promise I made, well, at least I found love for a while, and this confession is dedicated to the memory of Sarah de Klerk.

Alexander Howard

For a while, none of them spoke. Then Cameron said, 'So Shale was guilty. There was no miscarriage of justice. And then, when he came home, he fell apart completely.'

'And we now have a possible way of tracing our other dead girl. It's not much. Lucinda might well be a working name, but it's a start,' Joseph said softly.

'Aurelia knew her son better than anyone, didn't she? She believed he had committed murder, and he had. She just got the wrong girl.' Nikki felt almost pleased that Aurelia Howard had been right. It didn't make what she did any less reprehensible, but at least it hadn't all been for nothing. She looked down at some papers she'd been holding. 'Final forensic report from Rory. That partial print on the satchel belonged to Alex, and the pictures of Jennifer were taken with two different cameras. It looks like they stalked her together and shared the pictures.' She exhaled. 'Deacon has caused a world of pain over the years, hasn't he?'

'Now let's watch it come home to roost. I'm pretty sure he won't be a popular man inside. That world of pain could just go right back to hit him.' Joseph's eyes flashed.

Nikki laughed. 'Joseph and his karma. But in this case, I really hope it exists.'

'Oh, it does! Believe me. Quote . . . "If justice is denied, let the law of karma take the ride, nothing in this world is done without a price."'

'Oh Lord, not your mate Aristotle again?'

'No, it's good old Anon this time.'

Cameron smiled. 'So, what's left to tie up?'

'Very little.' Nikki pulled a face. 'Other than a mountain of paperwork that will need a JCB to shift it.'

'Then I suggest you make a start, Detective Inspector. I seem to be still waiting for the paperwork from the last case!'

'Ah, yes, well, I was meaning to talk to you about that, but then this body fell down the chimney, you see, and then . . .'

'Enough! That's the worst excuse I've ever heard! Go and find something believable, Nikki Galena.'

* * *

Hob's End Copse

Once again, an assortment of vehicles pulled into Hob's End Copse, lights flashing. This time there was only one police car. The rest were dump trucks, a pay-loader and a bulldozer, and the lights were orange, not blue.

On the edge of the field stood a group of people who had turned out to see the final moments of the witch's cottage and the clearing of the copse itself.

Even though Tamsin had told him to stay put, Niall had somehow made it from the car, hobbling on underarm crutches and cursing his damaged hand and the uneven ground. Nikki and Joseph duly told him off but seeing the remains of that evil little cottage being carted away in a dump truck was obviously worth the ear-bashing.

Richard and Jerrard Howard stood side by side. Richard had already told Tamsin that Jerrard would be coming home to work the farm with him. Next to them were the two volunteers from the village, Leigh Peacock and Claire Rhodes. It was apparently going to be down to them to bring in a small army of helpers to replant the copse with the native trees that Tamsin had suggested.

The only two people that Tamsin didn't recognise were an elderly couple with a small West Highland Terrier on a tartan lead.

Richard saw her registering interest in them and called her over. 'Tamsin, meet Mr and Mrs Goodacre. They answered an advert that I placed in the Greenborough Standard regarding the provenance of the cottage.'

Tamsin shook their hands, then patted the dog. 'So, you hold the answer to the mystery?' she asked with an excited smile.

The man nodded. 'Tilly here and I have been trying to trace our family tree. My family lived in Jacob's Fen for generations before we all went our own ways. Turns out that cottage was owned by a brother of my paternal grandfather. He'd been given a small parcel of land and the cottage as a token of thanks for years of faithful service to Sedgebrook. He left it to his two sons in his will but both boys fell during the war, and as his wife had predeceased him, it was left to rot and as far as we can gather, forgotten about, simple as that.'

'Looks like the copse took it over, don't it, Stan?' said Tilly, rather warily. 'It's like it was never there.'

'It certainly did take it over,' said Tamsin with a shiver, recalling her first sight of it. 'Tell me, did it have a name?'

'Not that we know of, Miss. But looking back at the comings and goings at the time, it never seemed to be a happy place — too many accidents, illnesses and deaths.' The old man took his wife's hand. 'We better get off now, but I reckon getting rid of the place is probably for the best. Good day to you.'

'Wise words,' said Richard quietly.

'I'll second that,' Jerrard echoed. 'I always thought this tangle of trees had a bad feeling about it. And right up to its dying day, it's been a magnet for bad luck.'

Tamsin remembered her father's suggestion that Hob's End was on a ley line of bad energy. It was hard to disagree. She went back to Niall and the others.

'Here they come!' A small cheer went up as the first dump truck, loaded with bricks and timbers and tree branches, lumbered slowly out of the copse. 'Good riddance to bad rubbish,' growled Niall, looking ruefully at his plastered leg.

The lorry stopped and the driver climbed up to attach a safety net over the top to stop loose debris escaping on the trip to the dump. As he climbed along the side to tie the net, he dislodged something. He looked down at an old bedroom mirror which crashed to the ground. 'Oh bugger!' he shouted. 'Seven years bad luck!'

'Bloody hell!' exclaimed Niall. 'That cottage is little more than a pile of rubble and it's still trying to get the last word. Come on, Tamsin, let's go home before it starts uttering curses and casting spells!'

'I'm with you, Niall!' called out Nikki, over the sound of a dumper truck engine. 'Come on, Joseph, I've had my fill of creepy stuff. Let's get back to the real world — you know the one, filled with villains, sweaty coppers, handcuffs and slamming doors in the custody suite.'

'Sounds good to me,' Joseph said. 'For once, I agree.'

Tamsin watched them walk to their car, and then she glanced back to the dark, sinister tangle of trees and shrubs. They were walking away from it, but she feared that they were all taking something of Hob's End cottage with them.

THE END

OTHER BOOKS BY JOY ELLIS

FREE KINDLE BOOKS AND OFFERS

Please join our mailing list for free Kindle books and new releases, including crime thrillers, mysteries, romance and more, as well as news on the next book by Joy Ellis!

www.joffebooks.com

Thank you for reading this book. If you enjoyed it please leave feedback on Amazon, and if there is anything we missed or you have a question about then please get in touch. The author and publishing team appreciate your feedback and time reading this book.

We hate typos too but sometimes they slip through.
Please send any errors you find to
corrections@joffebooks.com
We'll get them fixed ASAP. We're very grateful to eagle-eyed readers who take the time to contact us.

Made in the USA
Middletown, DE
06 May 2021